About the author

David Warr was born just before the end of the Second World War. He was schooled at a private boarding school in Surrey, leaving to join the Civil Service, and serving in the War Department. On leaving the Civil Service he joined the police, serving as a CID officer. He left the police to work as an insurance inspector before setting up his own brokerage and estate agency business after which he set up a renewable energy company. David retired from business in 2013 and now spends his time writing.

David lives happily with Ann, his wife of thirty-five years, in a small village in Hampshire.

George and The Dragon Warriors is David's third published novel.

www.davidwarr.com

GEORGE AND THE DRAGON WARRIORS

Also by David Warr

Kaine's Chronicles – The Haunting of Jack Kent

Visions of Death

David Warr

GEORGE AND THE DRAGON WARRIORS

Vanguard Press

VANGUARD PAPERBACK

A CIP catalogue record for this title is
available from the British Library.

ISBN 978 1 784653 63 7

*Vanguard Press is an imprint of
Pegasus Elliot MacKenzie Publishers Ltd.*
www.pegasuspublishers.com

First Published in 2018

**Vanguard Press
Sheraton House Castle Park
Cambridge England**

Printed & Bound in Great Britain

Dedication

My thanks to my lovely wife Ann

For being there!

ONE

The early morning mist crept over the brow of the hill, drifted down the gentle green slopes, slowly filling the lush green valley below, before rolling lazily along the length of the valley, completely enveloping a small grey stone temple positioned next to an ancient gnarled tree. An invisible force then appeared to swirl and lift the mist, sending it up the slopes and into the hills beyond.

The dawn's sun was rising over the opposite brow, casting bright beams of light down through the mist, eerily lighting the thirty sweating horses tethered in an arc around the old gnarled tree. They were restless, nervous, pounding their front hooves in the dirt, and emitting clouds of steaming mist from their flared nostrils.

Twenty-six alert and very wary warriors, with the insignia of a golden dragon emblazoned on the fronts of their black body armour, were standing grimly by their mounts with their swords drawn. They cut ghostly figures as the sun's rays played on them through the mist of steam emanating from their horses. All were showing the signs of recent battle, with varying degrees of injuries and damage to their armour.

Two warriors, at the far end of the arc nearest to the temple, held extra horses for their absent riders. One of the horses, a magnificent black stallion, was badly injured with a gaping wound in his left shoulder. The horse stood stoically, unflinching, whilst the warrior applied a poultice to the wound. It ignored the pain, and waited for its master's return.

The warrior standing under the carved figure of a dragon above the entrance was holding on tightly to a young boy. The boy was struggling desperately against his captor's grip in a vain attempt to get inside the temple to reach his father.

"Stay still, boy," the warrior warned gruffly, strengthening his grip and making sure there was no escape.

The warriors listened attentively to the voices reverberating eerily round the grey stone walls inside.

Wei Xuang, nursing a jagged cut down the right side of his face, was sitting crossed-legged in the centre of the temple. His sword, placed over his knees, was heavily bloodstained from the recent battle. The strain of continuous war had etched fatigue into his face, which was also shown by the strain in his dark brown almond eyes.

Second-in-command, Liu Mian, was sitting next to him. Like their soldiers waiting outside, they both proudly wore the insignia of the dragon on their armour. Their hair was smoothed and tied back in a small ponytail, signifying the status of a warrior.

A completely bald priest, dressed in orange robes, was sitting before them, partly obscured by the blue smoke rising from the incense burner between them. He was looking solemnly at the smooth, oily black hair of the bowed head of his feudal lord, and his most loyal follower by his side.

"Qin Shi Huangdi has overrun the entire territory with his armies, slaughtering all in his path. Not even the children are being spared," Wei stated harshly. The bitterness was mixed with sadness, as he added sarcastically, "The dog now calls himself the *First Emperor.*"

He lowered his head in hopelessness as his second-in-command turned to stare at him with sadness in his eyes.

The priest looked at the two bowed heads in front of him. "Lord, is there nothing to be done?" he asked in a whisper.

They both looked up, peering through the light blue haze of the incense at the priest, but before Wei could answer, Liu Mian spoke for them.

"Nothing can stand in their way now, Priest. Our warriors fought hard and died bravely," he answered as he gesticulated to the entrance and the waiting warriors. "Outside is all that remains. We could never compete against the numbers, let alone their new weapons of the material they call iron. Our softer bronze swords and spears of wood were too inferior. Together with their new type of crossbow, we were no match for them. They simply annihilated our ranks at will."

"Lord," the priest said, looking from Liu to Wei, "I have a boat a little way off from here, at a village on the coast. Take it and escape with your son and lieutenants whilst you have the chance. Huangdi's army cannot be far behind you now."

"No!" the voice rang out harshly, causing the priest to flinch. The sound reverberated round the temple, bouncing off the stone walls. "No, I will not desert my men. I will stand and fight with them to the bitter end."

Liu Mian grimly enforced his lord's defiant words. "We do not run, Priest. We won the last battle, but the next will be our last. We will die with honour, not hunted down like dogs. We will fight to the end, and join our illustrious ancestors in the afterlife."

Outside in the swirling mist, the warriors listened to the raised voices echoing around the hollow temple. On hearing the defiant words spoken by their warlord inside, they stood tall and proud. Their lord would rather fight and die with them than flee. They all stood defiantly with gritted teeth and jutting jaws, as they nodded sternly to one another, before once again staring at the entrance to the temple, and waiting.

Inside, the priest spoke urgently again. "Surely, Lord, it would be better for you to survive and to avenge your people?" he pleaded.

Wei looked at the priest and considered his reply carefully. "My day has come, and my day has gone. Liu Mian will take my son to the village and then board a boat to Tong Binh, the land of his mother. My son will grow strong, and when the time is right he will avenge his people."

"No, my lord," shouted Liu. It was his turn to shout his defiance with venom. "I have served you all my life, ridden into battle at your side for over twenty years, either to victory or death, this has always been understood, and this is no

13

different. Xhi can be trusted, and he can take your son. He will be safe with him."

Before Wei could answer the boy cried out from the entrance.

"No, Father, no, I will be by your side, as well as Liu Mian."

An angry Wei jumped to his feet and glared down at Liu, before turning to face his son. "First my loyal commander disobeys me, and now my son," he shouted, his piercing voice bouncing off the walls as it echoed fiercely round the chamber.

Liu rose slowly, deliberately, and faced his lord. "I... I have earned the right to be with you and fight at your side, Lord. You cannot send me away," he challenged, in a voice tinged with defiance, and yet servitude.

Wei held the steady gaze of his most loyal friend. Seeing the hurt in his eyes, he knew he could not deny him.

"Very well, Liu, we fight together for one last time." They clasped arms and Wei turned to the guard at the doorway. "Xhi, bring my son forward," he commanded loudly.

"Yes, my lord." Xhi moved forward, now having to pull the struggling boy to his father.

"Xhou, my son, you must go to your mother's family. Do not defy me. Do not make our parting an angry one. When you are old enough, and know the ways of the warrior leader, you will return to avenge our people."

Wei turned to his trusted guard. "Xhi, the fishermen will know of the land I speak of, they will take you there. His mother's people are monks with strange mysterious powers. They will keep my son safe until he is ready to return. They will recognise the scarf of the ancients he will carry. Keep him safe, Xhi. This will be your last service to me."

Xhi, standing erect, bowed low from his waist to his lord and master. "It will be so, my lord," he said reverently.

Wei took his son to one side, removed the bright yellow and gold silk scarf which had been tucked into his own waistband, and tied it round Xhou's neck.

"This was a gift to your mother from her people. They were holy monks blessed with very strong, mysterious, and magical powers from an ancient people. They told your mother it was worth more than jewels, or any other riches and it would watch over her. She gave it to me, and it has looked after me by warning me of danger in all of my campaigning across this great land. Keep it safe around your person at all times, my son, and listen... listen to what it tells you."

The boy was puzzled by his meaning. Tears filled his eyes as he tried hard not to cry. It was with a faltering voice and a trembling bottom lip that he answered. "Yes, my father, I will do as you say. One day I will return and avenge you... this I most solemnly swear."

They embraced for the last time with Wei proudly kissing his son on the lips before handing him back to Xhi. He moved towards the entrance with Liu walking by his side. Before they went out to meet their men, Wei turned to the priest.

"This temple carries the mark of the dragon, Priest, it would be better that you are not found here when the so called First Emperor arrives. He will not spare you, so go, and go quickly."

"My lord, you and your men will not die this day, you will live forever and become immortal," the priest predicted calmly, as they all looked up through the blue haze at the ghostly figures of their ancestors, peering down at them from the ceiling of the temple.

Wei and Liu Mian bowed to the priest, acknowledging him for the last time. As they emerged into the swirling mist, a loud cheer went up from the warriors, in a salute to their lord, and his heir. Wei looked at his son and noticed the scarf was glowing. His son felt the strange sensation and fingered the scarf in alarm.

"Xhi, you will leave immediately. Go now," Wei ordered. He had learned over the years to heed the scarf with its strange warnings.

Xhi, noticing the urgency in his lord's command, swung his son up onto the saddle of his horse, before athletically springing up behind him. With a wave in salute and a curt bow, he spurred his horse forward. After a few yards he stopped, turned his horse, and saluted his brother warriors for the last time. All the warriors raised their swords in a final gesture of farewell, led by Wei and Liu at their head.

Xhi turned once again, before urging his horse forward up the incline to the brow of the hill, stopping once more so that a son could wave his last farewell to his father. He saw the scarf on the back of Xhou's neck pulsating from gold to dark amber, and back again. Knowing the importance that his lord placed on this garment, he spurred his horse forward.

As he looked behind for one last glimpse of his comrades, he noticed that the swirling mist was coming together to form a wall, screening them from view of any watchers coming up the valley. The mist began to follow, keeping pace with them as they went over the brow of the hill. As he looked up behind him, Xhi caught his breath as he saw a mysterious, gigantic robed figure, with a fire-breathing dragon by its side, towering over the mist with its arms outstretched. The robed figure appeared to gather the mist and push it in front of him.

Outside the temple, Wei watched with satisfaction as the mist gathered to form a security blanket, which followed his son. He, too, noticed the strange figure in the heavens gathering the mist in front of him. As he waved his final farewell, he knew the magical protective powers of the scarf now belonged to Xhou. He was now without its protection and would stand alone with his men.

"Thank you, Ancient One," he murmured quietly, bowing his head in reverent respect and gratitude.

The warriors heard and felt the distant rumble of horses at the end of the valley as the armies of the enemy approached. The horsemen of the First Emperor had sensed their enemy, and were now galloping with all speed up the valley, ahead of a vast army of infantry.

The warrior, holding Wei's injured stallion, stepped forward. "Lord, your horse is badly wounded, take my mount, I will run like the wind by your side."

"Wang, my loyal warrior." Wei grinned as he took his arm. "I will ride my beauty for one last time. He knows, like every one of us, what is to come. He will not let me down."

Wei took the bridle of his horse and gently stroked his nose. "What do you say, Lightning, do we ride together for one last time?" The horse nudged his master, whinnied loudly, nodding his head vigorously with his consent and willingness to follow him into hell if need be.

"Mount," a grim and determined Wei ordered, mounting the proud Lightning as he snorted through inflamed nostrils, sending out clouds of steam resembling the fire coming from the dragon on its master's chest.

Sweating profusely, the magnificent Lightning started to pound the ground with his front hooves, making sounds like a deep throbbing drum beat. As he blew out steam from his flared nostrils, the other mounts picked up on the mood and rhythm, before joining the drum beat with their own hooves pawing loudly at the ground. The vibration, together with the noise, drowned out the thunder of the approaching hordes.

"Unfurl our standard. Let the enemy see the fearless dragon that we carry so proudly, and with such honour," Liu Mian shouted.

The warrior who was mounted next to Wei, lowered the covered banner, allowing another warrior to remove the green cover. The banner unfurled and started to flutter outwards in the breeze, showing the figure of a golden dragon on a black background. The dragon appeared to be breathing fire and ready to fight.

Wei, warlord and warrior chieftain, turned proudly to face his warriors, shouting loudly so that all could hear above the cacophony of noise caused by their own horses' hooves.

"My loyal warriors, it has been my privilege and honour to serve with each and every one of you. The priest says we will be immortal from this day on, our ancestors ride with us, I wish you all honours in the next life."

He wheeled round at the head of his men to face the enemy as they started to ride slowly and determinedly towards the advancing horde. Liu turned to look at his lord riding by his side, and as Wei became aware of his gaze, they both grinned at one another, before looking proudly along the line of their determined warriors and riding on.

Their swords of bronze were held high in front of them, catching the rays of the morning sun as they gathered pace. Onwards! Onwards they rode, towards the enemy, to glory, certain death, or immortality, as the ghosts of their ancestors looked down proudly on them.

"Death to our enemies!" Wei shouted to a loud cheer and wild screams from his men. "Charge them now, my warriors."

Standing in the stirrups of his mount, the streaming dragon banner breathing fire by his side, he raised his sword over his head, holding it there for all to see. It flashed and glinted in the sun, before he lowered his arm to point directly at the advancing hordes of the First Emperor, and charged.

As they got within crossbow distance of the marauding horde, a hail of bolts came out of the sky. Liu Mian was the first to go down as his horse took a direct hit. Wei looked behind and watched as his second in command rolled along the ground before springing to his feet and running forward, sword still held high in front of him.

Wei felt Lightning falter, stumble and then regain his momentum. He looked down and saw the wicked bolt embedded in his flank. Lightning whinnied, tossing his head in defiance as he carried his master forward into the fray.

His warriors were being decimated by the crossbow fire, with only twelve warriors left as they thundered into the enemy. Wei met the enemy horsemen full on, slashing and cutting with his sword, as Lightening reared and lashed out with his forelegs, smashing into horse and rider alike. He saw his loyal Wang go down, surrounded by the enemy's infantry.

Wei watched as his warrior laughed, cutting and thrusting at the enemy, taking down men before he was finally cut down.

Suddenly, feeling like a thunderbolt had struck him, Wei was involuntarily knocked from his horse's back. He hit the ground hard, rolling along the ground in spite of the pain in his shoulder. He finished up in a crouching position. Wei searched with his fingers for the source of the pain and felt the crossbow bolt that had almost passed through his right shoulder. Liu Mian came alongside him, and their arms locked as he hauled his lord to his feet. There wasn't any time for words as they were surrounded by the enemy. They grinned at one another then turned to face their foe, back to back, as the enemy started to close in around them.

The gallant Lightning wasn't finished, and burst through the heavy cordon of infantry in an effort to reach and protect his master. He reared up time and time again, lashing out with his front legs and then his hind legs, scattering the enemy before a further crossbow bolt hit him in the same flank as previously. He stumbled to his knees, but with superhuman effort he raised himself again.

Wei watched with sadness as he saw the pitiful state of his faithful steed who had served him so steadfastly and loyally for over twenty years. Back to back with his loyal lieutenant, surrounded by the dead of their enemy, they gradually succumbed to the overwhelming numbers that began to hack them to pieces.

It had taken just twenty minutes from start to finish, but now the battlefield was quiet. The victorious bloodthirsty hordes of the First Emperor had now passed through to continue their conquest.

A lone black stallion, with the banner of the golden dragon draped across its back, was standing quietly nickering, gently pawing the ground near the head of his master who lay amongst the dead of over one hundred soldiers and warriors. The two crossbow bolts, which had entered his left flank causing more blood to flow from the already stricken horse, was too much even for him to bear.

The magnificent Lightning weakened, shaking and shuddering involuntarily as his forelegs gave way as he began to fall slowly to his knees, before gently rolling over onto his side by his master. Whinnying defiantly for the last time, he eventually lay still.

A cold and eerie mist started to rise in spiralling columns from the ground. It gradually pervaded the battle scene, completely enveloping the fallen warriors and the gallant horse. As the mist rose and cleared there was no sign of any of the warriors… or the magnificent Lightning.

TWO

Battle of Trafalgar, 1805.

He opened his eyes slowly, painfully regaining consciousness as he squinted up through the dense smoke at the billowing sails above him. The young midshipman, stripped to his waist, was on his back, half propped up against the great cannon behind him. What on earth had happened, why was he lying down without his shirt or shoes? The pungent coppery smell of cordite mixed with blood hung in the air, stinging his dry throat and making him retch.

As *HMS Victory* passed slowly through the enemy line of battle, the smoke in front of them started to clear. He realised gratefully that he was still alive, but how he didn't know.

Suddenly an oriental face appeared over him, making him start. A fierce looking Chinese warrior, with a jagged scar down his right cheek, was looking down at him. He was dressed from head to foot in black leather armour with a golden dragon emblazoned across his chest.

"On your feet, young warrior, you have a battle to fight," he urged as he hauled him to his feet, but the sailor had been deafened by explosions and couldn't hear what he was saying.

Midshipman George Warwick, aged just nineteen, and with only a few months of service in the Navy, looked round at the devastation surrounding him. He noticed the bodies lying twisted and broken across the deck, the rigging and timbers brought down by enemy fire half covering the other mutilated bodies of his gun crew. Appearing to be the sole survivor of the slaughter, he looked round for the stranger, who had helped him to his feet, but he was gone, there was no sign of him amongst the carnage.

The silence was confusing. He couldn't hear a thing other than a faint buzzing sound and the dull constant throbbing of his temples. His head felt as if it was about to split in half. Raising his hand to his forehead, he became conscious of a warm sticky liquid running down from under his gold coloured scarf onto his fingers. Lowering his hand slowly, he watched mesmerised, as the blood trickled down his hand to his wrist.

Sliding in the thick oozing crimson gore beneath his bare feet, he started to move away from the horror. Puzzled, he looked down at his toes. Where were his shoes? Then he remembered. He had removed them, like the ordinary seamen had, in order that his feet would get a better grip on the sand covered deck, as it became increasingly sodden with their own blood.

The young midshipman stepped over the decapitated corpse of poor old Harry, only recognising him by the striped baggy trousers he wore. Harry, who had served with George's father under Collingwood. Harry, who had won battle after battle only to die at the point of what was to be the Royal Navy's greatest victory.

Harry had warned George not to be seen wearing his scarf, Nelson would not approve of one of his midshipmen dressing like a rating, but his father had worn the scarf in battle before him, and he had also served under Nelson. George, bewildered and alone, looked frantically around him. Where on earth was poor Harry's head?

"So this is war," he thought to himself, still stunned and in shock, as he stood in the middle of the slaughter, feeling sick and disgusted by the loss of life and limb.

The golden scarf around his head started to physically throb. A musket ball whistled past so close he felt the wind. Attempting to shake off the shock, he became aware of the continuing danger he was in.

"Jesus Christ!" he exclaimed involuntarily, as he threw himself to one side, scrambling for cover amongst the dead scattered alongside the big gun, still hot from the constant firing at the enemy ship.

The young midshipman looked around him and noticed Lieutenant Carstairs running forward towards him, jumping over debris and dead bodies. He appeared to be mouthing something. What did he want? George couldn't hear what he appeared to be screaming. Suddenly his ears popped, letting in the fearsome noises and deafening sounds of battle once again.

"Do you blasted well hear me, Warwick? Get that bloody thing cleared away and ready!" Carstairs was screaming at him, his face almost purple, with the veins in his neck bulging with the exertion or rage.

Still not fully comprehending what was going on, or what he was meant to do, George just stood there staring back at him, looking like an imbecile. Why was this lunatic shouting at him with such anger? What in God's name was he doing here? He started to retreat slowly behind the big gun, away from this madman running at him.

"Mr Warwick," he heard another voice shout out. "Pull yourself together, man. Clear the gun, another crew is on its way."

Somewhere deep in his subconscious, he recognised the calm, but urgent voice of Captain Hardy. It suddenly dawned on him; he was still expected to function in all this madness, in this horrific butchery and carnage.

"Aye, aye, sir," he responded automatically, as he obediently started to pull hopelessly at the rigging and the heavy timber which had fallen over the gun.

It was now he started to recall the beginning of the battle. The jerking headless body of Nelson's secretary, lying on the poop deck after a cannonball had literally blown his head off. Nelson had been surrounded by at least half a dozen dead Marines, some still twisting and writhing in their death throes. He recalled Nelson giving orders to the captain of Marines to disperse his men below, and brushing aside the captain's concerns for his commander's safety. Suddenly he realised he couldn't see Nelson anywhere, and then he remembered the biggest horror of them all, seeing him fall as a musket ball entered the back of his neck and went down through his spine. His apparently lifeless body was reverently lifted by a band of Marines, and he was taken quietly below with the minimum of fuss.

George became aware of a strange, cold, eerie mist starting to surround him. Still disorientated, he gradually became aware that he was no longer alone. Willing hands now joined him in his labour. Looking up he expected to see more of his fellow shipmates, but instead he looked into the strange face of the Chinese warrior with a jagged scar down the right side of his face. The warrior nodded curtly to him as he was surrounded by a band of strange, fierce looking Chinese warriors.

George immediately remembered the duel and ambush at Crompton Green, back in England a year previously, when he had first encountered these strange mysterious people. How on earth was this possible?

He was still stunned and in shock. What in damnation was happening? Where had they come from? How had they got on board? Were they real? Was he mad? They looked fierce and determined, but not threatening, at least not to him.

"Compose yourself, young warrior, you are in shock, it will pass. Prepare yourself to meet your enemy," the warrior rasped, as he helped George lift a timber from the gun.

The Chinese warlord turned to his men, pointed to the debris that lay over the cannon and waved his finger. Immediately they all set about lifting the heavy timber and rigging in complete silence, and throwing them overboard. Eventually the gun was cleared. The warlord and warriors turned to George, bowed and disappeared as mysteriously as they had come. Looking up at the darkening skies through the gun smoke, which had blotted out the other ships, he could have sworn he saw a smiling robed Chinese figure, with a dragon by its side.

Now, alone again, he looked round trying to comprehend what had happened, and where they had gone, but the only ones left were the dead and mutilated bodies of his comrades.

Other crew members were now running to join him. As the reserve gun crew arrived, and in order to continue the battle unobstructed, they began throwing the dead bodies of his crew members unceremoniously overboard.

"Well done, Mr Warwick, sir. How you moved all the timber and rigging is beyond me," remarked leading seaman John Briggs, as he grabbed the rope to the gun and started to heave her out with the rest of the team.

"Are you all right, George?" another voice asked.

He recognised the ex-colonial American drawl of Lieutenant Robert Gates of His Majesty's Royal Marines now standing at his side.

"I think so, sir. A bit dazed, but I think I'm all right," he answered, unsure of whether he was or wasn't.

"How on earth did you get the gun cleared so quickly, I saw the debris that was over it?" Robert asked, as he looked at the stern blackened haunted face that was normally so fresh and alive.

George didn't know how to respond. If he told him what had happened, or what he thought had happened, he would probably have him thrown overboard.

"I had a little help, sir," he responded, turning to the fresh gun crew. "Get the gun ready to fire, lads." He was now back and in control.

Robert Gates looked thoughtfully at the broad shoulders of the young man in front of him. As he saw the blood trickle down from under the glowing gold coloured scarf, he wondered if his own eyes could be trusted. He could have sworn that he had seen a band of Orientals dressed in black.

"Load with grape shot," the young midshipman ordered, as his crew readied the gun.

They looked over to the French line of ships that were spread out in a disorderly array, before eyes settled on the smashed and crippled *Bucentaure*. George recalled he had raked the enemy ship with his great gun loaded with a keg of over five hundred musket balls as they passed under her stern, devastating the ship's decks and killing or maiming a lot of its crew.

Before he could spot another enemy ship, a hail of musket balls ripped into the deck around him, causing splinters to fly in all directions. Two more men went down either by ball or splinter and lay writhing in the blood-soaked sand.

"Get them below!" screamed the lieutenant of Marines, as other crew members joined them. "Marines to me," he shouted.

Over twenty scarlet clad uniforms, with loaded muskets, took up position on the larboard side and readied to fire at the enemy. Then George saw the most fearful sight. The French warship *Redoutable* was bearing down on them, firing a full broadside.

"Pick your targets, get the ones in the rigging first," he heard Gates shout out to his Marines. "Fire at will as your target presents itself."

The Marines opened up, firing at their respective targets. George saw bodies and muskets falling from the rigging and hitting the deck of the French ship. He turned to his own gun crew who were now pulling the gun forward and preparing to fire.

Down below, the guns on *Victory's* lower decks opened up in unison with devastating effect. He held his breath, waiting until he couldn't possibly miss before giving the order.

"Fire!" he screamed as the gun sprang to life, sending its deadly load into the enemy, before recoiling violently, shooting backwards until it was arrested by the restraining ropes attached to it.

The gun crew couldn't believe their eyes as they watched their enemy hastily closing their gun ports, afraid of being boarded, as broadside after broadside ripped into her. The *Victory* was closing with it fast. Suddenly the inevitable happened as the two ships collided with a juddering impact. The *Victory* continued to fire into the enemy with devastating effect.

"Prepare to repel boarders," Gates shouted out to the crew on deck.

"All gun crews on deck to repel boarders," he heard Captain Hardy order.

The crew below responded, rushing up to the top deck armed with all kinds of weapons. George grabbed a cutlass and a hammer that had been stored by the cannon. This was his first battle and his first hand to hand combat situation, and he was scared. Not so much scared of getting hurt or killed, but scared of letting his comrades down and word getting back to his father that he had failed to do his duty.

"Please, God, help me keep my nerve and do my duty," he whispered to himself, as he looked through the acrid smoke to the heavens. The scarf around his head seemed to pulsate and he thought he saw the Oriental figure and the dragon, hovering way up above him in the sky.

George was made to concentrate as the French threw hand grenades over onto the *Victory*'s decks with devastating effect. He watched, horrified, as he saw members of his reserve gun crew getting ripped apart with the deadly shrapnel exploding all around them. Then he saw the screaming enemy face to face for the first time, as they dared to land on the *Victory*'s decks.

"Let's meet the French dogs, lads, let's pile them into the sea where they belong!" he heard Gates scream, as he leapt forward like the devil dressed in scarlet.

This action caused George's blood to boil and his adrenalin to flow. His fears now forgotten, he joined the brave and gallant American charging forward ahead of his scarlet coated Marines. The gun crews from below now swelled their ranks as they surged forward. Who was screaming the loudest, the enemy or his own men, he didn't know or care, as he also opened his throat, joining in the madness of battle with a blood-curdling scream of his own.

His first encounter with the enemy was with a French Marine who had charged forward, his sallow face contorted, screaming at the top of his lungs, as he lunged with his bayonet towards George's bare abdomen. He managed to arch his stomach backwards, his muscles taught in ripples, as he drew his hammer across the vicious looking blade, just managing to parry it away from his middle. The Frenchman was caught off balance as George slashed desperately at the man's side with his cutlass. He heard the escape of wind as the blade opened up the man's abdomen, spraying more blood to mingle with the already drenched sand on the deck. He stared wide eyed in disbelief as the man, already dead, fell heavily to the deck.

"Keep pressing men," he heard the drawl of the American yell, as he saw him parry and drive his sword through the lower stomach of a Frenchman, before taking on two more who had rushed at him. George managed to get behind the two enemy seamen and brought his hammer down across one of the heads in front of him, splitting his skull and felling him instantly.

"Thanks, George," Robert shouted, as he caught the second sailor in the shoulder with the tip of his sword, before hitting him under the jaw with the hilt, flooring him instantly and then driving down with his blade.

They watched mesmerized as more Frenchmen poured across to join their comrades. The situation was beginning to look very serious indeed, when more of Robert's Marines joined them. A volley of shots rang out, killing most of the leading enemy. More of the *Victory*'s gun crews joined them, turning the tide of the ferocious battle in their favour.

The gallant American suddenly jerked violently as a musket ball ripped into his shoulder, sending him spinning sideways to the deck. George rushed to his aid as more Frenchmen charged forward to finish him. His own men were falling back under the new onslaught of the French. He seemed to be the only one holding his ground as he desperately called out for the men to rally and push forward.

"Don't fall back, lads, press forward, we will win the day," he called out at the top of his voice, more in hope than conviction, as he straddled the fallen figure of the lieutenant. Two French Marines came at him as he cut wildly and viciously at them. Unable to parry one of their blades, it entered his shoulder. To his amazement there was no pain, although he knew he'd been injured.

He slashed out with his cutlass catching the enemy Marine in the throat. He watched as the gurgling man coughed up blood before sinking to the ground holding his throat in a vain attempt to stem the flow. George pushed him over with his bare foot as he faced the other assailant who was joined by two more enemy sailors. Beyond them surged a load more of the enemy.

He became aware of the strange cold mist around him once more, as again he realised he was no longer alone. The Chinese warlord and his men were forming a semi-circle around him, swords drawn and ready for battle. George watched as the enemy sailors lunged hopelessly at him as an invisible force seemed to check their blades. He stepped forward, slashing with his cutlass until they fell to the deck. The *Victory*'s Marines and crew rallied, and were now fighting back, coming alongside him and relieving the pressure. The mysterious Chinese figures disappeared once again, as his own men pressed forward to force the French off their ship.

George felt a hand grab his ankle. Alarmed, he was about to slash down with his cutlass, before staying his hand just in time to see Lieutenant Gates was awake and staring up at him.

"I saw them. I saw the Oriental warriors. It wasn't a dream, I actually saw them," he whispered hoarsely through a dry throat.

"I'll get you below, sir. You've been shot and need the surgeon," he answered in an attempt to deflect the man's attention. He turned to two seamen and beckoned them to him.

"Get this man below to the orlop deck, quickly." George looked down at Gates before they carried him off. "You've been dreaming, sir, you'll be all right when they patch you up."

The deck was clear of the enemy once again, and the *Victory*, now clear of the *Redoutable*, was able to rejoin the surrounding battle. By late afternoon, it became apparent that the battle had been won, with ship after ship of the French and Spanish fleet striking their colours. Ships that could be saved were being boarded by British sailors. Those that could not, were unceremoniously scuttled, set alight, and sent to the bottom of the sea.

George was now standing on the quarter deck in amongst the carnage with the other survivors of the crew, as they all looked hopelessly around them, searching for the faces of shipmates, friends who were now missing, and would not be seen again. He became aware of the acrid coppery smell of smoke mixed with blood and cordite hanging in the air. It dried and caked their throats. Never in his life had he been as thirsty as he was now.

"What of Nelson?" he heard a man ask.

"Died about an hour ago," someone murmured back sadly.

The loss of their comrades, together with the loss of their brilliant and courageous leader, was too much to bear for even these hardened seamen. Shoulders started to shudder and sag under the weight of grief, as the crew started to cry. With tears streaming down their blackened faces, they tried to avoid the stares of their fellow men, until they realised that they were all acting as one in their unashamed show of emotion and grief.

George's thoughts turned once again to old Harry. Old Harry who had related to him the exploits of his own father, who had served with Captain Sir George Fitzwilliam, George's godfather and sponsor, under Collingwood. He became aware of the pain in his left shoulder caused by the stab wound earlier. The throbbing in his head, caused by the explosion that had decapitated poor old Harry, became more intense. George gradually sank to his haunches and remained still. Propped against the side of the ship, he felt himself start to tremble and shake.

"Get below, Mr Warwick, and get seen to," Lieutenant Carstairs ordered, as he saw George's injuries.

"I'm all right, sir," George responded. "There are others far worse than me."

"It's not a request, Mr Warwick, now get below," Carstairs insisted, "and well done, it has been noted."

George was unsure of what he was referring to. Had he also seen the Chinese warriors like Lieutenant Gates? He made his way down between decks, acknowledging those he recognised on the way. The queue was long, with men with varying degrees of injuries waiting patiently to be seen by the ship's surgeon and his assistants. No matter how bad the injury, or the seniority of rank, traditionally men were seen in the order they arrived. He made his way down to the orlop deck stopping as he spotted Robert Gates slumped alongside the bulkhead.

Tapping him with his bare foot, unsure if he was still alive, he waited until he looked up. Gates recognised the young midshipman instantly.

"Hello, Warwick, still alive then?"

"Aye, sir," he responded with a smile.

"How bad are you hurt?"

"Head hurts a bit, my shoulder is throbbing, but I don't think I have a right to be down here, looking at you and the others," George answered ruefully. "How are you?"

"To be honest, I have had better days," Gates said, trying to grin, but failing hopelessly as it turned to a grimace.

"You'll be seen soon, sir, they'll sort you out."

George made his way back up to the upper deck, making sure to avoid Carstairs, and joined the crew members who were drinking copious amounts of beer. He was glad to get rid of the acrid taste in his mouth, as he gulped the warm ale greedily. Some hours later, when it had quietened down considerably, he rejoined the diminishing queue back down in the orlop deck. He was eventually attended to before going in search of the injured Robert Gates. He found him as he was coming out of Captain Hardy's cabin.

"Let's find somewhere to talk, Mr Warwick."

When they were sure they were alone, a very pale faced Robert turned to George, holding him by his good arm to prevent him moving away.

"I think you owe me some sort of explanation, and don't tell me I was dreaming. I saw them twice. First when they helped to clear your gun, and next when they joined you in combat over me."

"It's a long story, sir."

"I'm going nowhere, neither are you, and you can call me Robert. Now tell me what the hell is going on," he demanded.

George released himself from Robert's grip as they both turned to look out at the cold grey sea, which was starting to swell ominously. A storm was definitely on its way.

"I'll start at the beginning as I know it. It all began on a late September day this time last year, when I rode into Crompton village with my father after finishing a very arduous harvest time…" George started casting his mind back as he relived that fateful day.

THREE

November 1804. Sussex, England.

"My father and I rode down the main street of Crompton village on our heavy horses and entered the square, speaking to all the villagers we encountered along the way. About nine hundred people inhabit the village and its surrounds and we knew nearly all of them. Crompton was quite famous for its market, having being granted a charter in the thirteenth century. Because of its close proximity to Fareham and Portsmouth, it also housed a good deal of ex-naval personnel and quite a few of their widows.

"My father had been farming the area since leaving the Navy some ten years earlier, and we had struggled with the rest of the village, through bad winter after bad winter, until the bonanza harvest of that very year. Struggle after struggle had taken its toll on my father, and my mother, and although he was fit and reasonably healthy, his dark handsome face was now etched with the heavy lines that only worry and harsh weather can bring.

"We tethered our horses outside the hardware store on the opposite side to the Boar's Head Inn. I heard my father grunt with displeasure as he noticed the black coach, bearing the crest of a crow on its side. It was parked carelessly halfway across the road farther up, blocking part of the right of way to the square.

"'Good day to you, James,' he greeted the well-rounded red-faced shop owner. "'It looks like we are being honoured with a visit from his lordship,' he said sarcastically, as we entered his shop.

"'Good morning, Rodney, George," James said acknowledging me emerging from behind my father. 'I think it's his son,' James answered. 'Young Percival has taken to visiting our local hostelry with a few of his so-called aristocratic friends.'

"My father handed James a list my mother had made out earlier. 'Fill this for me, will you, or Martha will kill me when we get back.'

"James grinned as he took the list and scanned it. 'Most of these items we have, Rodney, the seed we will have to get in for you. What do you want me to do?'

"'Make the order up and order the seed. I'll collect the whole lot when it's in. Meanwhile I think it's about time I introduced my son to the wonders of ale.'

"James looked at me, grinned and winked. My father saw him, wondered why as he shrugged and let it go. As we got outside and started to cross the street, Sir George Fitzwilliam, my godfather and my father's best friend, cantered up on his magnificent chestnut stallion.

"Sir George lives at the local manor. He owns the village and most of the surrounding area, including the mills and the tanning factory. A more pleasant sort of chap you couldn't imagine. He's about five feet eight in height, of good and solid build, just starting to show the signs of an easier life and good living, with his middle starting to protrude over his thick leather belt.

"My father, who is still very wiry from working on the farm, is two inches taller and had served with him in the Royal Navy as his First Lieutenant aboard frigates. They had become good friends, as well as famous and rich, taking prize after prize from the French and Spanish ships. My father was able to buy our farm from Sir George, on the very riches made from their exploits.

"'Good day to you, Rodney, young George,' he said jovially, stroking his large greying handlebar moustache, as he dismounted. Landing lightly on the ground, he nodded in the direction of the black coach.

"'What's Crowe doing here?' he asked disdainfully.

"'Morning to you, Sir George," my father responded, as I touched my forehead in respect. He might be my father's best friend, but I still held this man in such respect and awe. "His son, I believe, with some of his friends. I'm just off to introduce George to a drop of ale."

"'I'll join ye, when I've spoken to James here.'

My father and I went across to the Boar's Head, ducking under the low oak lintel above the front door. As we approached the long bar, we noticed it was busy with plenty of noise being made at one end of the room.

"'Morning, Rodney. How are you, George? Haven't seen you for a couple of weeks,' Frederick Carter greeted us, letting the cat well out of the bag.

"At that very moment, Maggie, a very pretty buxom barmaid, passed by carrying two jugs of ale. 'Hello, George, how are you?' she asked innocently.

"My father looked at me with raised eyebrows as the penny began to drop. 'Seems this is not your first time in here, son,' he said to a raucous laugh from Fred behind the bar.

"'He's been coming in for this past year, Rodney. I'm hoping he will be coming in for some time to come.'

"I thought my father was going to explode, but he just grinned as he punched me in the arm, it blasted well hurt too."

"'You had better not let your mother find out, or it will be me that gets it in the neck,' he said as he turned to Fred over the bar, 'A jug of your ale for me, Fred, he can obviously order his own.'

"Fred had to compound my position by asking me if I wanted my usual. Anyway, I saw Black Tom sitting in the bay window as he waved across to me. When we were younger we always seemed to be fighting each other, but later we usually had a drink and a laugh, but that day he seemed to be sulking and scowling at the people at the end of the room. I soon realised why. Maggie, the barmaid who he was stepping out with, was being jostled and grabbed as she served the unruly crowd. This wasn't like Tom. He was very handy with his fists and could scrap like hell. He would never put up with behaviour like this towards his girl, so I went over to him."

"'Not like you, Tom, you wouldn't normally put up with that, what gives?'

"'Hello, George," he responded glumly. 'It's Percival Crowe and his cronies. What can I do? I live and work on his estate.'

"I looked to the end of the bar, and saw Maggie trying to free herself from young Crowe's clutches. The landlord shouted to them to behave, but they persisted in molesting her. Tom was about to lose it and started to rise. I put my hand on his shoulder, forcing him back in his seat.

"'Stay where you are, Tom, I don't have to watch any job or home, I'll go and get her,' I told him, as I made my way down the bar.

"'Maggie, we could do with some service down the other end,' I said, taking hold of her arm and wrenching Percival's hand from her waist. I turned her round away from them and pushed her towards the bar, it was then it all started.

"'Who the hell do you think you are, peasant, she is serving us!' shouted one of his friends. I told him, in no uncertain terms, that I considered them to be below contempt, and I turned to move away. 'Hang on there, oaf!' he screamed. 'Get back here this minute.' I ignored him and kept moving but then felt hands grab me, turning me back around roughly to face them.

"Percival Crowe was sneering at me, with his five friends at his side, all with clenched fists. 'Don't walk away from me, vagabond, or I'll have you flogged,' he spat out.

"'If you don't mind your language, you'll be feeling my boot," I said. They couldn't believe that I had spoken to them like that. One of his friends, no higher than the bar, thought he was a giant, probably the ale and his friends driving him on. Anyway, he took a swing at me and I responded by clipping him under the jaw. This seemed to incense Crowe and his lot, who all started to advance on me. I felt, rather than saw, Black Tom come up behind me, and I told him to stay out of it.

"'You had better keep out of this, Black Tom," Percival shouted at him, 'or you will be off the estate, out of a job and a home, as well as getting a good flogging in the bargain.'

"Tom didn't have time to respond as he was pulled away, with his place being taken by my father and Sir George.

"'Let's see how you handle some fighting men, you young puppies,' my father said as he laughed at them. 'I think you are going to get a lesson to remember, this day.'

"Percival, seeing his friends start to back away, checked himself. 'I have no quarrel with you, Warwick, nor Sir George, but I am not going to accept insults from your young whelp.'

"'Then keep coming forward, young man,' Sir George invited with a smile. 'I think this young whelp will give you an almighty thrashing.'

"He didn't know what to do. His friends certainly didn't want to know, as they backed off even further. He eyed me up and down, and decided against any action.

"'Very well, you have insulted me and my friends, and I demand satisfaction. You will be hearing from my second in due course. I will meet with you to settle this in a duel.'

"'You blithering young coxcomb, a duel, why not here and now with your fist, you young pup?' Sir George reacted indignantly.

"'I demand satisfaction on the field as a gentleman, Sir George, with him. It will be with swords and to the death.'

"I wanted to smack him there and then, but my father restrained me saying he had made a formal challenge, and we would have to meet it. I learned later that young Percival had received fencing lessons from the fencing masters of Paris during his stays there. He thought he was going to cut me to pieces and dispatch me without any problem. I must admit, when I thought about, so did I. Sir George took me in hand personally, it turned out that he, too, was a bit of a master with the blade and had also received instruction from the best in France and Spain.

"I was shoeing one of the horses on the farm one day, when Percival's second arrived at the house. I thought my mother was going to shoot him with my father's old blunderbuss, and he had to restrain her. The duel was to take place ten days hence, on the village green at Crompton. He wanted to show me up before dispatching me, as Black Tom later told me. Over the next ten days, I received comprehensive fencing lessons from Sir George. I thought I had become quite proficient, but my father thought otherwise.

"'Look, George, all this fancy stuff is all well and fine, but sometimes it just doesn't get the job done,' he said. 'The idea is to stay alive. This is not a game, and you can be sure that young Crowe has learnt some bad practices from his father. He was infamous for his dirty tricks and pushing those into duels he knew he could beat easily.'

"He proceeded to show me nearly every dirty trick in the book, and some that hadn't made it. I felt I was ready, but he kept me at it, day after day, morning to night.

"On the eve of the duel, Black Tom arrived at the farm with a very alarming message. Lord Crowe had received the news of the pending duel in a pique of anger. Evidently, he didn't want to take the chance of losing his son and heir, and was taking steps to make sure it didn't happen.

"'He's going to ambush you and your party,' he told me. 'Six men all armed with blunderbusses and cudgels, they have been told to do what it takes to stop you, including killing you if necessary.'

"I couldn't believe my ears, and when I told my father, he wanted to ride over to Crowe's estate and take him on. I persuaded him to seek the advice of Sir George before doing anything hasty, so we rode over to the manor. Sir George was of the same mind as my father until some common sense prevailed and he sent for the county magistrate. Anyway, it was decided that we would catch the footpads in the act with a surprise ambush of our own.

"At about eight o'clock that night, County Magistrate Thomas Fairbairn arrived at the manor for consultation with Sir George and my father.

"'Well of course I cannot do anything about Lord Crowe, Sir George, you know the law, he can only be tried by his peers, but I can try, and hang, any footpads that are caught and survive,' he said sternly. 'I will send two of my officers to assist you. How many men can you muster?'

"'Enough, Master Fairbairn, my estate is full of ex-seamen and soldiers who I have given work and homes to, fighting men who are prepared to stand. I will put six in the field. With surprise on our side, that should suffice.'

"'What time is this duel to take place?' the magistrate asked.

"'Some ungodly hour of seven thirty in the morning, I shall miss me breakfast, for God's sake,' Sir George replied indignantly.

"Tom went on to explain to us what he had overheard and where the ambush by Lord Crowe's men would be. We arranged that our people would be there earlier to thwart the ambush and then ride on to Crompton Green for the duel. Black Tom went back to the Crowe estate, but unfortunately, he was seen leaving the manor and captured as he entered his home. He was badly beaten within an inch of his life, and of course they realised he had informed on them. This did not stop Lord Crowe. He decided to let the ambush go ahead and not tell his own men. He knew that a skeleton party would be left to travel to Crompton. In fact, it was me, my father, and Sir George who went on. He arranged a second party to lie in wait for us.

"At five in the morning, with the frost still on the grass, our men, fully armed with pistol and sword, surrounded the bend in the lane where the ambush was to take place. The three of us were going to approach the bend as if we didn't suspect anything was untoward as we made our way to Crompton.

"This was my first sighting of the gold-coloured scarf which my father had tied round his head. It started to glow as we approached the bend. At first, I thought it was a trick of the early morning light. I didn't get any more time to think on it as we heard shots ring out. We galloped to the bend, getting there just as our lot finished off the footpads. Two were dead, and four injured and secured in chains.

"'Get these men to the magistrate straight away,' Sir George ordered. 'We ride on to Crompton to surprise Lord Crowe and his spoilt brat,' he added, not suspecting a thing.

"We cantered on with me following behind Sir George and my father. A mile further on I noticed the scarf starting to glow from dark amber back to gold again. It couldn't just be a trick of the light, I thought. I saw my father put his hand up to his head and feel it before shouting to Sir George to stop. Sir George pulled up abruptly, and as he turned to see what the problem was, he also noticed the glowing, throbbing scarf, only he seemed to know what it meant.

"'Into the wood, quickly,' he responded, as my father pushed me into the trees using his horse as a shepherd. 'What is it, Rodney?' he asked my father.

"'Danger, methinks,' my father answered. 'It doesn't lie, or let me down.'

"'Another ambush, perhaps,' Sir George pondered.

"I was amazed and puzzled as to what was going on. How did they know there was danger ahead? We had got through the ambush, why did they think there was another one? My father saw the questions in my eyes.

"'I will explain later, lad, suffice it to know there is grave danger ahead.'

"'Will your warriors come to our assistance, do you think?'

"'Like the scarf, Sir George, they have never let me down yet. I suggest we ride on. George, you stay well behind. Do you hear me?'

"I couldn't make out what this was all about. Warnings from a piece of cloth, was I dreaming? Warriors coming to help us, what blasted warriors, coming from where? I was about to remonstrate with my father when his stare said it all. I kept quiet and did as I was told, trusting in both of these men. We re-entered the lane and started slowly towards the village. As we approached the outskirts, a mist appeared to be coming from the ground, rising up and obscuring our visibility. It cleared in front of us as quickly as it had arrived, but only as far as the eye could see. My father and Sir George slowed their horses and edged forward. I peered over their shoulders to see the road ahead was filled by half a dozen well-armed men blocking our path.

"I felt uneasy and looked behind us to see that more armed men had filled the lane behind, and were closing in on us. I, like the other two, drew my sword and prepared to get cut down as the footpads started to rush at us. It was then I felt the cold that made me shiver. I didn't know if it was the fear or the cold that caused it, but my mind was soon racing as I noticed we were being surrounded by strange-looking Oriental warriors dressed all in black armour with golden dragons on their chests. One of them, with a jagged scar down the side of his face, was sat astride a huge black stallion which seemed to blow fire from its nostrils. The warrior smiled at my father and bowed his head to him, as his men turned outwards in a defensive line.

"The footpads were astounded to see so many men with drawn swords, but were unable to turn away in time before these fierce warriors leapt forward screaming at the top of their lungs.

"I just sat astride my horse, unable to move, not comprehending what was going on. I saw the warrior leader charge forward and lean over from his stallion as he slashed the first villain across his neck, almost severing the man's head. I then noticed another move forward to slash his bronze sword across another's stomach, opening him up as you would a deer's carcass. I can only describe the ensuing fight if you can visualise the inside of a knacker's yard when they are committing wholesale slaughter. The footpads were no match for these fierce and skilful warriors, who quickly put an end to them without mercy.

"When it was over, the warrior leader rode up to my father. The great black gleaming stallion seemed to tower over our own mounts, before rearing up on its hind legs, kicking out with its forelegs in some sort of defiant ritual. I just about managed to control my own horse as it physically jumped in fright. The leader grinned at us, bowed his head again and then just disappeared with the rest of his men into thin air. There was no point in me trying to understand, I was lost, I didn't have a clue as to what had gone on, or how.

"'Pull yourself together, George,' I heard my father chastise, as he noticed me trembling. He slapped me on the back as he said, 'We still have work to do, and I need you to stay sharp.'

"As we weaved our way through the carnage, I was nearly sick at the sight I can tell you. On arriving at the green, we saw Lord Crowe's coach parked in the middle. He had his son by his side, who was flashing about with a blade. His father was addressing the villagers who had assembled after receiving a summons to witness the duel.

"'My son is an honourable man and seeks satisfaction for the insulting behaviour of George Warwick, if he has the nerve to turn up, which I doubt,' he was saying. 'It will be to the death as my son has decreed...'

"His voice trailed off as he noticed movement at the edge of the green. Sir George, my father and I arrived astride our horses and made our way carefully over to the centre. Lord Crowe, open mouthed, couldn't believe it. What on earth could have happened? He had sent sufficient men to deal with and dispatch these men, even if the whole lot had turned up at the ambush.

"'You may well look surprised, my lord, your footpads were not good enough and have been dealt with in the most final way,' Sir George stated grimly as we all dismounted. 'I will be acting as George Warwick's second. In the absence of any other, I trust you will second your son?'

"It took the cruel mouthed Crowe a few minutes to compose himself as his cocksure son stepped forward to face them. I looked round to make sure no one else was going to surprise us again, when I noticed my father had moved beyond the edge of the crowd. I saw the Chinese warriors aligned along the edge of the green with the warlord standing in front of them. He bowed from the hips as my father approached. I couldn't hear what was being said, but my father told me later that this was a matter of honour and that he could not permit any interference from them. When he had said his piece, I saw the warlord grin and then bow towards me, and my father started to return.

"Lord Crowe soon returned to his normal bragging as he told the crowd that his son would soon dispatch this upstart, meaning yours truly of course. He stepped forward with Percival, and stood in front of Sir George and myself.

"'I take it that this upstart is prepared to die, Sir George,' he said callously.

"'Prepared to die and prepared to take life, my lord,' he answered smiling, as I drew my sword and faced his son.

"As young Percival heard this he gulped rather hard, as he realised what this had now come to. I must admit, I was scared, but I was determined not to show it and to see it through, no matter what the outcome. At the end of the day one of us would not be leaving this field alive. Percival took up his fencer's stance in front of me.

"'En garde,' he said suddenly, as he lunged at my middle without any further warning. I stumbled back and fell over, but my father's training suddenly kicked in as I rolled first to one side, and then to the other before springing to my feet to face him again.

"'Run the bastard through,' I heard Lord Crowe say as his son rushed forward relentlessly, forcing me backwards in defence.

"I parried his thrust, able to turn his blade away with small twists of the wrist as I had been taught by Sir George, but the biggest test came when I felt a hard thump and an excruciating pain in my side as I parried yet another thrust.

"'Foul,' I heard the shout from my father. 'The young bastard's got a knife.'

"I put my hand to my side over the pain and felt a warm trickle and knew instantly he had stabbed me. Sir George immediately aimed his pistol at young Percival whilst my father covered Lord Crowe.

"'Drop the knife or I will drop you where you stand,' he commanded, not taking his eyes off Percival for one instant.

"I didn't wait for the outcome, I was angry and so I kicked him in the knee, as taught by my father. He winced with pain as I lashed out with my sword catching him in the wrist. The knife fell to the grass without a sound as he let out a yell of pain. He backed off looking very shocked.

"'We are both wounded now, Warwick, honour is satisfied,' he whimpered as I circled him, ready to thrust.

"'To the death was yours and your father's decree, Crowe, and to the death it will be,' I maintained as I thrust at his middle.

"From that moment on I gained the upper hand, forcing him to retreat until I caught him high up in his right shoulder. He dropped his sword and screamed he could not continue. I picked it up and placed it in his hand and told him to fight on, I told him I would decide when enough was enough. He thrust at me a couple more times before I parried his blade for the last time, with my own going down his, passing up and over the hilt and driving right through his stomach and exiting out of his back. He fell slowly with my blade still in him and impaled himself into the soft ground.

"There was an eerie silence before I heard a hideous scream emitting from Lord Crowe as he rushed to his son's body jerking on the ground. He realised immediately that the movement was his son's death throes and turned to look up at me. As I held his mad stare through his cold black beady eyes, I looked into the depths of hell. His fierce hatred showed as he started to curse and swear at me. My father held his pistol pointed at his head, ready for any sudden movement, but none came.

"'I will see you dead for this, Warwick,' he spat at me, before I turned and walked away.

"My father came to me, took off his scarf as he moved behind me, and tied it round my head. I felt power that day, power as I have never felt it before as the scarf seemed to mould itself to my skull. My eyes were drawn to the edge of the green beyond the cheering crowd, and I saw twenty-eight Chinese warriors, with golden dragons emblazoned on their chest armour, raise their bronze swords in salute. As they put down their blades, the warlord stepped forward a pace and they all bowed. I looked up to the heavens to thank God for my deliverance, and there, in the bright morning sky, was the figure of a robed Oriental with a dragon by his side. The dragon roared fire from his nostrils, and when I eventually looked down the warriors had gone. They had simply melted into the mist surrounding the green.

"That night, after answering question after question from the magistrate about how three of us had inflicted such horrendous and fatal injuries to so many of the footpads, my father told me the story of how he had come into possession of the scarf and its strange powers. That is a story for another day, though. Sir George and my father impressed on me that Lord Crowe would not rest until he saw me dead, and that it would be best for me to disappear for a while, so I joined the Royal Navy under the patronage of Sir George and my father.

Captain Hardy had served with both of them, and under Sir George, and was only too willing to take me as a midshipman, and so here I am."

FOUR

After the Battle - Cape of Trafalgar, 1805.

George looked at Robert's bloodied sling on his shoulder. The wound still seemed to be weeping.

"How's the shoulder?" he asked.

"Never mind the blasted shoulder, what a story. If you had told me that before I'd seen the warriors with my own eyes, I would have had you clapped in irons and committed to an asylum the moment we reached shore. Besides, you seem to have your own injuries to contend with."

"Superficial, head and shoulder, just scratch injuries, really," George answered.

"How come I was able to see those warriors and no other members of the crew did?"

"I have no idea. Sir George, my godfather could see them as well as my father, but the only other witnesses were those that died. I think the scarf protects those that are close to me."

Robert just gazed at this strange but pleasant young man, not knowing what to say or how to react. What he did feel was a strong bond, and that he would be tied to him for life. What he didn't know was that George was feeling the same, although he too couldn't explain why.

As they looked out to sea and the aftermath of the battle, the ocean, which had been getting increasingly rough, was now getting quite violent, with waves tossing even the largest ships about like corks.

"I think we are in for one almighty storm," Robert commented in his American drawl, which sounded like a mix of Irish and West Country brogue. "Typical after a great battle, it must be the gunpowder that causes it," he added idly.

"Methinks we are going to lose a few ships tonight," George answered, as he watched one of the French ships list to port and then gradually slide under the surface. "Trouble is they are now manned by our own men, as well as the enemy prisoners."

They felt a violent shudder below their feet as a giant wave hit the *Victory*. More rigging came down on to the deck as members of the crew scrambled to get out of the way.

"We are going to have our own hands full keeping this old girl afloat, let alone worrying about others," George said.

"Get this cleared away and overboard," he shouted, as men appeared with axes and began cutting the timbers and rigging away.

The violent storm turned into one of hurricane force and lasted for over three days. Ship after ship succumbed to the ocean, or was driven against the rocks of Cadiz. The *Victory* had lost her means of steering and she was herself taken in tow, straining against the hawsers that threatened to break at any moment.

On the fourth day following the battle, a very weary George and Robert were standing on the weather deck, watching as they were towed into Gibraltar. They were the lucky ones, unlike a lot of other men in the fleet who had perished in the storms.

"I wonder if my family have heard news of our victory," he commented. "Will they know I made it through yet, do you think?"

"I wouldn't have thought so, George. They'll have to sweat it out a little while longer; it takes time for news to get back to England."

"What about you, Robert, where is your family?"

"Alas, I have no immediate family. I have an uncle and aunt in Kent who looked after me when I returned to England after my parents were killed."

George looked at his new-found friend and saw the sorrow in his eyes. Was this why he was so brave and reckless, did he care if he really lived or died?

"What happened to them?"

Robert watched as they tied up alongside the dock and workers from the port started to pour aboard the *Victory*. George thought he was going to ignore his question, but then he turned and smiled at him balefully.

"I haven't discussed this with anybody else, not even my relatives in Kent," he started. "I was eighteen years of age, and had enrolled at West Point Military Academy, north of New York alongside the Hudson River. I was one of the first entrants or cadets in the new academy, and I was doing quite well. My father and mother, together with my sister Alice, were at home running our farm eighty miles south. We had good fertile land and the farm was doing well. One day, early in October 1892, without warning Indians raided the farm, killing them all and burning the farm to the ground."

Robert's voice faltered a little before he cleared his throat and carried on. "I got the news from a neighbour two days later. I immediately finished at West Point and travelled back with him. There was nothing left but ashes and three graves. I swore vengeance on the barbarians who had done this until I learnt that white pioneers had massacred a whole tribe of men, women and children, and this was done in retaliation."

He hesitated again, his knuckles showing white with the pain and the futility of it all. "Where would it all end? I would avenge my family, they would retaliate even further, and so it would go on. I decided to leave and return to England where my parents were from, and stay with my father's relatives in Kent."

"I'm so sorry, Robert, I didn't realise. To lose one parent, let alone two, and your sister, must have been... must still be very hard to take."

"Water under the bridge now, George, life goes on, and I've learnt to live with it."

"Do you intend on staying with the Marines?"

"I suppose so. It's my substitute family, so to speak. I will have to accompany my colonel to London, as my commanding officer was killed in the battle."

"Your colonel," George asked, puzzled. "Who's he?"

"Nelson, of course," he admonished mildly. "He's the colonel of my regiment as well as an admiral in the Royal Navy, and as such we will afford him all military honours that befit his rank and status," he added with a rueful smile. "We will take his body back from here to Portsmouth and I will accompany him to London where he will probably lie in state. I'll know more when we get our orders on our return."

It was nearly three months since leaving Portsmouth when the *Victory* limped home, arriving on the 4th January 1806. George ordered his detail to stand down with the rest of the crew. Crowds lined the docks and surrounding streets to cheer the ship's safe arrival, but the celebrations were muted because of the death of the one man the nation loved above all others.

As the gangplanks were being secured, people started to climb aboard. Officers of high rank, as well as members of the government, entered a never-ending queue, until Captain Hardy ordered a stop. George saw his father and Sir George arguing with two Marines on guard and blocking the brow's entrance. Hardy saw the remonstration and grinned as he recognized his old commanding officer and his fellow shipmate, Rodney Warwick. He sent the Marine at the top of the brow to go down and to escort them up.

"Mr Warwick. To me, if you please!" Hardy shouted, above the cacophony of noise emanating from those milling on the top deck.

George saw his father coming up the brow at the same time he heard Captain Hardy's command, and went forward.

"Warwick, sir," he reported, saluting with a big grin on his face.

"You are excused for the moment, Mr Warwick. Tell Sir George I will await him in my cabin in due course."

George immediately rushed to the top of the brow as his father and Sir George emerged. Rodney Warwick didn't say a word. His mood seemed sombre for such a happy occasion and it was with tears in his eyes that he embraced his son in a bear hug that threatened to crush the life out of him.

"You have had us all so worried. Your mother has been driving us mad with her concerns. Welcome home, son, welcome home."

He opened his eyes and looked over his father's shoulder to see a smiling set of white teeth surrounded by whiskers, grinning at him. Sir George winked as his father let him go. He received the same treatment from his godfather as his own father. Bruised and feeling battered, George felt a welcome release as he was let go.

"Hello, Sir George, it's good to be back, sir." He grinned back at them. "Captain Hardy would like to see you, when you have a moment, sir."

"I'll just pop along and see him then. It will give you a chance to talk to your father and tell him all about your battle."

Before Sir George moved off, George saw Robert coming from the direction of Hardy's cabin.

"Just a moment, sir," he said stopping Sir George. "I would like to introduce you to Lieutenant Robert Gates of his Majesty's Marines. He knows about the scarf and the warriors."

Rodney and Sir George exchanged knowing glances as they both put out their hands to receive him.

"I am pleased to meet you, Mr Warwick, sir, and you Sir George. I've heard a great deal about you from George, although your reputation for prize-taking is legendary."

"It's good to meet you, Lieutenant. We do need to talk at some point, about what George has just said," Sir George responded. "But first I have to see the captain of this ship." With that, he moved off.

"I'll leave you to talk with your son, sir, he has a lot to tell you," Robert said to Rodney, before taking his leave.

The two of them moved to the side of the ship and watched the coming and goings of the traffic along the dockside as they talked at length about the battle and the warriors' involvement. An hour later, Sir George returned from his meeting with Hardy.

"Hardy's received his orders from the Admiralty. We will have to take our leave, Rodney. The *Victory* is to transport Nelson to London. We will meet you in Greenwich the day of the funeral, George. Make your way to the Volunteer Tavern in Broad Street. We'll meet there before the procession starts."

They said their farewells, both Sir George and his father understanding that duty came before family and friends. After they had disembarked the *Victory*, George bumped into Robert as he started to go below.

"A moment, George, please, I've just left Captain Hardy. We will be going up to the Thames before I escort Nelson to Greenwich where he will lie in state in Greenwich Hospital until his funeral procession. I'll be leaving you then, and I'm afraid there has been no provision for any of the crew to attend his funeral, so we will have to meet up afterwards."

On receipt of the news that no crew member was allowed at the funeral, bitterness and resentment abounded amongst the crew for the whole trip up the Thames Estuary, where they eventually moored at the Nore.

They took on board timber taken from the French ship *L'orient*, which had been blown apart at the Battle of the Nile, another of Nelson's famous victories. The timber was used to make a simple coffin for their commander in chief. Nelson's body was removed from the barrel containing brandy, which had preserved him for the past three months, and placed in the simple wood coffin. He was reverently lowered onto a barge that was to convey him up the River Thames to lie in state.

"It's time for me to leave with an escort party to take Nelson to Greenwich. What are your plans, George? Are you staying in the service, or are you leaving?"

"I'll be staying," George replied firmly. "I want to move into frigates, like my father and Sir George before me, but I'm definitely staying in."

"Who knows, George, we may even serve together. At least I hope we will," Robert said as he saluted, and then moved off to board the waiting barge.

George joined the whole crew lining the decks. They sadly said their farewell to Nelson, as he started his final journey. All hats were removed as men's faces streamed with tears, strong men, fearless men, who now, once again, unashamedly showed their emotions.

Two days later, due to a public outcry, stirred to a point of frenzy by the British press, they received the news that all available hands could attend Nelson's funeral in London.

***

At six in the morning, George arrived at the Volunteer Tavern in Broad Street. Despite the hour, he had to fight through the crowds to get there. Nelson's funeral was going to be a very busy one, with most of the country turning out for it, and it seemed to George that most of them were trying to get into the tavern.

The landlord was at the door, vetting people who were trying to get in. He saw George's uniform and immediately stepped aside to admit him.

"I am meeting Sir George Fitzwilliam and my father here, Landlord. Can I have a table, please?"

On hearing the name of Sir George, he sprang to life. "This way, young sir," he beckoned in a gruff voice, as he bowed his head. "I will clear a table for you."

He led George into the dimly lit interior of the tavern, told two men sitting at one of the tables to hop it, and cleared the plates and mugs. "Will this do for you, young master?" he asked as he pulled a third chair up to the table.

"It will do nicely, Landlord, thank you for your accommodation. I'll have a jug of your best ale whilst I wait, if you please."

"Certainly, sir, and I will look out for Sir George, who I do know of old."

George had got through three jugs of ale before Sir George entered the tavern, followed closely by his father. As they were shown to his table, George spotted them, and in his excitement overturned the table in his eagerness to greet them.

He received the same treatment as aboard the *Victory*. They eventually released their embrace and George noticed that Sir George was dressed in full captain's uniform. He didn't hold back either, embracing George and lifting him off his feet as they whirled round and round.

"You look quite resplendent, Sir George, got somewhere to go?" George joked as he was released.

"Don't be so impudent, young man," Sir George mildly chastised. "As a senior captain I am expected to form part of the guard of honour at Nelson's funeral. And talking about it, we must make our way there shortly, the crowds are becoming horrendous."

"We will make our way back here after the funeral, I have booked the table with the landlord and he will feed us on our return," his father confirmed.

They lost Sir George in the throng as they made their way to St Paul's. It was madness, with over ten thousand troops leading one hundred Navy captains behind the rich and famous, such as the Prince of Wales and Lord Hood. George lost count of how many admirals he spotted, all regaled in full uniform and honours. They briefly saw Nelson's ornate casket go past. What a difference it made compared to the simple wooden coffin in which he had left the *Victory*. Eventually his father had had enough.

"This is utter insanity, George, let's make our way back to the Volunteer and get out of this mob."

"That's if we can make it back, Father. Do you know the way through this lot?"

"Follow me, son, we'll head down through Ludgate, Broad Street is only two streets away from there."

George tucked in behind his father's broad muscular back as he elbowed and pushed his way through the crowd. They made it through Ludgate, even though it was just as mad, eventually emerging on Broad Street and forcing their way through to the Volunteer.

"You made it, sirs." The landlord stated the obvious, surrounded by some of his old cronies, and appearing slightly the worse for drink. "I still have your table kept... this way."

As they arrived at the table, they saw a uniformed soldier slumped over it with a broken jug by his side. The landlord took hold of his jacket at the back of his neck, and hauled him off of his seat.

"This is reserved for the Senior Service," he declared. "Not for the likes of you. I'll just get rid of him, sirs, and I'll be back to take your order." With that, he hauled the man backwards and disappeared into the throng.

His father laughed. "Could have been any one of us," he quipped.

They decided not to wait for Sir George before ordering food and ale for themselves. The landlord had reserved them three rooms for the night.

It was a good two hours later when Sir George eventually made his appearance. They watched him push roughly through the crowd, laughing loudly as he came towards them. *It could have been any one of them,* sprang to George's mind as he saw Sir George lurch forward. Rodney was on his feet in a flash and caught his friend before he fell headlong into the table.

"Hello, you two, had a couple of snifters with some old shipmates. Had a devil of a job getting through to here," he slurred happily. "Tomorrow, I need to talk to you, young man, but for now... we get drunk. Landlord!" he bellowed.

It soon became known to the tavern's customers that one of Nelson's own was amongst them, fresh from the battle, so to speak. The ale didn't stop flowing the whole night long and George was slapped repeatedly on his back so hard that he found it difficult to keep the ale down.

***

George was awakened most rudely by a banging on his door. He couldn't remember where he was. *Must be in the ship,* he thought as the movement of the room overtook him. He raised himself onto his elbows as his father entered the room. His head hurt like hell, his father laughed loudly and went over to the window, drawing the drapes back, letting in the glare of the morning sun which was shining between the buildings opposite. The searing light burnt into George's eyes. Bolts of lightning hit his brain, causing him to squint and shut his eyes tight again.

"Up, George," his father shouted. "Breakfast, and then we must travel."

"Breakfast, travel?" he queried. "What is the blasted time for heaven's sake?" he asked getting out of bed in just his shirt.

"No swearing, George, you're not aboard ship now, on your feet and get washed. I'll see you downstairs in ten minutes."

As his father was about to leave, a young serving wench came in with a towel and a large pitcher of water. She looked down at George's muscular legs and smiled in appreciation.

"Out, wench," he shouted. "Have you no modesty, girl?"

Tittering, she set the pitcher down on the sideboard, still keeping her eyes glued firmly to his legs as she handed him the towel.

"Out, out, out," shouted George as he turned around to great peals of laughter from his father as he slammed the door.

Washed and dressed, but not feeling any better, he made his way gingerly down the dark creaking staircase, and into the tavern's kitchen. Sir George had already breakfasted. His father was halfway through his, when he looked up at the pitiful sight of George entering the room. Sir George grinned as he looked at his father.

"Remember those days, Rodney?"

"We never got that bad, did we?" his father answered as they both laughed.

George failed to see anything amusing in his plight, he felt like death. He waved the landlord away, who was about to put a plate of food before him.

"I said last night, not that you will remember much about it, that we needed to talk about your future, young man."

He remembered Sir George arriving at the tavern rather the worst for drink, if he recalled correctly, but he couldn't for the life of him remember any conversation, let alone anything about his future. He kept quiet and let him continue.

"I think Sir George would like to talk to you before you get home, before your mother and sister get their claws into you," his father explained.

Quite why his mother and sister would have anything to do with this was beyond poor George at this time. All he could think of was his blinding headache and his double vision as he squinted across the table at the blurred figures opposite.

"I had a few conversations with some of my old shipmates last night," Sir George started, "Captain Hardy amongst them, as well as my old friend Captain John Brownlow. He's a frigate captain of experience and of some renown. The upshot of it was that Brownlow would like you aboard *HMS Broad*, young man. She's a thirty-eight gunner and as fast as any frigate afloat."

The message was filtering through his clouded mind. Frigates, this is what he always wanted, the same as his father and Sir George before him. What a stroke of luck. *No, not luck, who you know,* he thought as his vision started to clear.

"Before you answer, George, you had better listen further," his father advised him.

"Hardy will release your Marine's lieutenant, and Brownlow has agreed for him to serve aboard the *Broad*."

"Robert who, Robert Gates?" he asked as if in a trance. "Robert will be in the same ship, does he know?"

"Of course he knows. He was with Hardy when we spoke, he's all for it, young man."

"If I didn't feel so bad, Sir George, I would drink to that."

"Landlord!" Sir George bellowed.

FIVE

March 1806, *HMS Broad.*

Midshipman Grahame Johns frantically shook the lifeless figure from his hammock in his efforts to wake him.

"Come on, George, get out and get up top, your watch is about to start, man."

"All right, all right, I'm awake," George protested as he tipped himself out of his hammock, which was immediately filled by Grahame's small thin frame as the grinning youth took his place.

George looked down on the spotty pale face with the cheeky grin. "Talk about dead man's shoes, Johns," he quipped as he kicked the bottom of the hammock.

"Ouch!" cried Grahame. "You had better get moving, the old man's on the prowl," he warned.

Captain Abraham Brownlow, known as the old man to everybody on board, was master and commander of *HMS Broad*. The ship boasted thirty-eight eighteen pounders, ten nine pounders and eight cannonades in its armaments. She was a real fighting ship, a true raider of the high seas. George couldn't have been happier with this dream of a posting.

"It's a Leda-class frigate, Mr Warwick, named after Zeus's love interest in Greek mythology," Brownlow had said proudly when George had first come aboard.

"Sir?" he had questioned, not quite understanding the meaning.

"When he turned himself into a swan to seduce the lovely Leda," he tried to explain to his young midshipman, with a smile on his rubbery features.

George had been puzzled, who on earth was this Zeus? He had no idea, but to seduce a woman as a swan seemed madness in the extreme.

Brownlow had served with both Rodney Warwick and Sir George and was well aware of their prize-taking abilities. He hoped that a little of it had rubbed off on Midshipman George Warwick. At fifty-eight years of age, he was showing signs of slowing down and was looking forward to retirement in the near future, but he desperately needed to add to his prize monies for a more comfortable retirement.

George tied his scarf round his neck as he made his way up the stairs to the quarter deck. He heard the bells sound eight times as he emerged into a light drizzle being carried by the gentle breeze.

"Eight bells and all is well," the officer of the watch called out.

"Good morning, Bertie, thanks for rousing me," he said, greeting the sandy haired youth, who was turning the two sand timers over to start George's watch.

A pair of bright blue eyes looked back at him as Midshipman Bertram Harris smiled in acknowledgement.

"Hello, George, we are on course, just keep her on this heading," he responded cheerfully in his West Country accent. "I think I saw the old man about earlier, so you had better keep a sharp look out."

"Grahame's already mentioned it," he answered, looking down at the smaller man.

Being almost six feet in height, George towered over most of the crew, let alone the young midshipman. "You don't mind if I check our bearings, do you, Bertie?"

"Be my guest, I'm off below to get my head down."

George checked the course on the dimly lit compass which corresponded to the bearings given. The *Broad* was responding well in the light swell and gentle breeze. How he was starting to love this frigate. She acted as gracefully as the swans he used to watch on the coast at Fareham. She was aptly named, according to the captain, and he agreed.

George turned to the swarthy rating manning the wheel. "Keep her on this heading, Jennings, I'm going forward," he ordered.

"Aye, aye, sir," the rating on the wheel answered, but sneering at George's back, as he saw the scarf round his neck hanging outside his uniform jacket.

A few minutes later, after a turn round the deck, George returned to the wheel. He was standing with his back to the wheel when Captain Brownlow came up from his cabin. The captain remained standing there for a few moments before saying anything.

"Everything in order, Mr Warwick?" the booming Hampshire accent rang out. George jumped and sprang to attention. He hadn't heard him approach and turned around in a flash.

"All's fine," he answered as he tried to salute, nearly taking his own eye out. "On course and all quiet, sir."

Brownlow stepped forward, passed George and walked up the deck with a huge smile on his weather-beaten face. *It didn't do any harm to keep the youngsters on their feet,* he thought to himself.

"You're not a rating, Mr Warwick, be so good as to adjust your dress and place the scarf under your jacket," he said over his shoulder.

Jennings, on the wheel, smirked as he heard this.

"And if I catch you smirking at one of my officers again, Jennings, I'll have you flogged," he added as he walked off.

George watched the broad back of his captain moving forward on slightly bowed legs before turning to face a grim-faced Jennings. He just stared at the swarthy rating, no reprimand being necessary. Jennings knew his card had now been well and truly marked. The incident did tell George one thing: Brownlow either had eyes in the back of his head, or he knew his crewmen inside out.

"Was that the old man I heard, George?" The American accent was unmistakable as Robert Gates, fully dressed in his scarlet coated uniform, and looking as handsome as ever in the early morning drizzle, came up to the deck from below.

The fact that Robert was able to join the *Broad* was the icing on the cake. George couldn't have wished for a better companion than the daring Marine lieutenant who had fought alongside him at Trafalgar. His parents and Sir George had taken to him when he had visited the farm after their appointment to the *HMS Broad*, and so had his younger sister Rebecca, who couldn't find anything else to talk about after he left.

"It was indeed, Robert, he's just gone forward. He caught me with my scarf outside me jacket and ripped me off about it. Sloppy me, it won't happen again. He's a fair and just man, but a strict one for discipline and likes things just right."

"I don't think you need to worry where you stand with him, he thinks the world of you, thinks you are going to make it to the very top."

"I'm going forward again," George said, ignoring his last remark. He picked up his telescope and moved off. "Keep her on this heading, Jennings, and keep a sharp eye out."

"I'll keep you company, are you expecting anything?" Robert asked, trying to get a glimpse of George's scarf.

"Being at war with the French and Spanish keeps us all wary," he answered as he shouted to the men aloft up the main mast. "Keep a sharp look out, men. We're in dangerous waters from now on."

"Aye, aye, sir," the answer came from Briggs, a trustworthy leading seaman in his late thirties, who had served with George aboard the *Victory* at Trafalgar.

Briggs had started his service as a powder monkey at the ripe old age of twelve. He was now a strapping powerful man, well-liked and respected by the men and the officers alike. Men like Briggs formed the backbone of a crew. George had challenged him to a race to the top of the main mast, laughing with him as they descended, having beaten the experienced sailor to the top. George's reputation was growing, becoming that of an action man, a man you could rely on in a tight situation.

George and Robert were standing at the prow, looking forward, scanning the red horizon through their eyeglasses as the sun threatened to come up over the skyline.

"What time do your folks rise?"

"Do you mean, what time does my sister rise?"

"Am I that obvious?"

"Both of you are, I hope your intentions are honourable, Mr Gates," George stated sternly.

"Of course they bloody well..." Robert stopped as he saw the grin on his friend's face. "You are a bastard at times, George, do you know that?"

He didn't reply, his concentration being on a small black speck on the horizon to the left of the glowing red sunrise. The scarf around his neck started to feel warm and throb gently.

"To the left of the sunrise, what can you see?"

Robert scanned the line in front of him from left to right, and then saw the black spot in the form of a small white sail as it became larger. Before he could say anything a shout from atop echoed out.

"Sail ahead, sail dead ahead," Briggs's voice rang out.

"It's a sail all right," Robert stated, "but whose is it?"

"I don't bloody well care, I'm not getting caught out on my watch," George muttered. "Beat to quarters!" he screamed at the top of his lungs.

All hell seemed to break loose, as men started to run in all directions to the sound of a drum beating loudly and rhythmically. Powder monkeys suddenly appeared, frantically running backwards and forwards with assorted ammunition for the big guns, and placing pistols and cutlasses in strategic places around the ship.

"What is it, Mr Warwick?" the voice of Lieutenant Bray rang out, as he ran forward buttoning up his tunic.

Before George could answer a further voice boomed out. "Mr Warwick, to me immediately," the captain called out, having miraculously sprung from the bowels of the ship.

All three of them ran aft, dodging the crew as they moved to their posts and readied the main guns. They reached a very stern Brownlow standing by the wheel.

"Report, Mr Warwick, if you please," he said calmly.

"A sail dead ahead, sir, heading straight for us," George replied.

"Confirmation, Mr Bray."

Robert jumped in to back up his friend. "It's a sail, sir, I can confirm it," he said to nods of agreement from Lieutenant Bray.

Brownlow looked through the telescope and handed it back to George. "What do make of her, Mr Warwick?"

"Much too far away to make her out, sir, but I could hazard a guess."

"Could you by God," he replied with faint amusement, as George concentrated ahead of him. "And pray, what would that guess be?"

"She looks low in the water as she ploughs towards us, fully laden methinks, a Frenchie, sir. A French supply ship probably heading towards their garrison on the island of Naranga."

As they concentrated on the ship heading towards them, they saw it slowly start to turn and head east away from them.

Brownlow looked aloft and shouted at the crow's nest. "What do you make of her, Briggs?"

Briggs strained his eyes for some moments, squinting into the rising sun, before he answered, "Can't make her out, sir, but she's a fair size and looks fully laden. One thing for sure, she's seen us and is heading away as fast as she can."

The captain turned his attention back to George. "Just why do you think that, mister?" Before George could answer he continued, "All officers to my cabin, you as well, Lieutenant Gates."

The excitement was obvious as the young midshipmen entered the captain's cabin, together with Lieutenants Bray and Driscoll. John Bray was a promising officer, but always happy to leave decision making to others, an ethos that had to change if he wanted to progress in the Navy, according to Brownlow. Bartholomew Driscoll was old and staid in his ways, and it showed in his cynical manner and approach to things.

The captain's steward had cleared the table in the centre of the cabin and laid a chart out on it, with two weights placed on either side to stop it rolling up again. Bertie Harris and Grahame Johns' eyes were alive with expectation as they gazed at the map. George and Robert felt their excitement as they waited for their commander to lay out their plan of action.

He cleared his throat to speak as the slightly built dapper figure of Percival Rhodes, the fifty-year-old ship's surgeon, entered the cabin and stood by his side.

"Are we in for some action?" the surgeon asked despondently, before the captain could speak. George had never seen the man smile once since coming aboard.

"No need to clear away at this moment, Mr Rhodes, there will be plenty of time for that. If you would like to move back, my officers will be able to view the chart all the better."

A disgruntled Rhodes shuffled backwards, eyeing them over his thin spectacles as if the next time he saw them would be on his operating table. George and Robert quickly moved into his place alongside Brownlow, blocking out his view.

"Naranga, gentlemen," said the captain, pointing to an island in the east of the chart. "We are here and the ship... whatever she is, is now moving east," he said, looking up at George. "What now Naranga, Mr Warwick?"

George studied the chart studiously, looking for other possibilities, but he couldn't really see any. He looked up at his expectant commander.

"I still believe she's heading for Naranga, sir, where else would she be heading? The only other alternative is the Americas, and her course was all wrong for that."

"Reasons if you please, Mr Warwick?"

"Two reasons, sir. One, she was well laden, probably with troops and supplies to restock the garrison at Narranga which suffered an outbreak of cholera just after the defeat of the French at Trafalgar. They have had no chance to relieve the garrison until now, sir."

"And two?" Brownlow asked, raising his bushy eyebrows.

"As I said before, where else could she possibly be going? She was low in the water, sir, what a prize she would make, and we would stop the garrison from being able to raid our shipping," he added as an afterthought.

Brownlow grinned instantly, remembering the exploits of George's father and Sir George, who he had served with. Good times, he thought to himself, very lucrative times, times that he had not seen the like of since.

"You have done your homework, Mr Warwick, and I can see why you have the patronage of Lord Fitzwilliam."

"Sir George Fitzwilliam, sir," George corrected him, thinking he had made a mistake.

"Not any more, young man, he has been elevated to the nobility and sits on the Admiralty board. I received notification just before we left Plymouth."

George was stunned. He could imagine the festivities back at the manor in Hampshire, with his own family attending along with the rest of the surrounding inhabitants. What a party that must have been. He looked up to see Robert grinning at him.

"What a party that must have been," he whispered, echoing George's own thoughts.

Brownlow brought them back to the present. "Mr Bray, your thoughts, if you please."

"I have to concur with Mr Warwick, sir. It does seem to be the only logical explanation for its presence in these waters," he said, smiling at George and Robert, as Driscoll scowled.

"Very well, gentlemen, back on deck and let's see where the chase takes us."

As he made for the deck, Lieutenant Bray shouted up to the main mast. "Briggs, what's her heading?"

"She's still heading away, sir, and making heavy going of it."

"Let's chase her down, Mr Bray," the captain ordered, as more sail was hoisted and the course set to cut across her. "We should have her before nightfall at our rate of knots."

For most of the afternoon they dogged the ship, gaining gradually hour by hour. George could feel the apprehension of the ship's company as they steadily ran her to ground. Luck was not going to be with them for much longer as they noticed a mist coming towards them from the east. It was getting denser as it approached at quite a speed, soon becoming a thick fog.

"Damn it," Brownlow said through gritted teeth. "We are going to lose her if she gets in there."

The fog swallowed the ship up, but not before they made out the French Tricolour flying from the mizzen-mast.

"Damn it, damn it, damn it," Brownlow muttered in frustration. "No point in continuing through that lot, Mr Bray. Stand the men down if you please. Ships officers to my cabin," he ordered.

Gathered in the cabin, George looked at the chart still laid out on the table. There was nowhere else this ship could possibly go, unless it was going to head for America. He looked up at Brownlow and waited to be asked.

"Mr Driscoll, what do you think?"

He looked up from the chart, almost sneering as he eyed George across the table.

"Well it's not heading for that island now, is it? I think it goes to the Americas, probably New York. We've lost her in the fog, anyway."

"Mr Bray, your comments, if you please."

Bray looked at George and then down at the chart again before looking up at Driscoll.

"I think Lieutenant Driscoll is wrong, sir. I believe that Mr Warwick is correct in his assumptions. My wager is still on Naranga. Why would they have been on that course? Naranga is the only option."

Driscoll glowered at the lack of support from his colleague, and shot George a look that could kill, before moving away from the table and standing behind the midshipmen.

"Mr Gates, anything to add?" Brownlow asked.

"Yes, Captain. If Mr Warwick is correct, and I believe him to be so, I would urge some caution. There will be at least two to three hundred French soldiers aboard the ship if they are to garrison Naranga again."

"Your point is, Mr Gates?"

"My point is, sir, the prevention of troops reaching Naranga must be our priority." He looked at George almost apologetically as he continued, "Prize must be a secondary consideration. The destruction of the troops must be paramount."

Brownlow looked as if he was going to explode as he glared at Robert, and then stared at all of them around the table.

"Thank you for pointing out my duty, Mr Gates, it was a consideration I have already given some thought to," he answered, as Robert shifted uncomfortably from foot to foot. "If we are skilful, or should I say, lucky enough to track her down, we will of course go in for the kill… or until she strikes her colours."

"I apologise, Captain," Robert responded with his face reddening. "I didn't mean…"

"No need, Mr Gates, I understand your concerns, you felt it was your duty to speak, I respect that. Now let's plot our course to intercept this Frenchie." He grinned, relieving the tension that had built up. "Well, Mr Warwick, let's have your course, if you please."

George ran his finger along an imaginary line from their present position to Naranga. "At our present speed and with favourable wind, with their cumbersome cargo and their rate of speed, I would estimate our point of intercept would be… about here, sir."

"I agree, anybody else have any observations on this matter?"

Nobody answered as they all murmured their agreement. Save for one exception, Lieutenant Driscoll, who remained at the rear, scowling as his eyes bored into George's back. Robert noticed the look and winked at George as he indicated Driscoll at the back with a nod of his head. George turned, looked at Driscoll, and held his malevolent gaze until Driscoll sullenly looked away.

"Keep the crew stood down, but on standby," Brownlow ordered. "Everybody back to their posts and about yer duties." As they started to leave the cabin, Brownlow spoke again. "Mr Driscoll, remain if you please."

The cabin emptied out with the exception of the captain's steward.

"You too, Blackwell, I'll call for you if I need anything further." As he left, Brownlow turned to face a smiling Driscoll who thought his opinion was going to be asked for.

"What in damnation do you think you are doing, sir?" Brownlow thundered.

Driscoll was taken aback, the smile disappearing from his face to be replaced with a whitening pallor. He couldn't understand where this had come from.

"I am talking about your resentment of Mr Warwick, sir. If I've noticed, others will have too, and I will not have it, sir. Do you understand me?"

"I don't know what you mean, I... just don't agree with his reasoning..." he trailed off as Brownlow glared at him.

"It's more than that, man, your contempt is more than obvious, and unless you have any misgivings about Mr Warwick's duties, it will stop. Do you hear me? You are my senior officer and I look to you for harmony and the wellbeing of the crew. I cannot have you singling out any man for the sake of it, I won't have it. Now get out and about yer duties."

Driscoll came through the cabin door to see the grin on Blackwell's face as he passed him. He was now starting to seethe as he searched the deck for the object of his hatred. That object was standing on the quarter deck with Robert, both becoming aware of the hostile gaze in their direction.

"You'd better watch him, George, he's definitely got it in for you," Robert murmured, as they watched Driscoll move off and go below.

George shrugged as he went forward with Robert to keep vigil and watch for the French ship. George was slowly getting more apprehensive as the time for the intercept approached.

"Don't worry, George, it will turn up," Robert said encouragingly, picking up on his mood. "It's still early in the day yet."

The fog to the west was starting to lift to reveal a bright shining sun getting lower in the brilliant blue sky of the Caribbean. The wind was light and favourable as Brownlow ordered sail to be taken in to slow their progress so they didn't overshoot their intercept. They seemed to glide through the deep blue gentle swell of the sea without any effort.

George watched the sail being taken in by the many men in the rigging. Briggs was amongst them, making sure everything went smoothly. Suddenly, George felt the warmth of his scarf around his neck. He immediately put the telescope to his eye and scanned the vast ocean in the direction he thought the enemy ship would come from. Robert picked up on the new tension gripping his friend.

"What is it?" he asked.

"I think they are near and I think we ought to get ready for them," he replied.

Robert scanned the horizon, shutting his eyes as he passed the glare of the sun. Nothing, he couldn't see a thing.

"Briggs," George shouted. "Get up top and look for sail coming from the west."

"Aye, aye, sir," he responded immediately, passing through the rigging to the main mast which he scrambled up with ease.

They looked around the ship as they waited, spotting Brownlow by the wheel looking down at them. He felt their tension as he too looked to the west for sign of the enemy.

"Sail ahoy, sail ahoy!" Biggs's urgent cry went out from aloft.

All eyes looked to the front as they tried to spot the ship against the horizon and the glare of the sun off the sea. George picked her out as he pointed out the direction to Robert.

"Beat to quarters," shouted Brownlow from the poop deck as he also spotted the enemy heading towards them. "Officers to me," he added as he turned on his heel and went to his cabin.

For the second time that day they picked their way through the busy throng of crewmen rushing to their stations, as they made their way aft.

"Down you get, Briggs," George called up to the main mast.

"Aye, aye, Mr Warwick," he called back as he abseiled down the rigging, landing on the deck before George had time to reach the quarter deck.

"We seem to have it right, Mr Warwick," a happy Brownlow gleamed. "If we are right and it is a garrison supply ship, our first duty is to take her out of commission at all costs. As Lieutenant Gates has rightly pointed out, we must vanquish the enemy first before thinking of any prize." He looked at the excited faces of his officers as he continued. "We must ensure that we are ahead of her or astern. It is my intention to rake her and take out the French infantry as quickly as possible."

The excitement seemed to die on the young officers faces as they heard the term "rake her." This was a devastating action that fired over five hundred musket balls through either the stern or the prow of a ship, resulting in catastrophic injuries and death. George had used this to good effect aboard *HMS Victory* at Trafalgar. The thought of this ever happening to them filled them with horror.

"I am aware of your misgivings, gentlemen, but we have no choice, we cannot afford to let their soldiers get through. It looks as if we will be meeting them head on, in which case we will employ the forward guns to rake her before turning to larboard and using our main guns as we pass. We should be in a position to take out her rudder with our rear guns as we come astern of her."

"What then, sir?" Robert asked, "Do we board her?"

"If she strikes her colours, Mr Gates, we most certainly will, but if she continues to resist, I intend to send her to the bottom of the ocean with all on board."

This was a different side to Brownlow, which in a way, quite shocked George. This polite, mild-mannered man was talking about wholesale death and destruction. He knew he could be firm and resolute, but this ruthlessness was altogether something different.

"I understand your misgivings, gentlemen, but our actions are necessary for the safety of His Majesty's Navy and all who sail these waters. To your posts, gentlemen, good luck and may God go with you. Now let's chase the bugger down."

The ship was cleared for action by men with buckets of sand spreading it over the decks to soak up the blood that would be spilt if the enemy made any kind of fight of it. George noticed the French ship start to change course as they were spotted, but it was too late for them to get away. Brownlow ordered the helmsman to dog her and the *Broad* gradually closed the gap.

"She's changed her mind, sir," Briggs shouted out in surprise. "She's heading back at us."

"They're going to make a fight of it," Brownlow asserted. "My plan still stands, gentlemen. Mr Warwick, Mr Johns, get forward, if you please."

"Come on, Grahame, get your crew together," George said as he moved forward. "Briggs, get you team on the larboard gun and make her ready."

"Aye, sir," the stocky leading seaman answered as he shouted to several of his men to follow him.

George stopped and looked around at Robert. They grinned at one another before coming together and shaking hands.

"See you when we board her, George." Robert smiled grimly, as he moved off to join his detachment of Marines as George ran forward.

"Gibson, Meacher, move yourselves. Baldwin, Caukwell, Clarke, to me now." Briggs was shouting out his orders to his team as George arrived at the massive thirty-two pounder gun. They started to load it with the deadly canister of musket balls, determinedly ramming it down the gun's barrel. Briggs kissed the big gun as it was pulled forward ready to fire.

"I wouldn't do that after she's fired, Briggs," George quipped, thinking of the searing heat that the gun produced on firing.

"Aye, sir, no, sir," Briggs responded with a grin.

George looked over to the starboard gun and saw Grahame's team keeping pace with them. He acknowledged Grahame's thumbs up and smiled at him. The gun teams were tense and nervous. George noticed that they were stripped to the waist and barefoot, ready for action and ready for injury. He remembered the *Victory*, the gore of blood mixed with the sand forming a sticky morass below his feet.

Kicking off his shoes, he removed his short jacket and pulled his shirt over his head. He tied his scarf around his head resembling a pirate from the Barbary Coast. The crew at first couldn't believe what they were seeing from this officer and then they laughed, tensions disappearing before they let out a loud cheer.

Brownlow heard the cheer, and turned to look forward, knowing instantly what had caused it as he caught sight of a younger Rodney Warwick, George's father, from all those years ago. He was about to shout his disapproval and censure this unruly midshipman, but then realised how this had lifted the men. Perhaps he would speak of it later, he thought, and turned to watch the enemy ship coming straight at them.

George heard a whooshing sound overhead as a cannonball from the prow of the French vessel went harmlessly through the canvas sail aloft. As he turned to look up to see what damage had been done, he caught his breath as he noticed the smiling figure of the Chinese priest with the dragon in the sky directly above him.

Another shot went through the sails. The French were making the same mistakes as they always did, firing on the upward swell of the sea to take out as much of the ship's rigging as they could in the hope of rendering it powerless to sail. The British, conversely, fired on the downward swell in order to kill or maim as many crew as they could as well as hitting strategic targets aboard the enemy vessel.

A further shot from the French had a result, with Jennings, the cynical rating, falling headlong from the rigging and hitting the deck with a thud, staining the white sand with his blood. The ball had gone right through the middle of his chest, killing him outright. Crew members pounced on the body and unceremoniously heaved it overboard. They were now exposed to the enemy fire coming from high up in the *Chantelle's* rigging and they were hit by a hail of musket balls before they could regain cover. Three more injured men had to be dragged out of the firing line by their shipmates.

Robert's Marines lined the larboard side of the deck, keeping low before he gave the order to fire. Thirty Marines opened up with their muskets, firing into the enemy's rigging.

He watched, satisfied, as he saw bodies of French soldiers falling soundlessly to the deck.

"Steady, lads, keep your eye on the target and wait for my command," George ordered, more calmly than he felt. He had to get this right or they would most certainly be in for it. "We fire when we can see the nostrils of the Frenchie flare," he shouted to nervous laughter from the men.

He turned to see Brownlow watching both him and the oncoming ship. When he thought he had it right, he raised his left arm and Brownlow had the helm heaved over. George watched the enemy ship loom into sight as its prow presented itself.

"FIRE!" he screamed at the top of his lungs.

All sound was lost in the roar of the gun as it jumped and recoiled, driving itself back on its slide before being violently arrested and restrained by the hawsers attached. The heat from the barrel was instantaneous as the gunpowder fumes enveloped them in a blue-grey cloud.

They looked at the damage this deadly load had wrought on the enemy. The prow had been opened up as if made of paper, allowing the five hundred or so musket balls to rip along the decks in their deadly path.

"Oh my God," Caukwell, one of the gunners who was very religious, exclaimed, as he made the sign of the cross and closed his eyes.

They all watched as the ship passed by, almost close enough to touch, sending warm sea spray over the *Broad's* decks. George heard Brownlow order all guns to open fire.

"Fire as you bear," he called out, as cannon after cannon fired into the enemy, ripping through the side of the decks.

Musket fire sounded yet again from new French soldiers, who had climbed the rigging to be able to bear down onto the *Broad's* decks. George looked around in time to see Lieutenant Driscoll go down with a shot to his chest. As he writhed on the deck a further shot to the back of his head put him out of his agony. With the intense firing now coming from the rigging, no one went to throw him overboard. He noticed Robert stand up on the deck and call to his Marines.

"Now," he shouted as they all stood up and fired at their respective targets. More Marines, stationed on the poop deck, also opened up with devastating results, as screaming Frenchman plummeted to the decks below.

As the enemy ship drifted past, George noticed the name *Chantelle* emblazoned on its side, before it was obliterated by the cannon of the rear gunners, who also took out the rear galleries and the ship's rudder. She was now helpless and at their mercy.

Brownlow expected and waited for them to strike their colours. Instead they received a further shot from the *Chantelle* that hit a group of Marines. George looked for Robert and was relieved to see him rush to his men's aid.

"She's not done yet," shouted a grim and determined Brownlow. "Mr Warwick, get your gun ready for a further shot into her."

George's heart sank: he had seen what his first shot had done.

"Jump to it, Briggs. Get this gun ready," he commanded, obeying his orders. The scarf on his head started to feel hot and started to throb as he patted it. "I know, I know," he murmured softly in acknowledgement.

They were passing the stern of the *Chantelle* once more as Briggs concentrated on George's face, waiting for the order. Did he see his scarf glowing and changing colour? *Must be a trick of the dying sun,* he thought.

"FIRE!" George screamed once again to the deafening roar of the gun as it spat out its message of death, causing the deadly load to rip through the stern of the vessel, and along its decks.

"Oh, my God." He repeated the words of Caukwell that he had heard earlier, as screams of agony reached his ears.

Brownlow gave the order to come about. They tacked close to the *Chantelle*, giving them a good look at the damage they had wreaked on the vessel. Smoke was starting to pour out of the sides and the decks. No colours were being flown any more, but then most of the rigging and masts had been blown away. Explosions started to go off amidships as they moved in to board her.

Brownlow shouted to Robert, who was waiting for his orders with a detachment of Marines. "When you board, Mr Gates, we will stand off, we don't want the *Broad* catching fire. Mr Bray, get those fires under control as soon as you have secured the ship."

Grappling hooks snaked out from the *Broad*, pulling the stricken *Chantelle* to her. Marines and sailors screamed at the top of their lungs as they literally flew over on ropes and landed on the enemy's decks. George followed John Bray over and landed beside Robert on the vessel's poop deck. With swords drawn and bayonets fixed the complement of the *Broad* moved forward to meet the enemy.

Silence! It wasn't long before they all stopped gradually where they were. The carnage had been complete, the decks were actually running with the blood of the French, such was the ferocity of their attack. Mutilated bodies were strewn everywhere. Those that were still alive writhed in their death throes amongst their luckier dead companions.

They were all stunned. George looked at Robert's ashen face and knew it resembled his own. He felt sick as he remained stock-still in disbelief at what they were seeing.

"Where's your blood lust now, me lads?" asked Caukwell with tears streaming down his face. "They were sailors like you and me for God's sake."

"Shut up, Caukwell!" George screamed out, deafening everyone in the silence. "Below, check below."

No one moved. If this was the carnage up on top, what was it like below? Nobody wanted to find out. Smoke was starting to billow up out of the bowels of the ship as John Bray moved to the stairway leading below.

"Come on, men, follow me," he stammered as he started down the stairs. He was joined by Robert and George, with the rest of the men following reluctantly behind.

Nothing was as it should have been. Nothing was in its correct place. The decks had been raked from stem to stern leaving total devastation throughout the ship.

"Our Father, who art in heaven…" Caukwell started to pray and the whole of the boarding party joined in with their heads bowed. Their cutlasses and belaying hooks were hanging loosely by their sides.

Briggs, one of the hardest and most experienced men amongst them, was crying unashamedly with tears streaming down his face. He was not the only one to find himself affected by the horror all around him. George's mind went back to Trafalgar and the headless bodies of his old ship mate Harry and Nelson's secretary. That had been bad enough. This was on an altogether different scale. He was brought back to the present with men starting to be sick around him and moans coming from amongst the corpses.

"Check for any left alive lads, and be gentle with them," Bray ordered, as they began the gruesome task of checking the bodies.

Two hours later, the fires aboard the *Chantelle* had been extinguished and the ship secured. Out of four hundred and eighty men aboard the ship, only eighteen had survived, and it was doubtful some of them would live longer than a few hours or days.

***

George, trembling with the after effects of the carnage, had retrieved his shirt and jacket and was standing alongside John Bray in front of a grim-faced Captain Brownlow aboard the *Broad*. His lieutenant explained the scene that had met them and the numbers of the enemy who had survived.

"Get the survivors aboard the *Broad*, Mr Bray, so Mr Rhodes can attend to them. Leave a skeleton crew aboard the *Chantelle*. Oh, and Mr Warwick," he said almost absently. "Please be so good as to remove the scarf from your head, you are not a rating, sir."

As they closed the door behind them, they heard Brownlow speaking to himself. They looked through the small rectangular glass in the door to see him on his knees praying.

"Methinks it won't be the last prayer said today, George," Bray said, turning away from the cabin door. "What's with the scarf, is it some sort of talisman?"

"Something like that, sir, it belonged to my father," he said, removing it from his head and tucking it inside his jacket. "I'm going to check on the wounded prisoners below and see if Mr Gates needs a hand, sir, if that's all right?"

"Carry on, George. I'll call you if I need you."

He made his way down to the orlop deck to see a morose but attentive Robert listening to Bertie Harris as he translated the words of one of the French prisoners.

"Ask him again, Bertie," Robert urged, as Bertie questioned a badly wounded young French naval officer, who had blood-soaked bandages around his head and his left arm completely missing.

"What on earth is going on here?" George demanded to know. "He's in no condition to be interrogated."

Robert sprang upright, surprised at his sudden appearance. He took George by the arm and led him out of the orlop so that they were alone.

"Some interesting news," he started. "He's in shock, but he's talking all right."

"For Christ's sake, Robert, show some kind of decency, will you? I don't have the stomach for this at the moment," he replied, starting to move away.

Robert kept a hold of his arm and pulled him back to face him. "Listen, I didn't interrogate the Frenchie, he just started talking," he said defensively. "It's important, George."

He saw the seriousness in Robert's face. He looked down at the French officer's hurting baleful eyes, Bertie nodding his agreement by his side.

"All right, what has he said?" George conceded.

"They were on their way to Naranga, as you first thought, and you were right, they needed to garrison the fort and resupply it. Cholera has done a lot of damage to the population, and they had been carrying over three hundred soldiers to replace the dead."

"We had already guessed that much, why the excitement?"

"You don't know the half of it, George. They were not only restocking the fort, but their orders were to take on board the British seamen they had captured and imprisoned on the island, and return them to France." George was about to interrupt again when Robert continued excitedly. "Wait for it. They were also to take back all the booty they had captured throughout the Caribbean, a king's bloody fortune no less. It's just sitting there in a little ship in the harbour for us to take."

George started to take in what was being said. British seamen were never treated well by the French, he didn't give much hope to them staying alive en route to France.

"Get Bertie away from him, we must take this to the old man. I'll meet you up top."

George waited on the weather deck watching the clean-up operation as rigging was cleared away. He noticed the five hammocks, sewn up and laid out on the poop deck, awaiting burial at sea. Six British deaths, including Jennings, who had already been hurled overboard, as opposed to the heavy obscene loss of life of the enemy: it didn't seem to equate and he was at a loss for an explanation.

"Fortunes of war, Mr Warwick, there for the grace of God go I," Brownlow said from behind him, as if reading his mind.

They were joined by Robert, John Bray and young Bertie, as George addressed his captain. "We have some very startling news, sir. Mr Gates will explain."

As Brownlow heard the news he ushered them all to his cabin. Blackwell was ordered out and Brownlow addressed them.

"You can take the smiles off of your faces," he started, pushing his face into George's. "Unless it has escaped your notice, we now have two ships to crew, as well as eighteen enemy prisoners, and I am down an officer with Driscoll getting himself killed. That leaves me one officer and three midshipmen to do the job."

"Begging your pardon, sir, but we have Mr Gates and we would have the British prisoners on Naranga as well as our own men, if we are able to take them."

"The blasted operative word here, Warwick, is if! Who do you think is going to lead such a raid, and who do you think is going to command back here?"

He continued staring directly into George's eyes as realisation of what he was thinking dawned on him. "Ah! So you think you are up to it, do you? Well?" he demanded, with his hands on his hips.

"All the prisoners are aboard the *Broad*. Midshipman Johns is quite competent to handle the *Chantelle* and Lieutenant Bray could lead the party ashore. We also have Lieutenant Gates and his Marines with us to secure our seamen and the treasure, sir." George made sure to mention the treasure, hoping it would have the desired effect on the captain's decision.

Brownlow turned to face John Bray and Robert. "I suppose you two go along with this, eh?"

"The garrison has greatly depleted strength, thanks to the cholera, Captain. We have maps and charts of the island and we know where our sailors will be kept prisoner. With surprise on our side, it's feasible. Yes, I think it can be done," John Bray answered with nods of agreement from Robert and smiles from George.

"You can take that smile from your face, it won't be a blasted picnic, Mr Warwick," Brownlow said as he moved away from George and went behind his desk. He sat down heavily in his leather studded chair and remained silent as they all looked on. "I will give this some considerable thought, gentlemen, I will let you have my decision when I am good and ready. You are dismissed."

That night, George found it hard to sleep. After tossing about in his hammock for some time, he decided he wasn't going to drop off so he went up top and joined Bertie on watch on the weather deck.

"Do you think he will go for it? Do you think it's possible to take the island with our small force?"

"Yes, on both counts, Bertie." George's mouth hadn't moved, and then he realised that Bray and Gates had come up from behind them.

"Good morning, sir," Bertie acknowledged them.

"Couldn't you two sleep, either?" George asked quietly. "I wonder what his decision will be. Do you think he will go for it?

"As I said, I think he will," Robert said softly, picking up on the mood of conspiracy. "He is coming up to retirement and he has his mind on how to fund his pension. If this treasure is as vast as we have been led to believe, it should do him very nicely, and the rest of us as well," he added.

"He will weigh up the odds, but I think he will go for it," John Bray whispered as they huddled together.

"What gives, gentlemen?" a voice boomed out behind them. They had been so wrapped up in their conjectures they had failed to hear Brownlow approaching them from behind.

Every one of them jumped guiltily as they turned sheepishly to face him.

"What's this little cabal we have here then, eh?"

They all looked at him with blank faces, not understanding the accusation coming from their captain.

"Cabal, sir?" George questioned, red faced. "I don't quite understand your meaning, sir?"

"Cabal, sir," Brownlow mocked, realising none of them understood the term. "Cabal, conspiracy, plot, call it what you will."

"I can assure you Captain…" John Bray started to bluster before Brownlow interrupted him.

"I jest, Mr Bray. We have plans to make, gentlemen, all officers to my cabin in one hour's time."

Four very relieved officers watched their captain's back as he turned and went about. They carried on watching him until he disappeared into his cabin.

SIX

Raid on Naranga.

Three days later, after riding out a storm coming from the Caribbean Islands, they arrived off the north of the island of Naranga. Although the storm was fairly small for that area for the time of year, it had threatened to sink the unstable *Chantelle*. It was necessary to repair the ship before any raid on the island garrison could take place. George took a team of men, led by Briggs, across to the French ship to help Midshipman Grahame Johns and his crew make the vessel seaworthy for the journey back to England.

George was impatient to get the work done. He stripped to the waist and tied his scarf to his head before joining the men in their labours.

"The fore topgallant needs bracing, and the rigging to both the royal yard and the fore top gallant needs repairing. Briggs, pick two others and we'll go up."

"You, sir?" a surprised Briggs asked.

"Yes, me, Briggs. If I leave it to you lot we'll never get this done before the French send another relief force. Captain Brownlow will not move until the *Chantelle* is seaworthy."

Briggs grinned as he shouted to Meacher and Caukwell to join him aloft. "You'll have to be careful up there, sir, the rigging is quite bad."

He knew Briggs would race him aloft, and he was ready for him as they both climbed together, leaving Caukwell and Meacher way behind. Together they secured the split in the foremast with ropes acting as a sort of bandage and splint. The rigging was quite bad and a lot of work was needed to secure it to both of the top yards.

"I need a hand with this bit," Meacher called out as he struggled to grasp and hold the ropes, attempting to pull them together.

Briggs saw he was in trouble and made his way over to him, but before he could reach him, Meacher lost his footing. He managed to grasp hold of a rope hanging by itself, but was swung out over the open sea. In a flash Briggs grabbed hold of another rope and swung out to help his mate, grabbing him by the back of his pants before swinging him into the mast. Meacher grabbed desperately at the ropes hanging down the fore top gallant mast, just managing to hang on before there was a terrific crack. Briggs wasn't so lucky and was helpless to stop the timber from the royal yard crashing down on his skull.

George heard the sickening thud as he watched Briggs fall forty feet into the sea. He watched him pop up, but he remained face down on the surface, helplessly drifting slowly in a circle with his arms outstretched.

Grabbing a rope, George swung himself out over the bay and let go, landing feet first into the water some ten feet away from the stricken figure. George surfaced, swam over to him, and turned him over on to his back, before striking out to the side of the *Chantelle* with the unconscious Briggs in tow. A rope was thrown down and George secured it under the armpits of the unconscious seaman.

"Haul him up," shouted George, and he watched him being dragged up the side of the ship.

"Shark," a voice cried out as others joined in excitedly. "Shark, shark."

At the shout of "shark", George panicked. He searched the water around him frantically, looking for the tell-tale sign of a fin or its wake. Nothing sent shivers down a man's spine more that the sight of that fin cutting through the water. The scarf on his head started to throb as it changed colour from dark amber to gold and back again. As he felt the throbbing he became even more anxious. Then he saw it, travelling at a ninety-degree angle to him only thirty yards out. His worst fears were realised as he saw the fin and its wake change course, and head straight for him. Was this how he was going to die? Would there be time for any more ropes to be thrown over for him to clamber up? A quick decision made him swim frantically for the stern of the vessel, hoping to hide behind the rudder. He had no weapon to fight with, but it would have proved useless in the water against such a beast in any case. George said a prayer and prepared for the worst. *If I dive, will I stand a better chance underwater?* he wondered.

The shark, spurred on by the frantic thrashing of George's desperate strokes, was nearly on him. As he prepared to dive under, a strong hand gripped his arm. He looked up in alarm and stared straight into the grinning face of the warrior warlord, who was being held by his legs by the warrior above him. The warlord struck down hard with his sword in his right hand at the approaching shark, whilst at the same time, lifting George clear out of the water with his left.

"Climb, warrior, climb for your life," he said, and George did just that. Up the back of the first warrior on to the next, he desperately grabbed at whatever clothing he could in order to gain some purchase and leverage on his ascent away from those fearful jaws below.

"Be careful, oaf," a warrior shouted at him as he trod carelessly on his head and then his neck.

George looked up to see warrior after warrior forming a human chain, right to the top of the stern, as he scrambled and climbed to the top, eventually throwing himself over onto the deck. Breathless, he sat under the driver boom for a few seconds, before standing up and looking over the side. The warriors had gone. All that remained below was the blood trail left by the shark which was slowly zigzagging aimlessly away from the ship. Spotting a rope coiled up on the deck, George thought quickly, threw it over the side and watched it dangle in the water below.

"Are you all right, sir?" a flabbergasted Caukwell asked as he arrived, noticing George didn't have a scratch on him. "How on earth did you get back on board?"

"There was a rope at the stern and I climbed it," he answered, looking away from the man to hide his furtive embarrassment.

"I prayed for you, sir, I'm glad my prayers were answered," the devout Christian said reverently.

"Indeed they were, Mr Caukwell, indeed they were," a smiling George concurred as he looked to the heavens. He wasn't surprised one bit to see the smiling figure of the Oriental priest with his dragon by his side.

After changing his clothes, George was lying on the bunk in the captain's quarters of the *Chantelle* thinking of his close encounter with death and what could have been, when a knock came on the cabin door. Raising himself up on one elbow, he swung his legs over the side until he was sitting upright.

"Enter," he invited.

A sorry looking Briggs entered the cabin with his head heavily bandaged, wincing as he touched his temple in salute. "I've come to say thank you, Mr Warwick, sir, thank you for my life. Not many would have gone in the way you did, especially not for a rating."

"Are you trying to match me for headgear, Briggs?" George quipped with a big grin. "I wouldn't keep tapping your temple until it gets better, man."

"Yes, sir, I mean no, sir," he stammered. "What I mean to say, is thank you, sir."

"That's quite enough thanks, Briggs. You had better get some rest before going back to the *Broad*."

"Yes, sir," he answered as he was leaving the cabin, "but I won't forget it, ever, sir."

***

87

"Have you quite recovered from your ordeal, Mr Warwick? I understand you had a near brush with a shark," Brownlow asked as they all gathered round the charts in his cabin. Robert looked at George and gave him a knowing smile.

It was eight o'clock in the morning after his 'brush with the shark', and they had rowed back to the *Broad* to be briefed on the coming raid on Naranga.

"I'm fine, Captain, thank you, and none the worse. I took a leaf from their lordships manual, sir," George said mysteriously, with a knowing grin across his face.

"A manual from their lordships, what on earth are you on about, Mr Warwick?"

"Once upon a time a lord from the Admiralty fell overboard in shark infested waters, sir. He wasn't even touched, even though everyone else was savaged."

Brownlow looked at him, half suspecting some sort of jest, but the man seemed deadly serious. "Why was his lordship not attacked?" he asked.

"Professional courtesy, sir," George answered flatly.

Everyone in the cabin burst out laughing. Brownlow looked dumbfounded and just stared at him until the joke dawned on him and he too started to laugh.

"Very good, Mr Warwick, very droll, now let's get on with it, gentlemen. We are here, ten miles north of the port of Loba." He jabbed at the map with his finger. "Between our position and the garrison at Loba is dense jungle all the way, so it's going to be heavy going, but it should give you good cover."

They all studied the chart in front of them, wondering just how accurate it was, as their captain continued. "Two miles to the north of the port, away from the garrison, is the actual prison where our men will be housed. We are only expecting a skeleton guard at the prison due to their depleted numbers, and surprise should be well on our side, but, and I will emphasise this, speed is of the essence. Speed and silence, gentlemen, will win us the day."

Robert smiled at George as he asked the captain, "Who commands, sir?"

"Mr Bray will command, Mr Gates, he is the senior officer but you will assist him in the operations and attack. Now you are all in civilian clothes for a reason, just in case you are spotted on route, and I must say I have never seen a more likely band of cut-throats and brigands."

George was looking glum as there had so far been no mention of him taking part. Brownlow saw his face and smiled.

"Cheer up, Mr Warwick, you're dressed for the part so you will be going," he said, eyeing his scarf around his head. "You look like a pirate, so you had better assure our prisoners on Naranga that you are a British seaman, before they hang you," he added, to laughter from the rest of those gathered. "The boats will drop you ashore. God willing, you shouldn't need them for any return journey. If you take their prize ship, you should all make it out safely. I will hold off around the point until I hear the action."

As they piled over the side into the long boats, the officers stood on the deck to one side, before joining their men on the water. Brownlow stood on the quarterdeck to see them off.

"Good luck, Mr Bray, bring them all back safely, and may God go with you."

They saluted their captain, turned and grinned at one another as they went over the side to their respective boats. George sat down in the stern of the boat he commanded and was surprised to see a smiling Briggs sitting in front of him with oar raised ready to row.

All the men were armed with cutlasses, pistols and muskets. George looked to starboard to see his friend Robert leading two boats of Marines dressed in ordinary clothing, the same fashion as everyone else. Eight long boats pulled towards the shore through the clear turquoise sea that didn't even offer a ripple until they neared the beach. Gentle surf met them as it lapped the golden sands that stretched up the beach to the densely populated jungle beyond.

As they ran aground, the men jumped out and waded through the warm gentle waters to dry land. The sailors who would be returning with the boats stayed seated. Not so Briggs. He was on his feet in an instant and following the men up the beach. George spotted him in front, still wearing the bandage around his head and caught up with him.

"What do you think you are doing, Briggs? You're not fit enough for this, man, get back in the boat."

"I'm all right, Mr Warwick, really, sir."

George was about to order him back to the boats again when he noticed the grin on his face. As he turned he saw the boats pulling away from the shore and heading back to the *Broad*.

"I've a good mind to make you swim for it. I'll be having words with you later. In the meantime you stay close to me. Do you hear?"

"Aye, aye, sir," he answered, falling in behind George.

Forty Marines and thirty seamen made their way through the jungle, sometimes having to hack at the thick undergrowth and vines that barred their way. There were no signs of any paths, which in one way meant less chance of being discovered by the local inhabitants, but it made progress very slow and laborious.

"I'm not so keen on these creepy crawly things, sir, or the snakes," Briggs said as he followed behind George.

"You should have stayed in the blasted boat then, shouldn't you?" George retorted without turning around.

It was eight hours later when they stopped. George joined Robert and John at the front of the column. John Bray was looking at a compass and the chart as he arrived.

"We are not far off now. If this chart is correct, we should break cover and climb a hill before finding this path running down to Loba and past the prison."

"Silence is of paramount importance, John. With your leave, my Marines will head the assault on the prison."

"That's fine, Robert, but you'll take George and his section with you as well, you'll command, of course. We'll have a short rest before pushing on."

As they rested, Robert took George to one side. It was the first opportunity he'd had to ask him about the incident of the shark.

"Caukwell told me it was a miracle. He couldn't believe you got back on board so quickly... without help. He also said the shark drifted away from the ship with blood flowing from it. Now I believe in miracles, George," he said sarcastically, "but what on earth happened? Did you poke it in the eye?"

"I bloody well panicked," George blurted out. "I should have waited for ropes to be thrown over but I panicked. If you are ever in the water, and you see that fin making a beeline for you, you'll panic, believe me, you will. The thought of such a beast ripping me to sheds chilled me to the bone, so I swam for my life hoping to shelter besides the rudder. When it was getting nearer I decided maybe I stood a better chance under the water and went to meet it head on. I was about to dive when an arm went under my armpit and hauled me clear out of the water. The warriors had formed a human chain right up the stern of the *Chantelle* and I was able to scramble over them to the top. When I recovered I threw a rope over to make out that I had climbed back up."

"Well Caukwell was suspicious, but he's so religious he thought there had been divine intervention, your secret's safe. What happened to the shark?"

"The warrior chief struck out at it with his sword as he hauled me out of the water."

"My God, I'm glad I never met him in battle whilst he was of this earth," Robert whispered.

The chart was correct. They left the jungle behind and seventy men climbed the rocky slopes of the tor. At the top they looked down over Loba and the port of Naranga. They could just make out the silhouette of a ship moored at the quayside of the dock and some small fishing vessels dotted around the bay. It was starting to get dark as the larger than life sun set far out to sea, bathing the whole land on this side of the island in an orange glow.

"There's the prison, just as marked on the map. The garrison should be to the east of it overlooking the port. There it is," John pointed out triumphantly.

"I think we should get some rest at the edge of town and wait for them to fall asleep," Robert suggested.

"We'll do just that, let's move," John replied as he started to stride away.

They stayed half a mile away from the prison, camping in a bushy area which provided excellent cover. At half past two in the morning they made their move. John Bray, with most of the seamen and twenty Marines, formed a cordon around the perimeter of the prison, whilst Robert led his men, and George's section of ten sailors, for the assault on it. The town of Loba was quiet, thanks to the cholera epidemic, not even a dog could be heard barking.

They crept forward silently to the walls of the prison with Robert indicating with his hands that they should keep tight against the stone walls. George spotted the sentry post positioned outside of the main gate and tugged at Robert's sleeve to point it out. They crawled forward, not knowing how many guards would be on duty. They came across the sole sentry who was happily snoring and dead to the world. Robert looked on him with disdain as he raised the butt of his pistol and brought it down with a sickening thud on the man's head. He couldn't care less if he had killed him. If it was one his own sleeping at his post, he would have had him shot.

George winced at the sound of the blow. He moved forward silently, past the post and through the open gates of the prison. No other guards were on duty. He signalled the men to follow him as Robert dispersed his men along the inside walls of the prison, all ready for action.

John Bray joined them with some of his men, as Robert signalled them to move inwards towards the buildings. George made for what he thought was the main gaoler's office. He went past the door to a window showing a light on the inside and peered in. Four French soldiers were slumped in chairs around a table in the centre of the room. George held up four fingers to indicate their number to Robert and three of his Marines who stood waiting outside the door. Robert nodded his understanding as George joined him.

"Four, sitting round a table, they look asleep," he whispered.

They opened the unlocked door very quietly and went in. The Marines jumped forward bringing the butts of their muskets down on the heads of two of the soldiers nestled on the table. The commotion brought instant reaction from the other two on the opposite side who were able take advantage of the obstruction caused by their own men falling over. They grabbed their weapons that had been laid on the table and quickly unsheathed their swords. Robert moved forward to face the one on the right as George moved to confront the one on the left.

The Frenchman lunged, but he was no match for the skill of Robert, as his own blade travelled down the length of the sword and entered the enemy's stomach, dispatching him instantly. George's opponent proved more adept with a blade as he simply turned his wrist to ward off a lunge, and then turned defence quickly into attack as he pressed forward. George had his hands full as the Frenchman started to call an alert as he warded off a counter attack. Suddenly, and mysteriously, the man fell to the ground as if he had been hit with a sledgehammer. George looked up from the fallen figure into the smiling face of John Bray who was holding his pistol by the barrel.

"Sorry, George, no time for niceties," he apologised. "We couldn't have him waking up the whole of Loba, now could we? We need to push on." John moved over to a board on the wall and removed the large bunch of keys hanging on a peg. "This way, gentlemen," he said, leading the way to some stone steps the other side of the room.

The dimly lit steps led down to the underground dungeon, where the smell of decay and human incarceration became stronger on their descent. The torches on the wall threw out long flickering shadows, reminding George of the great hall back home at the manor. This couldn't have been farther from the welcoming smells and sights of the house in Hampshire.

As they reached the bottom step they entered the dungeon to see rows of bars from floor to ceiling. They could hear the laboured breathing, snoring and coughing of the inhabitants. The smell of excrement and body odour was horrendous. They all tried to cover their noses whilst they peered into the gloom beyond the bars.

George tried to clear his throat as he almost retched. "Are there any Englishmen here?" he called out.

They detected some movement behind the cages as some of the occupants started to stir. Eventually George saw one man rise from the floor to stand unsteadily on his feet.

"What the hell is this?" he spat out. "You Frenchie bastard, what are you trying to pull now?"

Other inhabitants of the cages were now stirring and starting to murmur as George turned to one of the Marines. "Fetch that torch over here so they can see us," he ordered.

The flickering light licked out across the wretched inhabitants of the cage, lighting up the man standing amongst his fellow prisoners as well as George and the rest of his men.

"They're English," a hesitant voice announced from within. "For God's sake, they're English."

Robert took the keys from John and tried each of them in turn until the door opened. They walked into the cesspit of humanity to cries of doubt from the inmates.

"Who are you?" the unkempt bearded man who had been the first to stand asked.

"We are British seamen and Marines and are here to take you home," Robert said softly. "We would appreciate you being very quiet so as not to wake the neighbours."

George was standing facing the man who had spoken. "Who are you and what ship are you from?"

"Lieutenant Briars, late of *HMS Alma*," the wretched man replied.

John Bray couldn't believe his ears as he moved forward. "The *Alma* was taken over two years ago," he said incredulously.

"Aye, sir, and we have been here ever since. There were fifty-six of us last night, out of an original complement of two hundred and sixty men. This is all that is left and I don't think many of them will survive much longer."

The rescuers looked at one another in astonishment as they realised just how long these men had put up with this horror.

"Let's get everyone up that can walk, sir, we're going to get you all home," George vowed to Briars.

"God bless you, sir," Briars said as he grabbed George's hand. "Who do I have the good fortune to address?"

"Midshipman Warwick, sir, and this is Lieutenant Bray of *HMS Broad* and Lieutenant Gates of His Majesty's Marines. Now we really must get you all moving."

As they started to move the pitiful prisoners out of the cells, the Marines were refilling them with French soldiers from the prison's barracks. They were going to get a small taste of what the British seamen had endured for the past two years.

Weapons were seized from the prison's armoury and given to those strong enough to carry them. Others, who could hardly walk, were carried by the able prisoners and the men from the *Broad*.

They cut a pathetic sight as they trudged silently through the sleeping settlement, with Lieutenant Briars gallantly encouraging his men on with whispers and pats on their backs.

The dark was starting to lift, as the dawn crept up on them. Soon the sun would be breaking through and the inhabitants of the settlement would be awake.

George tugged at John Bray's sleeve as he pulled him to a stop. "Sir, we are making very slow progress. Can I suggest we send men forward to secure the ship and the dock area so we don't get held up at that end?"

"Good thinking," John Bray answered. "We'll leave twenty men here under the command of the sergeant of Marines, if that's all right with you Robert?"

"It's what I had in mind, I'll let him know."

Forty-nine armed and determined men set off at a trot through the silent settlement to the dock. It didn't seem like a garrison town, it was that quiet, so quiet it felt like a trap.

Relieved and slightly out of breath, they eventually made it to the outskirts of the dock. They edged their way through bales of linen and crates of all kinds of goods, which had been piled high ready for loading on a ship when the garrison was relieved.

George and Robert spotted the berthed ship with the name *Melissa* on her side. She was lying fairly low in the water. A sentry was in a sitting position at the end of the gangplank. He was moving so he wasn't asleep, but he wasn't very alert either. George removed his cutlass, which had been strapped round his chest, and handed it to Robert. At the same time he drew his knife from its sheath and removed his shoes. Robert realised his intentions and nodded silently his approval, and George prepared to rush forward.

As he crouched, ready to run forward, there was a metallic clinking sound at the sentry's feet. He watched with bated breath as the soldier stooped and searched for the cause of the noise. George took the opportunity to rush forward whilst the guard was distracted. Robert held his breath and watched in silence as his friend flew over the cobblestones, knife in hand and his scarf around his head, which was glowing from gold to dark amber.

The sentry became aware of something approaching, but the attack was so fast he had no time to react before George had him around the neck, turned him and plunged the knife up through the man's ribcage. In his death throes, he tried to call out but his cries were quickly stifled with a hand over his mouth. Lowering him to the ground, George looked around, curious as to what had distracted the sentry. A silver coin lay at his feet. Whatever the value, it had cost its owner dearly.

Robert, seeing that the way was now clear, urged his men forward, followed by John and the Marines. They rushed past George and up the gangplank. Two French soldiers, who had been deep in sleep at the top, woke up just in time to be clubbed senseless by the Marines and thrown over the side.

Briggs handed George his shoes and cutlass as he made it to the top of the gangplank to join the others. Robert indicated to him to move forward and they crept stealthily towards the captain's cabin as the seamen and Marines dispersed around the ship.

They listened at the cabin door for a few seconds before Robert stepped back and then gave it a mighty kick with his boot, sending it inwards and almost off its hinges. Both of them rushed in with George slightly in the lead. A French officer was dressing, oblivious to the insurgency aboard his vessel. Startled, he looked up in amazement at the two pirates in front of him. He was young, but he was also very quick. Diving backwards away from them, he reached for his sword hanging on the wall. George had anticipated this and leapt forward, meeting him with a vicious uppercut that lifted the man clear off his feet. Robert winced at the sound of the man's jaw breaking and watched him slump to the cabin's floor.

"He's out cold," Robert said as he went around to check on him. "That was worthy of any prize fighter, George."

George cursed in response as he rubbed at the pain in his injured knuckles. As he nursed his hand, they heard firing coming from below deck.

"Never mind him, he won't be conscious for some time," Robert shouted as they both rushed from the cabin and down the stairs through greyish gun smoke to the deck below.

John Bray and the Marines had come across five French soldiers, the only ones on board left to guard the ship. Four of them were killed and one other, who was blabbering away in French, was about to be dispatched by Meacher's cutlass.

"Belay that," Robert called out as he grabbed the sailor's arm "We may need him. Take him, clap him in irons, and then go and get his officer up top."

"Aye, aye, sir," a disappointed Meacher replied, as he kicked the Frenchman in the stomach, before dragging him to his feet.

When they were sure the ship was secure, Robert sent a further ten Marines back along the route to help with the helpless prisoners. The remaining Marines formed a wall of steel around the perimeter, cutting off any access to the ship. The seamen, under John's command, made the ship ready to leave the port the moment the rescued prisoners were aboard.

There followed an agonising wait for their arrival until the first Marine came through the bales of linen half carrying, half dragging one of the feeble men. The rest followed on slowly, with their gallant and brave officer bringing up the rear with the Marine's sergeant guarding their backs, just as the sun rose over the horizon, lighting up the dock and the garrison's ramparts with their gun emplacements.

As soon as they were on board, the gangplank was discarded and all lines to the dock were let go. John ordered full sail to be hoisted as they slowly and painfully moved away from the dock and headed out to sea.

George watched as the rescued prisoners pitifully tried their utmost to help the crew get the ship sailing out to the open sea. He looked up to see the sails start to billow against the blue morning sky. The wind picked up slightly as they made slow headway out of the harbour. If they didn't reach open sea and a full wind before the garrison woke up, they would be at the mercy of the guns lining the fort's walls.

Suddenly he heard it, the sound of a cannon firing on them from the garrison. George watched apprehensively as the ball hit the water harmlessly, going wide and long of its mark. How long before they corrected the range and direction? How long before they started to hit the ship? His questions were answered a few moments later as a ball ripped through the Mizzen topsail.

SEVEN

On deck the whole crew ducked instinctively as rounds of shots went whooshing overhead. George wondered why they weren't taking casualties, then he realised the whooshing sounds were passing them from forward to aft. He scanned the open sea in front of them. They had been too busy watching their tails and the garrison behind them to notice the *Broad* bearing down on them under full sail, with smoke billowing from her forward guns.

He ran aft to the upper deck through a cheering crew as they all realised what was happening. An excited and relieved John joined him with Robert following closely behind.

"How goes it, Mr Warwick?" John shouted.

"The *Broad* is hitting the target, sir," he shouted back as he saw a ball smash into the ramparts of the garrison fort.

They cheered as they watched the *Broad* sail swiftly past with all its sails billowing in the stiff morning onshore breeze. They thought it was going to sail through the garrison's gates until it heaved hard over to starboard at the far end of the bay in front of the fort and headed broadside on to the walls. A thunderous salvo met their ears. Smoke poured from the other side of the *Broad*, as she fired her port side cannon into the garrison.

Through their telescopes they watched the granite ramparts disintegrate under the blows, as enemy cannon after cannon were blown apart, or ripped from their emplacements to topple forward on the defenders below. Not one enemy cannon fired in response on the *Broad* or the *Melissa*. The *Broad* turned hard to port, taking it even nearer the garrison, before opening up once again with devastating effect as each gun fired in turn, sending iron balls into granite walls.

Satisfied, the *Broad* turned to the open sea and sailed towards them.

"What's she saying, Mr Warwick?" John Bray asked as he noticed signal flags being hoisted aboard the *Broad*.

George waited until the signal had been hoisted completely before answering. "We are to continue on this course away from the island until we rendezvous with the *Chantelle*, sir."

The crew were still cheering as George made his way past John Bray and headed for the quarterdeck. Looking around the ship he became aware that he couldn't see the scarlet tunic of Robert.

"Briggs, have you seen Lieutenant Gates?"

"Aye, sir," a very happy Briggs replied. "He's gone below, probably to inspect the cargo."

George wasted no time in following his friend down to the lower hold. It was no wonder the *Melissa* was so low in the water. She was packed to the gunnels with all kinds of goods making it very difficult to force a passage through. Eventually he came across Robert examining a large iron cage. He was trying all kinds of ways to prise the large padlock from the iron casing.

"What are you doing, Robert?"

Robert jumped like a naughty boy caught scrumping apples from the local lord's estate.

"It's locked," he said simply.

"I can see that, why the urgency?"

"Have a peek, George. Can you see what I see?"

His eyes slowly became accustomed to the gloom as he peered through to the dark interior. He thought he saw a glint coming from the top of one of the open boxes, as he examined the unforgiving lock.

"Just a minute, I'll be back," George said as he went out of the dark hold to the stairway, where he saw a Marine. Relieving him of his pistol he returned to a very frustrated Robert.

"Stand well back," he ordered as he aimed at the lock covering his eyes with his left hand. The explosion was muffled due to the densely packed cargo. As the blue smoke cleared, they noticed the lock was now hanging from its hasp.

"Careful, it might still be hot," he warned.

Robert reached gingerly for it, removing the lock altogether and pulling open the iron grill that was acting as a door. George watched him enter the cage and move to one of the boxes.

"Oh my God," he whispered, pulling back the sacking over one of the crates to reveal it was full of English, Spanish, Portuguese and French gold coins.

Wondering why his friend had suddenly gone so quiet, George followed him in. Reaching his shoulder he looked down and stood in awe at the sight in front of him. Case after case revealed jewels and gold, riches beyond their wildest dreams. Robert fumbled with one box as it toppled over, spilling the contents on the floor of the cage.

"Oh my goodness, it gets better and better," an excited, almost demented Robert beamed, with golden light being reflected in his eyes, "Spanish doubloons, lovely golden, Spanish doubloons." Running his strong fingers through the coins, he sighed loudly.

George was getting worried about his friend, he had never seen him act like this before, but there again, they had never seen such a treasure before.

"Are you all right, Robert?"

"A king's bloody ransom on its own, a king's bloody ransom, man, don't you understand?" he said huskily, as he looked up. "George, it's a bloody fortune, man."

"I think you had better sober up and pull yourself together, Robert, none of it is yours. It belongs to His Majesty or at the very least the Admiralty."

"The Admiralty," he repeated. "They will take more than their share, you wait and see. We will get a pittance as its downgraded, I've seen it before."

"Nevertheless, Mr Gates, you will step away from it now, if you would be so good." John Bray was standing outside the cage with a pistol in his hand and had been privy to all that was said.

"He doesn't mean it, sir, it's just the excitement at seeing such a vast fortune." George intervened on Robert's behalf.

"Step outside the cage, Mr Gates, and leave all behind you, if you please."

"If you please, if you please, you're bloody well sounding like Brownlow, John," Robert protested, pushing roughly past George and standing outside the cage.

"Let's leave this as it is, sir. Lieutenant Gates meant no harm and I will testify to that if I have to."

"There's no need for that, George, I understand," John said, looking at Robert with suspicion. "Nevertheless, I will be putting a guard on this cage until further orders from Captain Brownlow, even if I am beginning to sound like him."

After rummaging aboard, a new lock was found to secure the cage. Two armed Marines were placed on the door and given orders that no one should enter without Bray's say so, or until Captain Brownlow relieved him. This order remained until they rendezvoused with the *Chantelle* and the *Broad* five hours later.

***

"Well done, everybody, and congratulations. Their lordships will be most gratified and pleased when we get back." Brownlow was positively beaming; comfortable retirement was looking a distinct possibility, if their reports on the treasure were true. "I will inspect the cargo first thing on the morrow, but first, Mr Rhodes, I want you to see to the rescued men aboard the *Melissa*."

"What about our French prisoners, Captain? Some of them are still in a bad way."

"The French have inflicted horrific injury on our own, Mr Rhodes. Ours will come first, get over there without delay. You can leave one of your assistants to tend to the prisoners here."

The *Chantelle*, still not looking very seaworthy, was anchored off to their starboard with the *Melissa* alongside. Brownlow decided that an inspection of the stricken ship would have to follow after viewing the cargo aboard the *Melissa*.

***

Accompanied by Robert and George, Brownlow climbed the rope ladder from the long boat onto the *Melissa*. In the captain's absence, Bray was left in charge of the *Broad*. He had kept silent about Robert's indiscretion. Although the captain was eager to see the treasures that had been lauded to him, he knew his first duty was to see the rescued sailors.

"This is Lieutenant Blair," George said introducing the rescued prisoner. "Sir, this is Captain Brownlow of *HMS Broad*."

"I am very pleased and honoured to meet you, Mr Blair. I understand that you have had to contend with a French hellhole for over two years."

"The honour is mine, sir, and I can't thank you and your men enough for what you have done," he replied as he saluted.

"If you feel up to it, please be so good as to accompany me whilst I meet your comrades and inspect the ship and its cargo. If you feel up to it, that is?" Brownlow added, noticing just how frail the man was.

"Again, I would be honoured. Mr Rhodes, your surgeon, is tending to the sick at this very moment, and I thank you again, sir."

"Not at all, man, it's the least we can do for such gallant men."

Because of his frailty, Lieutenant Blair retired halfway around their inspection of the ship leaving Brownlow, George and Robert to continue down to the hold. Lanterns had now been lit, illuminating the large cargo and the way through to the treasure. The anticipation was quite exhilarating as they approached the great iron cage with two Marines on guard at its door.

"You may stand down, I'll call you when you are needed," Robert ordered as the two Marines came to attention and then moved off through the hold.

Producing the key that John Bray had handed to him, Brownlow moved forward, inserting it into the lock with a slight tremble of his hand. The lock opened and he removed it from its hasp. Slowly, almost warily, he entered the iron cage watched intensely by Robert and George.

"Good heavens above," he exclaimed as the full extent of the treasure hit home. "For once, young officers do not exaggerate. It is indeed a king's ransom."

George and Robert looked on, smiling contentedly, as if they had produced this vast wealth themselves. The smile was soon to disappear from George's face as Brownlow spoke to them as he rummaged through the gold coins, letting them slip through his fingers back to their box. He eventually tired of the exercise, turned on his heel and exited the cage. He made sure it was locked tight before asking Robert to get his Marines back on guard.

"I want you stay on board this vessel with a detachment of Marines, Mr Gates. You will be responsible for its safe passage back to England. I will send a man over to make out an inventory of everything on board." He then turned to George. "Mr Blair is not fit enough to command, but, Mr Warwick, you are. I therefore promote you to lieutenant in command of the *Melissa,* you have absolute command. Is that understood?"

George couldn't believe his ears. He was apprehensive enough at the thought of Robert being in charge of the treasure, a fox in charge of the henhouse came to mind, let alone taking such a command.

"Lieutenant, sir, you are promoting me? What about Mr Bray, he could command," he blustered, not knowing how to accept this.

"I need Mr Bray on the *Broad* and we also have the *Chantelle* to crew. No, you take charge, Lieutenant Warwick, that's final, now I must return to the *Broad* and prepare for our journey back."

As they watched Brownlow returning to the *Broad* in the stern of the longboat, Robert grinned at his friend.

"Lieutenant, eh, congratulations, George, or should I say, Captain?"

George remained looking at the back of his commander with a sombre face, wondering what he had landed him with. Robert slapped him on his back.

"What's the matter?"

"Nothing, Robert."

"You look as if you've just messed yourself, George. You've been promoted, man, for goodness sake, so what is it?"

"I'm wondering if you are going to behave, or if I have to have one eye in the back of my head at all times."

"Oh, you mean my demeanour in the hold in front of John Bray. Well you don't have to worry on that point, George. I've got over the initial excitement, I'll behave, cross my heart," he said as he winked.

George was not encouraged by the words, or the gesture, but he had other things on his mind as he cast an eye over the *Melissa* and his makeshift crew.

"What do you make of her?" Robert asked, seeming to read his mind.

"She's a twelve six pounder gun lugger of the *Reynard* class, having been converted to carry cargo, not as much as she is carrying now though, which does pose some problems if we hit rough weather," he answered, spotting Briggs giving orders to the deck crew. "Briggs," he called out, "To me." He watched as he touched his forehead in salute and acknowledgement before making his way aft to join them by the wheel.

"What do you think of her, Briggs?"

"A bloody big whale, sir, if you pardon the expression, she's heavy and cumbersome and is going to take some handling. I have had experience of one of this class before. We captured one off Brest in ninety-three and took her in to Portsmouth."

"Well, we will have to do our best. Have you got enough men for the job?"

"Aye, sir, but more ratings are neither here nor there. It's what we are carrying that makes the difference. I've been down in the hold, and I hope you don't mind, sir, but I have had the cargo's weight distributed a little better."

"Well done, Briggs, back to work and keep the men at it."

"It seems we have a very good man there, George, you had better hang on to him."

"I intend to do just that, Robert, believe me, I do," he replied as he turned to the crew. "Weigh anchor, let's get under way."

Briggs looked up to George at the wheel and grinned. "Come on lads, put your backs in to it," he shouted to a willing crew.

"Keep the sail short," George ordered. "Remember the *Chantelle* has to be able to keep up. He looked through his telescope to the *Broad* whose signals were telling them to do just that.

"The old man's keeping an eye on us," Robert responded as he saw the message.

I wonder why, thought George, as he looked sideways at his friend.

September was a time for storms that far west in the Atlantic. One morning they woke up to a brilliant bright red sky signalling the approach of bad weather. By ten o'clock the sky had changed to a dark greenish brown colour and the gentle swell of the sea was starting to toss as the waves grew bigger and bigger. George expected enormous problems with the *Melissa* in the stormy conditions, but she handled it far better than expected, and although it was rough going, she was manageable. The *Chantelle* was not to be as fortunate, as Grahame Johns fought a losing battle to save her. He managed to save all hands on board, as the long boats from the *Broad* assisted in their rescue. As the boats pulled away, they watched the *Chantelle* lift from the water one more time, before turning over and disappearing, stern first, under the enormous waves. The storm lasted for a further two days, with George blessing Briggs for his excellent work in ballasting the ship with its heavy cargo.

On the fourth day the storm abated, and within a very short time, the sea had become a millpond again with just a gentle swell and breeze to help them on their way.

Late on in the afternoon, George felt the scarf vibrate under his tunic. He took it off to see it glowing from gold to dark amber, the sign of danger.

"Get up top, Briggs, and keep an eye open for sail."

"Aye, aye, sir," he answered as he started to climb the rigging on the main mast.

"Problem, George?" Robert asked as he appeared by his side.

"Managed to leave the treasure for a few moments?" he retorted sarcastically.

Robert ignored the remark and smiled as he raised his telescope to his left eye and scanned the horizon in front of them. He was the first to spot the sail appearing like a small dot against the distant skyline.

"Your scarf is an early warning signal, George. Right ahead at eleven o'clock, it's a sail all right. How big is anyone's guess?"

"Sail ahoy!" Briggs hollered from on high. "Sail ahead, Mr Warwick, she's too far to make out."

"Signal the *Broad*, and let Captain Brownlow know we might have company, and that we await his orders," George ordered. "All hands to stand by."

By early evening, the distant ship was becoming visible to the naked eye. She was a British ship of the line, almost three times the size of the *Broad*, and accompanied by two other frigates. *Why was the scarf warning him of danger? These were our own people.*

A signal from the *Broad* told them to stand down and that they would receive the new arrivals. George reluctantly gave the order to stand down and heave to.

"What's the problem, George? You don't seem too happy at seeing our guests."

"I have a very uneasy feeling about this, Robert," he replied as he shouted up to the main mast. "Keep an eye out for any further sail, Briggs."

His uneasiness continued as he watched the new arrivals heave to and the ship of the line admiral's barge disembark. Then he realised why he had been warned of danger. Sitting in the back was the thin, cruel, twisted face of Lord Crowe.

EIGHT

"The *Broad* is signalling for you and Lieutenant Gates to join them, sir," Caukwell said, reading out the new signal.

"Signal our acceptance, Caukwell."

"So, your old adversary is here to haunt you," Robert said, smiling at him.

"No smiling matter, Robert, he's the evillest man you could wish to meet."

"You killed his son in a fair duel, what can he do to you out here?"

"What indeed?" he responded as he moved to the long boat that had been lowered for them. On seeing Briggs by the side ready to go down into the boat, he stopped.

"You stay aboard, Briggs, and keep an eye on things. No one is to come aboard without mine, or Captain Brownlow's expressed permission, and that means even an admiral. Is that clear?"

"Aye, aye, sir," he answered determinedly but puzzled, as George and Robert went over the side.

Twenty minutes later, they went aboard the *Broad* and were shown to Brownlow's cabin. George tapped the door and on command to enter, they both removed their headdress and stepped in. Brownlow was sitting at his desk and smiled as they both appeared. Lord Crowe was standing looking out of the gallery window with his back to them. He didn't move until they were standing in front of the desk.

"This is Admiral Lord Crowe, who has asked to meet you both. I understand that you are already acquainted with his lordship, Mr Warwick. This is Lieutenant Gates, our gallant Marine officer," Brownlow said proudly.

Crowe gave a small twisted smile in response, but there was no mistaking the hatred in his beady little eyes as he looked George up and down.

"Life has been good to you, Warwick. Promoted to lieutenant, eh? Well, we will have to see that confirmed by a proper panel when you get back to England."

George didn't respond. He looked straight ahead of him and held the gaze of his captain. It was Robert who spoke for him.

"I have heard of you, my lord. I can assure you that Mr Warwick has earned his commission, as can be borne out by his commander," Robert said firmly as he, too, looked at Brownlow.

Captain Brownlow sensed that there was history behind this tension, and not just some acquaintance of old, as he stood up and faced Crowe.

"When we get back to England, my lord, I will offer Mr Warwick up for proper examination, but in the meantime his commission stands according to naval orders, and he remains master and commander of the *Melissa,* which is now under British colours."

"Of course, of course, Captain Brownlow, I wouldn't presume to impose on your authority. Now, I would like to see this vast treasure aboard the *Melissa*, as well as the inventory when it is completed."

"Certainly, my lord, but I must caution you that not one item will be released. Lieutenant Gates has his orders to that effect, and those orders will not be countermanded by anyone."

Crowe smiled as only Crowe could. A twisted smile of contrition played evilly on his lips.

"That goes without saying, Captain. I am surprised that you of all people would feel that you had to mention this to me. I have changed my mind. I will not be staying for dinner. I wish to return to my ship and dine with my own officers. I do not think I can accommodate you with fresh provisions, Captain. On reflection we barely have enough for ourselves. I will inspect the *Melissa* tomorrow morning," he rasped as he picked up his hat and barged out of the cabin.

"Good riddance," Blackwell, the captain's steward, muttered under his breath as Crowe left the cabin. George and Robert, standing with their backs to him, grinned as they heard him.

"Get back to the *Melissa*, gentlemen. Have no fear, Lord Crowe cannot, and will not, go against naval orders. Thanks to the tedious tantrums of Lord Crowe, we will have to rethink our plans for fresh provisions. I will signal you later."

They both saluted their captain as they turned and left the cabin. Blackwell was standing outside, looking a little sheepish, realising that the two had overheard his indiscretion.

"Ah, Blackwell," George acknowledged him. "You have previous knowledge of his lordship, methinks?"

"I apologise, Mr Warwick, sir, please forgive my foolishness."

"Forget it, man, tell me why the remark."

Blackwell shifted from foot to foot, clearly uncomfortable in his present circumstances. He wasn't to know he was on safe ground with these two officers. He reluctantly decided to bare all.

"It was about a year ago, sir. Lord Crowe insulted the wife of my brother's employer. When he took him to task, Lord Crowe challenged him to a duel, knowing that as a merchant, he would be easy meat. He slew him, he could have spared him, but he slaughtered him as he leaned against a door, seriously wounded and unable to defend himself. My brother and his family, along with many others were put out of work and out onto the street because of it. The man is pure evil, sir."

"All right, Blackwell, about your business. The captain didn't hear, and neither did we," Robert said, dismissing him.

They made their way back to the *Melissa,* and as they climbed aboard they noticed the side of the ship was lined with Robert's Marines, headed by Briggs.

"Report, Briggs, what's going on?"

"We have had visitors whilst you were over at the *Broad*, sir. A detachment of Marines came over from Lord Crowe's flagship. They said they had the authority to board and inspect the cargo of the ship."

"What happened?" Robert asked.

"I told them that no such authority existed without Mr Warwick's, or Captain Brownlow's expressed permission, sir. Your Marines did the rest. They resisted orders to stand down and aimed their muskets at the long boat until it pulled away and retreated."

"Well done, Briggs, well done all of you," George congratulated. "Get Caukwell to signal the *Broad* and let Captain Brownlow know what has happened."

A few minutes later, a grinning Briggs reported to them in George's cabin.

"What's amused you?" Robert asked, unable to resist grinning in response.

"I don't think I had better repeat Captain Brownlow's answer, sir, but the upshot of it is, Lord Crowe could go to blazes and that we are to resist any further attempts for him to board, including his inspection tomorrow. The captain is sending over more Marines in the morning, sir."

"What do you think Crowe's reaction is going to be?"

George thought deeply for a moment before answering Robert. His scarf was no longer throbbing so he believed any danger to have passed, for the present.

"That will be all, Briggs, well done, keep the men alert," he said as he dismissed him. Once he was out of the cabin he turned to his friend.

"He is a vindictive bastard. I wouldn't put it past him to fire on us, although he would also have to fire on the *Broad*, and I don't know how he would explain that with so many witnesses."

"I suspect he will make haste back to England, and get his story to the Admiralty. He will be back long before we are able to dock at Portsmouth. I believe that is where we will get our reception from Lord Crowe," Robert responded thoughtfully.

The next morning, George was in his cabin when Briggs summoned him to the upper deck. He handed him a telescope and pointed out to sea.

"What am I looking for?" George asked as he scanned an empty skyline.

"Nothing, sir, simply nothing." He grinned at him. "Lord Crowe and his escort have gone, they have done a bunk during the night."

"Wake Lieutenant Gates, Briggs, ask him to join me on deck."

A few minutes later, he was joined by Robert, eager to have confirmed what Briggs had told him.

"Has he really up stakes and gone, George? I bet you all the money on board he is hightailing it back to the Admiralty with his own version of events."

"You are probably right, my colonial friend. In the meantime, the old man's noticed his absence and has summoned us to go over to the *Broad*."

***

"Sit yerselves down," Brownlow invited, as they entered an already full captain's cabin.

Already seated around the table were John Bray, the surgeon Percival Rhodes, and Midshipmen Bertie Harris and Grahame Johns. All of them were examining a chart of the Caribbean, weighted down on the table.

The captain's steward arrived with a tray of glasses filled with port, and handed them around. When each had a glass in front of him, Brownlow proposed a toast.

"To His Majesty the king," he toasted.

"To His Majesty," they all repeated as they drank their port.

"Right, gentlemen, we need to make some plans. Lord Crowe's refusal to supply us leaves us very short of fresh provisions. We need most items, but most of all we need fresh fruit," Brownlow declared to manic nods from the ship's surgeon.

Robert looked up expecting the captain to say he was going to America where he would be able to visit old friends, but this was soon dashed.

"I do not intend to go backwards, gentlemen, so the only alternatives are the islands of the Caribbean, most of which, unfortunately, are occupied or garrisoned by the French or Spanish."

"Ahem!"

"Yes, Mr Gates, you have something to say?"

"If I may be so bold, Captain. Napoleon has sold off the state of Louisiana to America, and after the massacre of his troops on Hispaniola, added to the typhus and cholera outbreaks, especially in the north of the island, he is fast losing interest in the colonies. He would rather concentrate on building and securing his European empire. The islands should provide us with what we want, and the French will be kept busy by the black slave army that has emerged."

Brownlow looked at the chart on the table in front of him and put his finger on the island of Hispaniola, pointing at the French colony of Saint-Domingue in the south.

"There seems to be plenty of small bays and inlets in the north, away from the colony. What do you know about these?"

"I'm sorry, sir, that's as far as my knowledge goes on the islands," Robert confessed apologetically.

Brownlow thought for a moment, looking at each one of them in turn, and when no other comment was forthcoming he made his decision.

"We have very little choice, gentlemen, Hispaniola it is. Mr Bray, please chart our course and let's get underway."

NINE

Hispaniola.

As they neared their destination, George received orders to anchor the *Melissa* and return to the *Broad* with Robert. As Briggs tied up alongside they scrambled up to the deck.

"Is that gunfire, or a storm?" Robert asked as he heard the noises coming from the island of Hispaniola. He scanned the land in the distance, but couldn't make out any ships at sea, or anchored.

"It will be a peculiar storm in these clear blue skies," George answered as he, too, scanned the island ahead. "I'll alert John and the old man." He turned to see Blackwell about to go into Brownlow's cabin. "Blackwell, tell the captain he is wanted on deck, and summon Lieutenant Bray."

"Aye, aye, sir," he responded as he went inside.

John Bray had heard the shout to the steward and appeared on deck, closely followed by Captain Brownlow.

"Welcome aboard, Mr Warwick, report please."

"Sounds like gunfire coming from ashore on the island, Captain. We can't make anything out yet, but I thought you should be aware."

"Thank you, Mr Warwick," he answered before turning to Briggs, who was standing by the main mast, ready for the command. Brownlow smiled at the man's anticipation. "Up you go, Briggs, take an eyeglass with you."

As Briggs skilfully scaled the mast, they all returned to concentrate on the island. If it was gunfire, and it seemed most likely that it was, it would be coming from the other side of the point.

"Set a course to keep the point to starboard until we get within range, Mr Bray, if you please. To your stations, gentlemen, let's prepare for battle."

"Beat to quarters!" shouted John.

The ship sprang into life with seamen and powder monkeys dashing to their posts in a well-rehearsed routine. Soon the guns were charged and run out ready to fire on any enemy that should present itself.

As they neared the point, the sound of gunfire increased: they could even hear the cannon balls smashing into rocks as the enemy searched for their targets. Brownlow ordered the sail to be shortened to slow them down. They crawled past the point into the open bay which gave them a panoramic view of the island's landscape. All telescopes were concentrated on the explosions in the rocks and crevices, before traversing up to the direction of fire on the cliffs above.

"French infantry and guns," Robert said as he saw the Tricolour fluttering on the clifftop.

They watched intently as fire from the cannon was directed down below. Attempting to hide behind the rocks and crevices of the small ravines leading down to the beach were members of the black slave army. They were being systematically blown to pieces.

"Maximum elevation," shouted Brownlow to his gunners. "Fire on my command." Whilst he waited for the guns to be raised, he estimated the maximum firepower of the French artillery positions.

George was standing with his hand on Briggs's shoulder as they waited for the command to fire. The French were so intent on obliterating the black slaves that they were quite oblivious to the ship's presence in the bay, broadside on and preparing to fire.

"Fire!" Brownlow bellowed.

The sound was deafening as the *Broad's* guns sent their iron balls upwards towards the enemy. George watched as the concentrated fire smashed into the guns and men on the clifftops. They now had the enemy's attention.

"Reload." The unnecessary order came as they were already setting about re-charging the guns. Less than two minutes later the order came again, "Fire!"

The French were getting over their shock and trying to recover as they watched the *Broad* start to turn slowly in the bay and head back to them. What guns were left, were now pointing down and out to sea.

The black slave army also realised that they had an ally in their fight and were rallying, firing up at the French, keeping them from accurately aiming at the *Broad*.

It seemed like a lifetime to George and his gun crew as they slowly made headway back along the bay in the gentle breeze.

"Wait for the order, Briggs," he commanded as he saw his gun captain eager to engage the enemy.

French fire was now being brought to bear on their new target. The smooth sea around them started to be stirred by splashes as enemy fire sought out the ship.

"Fire!"

The same deafening roar repeated itself as the guns fired. The acrid smell of cordite, mixed with the blue-green smoke, wafted over the decks causing some of the crew to cough.

George looked through his telescope and was surprised to see that most of the guns had been destroyed. The black slave army was on the move up the crevices towards the French, who were now starting to retreat and withdraw. He could hear the small arms gunfire and excited triumphal screams of the black army as they advanced.

"Cease firing," Brownlow ordered, as he saw the scene unfolding before him. "Mr Warwick, Mr Gates, to me please."

"Tidy up here, Briggs, and stand the men down. Be ready to man one of the boats. I think we will be making a visit," George ordered, before he joined Robert on his way to the captain's cabin.

"I think we will be forming a shore party," he said as they met and went to join Brownlow.

"Get the longboats ready, Mr Warwick. You will be going ashore with Mr Gates and his Marines," Brownlow confirmed. "They should be grateful, but you never know how these people are going to react to our presence, be on your guard at all times. Remember, provisions are of the utmost importance."

George led the three fully crewed longboats, with a detachment of Marines, to the shore. The black army had defeated the French and were returning to line the beach. He was heartened to hear them cheering, at least they didn't want to fight them… yet. George took his scarf from under his tunic and tied it around his head. It was benign, he felt comforted.

"Be on your guard, men, but be civil," Robert ordered as they neared the shore and prepared to leave the boats. "No man acts without express orders."

They ran the boats aground as the seamen jumped out, dragging them farther onto the beach, but not so far that they couldn't reverse the process if they had to. The Marines, in their bright scarlet tunics, fell in behind Robert whilst the seamen formed up behind. The black army was in good spirits and happy to see them as they waived their guns in the air and cheered, whilst advancing to greet them.

George moved through the line of Marines to join Robert at their head. He stepped forward to greet whoever appeared to be the leader of this ragged army. One man stood out from the rest. Half dressed in French uniform, and armed with a French officer's sword, he was much taller than the rest. The blacks deferred to him and allowed him to move forward to meet George.

"English?" he asked in a French accent.

George nodded. "British Royal Navy. Who do I have the honour of addressing?"

"Colonel Jean Baptiste of the free island of Haiti," he proudly answered. "Any enemy of the French and Spanish is our friend." He grinned, showing a large set of gleaming white teeth. The leader looked Robert up and down. Impressed by his appearance he asked, "You are a general, *monsieur*, yes?"

George didn't want Robert to deny it, if it gave them some headway with this man. "We are after provisions for our ship, can you help us?" he asked.

Jean Baptiste looked at George a little more closely, as if it was the first time he had seen him standing there. "You are... *Le Scarf?* he asked, pointing at him in amazement. "We have heard of you for many years, the scourge of the French and Spanish, but we didn't think you existed."

George shook his head as he answered. "No, that is my father, he is back in England. It is he who is known as *Le Scarf.*"

Baptiste looked disappointed but then suddenly grinned. "No matter, you are of his blood, you will do."

Oh my God, thought George, *he's going to try and abduct me.* He placed his hand on the hilt of his sword to be ready for any hostile action. Robert picked up on his concern and stepped forward.

"We need provision for our ship, are you able to help?"

"Of course, *Monsieur General*, but we would like your help a little further, then you can have all that you want."

"What kind of help?" George asked.

"Let us say we need your expertise as fighting men for a little, how do you say it? Ah yes, a little skirmish, a little skirmish against a French garrison."

"You want our forces to get involved in your war?"

"No, no, no, not your ship, or your men, just you two." He indicated to George and Robert. "My men will do the fighting but we need your planning to take the garrison. In return we will give you all the provisions you want. What do you say?"

George and Robert looked at one another. They stepped back behind the Marines, out of the hearing range of Baptiste, to discuss their position.

"What do we do here then?"

"We need those provisions, Robert, what choice do we have?"

"None, I suppose, only let's have the provisions first, and let's have them safely on the ship."

They returned to face Jean Baptiste, who was standing patiently in front of his men, grinning like a card player who knew he had the winning hand.

"We agree," George said with nods from Robert, "but, we must have the provisions on board our ship first."

Baptist laughed loudly. "Of course, my friends, but you two stay firmly on Haitian soil while it is done. You may return when your mission is completed." The smile was replaced with a determined scowl on his face.

George signalled Captain Brownlow on the *Broad* and apprised him of their predicament. They received a signal in reply telling them to use their own judgement and to make the decision they felt was best.

"Well he's got away with that one," Robert said sarcastically.

"What else could he do? If he tells us to return then we have to fight for provisions, if he tells us to stay, and it goes wrong, he will have some explaining to do to his lordships back in England." George turned to Baptiste who was still waiting patiently with his men. "You have a deal Jean Baptiste, as soon as we have the provisions, we will comply with your wishes."

"A very good decision, *Le Scarf*, you and the general will make plans for us to use in our attack. My people will help with whatever you need for the ship," he said, grinning from ear to ear.

George left Briggs in charge of the beach party, and for the carrying of the goods to the ship, whilst he and Robert accompanied Baptiste and his men inland through the jungle to make their plans for the assault on the garrison. How many French troops were at the garrison? No one seemed to know.

"I suppose we'll find out the strength of the enemy when we get there," Robert whispered to George, as they hacked their way through the dense undergrowth.

An hour later, they emerged from the jungle, stopping on a mound overlooking a ramshackle fort. They watched the comings and goings of the French through their telescopes, trying to estimate their strength.

"There's only about forty infantry in there, Robert, why does he need our help in taking this? He has enough men to swamp the place."

George got his answer when Baptiste had finished observing the garrison himself. "Last night there were over three hundred infantry and cavalry in and around the fort. I think Napoleon is ready to withdraw from here," he said smiling. "I don't think we will need you after all, General, but if you wish you can accompany my people in taking the fort."

Robert looked at George as they both considered their position.

"Why not?" George responded. "We could do with a little exercise, but if Napoleon is on the move, it means French ships to the south of the island. We must get back in case of attack on our ships."

Baptiste laughed, showing his large white teeth, as he faced them. "It will be an honour to go into battle with *Le Scarf* and the Scarlet General by my side."

Robert shrugged his shoulders at the Scarlet General label, as George looked at him with an amused smile on his face. Surprise would be on their side. It was decided to split the black army in two, and approach the fort from both the east and west at the same time. George and Robert were to lead the west section, whilst Baptiste led the east section. They waited for an hour before George spotted that the west, under Baptiste, was ready to move in. On George's signal they all moved together and advanced on the fort.

The French were busy packing up, being very sloppy in their sentry duties. They got to within thirty yards of the garrison's gates before the enemy realised that they were even there. Suddenly a shot rang out. George watched as a puff of smoke drifted up from a Frenchman's musket. He heard the thud and the scream as one of his section went down in agony.

"Charge!" Robert screamed. Nobody moved.

"Avancez, avancez!" George screamed out, mimicking a French accent as best he could, to instant reaction from the black army. He was aware of the scarf now throbbing on his head.

Everyone, without exception, sped forward, screaming at the top of their lungs. The French were taken completely by surprise as the two sections arrived together, and surged through the gates before they could completely close them.

George got caught up in the excitement as he ran forward to meet a French soldier who was trying to load his musket. He realised that it was a hopeless task, and turned his musket with bayonet attached to face the onslaught. George easily turned the bayonet and rifle to one side with his sword, before driving the blade home in the man's stomach. He had to put his boot against the man and shove in order to free the blade. He noticed Robert fighting two more soldiers, before five black men mobbed and cut them to pieces. They didn't stop when the enemy went down, and were quite obviously dead. Robert stood back in horror and amazement at their merciless ferocity, as they slashed and mutilated the bodies.

George looked around him at the slaughter and senseless mutilation, which was happening everywhere. French soldier after French soldier succumbed to the superior numbers, as they were butchered mercilessly by the rebels. He looked across at Robert, who he could see was as shocked by this horror as he was. He nodded to him, indicating their withdrawal from the scene.

"Let's get back to the ship, Robert, I can't stand this butchery, and I have no desire to be around when Baptiste has finished."

"I'm with you. Let's get back as fast as we can."

They both ran forward to the jungle and went back along the path they had helped hack out just a short while before. It had taken them over an hour to reach the garrison, but only forty minutes to emerge from the jungle and make the shore.

The beach was empty. There wasn't a sign of anybody as they frantically scanned the whole beach, and then looked out to sea. They had been abandoned and left to fend for themselves the best they could.

"It looks as if we are on our own, George."

"Probably activity at sea with the French," he replied as something caught his eye at the far end of the beach. "What's that, at the end of the beach?"

They made their way over to see a pile of timber had been stacked in the form of a beacon. Perhaps they were to light it to bring the *Broad* back. George noticed a small plume of smoke coming from the edge of the jungle and then saw Briggs rush out with a lighted torch, clumsily carrying pistols and dragging a musket with a bayonet attached.

"Well I never, it's Briggs, and he's got a lighted torch with him." Robert confirmed the obvious as they waited for him.

"Hello, sir, thought you would be back. I'll just light the beacon and signal Captain Brownlow to come and pick us up. We saw a bit of French activity far out to sea and the captain thought it wise to move around the point a little."

"It's good to see you as well, Briggs. Thank you for waiting for us," George replied as he watched the smoke go up the instant he lit the beacon. "Armed as well, I see."

"I didn't know how long I would have to wait, or what I would encounter, sir." He grinned. "Best to be safe rather than sorry though."

As the smoke gained height and curled away out to sea, George suddenly thought that if the *Broad* could see it, so could the black rebels.

"Oh Christ," he blurted out. "If they can see it so will the rebel army."

"Chances are they won't bother with us, George, or the *Broad* gets here on time anyway," Robert said hopefully.

"Keep your eyes peeled on the jungle, Briggs, you may wish that you hadn't stayed behind," George warned as his scarf started to throb and glow from gold to dark amber.

"All right, sir, but the *Broad* is looking for the signal."

A few minutes later, their worst fears were realised as black rebels started to emerge from the jungle and line the beach. They counted forty of them. Forty to three, George didn't give them any chance at survival.

The rebels started their advance with Jean Baptiste at their head. They heard him shouting in his heavily accented English.

"You insult me, *Le Scarf,* you left the battle without completing your mission. You and the Scarlet General are cowards and not worthy of your reputation."

"We are no cowards, Baptiste, but we are not butchers either. Yes, you turned our stomach with your senseless slaughter and mutilation and if that insults you, I couldn't care less."

"Why don't you tell him what you really mean?" Robert said grimly. "We don't want him misunderstanding, do we?"

"Briggs, make for the sea, you're a good swimmer. You might make it out to the *Broad*, or meet the longboat."

Briggs swallowed hard, his mouth becoming dry. He was scared, but he was no coward. "I owe you my life, Mr Warwick, and I have no intentions of abandoning you to this Godless rabble. I stay, sir."

"You can't make a difference, man, for goodness sake, bugger off into the sea."

"Leave him be, he has a right to make his choice. Welcome, Mr Briggs, I am honoured," Robert said solemnly. "We could do with your Chinese friends at this moment though, George."

Briggs puffed out his chest. No more fear for him, he accepted what was to happen and was prepared to sell his life dearly. He looked across at George and held out his hand.

"Thank you, Briggs. Likewise, it is my honour that you should stay," George said as he grasped the outstretched hand.

The rebel army started to advance towards them with Baptiste still shouting out his insults. The three stood firm, ready to meet them, ready to die. George was in the middle armed with pistol and sword. Briggs was standing on his left with a pistol in each hand and his cutlass strapped across his chest. Robert, on the right, sword in its scabbard, pointed his musket with bayonet at their newfound enemy.

The rebel army suddenly halted their advance for no apparent reason. They seemed to be looking beyond them, and out to sea. Had the *Broad* appeared? Were the longboats making for the shore? Briggs was the first to glance behind.

"God Almighty," he whispered. "They're behind us."

George turned quickly, ready to face the extra enemy, which was coming from behind, as a now familiar voice rang out.

"You seem to be in trouble yet again, young warrior, and prepared to meet such odds, and pay with your life if needs be. We honour you," Wei said as he bowed to George.

He was standing in front of his twenty-seven warriors, arranged in an arc behind him. Their backs were to the sea which was blocked out by a heavy rising mist. They all, like their warlord, bowed to George, before drawing their swords of gleaming bronze.

"Are they with us, sir, do you know these heathens?" Briggs asked incredulously, as he noticed the sign of the dragon on the warriors' chests.

"Angels not heathens, Briggs, and they most certainly are with us. Standby for the thrill of your life, Baptiste is about to find out what slaughter really is."

George pointed out the rebel army to the warlord, which almost filled the beach. "They are many, we are still too few."

The warlord smiled through white gleaming teeth, accentuating the battle scar that ran down the side of his face. "The last battle we fought, we were outnumbered by over one hundred to one. Numbers are of no consequence to us, young warrior."

The rebel army had taken stock of the newcomers and decided that their own numbers were far superior. Baptiste gave the order to advance and the black army came at them, slowly at first, but then, screaming like devils, they increased their pace to a run.

All eyes suddenly turned to a black blur hurtling along the beach towards them. Lightning, the magnificent stallion, had turned up to support his master, and whinnied loudly as he rushed to his master's side.

"Where have you been, Lightning, you are late?" Wei chided good naturedly as he sprang up astride him. "Let us sort this rabble who dares to threaten our young warrior."

As Lord Wei turned Lightning to face the enemy, the three comrades stood firm, and turned to face them. Briggs with his two pistols and cutlass slung across his chest, Robert with the musket and bayonet at the ready, and George armed with his sword and a knife in his belt.

The Chinese warriors followed their warlord as they pushed roughly in front of the three comrades, and advanced determinedly on the enemy.

The three of them stood mesmerized as Wei, on Lightning, charged forward, scattering the slave army as the Chinese warriors advanced, seeming to dance in carefully choreographed movements, as they cartwheeled and sprang through the hordes being scattered in front of them. They moved like lightning, cutting, thrusting and slashing their way through the black rebels at will.

Baptiste faced them with his eyes almost popping from his head as the fearsome black beast, with fire seeming to come from its nostrils, rode mercilessly towards him. He was the first to go down in a hail of slashes from Wei, with his own sword being swept aside as if it was a straw.

Wei's warriors were relentless in their ferocity, with lightning speed and agility, as they sprang sideways and forwards, cutting with their awesome bronze blades, decimating the slave army's ranks, until not one of the rebel army was left standing.

George was the first to recover from the awesome sight confronting them. As Robert and Briggs stood open-mouthed in awe at what they had witnessed, he moved forward slowly, gradually approaching the battered and mutilated body of the rebel leader Baptiste. He looked down at the butchered mess, still writhing it its death throes. Baptiste's eyes opened. He was barely alive as he looked up at George, his eyes glazing and clearing as he tried to focus.

"I thought you didn't believe in slaughter and mutilation, *Le Scarf*," he whispered, as he recognised George before letting out his last breath.

"There is always an exception to the rule," George whispered down at the dead man, "and you are most certainly that exception."

When he looked up, the Chinese warriors were on their way back, led by a smiling Wei astride a much calmer Lightning.

"Your rescue is at hand, young warrior, a boat comes for you and we must go," he said, bowing his head, as Lightning whinnied, and then suddenly disappearing with the rest of his band.

"Where the hell have they disappeared…?" Briggs trailed off, not understanding what had happened, but grateful to be alive.

They looked around for them. They had disappeared as quickly and as mysteriously as they had come. They saw the longboat from the *Broad* emerge through the rising mist, round the point, and head towards them.

"Not a word of this, Briggs, on your oath, not one word. Is that quite clear and understood?"

"Mr Warwick, I don't for the life of me understand what has gone on today, it most certainly isn't very clear. I do believe that we have had divine intervention; quite what it is though, is beyond me. You have my word, sir. Anyway, if you and Mr Gates didn't back me up, they would have clapped me in irons as a madman."

"Good man," Robert said as he slapped him on his back. "Now let's get to the boat."

"I won't forget the way you stood with us, Briggs, when you could have made good your escape. As far as you were concerned you were going to pay your debt with your life," George said, as he grasped the man's hand. "I know you don't understand, but suffice it to say, you have been honoured if you have seen the warriors."

Briggs shook his head and looked up to the heavens. *Surely not,* he thought, as he looked above and let out an involuntary gasp. George and Robert looked up, following his gaze as they noticed the smiling figure of the robed priest drifting in the heavens above.

They waded out to sea to meet the longboats until the water was under their armpits and they could go no further. The rescue boat was under the command of Bertie Harris, who was sitting bolt upright at the stern. He stood up to help them in, but more to try and see the scene of devastation in front of him. He tried to count the many bodies, littered right across the beach, before turning to George.

"You've had quite a battle, sir, and not a scratch on any of you," he said incredulously.

"Yes, Bertie, quite a battle, we did have a little help," George said, winking at Briggs as they pulled towards the *Broad.*

TEN

A Hostile Homecoming.

As they arrived on board, they saw Brownlow looking through his telescope observing the scene of the massacre on the beach. As he turned to go down the stairs to his cabin, he beckoned the three of them to follow.

"It had better be good, Mr Warwick. I want to know how the three of you escaped that carnage without a scratch."

George tried to think quickly. The *Broad* was round the point and out of sight of the beach when the actual fighting took place. He was going to have to gamble that the captain and crew were in the dark, and didn't see anything. His mind fumbled for an answer.

"We were lucky, sir. The rebel army took exception to us objecting to the way they massacred prisoners, so Mr Gates and I made good our escape to find Mr Briggs waiting on the beach for us. The rebel army caught up with us, they were about to fall on us, when a large French detachment of infantry turned up and routed them."

"Why? Why would they come to your aid, Mr Warwick?"

"They didn't know who we were, sir," Robert answered. "They couldn't see the ship as you were round the point. In any case, their one aim was to smash the rebels in the same way as the rebels had massacred their people."

"That still does not explain why they didn't take you when they had the chance," Brownlow said as he puzzled over the explanation.

"They must have seen the *Broad*, and the longboat, as you came around the point, sir. They probably went to warn their forces we were in their waters," George added, biting his lower lip.

Brownlow watched all three of them standing in front of his desk. He decided there was no point in questioning Briggs… yet.

"I can't waste any more time on this, gentlemen, if what you say is true, we may get visitors at any time. We do have the *Melissa* to get back to England. We will have our work cut out doing just that. To your stations, gentlemen, let's get underway without any further delay."

Nursing the *Melissa* through the sometimes hostile Atlantic proved arduous, and took them far longer than the journey should have. They were grateful for the fresh supplies of fruit, coconuts and meat, as well as the water taken on at Hispaniola.

George had taken over the command of the *Melissa* once again, aided by the able Bertie Harris and Briggs, who had been promoted to petty officer, filling the role of bosun. Robert and his Marines still provided the security for the vast treasure in the hold and iron cage. The three of them were grateful to be away from any more questioning from their captain with regards to the beach incident on the island.

Three days later, Briggs sighted two ships sailing towards them. George signalled the *Broad*, which immediately put on all sail and went to intercept. They watched as the two ships took evasive action away from the *Broad*.

"Can you make them out, Briggs?"

"No, sir, but I think the *Broad* is about to fire on them. Yes, they are, sir."

They watched blue smoke come from the prow of the *Broad* and then heard the sound of two cannon shots echo across the ocean towards them.

"What's going on, George?" Robert asked as he appeared on deck beside him.

"The old man's seeing off what appears to be two French luggers. They're making a run for it."

Half an hour later, they saw the *Broad* change course and head back towards them. Soon it was travelling in close proximity to the *Melissa*, making sure of its protection.

They were still about two weeks away from reaching England, when they spotted another sail approaching them fast from the stern.

"Moving like that, she has to be a schooner," George said to Briggs. "Signal Captain Brownlow, let him know, if he's not already seen her."

The *Broad* had seen her, and was already turning to starboard, turning to meet the possible threat. As the ships got closer, they watched as the *Broad* drew alongside her before both ships made their way back to the *Melissa* together.

That evening, they were told to heave to and await further orders. They watched as a longboat was lowered from the *Broad* and pulled away towards the schooner. Once it was alongside, George made out the distinct figure of the old man climbing aboard.

"What's all that about?" Robert asked as he too watched through his telescope. "Only the captain's gone aboard the clipper, no one else."

"Your guess is as good as mine, but the schooner will be in England way before we are, maybe Brownlow is sending someone a message."

"What kind of message?" Robert asked.

"Again, your guess is as good as any."

After saying farewell to the schooner, there were no further incidents and they continued their journey to England. Entering the English Channel, they made their way through the Solent keeping the Isle of Wight on their starboard and headed slowly towards Portsmouth harbour. They passed by Southsea Castle, built by Henry the Eighth, and from where the Tudor king had watched as his flagship, the *Mary Rose,* turned turtle and went to the bottom with all hands lost.

As the *Melissa* neared the harbour, closely followed by the *Broad*, they hauled in sail and went into berth at a snail's pace. They docked with the *Broad* eventually coming to rest astern of the *Melissa*. Captain Brownlow had given orders that no one should leave the *Melissa* until he was standing on the dockside.

"I don't think the old man trusts us," laughed Robert, looking across at George.

"I wonder why?"

"Oh, come on, George, that was one little indiscretion in the heat of the moment."

He let the comment go, but he would be relieved when his valuable cargo was under lock and key at the Admiralty, and no longer a temptation to his friend.

"I'm just going down to the hold to check on the cargo one more time before Brownlow comes aboard."

"I'll come with you, George. One last look won't do any harm."

They made their way down and through the bales that were neatly stacked and stowed, thanks to Briggs, until they reached the iron cage. Standing in front of it, all appeared in order.

"Aren't we going in for one more feel, George?"

"No we are not, and in any case I couldn't open it even if I wanted to, Brownlow has the key."

"He really does not trust us at all. Does he?"

"Can't say I really blame him, Robert, after all he is the one responsible for it."

Briggs called down through the hold, "Captain Brownlow is coming aboard, sir."

"Thank you, Briggs. Give him my compliments and tell him where we are, please."

"Aye, aye, Mr Warwick, sir," he called back as Robert looked at him with a rueful smile.

A few minutes later, they could hear Brownlow moving through the hold. He was accompanied by John Bray, with Grahame Johns bringing up the rear.

"Ah, Mr Warwick, and Mr Gates, how are things? Everything is still as it should be, I trust," he said, as he produced the key to the iron cage.

"Aye, Captain, all is secure and intact," George answered, apprehensively looking at Robert, who was standing by his side nodding his agreement with a big smile.

Brownlow handed the key to Robert. "If you would be so good, Mr Gates."

Robert accepted the key, unlocked the cage and stepped in. He held the door ajar for Brownlow to follow him. The captain produced two large pieces of paper, selected the list for the cage as he entered, and started to mentally count the items off as he moved through. George watched Robert's face, not quite sure whether he had been up to anything, but his smiling countenance didn't change in the slightest as Brownlow came to the end of his inspection.

"All present and correct. Well done, Mr Gates," Brownlow congratulated. He then stunned them both with the rare gesture of holding out his hand and shaking both Robert's and George's. "You are both relieved of your duties here and can take a well-earned break. I will be placing new guards on the hold until an escort arrives to take the treasure up to the Admiralty, with the rest of the cargo going to storage in the dockyard."

Back in George's cabin, they both smiled contentedly at the thought of the bounty they would receive from their share. George in particular was happy because he would receive a lieutenant's portion of the prize instead of a midshipman's. Robert stripped off his uniform and put on civilian clothes, still managing to look like a gallant officer, even in civvies.

"Can I leave my gear in here whilst we go ashore to celebrate, George? You are coming ashore, aren't you?"

"Too right I am, Robert, let's go and play merry hell with the locals." He beamed as he removed his uniform jacket and donned a short reefer coat.

They were on their way down the gangway of the *Melissa* when a host of horses and infantry came alongside the dock. The riders dismounted and joined the fully armed infantry that had lined up alongside the ship. George and Robert froze and stood where they were as they tried to work out what was going on. Briggs appeared on the deck above them.

"I think we have a visitor, sir," he said, pointing up the dockyard as a coach made its way down towards them.

They gradually made their way back along the deck, watching the coach as it arrived. George's face darkened as he saw the coat of arms on its side. Lord Crowe. He should have expected as much.

Crowe stepped off the coach with a triumphant air, and looked up at them, still with that twisted smile playing on his cruel lips. They watched him speak to a sergeant at arms before seeing the soldier start to move up the gangway.

"Stay where you are. I am the commander of this vessel and demand to know what your business is here," George shouted down to him.

"I have a warrant from the Admiralty for this vessel's cargo. You will stand down and allow my forces on," Crowe shouted up at them.

"You may come up, Sergeant, and present your warrant. All others will stay off this vessel until then," he replied as Robert and Briggs, stood by his side.

"If you do not comply, Warwick, I will take this vessel by force," Lord Crowe shouted from the bottom of the gangway.

"We have to play for time," George whispered. "I'll take the sergeant and his warrant to my cabin. Get some more men here, including the guards below deck." He beckoned the sergeant to come up with his warrant before calling down to Crowe.

"My lord, if the warrant is correct, I will accede to your wishes, but until I clarify this, I am still under orders from my commanding officer, and that is Captain Brownlow."

"Just get on with it, Warwick, I am running short of patience."

George didn't reply as he led the sergeant down to his cabin. He made a big play of looking for an eyeglass to enable him to see more clearly in the poor light of the cabin.

"May I suggest we go back on deck, sir, where the natural light will help you?" the sergeant proposed.

"It's around here somewhere, I had it before I went out," George blustered as he fumbled around his belongings.

They heard a further commotion on the deck above as Briggs arrived at the cabin's door. "Captain Brownlow's arrived, sir, with a full complement from the *Broad*. He's in a stand-off with Lord Crow below, sir."

Both George and the sergeant joined Briggs in returning to the deck. Robert was now armed with musket and sword, together with his Marines who were on board to guard the cargo. They looked down at the docks to see Brownlow strutting along on his bow legs, fearlessly confronting an irate and indignant Crowe.

"I don't give a tinker's cuss who you are, sir. This command can only be removed from my jurisdiction by the Admiralty Board, and I've yet to see that."

"That is because the warrant is being served on your man aboard this vessel, Captain Brownlow," Crowe stated frustrated. "Now order you men to step aside, or I will declare that you are in a state of mutiny."

"Don't talk of mutiny to me, sir, I know my duty to my king and country, and I will fulfil that duty to the letter."

"Bring that warrant back down here, Sergeant, this minute," Crowe shouted, with his face getting ever redder.

Before the sergeant could get past Robert and his men, a further commotion happened at the far end of the dock. More cavalry and more infantry started to pour down onto the little *Melissa*.

"What the hell is going on now, not more of Crowe's men?" asked a puzzled Robert, as he saw the vast army approaching. "There is hardly enough room to swing a cat down there."

"It's Lord Fitzwilliam," George shouted out with glee. "He hates Crowe, now we should get somewhere."

"Not even he can overturn an Admiralty warrant. All we are doing is playing for time," Robert muttered as the sergeant pushed past him, waving his piece of paper as he descended the gangway.

Lord Fitzwilliam rode straight up to Crowe and dismounted, before standing in front of him with his legs wide apart and his hands on his hips. They saw his defiance and started down the gangway towards the confrontation that was about to take place. This was going to be settled here and now.

"You intercepted the letter from Captain Brownlow to the Admiralty, Crowe, but what you didn't bank on was a second letter given to a junior officer aboard the cutter, who just happens to be a nephew of the good captain... and it was addressed to me personally."

"Lord Fitzwilliam." Crowe addressed him sarcastically. "I have a warrant to take command of the cargo of the *Melissa,* and take it into safekeeping."

"Don't brandish your blasted warrant in front of me, man. Sergeant, come here and read this." Fitzwilliam beckoned him over, with the sergeant still holding his piece of paper in his hand as he was handed a further warrant. He read it carefully, and then read it again, before turning to face Crowe.

"I am sorry, my lord, but this warrant supersedes ours. I am afraid that we will have to withdraw."

"What are you blethering on about, Sergeant, give it to me," Crowe screamed as he snatched the new warrant from his hand. He read it with his beady little eyes growing wider and wider. His face was now purple, with his thin white lips twisting back and forth across his cruel mouth.

"I don't know how you have done this, Fitzwilliam, but you haven't heard the last of this." He scowled, looking at

George, who had joined them. "Or you, Warwick, mark my words you are a marked man."

"As your lordship, pleases," George responded sarcastically, with a bow of his head to howls of laughter from Fitzwilliam.

"Perhaps the dockyard can get back to normal now," Captain Brownlow conjectured, laughing with Fitzwilliam at the retreating figure. "I'll be glad and relieved to get this treasure off my hands though, my lord."

"Never fear, my dear Captain, that is about to happen now," Fitzwilliam said as he eyed Robert. "Ah, Mr Gates, one other thing Lord Crowe didn't mention to you out in the Caribbean. You received your promotion the day after you left England. You are now Captain Gates of His Majesty's Marines."

Robert didn't quite understand. a captain, a promotion? "Thank you, my lord, thank you for letting me know."

"Let me be the first to congratulate you, Robert, I mean, sir," George said, shaking his hand. "Oh, by the way, your share of the prize has just gone up a notch."

Three hours later, after the iron cage had been emptied and put in the charge of a detachment of Marines, George and Robert were sitting with Lord Fitzwilliam in The Benbow Arms public house, just off Broad Street in Portsmouth. They were getting a little drunk. Robert was celebrating his prize money being upped, as well as his station in life. He suddenly stopped drinking and got to his feet.

"I've left some letters I wanted to send urgently to my relatives in Sussex and America. They're in your cabin, George. I have to get them, it won't take me long. You carry on drinking until I get back. With your permission, my lord?" he ventured.

"Carry on, Robert, don't take all night about it, you'll be missing some fine ale. George and I will hold the fort."

It was almost two hours before he returned, explaining that he didn't want them to be delayed, so he to find someone to deliver them. By this time George and Fitzwilliam were too drunk to bother about it.

***

George was sitting outside the hall where the admirals were assembled, with Captain Brownlow on one side of him and Robert on the other. They could hear muffled voices coming from behind the large double oak doors, recognizing the booming voice of Lord Fitzwilliam, but they couldn't tell how it was going.

George's thoughts took him back to when he had got home to the farm, taking Robert with him. The *Melissa* had seemed a distant memory as they were welcomed by his mother and father, as well as his blossoming sister.

He had gone out to the barn to tend to the horses, when once again he had felt a distinct change in the air. Looking up, he knew instinctively who he would see.

"Warrior, you have done well, you have brought honour to the scarf. It will aid you when you act with courage and gallantry, and your bravery has earned its protection."

"Thank you, Lord Wei, for the protection and assistance it has rendered me," George had said, with reverence and gratitude.

"You must be on your guard," Wei had warned. "Your enemy, who sits with your rulers, means to take away your honour, but never fear, your warlord of the ship will stand by you, as will your adopted father, who sits with the rulers."

"I would like to know one thing, Wei."

"And what is that, young warrior?"

"The giant black steed, was he yours many years ago?"

"Lightning!" he exclaimed with a smile. "You only own a horse such as him with his blessing, but yes, he carried me into battle many, many times, striking fear into my enemies. He was with me at the end of my mortal life, and will be with me for ever more."

"Why do we not see him more often?"

"My warriors and I only turn up at points of grave danger, and Lightning only when he is needed. But one thing, young warrior, he is not a seahorse and will never go on the great waters, which he hates."

George had been about to answer when he heard a voice from outside the barn. Alarmed, he had turned to see his sister coming through the open barn door.

"Who are you talking to, George?" Jessica had asked, as she peered round the barn.

George had turned back to Wei, but he was no longer there, "To the horses, sister, who else?" he'd answered hesitantly, making sure that Wei had gone.

George's thoughts were interrupted as he was brought back to the present by the sound of the great oak door opening. A steward came out carrying a sheet of paper. Did it refer to him, he wondered, as the great door gradually eased shut again. Inside the chamber, the lords continued their discussion.

"Why do you want us to rule on this matter, Fitz? Surely this should go before the normal examination panel of three or more senior captains?" Admiral Lord Grenville, presiding over the panel, asked.

"True, my lord, but there are exceptional circumstances in this case, one being Warwick's length of service. He has only completed three years in the Royal Navy, even though he has served with distinction in every command."

"The coming rules state no less than five years, my lord Grenville," Crowe, sitting on the other side of the table, asserted. "Has he the experience in gunnery, does he understand the azimuth compass and the proper use of sextants?"

Fitzwilliam, holding his protruding stomach, laughed out loud. "Crowe by name and crow by nature, just listen to him, he's nothing but an armchair warrior, a civilian sailor who's never commanded a proper fighting ship in his life. You got where you are through rank and privilege, man, not like the rest of these members who got here by merit."

The smirks suddenly appearing on the faces of the admirals, told Fitzwilliam he had hit home, and his words had made a lasting impression on them.

"My lords, I must protest," Crowe blustered as Grenville held up his hand to silence him.

"He has a point, Fitz, what do you say?"

"Captain Hardy has sent in a letter of commendation for Lieutenant Warwick. As you know, he is in Lisbon at present as the flag captain to Lord Berkeley, but commends Warwick's actions aboard the *Victory* at Trafalgar." All heads turned to smile at one another at the recognition of their most famous sea battle. Fitzwilliam had their undivided attention.

"He has commended him for his devotion to duty, his superhuman efforts in clearing the rigging and timber away from his gun, after his whole gun crew had been killed, and making the gun ready to fire for the reserve gun crew." Fitz paused for the effect to take hold, and then continued. "Captain Brownlow of the *Broad* waits and will also testify to the fitness of Warwick's commission, which he gave without the slightest hesitation I might add, as he did the command of the unstable *Melissa,* which Warwick brought back to England with vast riches such as we have never seen the like of before. They are safe and intact, my lords."

"That doesn't excuse the fact that he does not have the necessary service in," Crowe insisted over the murmurs of contentment coming from those present, who were thinking of the riches they had already inspected.

"A mere suggestion to the rules that may, or may not be adopted, my lords," Fitz added with a broad grin, showing his nice even teeth under his large moustache. "But even so, since when did proposed regulations get in the way of the better judgement of the Admiralty?"

"My lords, if you please." Lord Grenville called them to order. "I think we will have Captain Brownlow in next and then see Lieutenant Warwick. Steward, be so good as to summon Captain Brownlow."

It didn't escape Lord Fitzwilliam's ears that the term of lieutenant was used by Grenville, as the steward pulled at the left handle of the large double oak doors to the outer corridor. In marched Brownlow with all the confidence in the world. He was invited to sit opposite Fitz.

"You know why you are here, Captain Brownlow, do you not?" Grenville asked politely.

"Yes, my lord, I do, for the confirmation of the commission of Lieutenant Warwick," he said proudly.

"My lord, I must strongly object. Warwick has not been commissioned yet," Crowe sneered.

"Begging your lordship's pardon, he has, under the regulations and authority granted to me by His Majesty, and as directed by yourselves. That commission has been granted but is subject to your lordship's examination and acceptance," Brownlow asserted firmly.

"Quite, quite so," Grenville muttered. "Let's get on with it please."

"Captain Brownlow. Why was Warwick given a commission and command of the *Melissa,* when you had a senior lieutenant on board?" Crowe asked triumphantly.

Brownlow did not hesitate with his answer. "Mr Bray is a first-rate officer. He follows orders to the letter, but he does not have what I feel to be, sound leadership qualities or imagination. I believe that this will change as he gains more experience, but I needed an officer who could command with verve and unfailing determination, one who I knew would see the job through to the end. That man was Lieutenant Warwick, who has proved my judgement to be correct."

Grenville looked around the table at his fellow lords, all of whom were nodding, apart from the notable exception of Lord Crowe.

"Thank you, Captain, I find your conduct in all of this both acceptable and commendable. Thank you for your testimony. On your way out, please ask Lieutenant Warwick to come in."

George sat uncomfortably facing Lord Grenville, this man of legend, a man only second to Nelson in reputation. He glanced nervously around the table, noticing the hostile sneer of Crowe, before settling on the grinning face of his patron, Lord Fitzwilliam.

What will be their decision? he wondered. *Will Crowe win the day, or will I retain my commission?*

ELEVEN

Crompton Manor, set in the most beautiful Hampshire countryside, looked splendid for the time of the year. It was late September and the trees were turning from their summer greenery into different shades of red, brown and gold. The flower beds were being tidied by the gardeners. Seed heads had been collected from the various blooms which were now dying, unlike the roses which, with dead heading, continued to produce wonderful flowers, and would do so well into the onset of winter.

Lord Fitzwilliam had invited the Warwick family over for a late picnic on the well-manicured lawn in front of the house. The grass was lovingly cared for by Harold, the estate manager himself, who was the only one permitted to use the new-fangled lawn mower.

The invitation stretched to Robert, who was staying at the farm with George's family.

"My brother should be arriving anytime now with his wife and daughter. You'll like Barbara, Jessica. She's your age and quite a fun-loving girl. You should both get on well."

I'm more interested in getting to know Robert more, Jessica thought to herself, *what a handsome man, and that voice with its accent, simply divine.*

Sir Henry Fitzwilliam, younger brother of Fitz, was a merchant banker living on the Kent border near East Sussex. He had been married for thirty years, with his wife bearing him a daughter who was now aged eighteen, and if the stories George had heard were true, quite a looker.

Jessica and her mother were inside the manor with Mrs Baird, a widow and Fitz's housekeeper and confidante, if rumour was to be believed. True or false, the relationship was good for Fitz, and he was certainly a man reborn following the death of his wife some eight years earlier. The four men, Fitz,

Rodney, Robert and George were seated under the giant beech tree facing the driveway's entrance and the large, ornate iron gates.

"Thanks for what you have done for George, Fitz, I do appreciate it," Rodney said quietly, as the two younger friends looked on.

"Nonsense, Rodney, how many times did you haul my nuts from the fire?" He laughed. "Besides, he earned his promotion the hard way; I don't think I could be more pleased. Robert also had a hand in it, as well as Captain Brownlow."

"Robert, my lord, what was his part in my examination?" asked George, as Robert smiled and started to redden.

"After their lordships had seen you, Captain Gates was called in. He told them that if George didn't retain his commission, his colonel had authorised him to offer him a commission in the Royal Marines. That settled it. Grenville ruled, there and then, that George would keep his commission and continue to serve on *HMS Broad*."

"You never said," George accused.

"I didn't know if I had any effect or not. In any case, I think they had made up their minds before I entered the room."

"You could at least have mentioned it, Robert," George protested.

"Come on, you two, don't make an issue out of it," Rodney said, intervening. He was about to say something further, when they all noticed the coach, being pulled by two beautiful chestnut horses, enter the drive at the trot, and head straight for the house.

They all made their way to the front of the manor to see that the buxom Mrs Baird, with Jessica and George's mother, Rebecca, together with Harold, the estate manager, were already descending the stone steps to the carriage as it came to a halt. Fitz and Rodney strode on ahead, leaving George to take further issue with Robert.

Harold opened the carriage door, pulled down the attached step, and helped a portly gentleman alight. George caught sight of him over the shoulder of his father.

"Good heavens!" he exclaimed. "Another version of Fitz, he's the spitting image."

Robert agreed. "You're not wrong there, George," he commented, with a big grin stretching right across his face.

"Henry, you old rogue." Fitz greeted his brother with enthusiasm as he hugged him warmly.

"Let me have a look at you, you old pirate," Sir Henry responded, holding Fitz at arm's length whilst looking him up and down.

"Hello, Uncle," a voice came from the within the carriage, as George spied a well-turned ankle stepping down.

What followed took his breath away. She was a goddess, a goddess dressed in an emerald green dress, which showed off her golden hair as it cascaded down around her beautiful shoulders. It also showed a modest amount of cleavage, which definitely promised more.

"Fitz, how lovely to see you again." Another vision alighted from the carriage, older, but just as beautiful.

"Hello, Miriam." Fitz welcomed the elder woman. "Hello, Barbara," he greeted the goddess. "It's lovely to see you both again, it has been too long."

George was now pushing in front of Robert to be the first to be introduced and stood to one side of his father. He didn't, he couldn't, take his eyes off Barbara and just stared at her with his mouth gaping open.

"You've all met Rodney before." Fitz introduced George's father to nods of recognition and smiles. Sir Henry stepped forward to shake his hand and then turned to George.

"And who have we here?" he asked as George continued staring at Barbara, who was standing behind her father.

"Close yer mouth, George," Fitz ordered with a smile, to the amusement of Barbara and her mother. "This is Rodney's first-born, George or should I say, Lieutenant Warwick of His Majesty's Navy."

"Glad to meet you, young man, and you are not the first to experience a jaw dropping moment upon meeting my daughter," he said, shaking his hand and slapping George on the back.

"Please, Father, don't embarrass him, or me," Barbara said, stepping forward to take George's hand in hers. "I am very pleased to meet you, sir."

George was dumbstruck. He didn't know what to say, he just stood there holding her hand, forgetting to let go. Robert pulled him gently backwards as he smiled at her.

"I'm Robert Gates, captain of His Majesty's Marines," he said boldly. "You will have to forgive my young friend; he has been starved of such beauty for these past years."

"Well said, Captain," Lady Miriam said, shaking hands with Robert, before smiling warmly as she turned to George. As he took her hand, he was speechless again and forgot to release it.

"You're a greedy young fellow, Warwick. What? Do you want them both? That one's taken, young man, so let go of her hand, or you'll feel me slipper," Sir Henry boomed as everybody laughed at George's discomfort.

"I'm terribly sorry, sir, I didn't mean any harm, what I mean..." George started to bluster in his embarrassment.

Jessica came forward to save her brother any further awkwardness and to be introduced, but not before firing a vicious look at Robert for daring to compliment the opposition. Robert caught the withering look, realising what it meant, and smiled to himself. *At least now I know you feel the same about me,* he thought. After introductions all round they moved off to go into the manor.

"After you, Lady Miriam," Mrs Baird invited.

"Forget the lady, Anne, we both know your true position in this household, and it's about time he made an honest woman of you. Just call me Miriam, please."

Fitz suddenly developed a very violent coughing fit with Rodney pounding his back and laughing at the same time. Anne Baird led the way in through the large single oak door, with a secretive and mysterious smile on her face.

Over the next two weeks, George and Robert became constant visitors to the manor, as Jessica visited to get to know her new friend. The four of them took to riding across the estate and venturing out into the countryside, sometimes ending up at the farm for afternoon tea with Rodney and Rebecca. They were often invited to have dinner at the manor with Barbara's parents. Fitz insisted that they wear full uniform for such occasions. "Adds to the occasion and the ambience," he would say.

Robert and Jessica were getting very close and often tried to find a place to be alone. George, on the other hand, continued with his shyness, much to the disappointment of Barbara.

"What is it with you, George, don't you like her?" Robert asked him one morning, as they went around the farm, stopping to sit outside the barn. "Barbara's spoken to Jessica, and she tends to think you can't wait to get away from her."

"Good heavens no, man, I adore her, I don't want her to leave," he said, beside himself with the thought that he had spoilt things.

"Then why don't you tell her so, you idiot?"

"Because she frightens me," he blurted out.

Robert couldn't believe what he was hearing. He just stared at his friend before bursting out laughing. "*Le Scarf,* the scourge of the French and Spanish! The great George Warwick, Navy lieutenant, not afraid of any man… afraid of a slip of a girl?"

"Shut it, Robert, or I'll knock your blasted head off," he responded, through embarrassment more than anger. "I have it all worked out, what I'm going to say, how I'm going to say it… and then, I just fold. I can't explain it, and I don't know what to do about it."

They remained sitting for a while, deep in thought before Robert eventually broke the awkward silence. "When you first went into battle, were you afraid? When the French swarmed over on to the *Victory*'s decks, were you afraid?"

"We've had this conversation before, you know I was, and probably will be again in the next battle."

"But you still went forward, no matter how scared you were, you still went forward and engaged the enemy, you even saved my life in the process."

"It's bloody different, Robert, those were ugly French sods. Barbara is the most beautiful thing I have ever imagined, and more, the thought of her saying no to me leaves me with such dread I'd rather not ask."

"Oh, it's rejection that you fear. If you don't ask, you are not refused, is that it? Well, let me tell you something, mister, if you don't say something, you most definitely will lose her, and she'll be snapped up by the first man of means to come her way. I'll give you the best piece of advice a friend can give anyone: conquer you nerves, bite down on a piece of wood if you have to, but tell her how you feel."

George studied his friend's face and knew he was right. If he didn't say something she was going to be off without her knowing just how he did feel about her.

"You're right of course, I do have to say something, and I will... next time we go over to the manor."

***

They rode through the gates to the manor and made their way slowly up the drive to the front entrance. George was astride the farm's large chestnut mare, normally used for ploughing or pulling carts, and Robert was astride the beautiful black stallion loaned to him by Lord Fitzwilliam.

The weather was very clement for the time of the year, with the autumn late morning sunshine still managing to bring warmth to the air. They spotted the party assembled on the green under the large beech tree. A long table, covered with a white damask cloth, had been produced and prepared by Anne Baird, and the food was about to be put out. Fitz saw them coming and told Harold to tend to their horses.

"Come and join us, you're just in time for some lunch. Harold will deal with the horses," he said, as they both dismounted.

"We don't wish to intrude, my lord," George said, eyeing Barbara, who was sitting next to her mother.

"Not at all, young man," Sir Henry answered for Fitz, "The ladies will be pleased of your company." He had noticed his daughter's cheerful countenance at their arrival.

"Come around here, the pair of you," Lady Miriam invited.

As they went around the table to join them, George was determined to ask Barbara if he could talk to her alone. He had resolved to 'bite down on the piece of wood,' and would tell her how he felt about her.

Robert was the first to notice the courier as he entered the drive and rode up to them. His mount was sweating, he had obviously ridden long and hard to get here. All eyes turned to the middle-aged rider, who had dismounted and was approaching Fitz.

"My lord, I have urgent documents from the Admiralty that need your immediate attention."

"I dare say, Mr Harris, sit yerself down, man, and get a drink inside you. My manager will deal with your horse which looks all in." Fitz knew the courier, who was a regular visitor between him and the Admiralty. "It must be important for you to ride so hard."

Barbara was looking at George, half expecting him to ask her to one side, only to see that he, together with Robert, was only interested in what the courier had brought. Fitz broke the seal on the leather case and took out the contents, laying them out on the table in front of him. He carefully read document after document. His mood seemed to darken and his temper started to increase. Eventually he looked up from the papers at Robert and George.

"With me please, gentlemen," he commanded rather than invited, and on seeing his brother rise added, "No, not you, Henry, this is official business."

He led the two of them back inside the manor to his library. "No visitors, Anne," he instructed Mrs Baird, as he closed the door behind them.

"What is it, my lord? You seem upset by the news."

"It's still Fitz in private, George, and yes I am, as you two will be."

"What on earth can be that bad?" Robert asked.

"Let me tell you the good news first. Your promotion has been confirmed, George, and you are both to report to your ship in Portsmouth without delay. You are to rejoin *HMS Broad* under Brownlow."

"And… the bad news, sir?" Robert ventured.

Fitz looked at them both and was obviously having trouble thinking of how to put something over to them. He cleared his throat.

"Now remember, I had nothing to do with the valuation or disposal of the cargo brought back aboard the *Melissa*, and I am afraid I was not privy to their lordships assessment of it, but here goes. I might as well tell you as it is. Robert, your share of the cargo is one hundred and twenty-eight pounds and ten shillings."

"Of the cargo, but what of the treasure, my lord, surely we get a cut of that as well?"

"That is it, Robert, the total sum. I will take issue with them, but in my experience, once a decision has been made, every greedy little palm has already been greased."

"And what do I receive, Fitz?" George asked

"One hundred and two pounds five shillings," he answered simply and to the point. "I'm sorry, George, we both know it should have been over a thousand pounds. Look, as I said, I will take issue with their lordships, but I doubt it will make a difference. I smell Crowe's hand in all of this, and I will have it out with him."

"It's a princely sum, but I can't get married on that, can I?" Robert said bitterly, letting the cat out of the bag as to his intentions towards Jessica.

The two friends stood in the library just looking at one another, as Fitz wondered what to say next.

"Oh well, it was only money, George, we'll make it again, just you wait and see," Robert added flippantly.

George couldn't believe his ears. A greater disappointment he couldn't imagine. And Robert intended to marry his sister. Why was he so philosophical over the matter? George couldn't make his friend out, but if he was accepting it, so must he.

They rode back to the farm, George cursing himself for not telling Barbara how he felt and noticing the disappointment in her sad eyes.

"Don't say anything to Jessica about what I said back there, it'll have to keep until we return."

Two hours later, they said their farewells to George's mother and father. George thought that Robert and Jessica had become joined together; such was the length and intensity of their embrace.

They rode to the coach station in silence, said farewell to Harold, who took control of their mounts, and boarded the carriage that would take them to Portsmouth. They were the only passengers on this leg of the journey so they could talk with some privacy and not be overheard. For the first mile they travelled in complete silence, each with their own thoughts of those they had left behind.

George got the feeling that his friend wanted to confide in him, but decided to wait until he said something. When he eventually spoke, George was hit with a thunderbolt.

"I have something to tell you, old friend. You might have wondered why I took the news of those thieving bastards from the Admiralty so well. Well I'll tell you. Do you remember when we were with Fitz in the tavern in Portsmouth, after we docked? Do you recall me having to leave to post some letters to Sussex and America? Well there weren't any letters. I went back to the *Melissa* to retrieve those beautiful gold doubloons that were in the iron cage."

George looked at his friend, not quite understanding what he was being told. He remembered him going to get the letters, but couldn't remember much after that. How on earth had he done it? Several copies of the inventory were made and checked on docking and everything was found to be correct.

"You couldn't have, the treasure and cargo were listed as correct when we got back to Portsmouth."

"I could, and I did. I removed the doubloons well before the inventory was taken."

"Where on earth did you stash them? They would have been found."

"You'll love this, George. I hid the box under the bunk in your quarters. You had them the whole time, you were sleeping on them."

George stared open-mouthed at this news. What it meant, and what it could have meant if it had been discovered, filled him with horror.

"You blasted fool. Not only do you steal from the King, but you risked my neck on the gallows for it. Don't you understand what you have done?"

"Oh, do stop it, George, you're being a bit melodramatic, aren't you? If it had been found, the previous captain of the *Melissa* would have been blamed, and he was still in Lobo. No harm done!"

George sat quietly, looking out of the coach's window at the passing hedgerows and trees as they flashed by. He refused to talk to his friend, and at the next station they were joined by a man and woman, also travelling all the way to Portsmouth. Robert kept shooting furtive looks across at his friend as he watched him quietly seethe in the corner of the carriage. How was he going to get back on good terms with him? A ship, even the size of the *Broad*, could be a very small place if you were not getting on with someone.

He was starting to regret telling his friend of his bounty, but not the taking of it. Their lordships had justified his actions. Robert sat back, resigned to what lay ahead, but satisfied as to what he had done.

TWELVE

As they gathered in Brownlow's cabin, they were all obviously pleased to see one another, but the meeting was muted by the news of just how small their prize money had been in relation to the cargo handed over to the Admiralty. Captain Brownlow appeared to be the most upset, having put his faith in his share bringing a well-earned comfortable retirement.

"I know how disappointed you all must be in the somewhat dubious behaviour of some members of the Admiralty, reflecting in the paltry purses you have received. I am well aware of the worth of the cargo, as I took the inventory, but we must move on, gentlemen," Brownlow said, as he looked round at the officers presently seated at the table.

George looked accusingly at Robert, who had the audacity to look as upset and disappointed as the rest of them. Robert ignored him and continued to listen attentively to Brownlow.

"Is there anything that can be done about this blatant misappropriation of the cargo, sir?"

"I am afraid not, John," Brownlow answered. "I understand that Lord Fitzwilliam is attempting to address the situation and acquire a more appropriate payment, but even he does not hold out much hope."

Bertie Harris and Grahame Johns looked at one another with obvious disappointment, but still happy that their captain had taken them both on again. Their devotion to him, and the *Broad*, was well known, and besides, with George Warwick on board, there would still be more chance of prizes.

There was one absentee from the last crew, as well as three more additions. Percival Rhodes, the ship's surgeon, had refused to sign on again because of the lack of bonus payment, so he had been replaced by a younger, far more genial sort, in the form of twenty-eight-year-old William Delaforce from Jersey. Two more midshipmen, Owen Bright and Roger

Knowles, sixteen and seventeen years of age respectively, brought the ship's complement up to strength. Young Bright was the son of an army officer, disappointing his father with his preference for the Navy. Knowles was the son of Lord Craig, who was also expected to be made a member of the Admiralty in the near future.

"We must put this behind us, gentlemen, and I will now deal with our orders and destination. Parliament, in its infinite wisdom, has now ordered the abolition of the slave trade, and has charged the Admiralty with putting a stop to this wherever we come across it. Our destination is the Caribbean, the Americas, as well as South America."

"What are our orders when we come across these slavers, sir? Some of them, like the Portuguese, are our allies."

"That is correct, Mr Warwick, but our orders are no exceptions. If the slavers refuse to desist from this vile and wicked trade, my orders are to sink and hang them."

"Without any trial, Captain Brownlow?" a worried Robert asked.

"Caught in the act, Mr Gates, they will desist, or we will send them to the bottom of the sea, and hang any survivors for this insidious trade."

Brownlow looked around the cabin for any further comments. There were none. "Right, gentlemen, we are fully provisioned and crewed, let's get underway."

As they emerged from the captain's cabin into the grey mist of the early morning, George spotted Briggs instructing a gang of seamen. Briggs saw George and Robert, grinned and doffed a salute to them.

"Still with us, Briggs," George said, acknowledging the salute.

"Aye, sir, once I knew you had signed on again, I didn't want to miss anything," he said grinning.

"We'll be getting underway soon, so you had better get the men ready." No sooner had George spoken than Captain Brownlow appeared with John Bray at his side.

"Get her underway, Mr Bray, if you please."

***

Three weeks later they were riding out one of the worst storms they had ever encountered in the western Atlantic to date.

"It's what we Americans call the 'hurricane season', George," Robert pointed out, lurching to one side as he struggled to keep his balance. He pulled his cloak up tightly around his face to guard against the howling wind and stinging spray.

Even with the passing of three weeks, George had found it hard to acknowledge him, let alone hold a conversation, but his curiosity was getting the better of him.

"What did you do with the coins?" he suddenly asked him.

Robert looked at his friend and grinned. "Ah, curiosity getting the better of you, is it? Not here, George, I would have to shout in this wind. I'll see you after your watch."

Down in their quarters they found themselves alone. George had bottled this up for too long, he wanted to know, but he waited for Robert to start.

"My uncle over in Kent is a banker, and the soul of discretion. He lodged the coins at his bank and changed them into sterling," he said as he smiled at George. "You now have an account at the bank with the princely sum of one thousand, one hundred pounds and ten shillings. I have an extra three percent, as the more senior officer, and for my anticipation of events."

George shook his head, but grudgingly started to smile ruefully. "You are a foolhardy idiot, but I must admit, in hindsight the circumstances did warrant your actions."

"That's my boy." Robert grinned. "I knew you would come around eventually. It does mean that I can get married to your sister, after a decent interval, that is."

Later that evening, George was alone, leaning on the bowsprit and looking out to sea. The storm had abated, leaving a large but gentle swell on the grey ocean, which was lifting him up, before slowly dropping him down again. His thoughts, once again, turned to Barbara. Would he get another chance with her? Would she still be available when he got home? Robert's words preyed on his mind. Would a suitor turn up and sweep her off her feet?

"Warrior, you seem deep in thought."

George was so wrapped up in his reverie, he almost answered as if he were speaking to Robert.

"Your mind should be on battle, warrior, not women."

"Lord Wei, what is wrong?" George acknowledged the warlord, embarrassed that he hadn't realised who it was when he spoke.

Wei grinned at him, making the jagged scar running down the side of his face more pronounced. "Tomorrow you will face new dangers, you must be ready."

George looked out to sea, but everything seemed calm after the hurricane. "What new dangers, my lord?" he asked as he turned back to him.

"Dangers, George, what's this all about?" John Bray asked from behind him.

He jumped. Had John seen and heard? He thought quickly. "Daydreaming I'm afraid, John," he said looking around for Wei.

"It's unlike you, George. You are normally so full of common sense."

George turned to face him and saw Briggs watching them from behind.

"I think I'll go and get me head down for a while, John. I'll see you later."

As he made to go past Briggs, he stopped. "Are you all right, Briggs?" he asked.

"I'm fine, sir, I hope the visit doesn't mean more trouble like on the island, sir."

George realised that Briggs, once again, was privy like Robert, to seeing the Chinese when they appeared. The warriors obviously thought his gallantry was worthy of them.

"We'll have to wait and see, won't we? Get some rest, Briggs, tomorrow could be an interesting day."

John Bray watched them both walk away and disappear below, and wondered what it was that these two men could possibly have in common.

***

George was awakened by Bertie Harris who, on trying to wake him, almost tipped him out of his hammock.

"What is it, Bertie? This is getting to be a habit. You don't have to be so rough."

"It's almost your watch, sir, but I think you had better come on deck and listen."

"How many times have I told you? Call me George in private, for goodness sake. We served at the same rank together."

"If the old man heard me, sir, I would be in deep trouble. You know what he's like for discipline and status."

"Quite right, Midshipman Harris, let's have it right," Robert responded as he woke. "What's up anyway?"

"Noises, rumbles, flashes, all coming from off the larboard bow far ahead, sir," the smiling young midshipman answered as he moved away.

Three minutes later, they both joined him on deck with their telescopes at the ready. The night was starry and quiet, with a warm gentle breeze forming a slight headwind to the eastern horizon. They noticed flashes coming from ahead with a very distant rumble.

"There, sir, coming from the eastern sky. Do you see them?"

"We can see them, Bertie. What do you make of it, George?"

"In a night as clear as this, I shouldn't think it's a storm. It looks as if we have found a small war going on."

"But whose war?" Robert wondered quietly to himself.

"It's now my watch, and I'm not going to be caught wanting. Request the captain to join us on deck please, Bertie," George said, overhearing what Robert had said.

"Aye, aye, sir," Bertie saluted and scampered off below.

When he had gone, Robert turned to George. "What does your scarf say?"

"Nothing as yet," he answered, feeling it under his jacket.

"Well that's a relief."

"What is, Mr Gates?" the captain's voice asked behind them. "Report please, Mr Warwick."

"Flashes and sounds like thunder or gunfire coming from the eastern horizon, Captain, though I have a feeling it is gunfire."

Brownlow scanned the eastern sky, noticing the flashes and the muffled sounds coming from over the horizon. He gazed for some minutes, taking in the sounds, before looking up at the clear sky, now showing the first signs of dawn. If it was a battle, it was certainly some way off and not presenting any immediate danger to them.

"No need to beat to stations yet, Mr Warwick, but let's put on more sail and head in that direction. I think you are right, gentlemen, something is definitely happening."

As Brownlow returned to his quarters, Briggs appeared at George's side as if he had been summoned.

"You know what to do, Briggs, let's chase this little war down."

"Aye, aye, sir," he responded with a willing grin as he alerted the crew to their stations.

Three hours later, under full sail and a quickening wind, the *Broad* was in telescope range of the men blasting away at each other. A Portuguese warship was listing heavily as it was being mercilessly pounded by a French ship. By the state of it, the Portuguese vessel wouldn't be lasting much longer as it received blow after blow.

"Beat to stations, Mr Bray, let's close with the enemy."

"Beat to stations," he screamed out loud as the ship came alive with men running backwards and forwards, carrying cannon balls and small arms to their respective stations.

George watched as the ritual spreading of sand on the *Broad*'s decks was carried out in preparation for taking casualties. The ship's surgeon cleared away and readied his instruments for the butchery, which normally followed an engagement.

They were making good headway and closing in on the battle scene, when they heard an almighty explosion which ripped the Portuguese ship apart. Unbelievably, it just disintegrated before their very eyes. George shuddered as the shock wave of the explosion reached them.

"God have mercy on them. Let's get to grips with this bastard, Mr Bray, I mean to have him."

"Aye, aye, Captain, we'll chase him down all right."

George's scarf started feeling warm around his neck. He remembered that he had left his sword down below and went to collect it from his quarters. As he entered and reached for his sword, he became aware of someone else nearby. He instinctively knew who it was.

"Lord Wei," he said as he turned to face the Chinese warlord.

"You are getting the feel of me, young warrior." He grinned. "Your enemy is after a bigger fish than the ship it destroyed. Be careful, young warrior, she will not be what you think."

George looked down to buckle on his scabbard and when he looked up, he was alone again. What on earth did he mean? He was going to have to find out the hard way, he thought.

"She's turning away, sir, she must have seen us," John Bray said, eyeing the French ship through his telescope, as George rejoined them.

All eyes were trained on the ship as she defiantly showed the *Broad* her stern. George trained his telescope farther forward and picked out another sail in the distance ahead.

"She's not running, she has sighted further prey, look ahead of her," he said to the watchers. All eyes now switched to search for the new sail.

"I want every bit of sail aloft, Mr Bray. We may be lucky and nail her before she becomes aware of us," said the captain.

"It looks as if the protector has suffered the ultimate price, Captain."

"I think you may well be right, Mr Warwick. Let's hope the French concentrate on their new target."

Just after midday, the French were closing in on their new prey, still unaware of the *Broad* bearing down on them from their stern. They watched as the French fired at the Portuguese from their forward guns, the shots falling short and causing eruptions in the water behind her.

"Can anyone make her quarry out?" Brownlow asked as he strained to make out the ship ahead of the French.

"I'll go up the fore topmast, sir, I should get a better view up there," George said as he joined Briggs, who was already scaling the front mast.

As they both reached the top, they looked through their telescopes and watched the two ships ahead, riding and cutting the gentle swell with all sails billowing in the wind.

"Can you make her out, Briggs?"

"She's definitely a Portuguese ship, Mr Warwick, and I do believe she carries the Royal Standard."

"Are you sure? The Royal Standard, that must mean royalty on board," George responded as he abseiled down the rigging leaving Briggs to concentrate on the ships ahead.

"Report, Mr Warwick," Brownlow ordered, as all the officers concentrated on him.

"A Royal Standard flies on the Portuguese ship, sir. The other ship did pay the ultimate price."

Brownlow concentrated his scope on the lead ship and studied the standard that was becoming more evident as they closed on both ships.

"The Braganza Standard," cooed Brownlow. "The royal family is on board. Napoleon has promised to wipe out the whole dynasty. No wonder the French haven't seen us, the prize is worth a fortune to the captain, not to mention the honours Napoleon will heap on him. Let's scupper his little game. Gentlemen, to your stations."

"Briggs, down you come, man, and get your gun team ready," George called up to him as he went to the forward gun.

Fifteen minutes later, they were in range of the French ship. George couldn't believe that they had not been spotted, although he suspected the Portuguese had seen them on the French's tail. *At least it would hearten them and give them some hope,* he thought.

"Hold your fire, Mr Warwick. Set your charge for canister. I want to blow their stern off," Brownlow shouted from the quarter deck.

Robert came up to him and held out his hand. "I have to get out of sight with my Marines. I'll see you when we board her."

"I don't think the old man has any intention of boarding her, Robert. I believe he intends to sink her."

"They never gave the Portuguese escort a chance, George. I'm happy with that. I'll see you later." He smiled as he saw George remove his hat, take out the scarf, and tie it around his head to cheers from the gun crew.

Brownlow, and the rest of the crew on deck, heard the cheer, all joining in as they realised the object of the exultation. Brownlow looked at John Bray and just raised his eyebrows in resignation.

"The men are in good spirits, sir," John said as Brownlow smiled.

"They must see us now, sir, unless they're bloody blind," Briggs said incredulously as they approached the stern of the French ship.

George looked around at his men, their cutlasses and pistols stored around the big gun in case of being boarded, and then at Brownlow. He was still concentrating on the enemy through his telescope, but was now standing on the poop deck. He saw him lower the spyglass and look forward.

"Right, Mr Warwick, open fire."

"Fire!" screamed George, bringing the large gun to life and sending its deadly load of over two hundred musket balls into the stern of the French warship.

The sound of the gun hurt his ears. He only just had time to move aside, as the gun recoiled viciously before being restrained by the hawsers attached to it. As he looked up with the rest of the crew, the stern gallery of the warship disintegrated before their eyes.

"Reload!" he screamed at his crew. "We need to knock out the rudder."

Briggs drove his crew mercilessly, and within two minutes they had reloaded with grape and chain, run the gun out, and were aiming at the wrecked stern of the ship as they started to drift by.

"Fire!" George screamed again as the gun roared its message of death and destruction at the enemy. He didn't wait to see the damage wreaked on the enemy as he ran back along the line of guns, tapping each gun captain on the shoulder as his gun came to bear. Each gun fired in turn, thudding into the target. George's scarf started to throb and feel warmer.

Cannon balls, although belated, were now coming back from the enemy. One shot took out the fore topgallant mast, sending the rigging and timber crashing down to the deck below. George was unable to get out of the way as he and the crew were struck by the debris. He managed to hug the big gun which afforded him some protection. Caukwell wasn't so fortunate. The timber from the fore topgallant yard struck him and he was knocked unconscious to the deck. Briggs, who was on the other side of the gun, scrambled his way under the rigging to reach him. George couldn't see any other member of the gun crew and was trapped by the rigging pinning him down against the red-hot barrel of the cannon. He felt hands tear at the rigging, the ropes being cut, and then he was dragged clear. The face of Wei looked down at him.

"Back to the battle, warrior." He grinned as he disappeared.

"Back to the battle indeed," George mimicked. "I was hardly taking time out."

"Nobody said you were, George," John Bray said, pulling him to his feet. "But it is a good idea to get back in the battle," he quipped as he saw that he hadn't been understood.

Briggs had gathered the gun crew, minus the injured Caukwell, and set about readying the gun once more. Brownlow looked on with satisfaction as he saw the training and discipline take its effect, as all hands went about their duties.

"Hard to starboard, Mr Bray, her rudder seems to have gone. Let's cut her bow." He turned to George and shouted, "Mr Warwick, ready with grape and chain, if you please."

"If you bloody well please," George muttered to laughter from the rest of his gun crew. He smiled at them in return. "You heard the captain, load," he shouted at them.

As they slowly cut across the bow of the enemy, visions of the death and destruction they had wreaked on the *Chantelle* flashed before his eyes. The gun was ready and aimed at the target, but he hesitated. He didn't want to complete the devastation.

"Fire!" The order was shouted as the gun roared and recoiled, sending its charge across the short journey to the French ship's bow.

George looked around to see who had given the command. Briggs was staring at him with concern written all over his face. George closed his eyes, not wanting to look, not wanting to see the death and destruction he had brought to his enemy.

The *Broad* was now travelling along the starboard length of the French ship. He heard Brownlow order every gun to fire as they bore. The sound of explosions, screams, shouts and timber being blown apart ripped through his skull leaving him senseless. George jumped out of his skin as an almighty explosion filled the air. Heat and shock waves, followed by large splinters of wood and even whole pieces of mast, flew through the air and across the *Broad*. The whole crew, to a man, threw themselves down and hugged the deck to avoid the searing heat and debris coming over them. When they eventually dared to rise they stared out over a boiling sea. No ship, just a bubbling sea covered in blue smoke. When he eventually started to comprehend what had happened, George looked aft to see Brownlow picking himself up off the deck and shouting orders. It was then he realised that he, like a lot of his men, had been deafened by the explosion. Brownlow's mouth was operating, but no sound was coming his way. George made his way to Brownlow, holding his ears to indicate he couldn't hear him. As he reached him, his ears popped and the noises rushed in once again.

Robert and John had joined Brownlow as George reached them. The four midshipmen followed and waited for orders.

"Get the injured below, Mr Bray," Brownlow ordered. "I hardly think there is any need for a boarding party, Mr Gates, stand your men down, if you please."

They all looked over the side at the now still waters, watching the debris that was once a fighting ship drift idly away.

"What the hell happened?" Robert asked, not believing his own eyes.

"Just that they have been sent to hell, God rest their souls," George answered.

"Mr Warwick, set course for the Portuguese, let's see what royalty we have, and where they are headed."

The Portuguese ship, with its Royal Standard fluttering proudly in the breeze, had taken in sail and was heaving to.

"You and Captain Gates will accompany me with a party of Marines. I want them smart, Mr Gates, and you, Mr Warwick, in proper uniform and without the scarf showing. Mr Bray, you command whilst I'm away. Keep a sharp look out, if you please."

George removed the scarf from his head and placed it under his jacket, as Briggs came forward with his naval hat.

"Thought you might need this, sir." He smiled.

"Get your party together, Briggs, you can row us over."

A party of Marines, dressed in their scarlet jackets, and accompanied by Robert and Captain Brownlow sitting in the stern, were ferried across to the Portuguese ship. George, sitting just behind the Marines, was watching as Briggs called out the time to his oarsmen.

As they neared the vessel, they could hear the raucous cheers of the sailors aboard, who were lining the starboard deck and hanging from the rigging in their excitement to see the conquerors of their enemy.

THIRTEEN

Willing hands reached down, hauling George up off the rope ladder and over the side, where he joined an indignant Captain Brownlow. He was being manhandled by the seamen and slapped on his back so hard it was making him cough. Robert came over next, followed by his Marines, who lined up as best they could in the chaos. Suddenly, a Portuguese voice rang out above all others, and the crew stood back, allowing a man to come forward.

"I am Captain Luis Garcia, commander of this ship and protector of the royal family. Who do I have the honour of addressing?" he asked in heavily accented English.

A red-faced Brownlow smoothed himself down and straightened his hat as he stepped forward. "Captain Brownlow of his Majesty's Royal Navy, at your service, sir," he managed to cough out.

As the two captains shook hands, Brownlow turned to his own men. "This is Lieutenant Warwick." He introduced George. "And this is Captain Gates."

"His Royal Highness, Prince John, has asked that you join him below, gentlemen, so would you please follow me."

"Order your men at ease, Mr Gates. You and Mr Warwick, come with me."

They filed down the stairway, and after a short knock on the door, they entered the state room. George looked around in amazement to see such opulence that would not have been out of place in any palace in Europe.

Directly in front of them, a man rose from his settee. He was short and quite slender in stature, almost effeminate looking, with a small goatee beard protruding from a small pointed chin. He was dressed elegantly in a rich dark green doublet embroidered down the front in gold braid. His knee-length boots were so highly polished you could see the ceiling reflected in them.

"Your Highness, may I present to you Captain Brownlow, our saviour and deliverer, and his officers, Captain Gates and Lieutenant Warwick."

Prince John, Regent of Portugal, stepped forward offering his hand to Brownlow. Unsure of how to proceed, he accepted it awkwardly, not wanting to crush the delicate hand he held in his rough mariner's fist, and not knowing whether this was correct or not. He bowed low and clumsily from his waist.

"Ah, my gallant Captain, it is a great pleasure and relief to see you. You have done Portugal and her queen, a great service today." He smiled warmly as he looked down at his hand to make sure nothing had rubbed off on it. He then turned to George and Robert. "I take it that you are Captain Gates of the British Marines?" he asked observing the scarlet uniform and shaking Robert's hand before turning to George. "And you are…?"

"Lieutenant Warwick, Your Highness," he answered, bowing from his hips as he had seen Brownlow do.

"Bravo, Lieutenant. It is nice to see such protocol in one so young. I thank all of you," he said, still smiling broadly. "Will you all join me for dinner, Captain?"

"It would be an honour and a pleasure, Your Highness," Brownlow answered, having recovered his composure.

They were shown to the dining room, where they were seated around a long, highly polished table. George noticed that all the tableware was of silver with the food being served on the finest porcelain dishes.

"Her Majesty the queen, will she be joining us, Your Highness?" Brownlow asked innocently.

"I am afraid not, Captain. She is… what do you say… ah yes, indisposed. She does not travel well on the water, and with the terror of the French she has taken to her bed."

"Understandable in the circumstances," Brownlow said gallantly. "Would you permit me to escort you to your destination, Your Highness? I know my government, and King George, would want us to ensure your safety as Britain's oldest ally."

"I accept your kind offer, Captain Brownlow. Your king will hear of your gallant service to us today. We go as far as Brazil, to Rio de Janeiro."

***

Not once on their many visits over the ensuing two weeks, did they catch hide or hair of Queen Maria of Portugal. George thought he heard her ranting at the servants a couple of times, but never laid eyes on her. The rumour was that she was quite mad, given to fits of temper, and that the Prince Regent really ruled in their exile. Rio de Janeiro would be their home and where the Court of Portugal would be placed, until Napoleon, who had set up a puppet government in Portugal, could be defeated.

They eventually docked in Rio de Janeiro, bidding their royal charges goodbye. They took the opportunity of the goodwill of the people to provision themselves and take on fresh water.

"Thank God we can now get back to our business, gentlemen," Brownlow said, confessing his relief at sailing out of Rio, without their charges. "Let's get back to our hunting grounds. Full sail, Mr Bray, no time to lose."

A week after leaving Brazil, George was on watch when they spotted sail due north of their position, appearing to be heading for North America.

"Make for her, Mr Warwick," Brownlow ordered, as George ordered the helm over to starboard and hoisted more sail.

They were gaining on the ship fairly quickly. George guessed it must be a cargo ship, well laden and unable to move very fast. As they got nearer they could make out that she was some sort of merchant vessel, and very low in the water.

"Can you make her out, Mr Warwick?" Brownlow called out to him from the poop deck.

"Not yet, sir, but she seems to be heavily laden with cargo."

"A prize or friendly, that's the question," he called back. "Beat to quarters, Mr Warwick, its best we are prepared for the unexpected."

"Aye, aye, sir," shouted George, relieved at some more action at last. "Beat to quarters," he shouted as the ship once more became alive to the noises of preparing for war.

The foreign ship must have seen them, as they put up more sail and altered their course away from the *Broad*.

"I can't believe they are going to make a run for it, sir," John Bray laughed as he watched them trying to make a getaway.

"Chase them down, Mr Bray. Mr Warwick, prepare the forward guns, and when we are in range, put one across her bow. Not too near though, we don't want to sink her," Brownlow warned.

As ever, Briggs was awaiting his orders and had already started to move forward, shouting orders to his gun crew. By the time George reached the forward gun it was being loaded with ball and ready to be hauled out.

"Well done, Briggs, run her out," George ordered. "The aim is to warn her, not to sink her, so make sure the shot is wide, but near enough to get their attention."

"Aye, aye, sir." Briggs smiled. "We'll wet them a little, sir, but we won't damage them.

The hopelessness of the Portuguese's flight was becoming obvious as the *Broad* started swiftly closing the distance between them. George, looking through his telescope, noticed the name on her stern as being the *Santa Anna* out of Oporto. He could also make out the vessel's crew running backwards and forwards along the deck. They were arming themselves, preparing for a battle.

"They have to be jesting," he muttered.

"Sir?" Briggs asked, catching his comment.

"They appear to be preparing to make a fight of it, Briggs," he answered in explanation.

"Fire when you are ready, Mr Warwick, we are well in range now," Brownlow called out as he observed the activity on board the Portuguese ship. "Let them know we mean business."

"All right, Briggs, fire when you are ready."

George put his hands over his ears as the gun roared to life, sending a cannon ball towards the fleeing Santa Anna. They watched as the shot fell close enough to the ship to wet the crew as Briggs had promised, but without actually hitting it.

Brownlow looked on with a great deal of satisfaction at the accuracy of the gunnery. He lowered his telescope and shouted, "Well done, Mr Warwick, I couldn't have done better meself."

"Well done, men," George complimented the gun crew, as he noticed the increased level of panic on the ship. "Reload, Briggs, just in case they do not heed the first warning."

"Stand down, Mr Warwick, methinks they have got our message," Brownlow ordered as he watched the *Santa Ann* take in her sail and begin to heave to.

"What the hell is that smell?" George asked, as a foul stench wafted towards them on the breeze.

"I've smelt that before, the vile smell of a human cargo," Robert answered through gritted teeth. "They're slavers, George, filthy, stinking slavers."

As they closed alongside her, the smell was even more horrendous. How the crew were able to stand it at close quarters was beyond George.

"Lower the longboats," Brownlow ordered. "A full detachment of Marines with fixed bayonets, Mr Gates, if you please. Mr Warwick, you will accompany them and deal with those on board as appropriate. Signal me when you are ready. Be on your guard, I saw activity of weapons being issued."

A few minutes later, George was sitting in the stern of one of the longboats, next to Robert.

"Pull away, Briggs," he ordered as they made their way over to the stinking hulk which bore such a lovely name.

They pulled alongside the ship, noticing a very hostile Portuguese crew sneering down at them. No ropes or ladders were dropped over the side. George shouted up to them to lower ropes but he was ignored. Brownlow had anticipated just such action from them. A further shot from the *Broad* rang out as another cannon ball just missed the vessel's stern. It had an effect, as a single rope was thrown over the side. George started to climb the rope, under strong verbal protests from Robert.

"Wait for them to throw more rope over, George, we need to go up in numbers."

Ignoring the warning, George reached the top on his own, and was bundled over by the Portuguese crew who then cut the rope to prevent anyone further coming up. George felt the scarf under his jacket start to throb and become distinctly warmer, as he became aware of the danger he was now in. His arms were pinned behind his back as he was surrounded by the threateningly filthy crew.

"Let go of me this instant," he warned. "I am an officer in the king's Navy and if you don't yield to me and my men, you will be sunk without trace."

"What is your name?" a man with several days' growth of beard asked in heavily accented English.

"I am Lieutenant Warwick from His Majesty's ship *Broad*, and if you are the captain of this stinking ship, you had better release me now."

"Brave words, Lieutenant, I am Captain Mendoza of the *Santa Anna*. When I last heard, we were your allies, so why are you firing on a friendly ship?"

"You are a slaver, sir, and you are not to be treated as a friendly ally of Britain. Release me immediately, or be sunk."

"I don't think so, my young friend, I don't think your captain will want to lose you. I think we will take our chances with you on board," he sneered.

"You are a bloody fool, Mendoza. My captain will sink you, with or without me on board."

"We will see." He turned to his men. "Strap him to the main mast where he can be seen by his captain."

George wrestled himself free from his captors and drew his sword. As he held them at bay, Mendoza laughed loudly, showing his broken teeth.

"What do you expect to do against so many men, Englishman?"

"I mean to fight to the death if necessary, Mendoza, and then you will be sunk," George vowed.

"So be it, we will tie your body upright to the mast. Kill him," Mendoza screamed as his men lunged forward.

George felt that this was the end, but he was going to make them pay before he went down. He became aware of a change in the temperature as he looked to one side.

"Warrior, this is becoming a habit," Wei said, as the Portuguese crew, armed with all kinds of weapons, became aware of a strange band of warriors in their midst. With a nod from their warlord, the Chinese warriors drew their swords and started to engage the enemy crew. Three of Mendoza's men went down with horrific injuries before the crew backed off, leaving him isolated in front of George, who advanced on him. He threw down his sword before ordering his men to do the same. Wei went up to him, raising his sword above his head with the intention of decapitating him.

"No, Wei, he is for the hangman, he is not fit for a warrior's death."

Wei stayed his arm as he thought on George's words, and gradually lowered his sword, as he grinned at him.

"Spoken like a true warrior. I agree with you, young Warwick," he answered, using George's name for the first time.

Mendoza looked at the strange band of warriors and their chief standing menacingly over him, and was at a loss as to how they had got on board.

"How?" he asked, trembling uncontrollably before Wei. "Where have these fierce pirates come from?"

"Throw rope ladders over the side, Mendoza, before I allow him to decapitate you," George answered, ignoring the question.

Mendoza didn't hesitate. He ordered his crew to comply, with several ropes and ladders going over the side to Robert and his men, who quickly scrambled aboard. By the time Robert was standing next to George, the Chinese warriors had completely disappeared.

Robert looked at the strange sight in front of him, with Mendoza still trembling on his knees. "Been having some fun, George?" he said lightly, as he saw the mutilated bodies of the three crewmen lying on the deck, and Captain Mendoza kneeling at his feet.

"Had a little help." George winked, knowing that Robert understood what had happened.

The Marines formed a line along the side of the ship, with muskets fixed with bayonets pointed at the hostile, but cowed crew. Mendoza was pulled to his feet and hustled to the side.

"Over you go, Mendoza, resist and I will hang you here and now, but before you go, I want to hear you order your men to surrender and comply with all orders from me and my men."

Mendoza ordered his men to comply in Portuguese before looking at George and nodding, as if he had complied willingly.

"Not good enough, Mendoza, I want to hear them all agree, tell them to sing out loud and clear. If they don't, they will join the cargo below."

He spoke again in a loud voice and demanded that his men reply. *"Si, Si, Capitano,"* the crew shouted back for fear of being incarcerated with their human cargo.

George nodded to the side of the ship. Mendoza moved to the side before going over and down the rope to the longboat below. He sat compliantly in the prow, resigned to his fate.

"Get this man over to the *Broad*, Captain Brownlow will take custody of him. If he tries anything, throw him over," George ordered as the crew pulled away. "Briggs, signal the *Broad* that a prisoner is on his way, and confirm the status of the *Santa Anna* as a slaver."

Three Portuguese crew members were standing apart from the others, surreptitiously watching what was going on. Robert noticed that the rest of the crew, who on the whole were compliant, stayed well clear of them. As he looked over at them they became aware of his attention. All three instantly grinned from ear to ear.

"Greasy, filthy bastards," Robert said out loud.

"What's up?" George asked.

Those three, the ones apart from the others, the ones with the instant greasy smiles, I wouldn't trust them an inch."

"Get your sergeant to keep an eye on them, one wrong move and they can go below with the cargo."

"Talking about the cargo, what are we going to do with them?"

"Hispaniola, I think, Robert, the only place we can take them."

"You have to be joking, what after our last escapade there? We were lucky to get away with our lives, man."

"The slave army must have thought the French had slaughtered their members in retaliation for the settlement. In any case, we don't have too many choices. Let's check on the cargo," George ordered.

Robert looked horrified at the thought.

"It has to be done, I'm afraid. Bring some of your Marines with you. Leave the rest to keep an eye on the Portuguese," George confirmed his last order.

"Get those hatches open," Robert ordered, as his men and the Portuguese crew worked together to lift the hatches clear.

The smell was even viler as it hit their nostrils. Human excrement, mixed with vomit and sweat, was overpowering. The noises emanating from the hold grew more pathetic as the wailing echoed up on to the deck above. Robert looked at George, who just nodded. They had to go down, no matter how bad it was. As they entered the hold, they held cloth over their mouths in order to stop themselves retching. As the captives caught sight of the Marines with their weapons fixed with bayonets, their eyes started to bulge in abject fear and the wailing grew even more intense.

"Robert, tell your men to lower their weapons, they think we are here to do them harm."

"Lower your weapons, men, they are no threat to us," Robert ordered as his hatred and revulsion for the Portuguese grew inside him.

"Send two of your men up top, Robert, and find me a crew member who can converse with the slaves. If he refuses to attend, shoot him, and the next, until we have one down here," he instructed as he removed his scarf from round his neck and placed it on his head.

A few minutes later, a crew member appeared at the entrance to the hold and waited with the two Marines for George to join them. He was a small, but stocky man of about thirty-five years of age, and looked petrified. His shabby and tattered appearance told George he was one of the lowly deck crew.

"Do you speak English?"

"*Si, Capitano*, a little."

"Do you understand the tongue of these people?" he asked, pointing to his own mouth and then to the slaves.

"*Si, Capitano*, a little," he replied, as he saw George's headgear. Recognition seemed to enter his frightened eyes, which were now as wide as the slaves in the cargo hold.

"You are the one they call Scarf," he stated, rather than asked.

"Yes I am, and you will tell these people exactly what I say. My orders are to hang all slavers, so do what I tell you."

"I am… what you say it, Capitano, a forced man on the *Santa Anna*. I am not here by…"

"By choice," George finished for him.

"*Si, Capitano*, not by choice. I will obey you."

"Do you know who the leader of these people is?"

"*Si*, he is," he answered, pointing at a well-muscled black slave, manacled to the wall.

On being singled out, the man stood up. He was tall, as tall as Robert and George. His eyes were wary, but did not show the fear that the rest of the natives portrayed.

"Tell him his shackles, and those that bind his people, will be removed. Tell him I cannot release them all on deck at the same time, but they will be allowed up in small parties… and the hatches will not be put back on. Now tell them."

The Portuguese started to tell them in their own language as best he could, as the native stepped forward to face George.

"I understand some of your language," he said, surprising both George and Robert. "We had a mission near my home. They taught us the ways of your God and then we were taken slaves and we ended up here."

"What is your name? I am George, he is Robert," George said, pointing to each in turn to explain.

"I am Biko," he said simply as he tried to smile with his haunted eyes. "Can we have water, please?"

"Biko, you may have all the water you and your people need from now on, together with food. Is there anything else I can do for you?"

Biko stared at George, wondering whether he should ask. "The women have been separated from us in another hold. My woman is among them, can they be freed to join us?"

"Robert, can you open the other hold and free the women? Let them join their men."

Water and food was sent down to the freed captives and the women rejoined their men. They learned from Biko that all the women and young girls had been systematically raped and abused by the Portuguese crew, furthering their hatred and loathing. George and Robert located the captain's cabin and went through the various papers and charts they found. From what they could make out, the *Santa Anna* had set sail from Zanzibar some six weeks earlier and travelled down to Rio de Janeiro. Why? Why had they detoured? What had taken them away from the market for their cargo?

"Most of this is in Portuguese, Robert. I understand a smattering of French and Spanish, but I think we have need of our little crewman once again."

"I'll send for him," Robert replied as he went out to fetch a Marine. He came back into the cabin. "Put your scarf back on, it seems to frighten the little bugger to death."

The Marine returned with the stocky little crewman, who was showing signs of some fear at being summoned once again by The Scarf. George started to tap the charts in front of him.

"Why did you go to Brazil?" he asked.

"Brasilia?" he queried, with a puzzled look. "The capitano is the only one who knows. I do know that a chest came aboard when we docked. That chest in the corner," he explained, pointing to it, "The one with the iron straps and lock on it."

"All right, you can go, but stay where I can find you if I need you."

"Si, Capitano," he answered obediently, leaving the cabin and closing the door.

Robert went over to the chest and dragged it out into the centre of the room. His eyes had come alive all of a sudden, and George got a feeling he'd been here before. He remembered the Marine's reaction to finding the treasure on board the *Melissa*, and his subsequent actions in purloining the gold coins.

"Let's force the lock off this thing," he said, grinning as he put his pistol to it.

"Hold your horses, for goodness sake," George pleaded. "I searched Mendoza before he left for the *Broad*. There was no key on him, it must be here somewhere."

They searched the cabin from top to bottom as Robert got increasingly impatient at not finding it. He was about to take aim at the lock when George felt under the captain's desk and found it on a hook.

"Eureka," he exclaimed. "I have it."

Robert watched him with bated breath as he inserted the key in the lock, causing the hasp to drop open. They both held their breath as they expectantly lifted the lid. Papers littered the top, papers and more charts. A disappointed Robert started to pull them out, dropping them on the cabin floor as he delved further down.

"What have we here?" he asked himself, as he pulled out small sack after small sack, placing them on the table in front of them. "Would you like to do the honours, or should I?" he asked, as he weighed one of the bags in his hands.

"Get on with it, man," George replied as he took hold of another bag, untied the string around its neck, and poured the contents onto the table together with Robert's. George could see the sparkle come alive in Robert's eyes as they reflected the light from the purest diamonds he had ever seen. Five sacks, all containing diamonds.

"My God," Robert whispered as he ran his fingers through them. "How much are these little beauties worth?"

George gasped, letting his breath out in a long sigh. "I have no idea, but I am not having a repeat of last time. Put them back in their bags and let's lock the chest."

"Oh, for Christ's sake, you know what happened last time, we were damn well robbed by their lordships."

"I don't care. I am not putting my neck in a noose over these little baubles, now put them back."

"All right, I'll put them back. We don't tell anyone about this, but we will tell the old man, let him decide what to do. I think after being cheated the last time, he may be more amenable to a little deal."

After the excitement died down a little, George got to wondering why the captain was off his normal route. Robert decided he needed some fresh air and left the key in George's possession. He sat there in the captain's chair and thought hard. His thoughts drifted back to England and he wondered what Barbara was doing and if she was waiting for him. He was brought back to the present when the scarf started to throb and change colour. He unsheathed his sword as he sprang up and went out of the cabin to the poop deck.

"Captain Gates, muster you men at once," he shouted.

Robert heard the orders and started to shout to his men as he ran to join him on the poop deck. "What is it?" he asked urgently.

George didn't answer. He was busy scanning the horizon for any approaching danger. All he could see was the *Broad*, rising and falling gently in the ocean's swell.

"What is it?" Robert repeated his question.

Before George could answer, shouting started to come from the Marines below. They rushed to the stairs and went down to find the sergeant was standing with his men.

"Report, Sergeant," Robert ordered.

"Dicks is missing, sir," he answered.

"Who the hell is Dicks?" George asked.

"One of my Marines, a good man, he wouldn't go missing unless there was something amiss," Robert answered. "Let's search the ship, Sergeant, no corner left untouched."

Fifteen minutes later, they heard further excited shouts coming from the stern quarters. They rushed there to find a bunch of Marines kicking the hell out of the three surly sailors they had first seen on deck. George joined Robert and the sergeant in trying to pull the Marines off of the men, as they refused to stop their incessant beating and kicking. Eventually they got them off and stood back panting and sweating.

"They killed Dicks, sir, they slit his throat like an animal," one of the Marines gasped, to justify their action.

"Secure them and take them up top," George ordered, as he followed the three who had been kicked up the stairs and into the daylight. Once on deck, he ordered everybody, Portuguese and British, to assemble. "Find me a crew member who speaks either English or French and who can read Portuguese."

A little time later, an ageing seaman shuffled forward, unable to take his eyes off the fearsome looking pirate.

"Do you speak either English or French? Can you read papers and charts?"

"Si," he answered plainly.

"What is your name?"

"Miguel Pedroza, *Capitano.*"

"Come with me, Pedroza," George ordered, leading him back to the captain's cabin. Once inside, he laid the charts out on the desk and placed the papers from the chest on top. "I want you to interpret, word for word, what these papers say. I am going to hang those three outside. You make up your mind whether you wish to join them."

Pedroza was physically shaken at hearing this awful news. "What if I do not understand, *Capitano*?" he pleaded.

"Then you will tell me precisely that, and then make an educated guess. Do you hear?"

Pedroza nodded as he sat down in the chair at George's invitation and started to read the papers. As he explained what they meant, Robert entered the cabin.

"What's going on?" he asked, as George indicated for him to keep quiet.

"It appears our Captain Mendoza is not who he seems to be. There is much more to him than meets the eye. I must get back to the *Broad*. Stay here, Robert, and make sure your men don't take the law into their own hands whilst I'm gone. Oh, and I'll be taking the key with me," he added as an afterthought.

As they loaded Dicks's body into a longboat, George realised he had known the man. He had fought alongside him on the *Victory* at Trafalgar.

As he climbed the side of the *Broad* and scrambled over onto the deck, he was surprised when Brownlow had him piped aboard.

"Welcome, Captain Warwick." He smiled. "What seems to be the problem?"

"Can we avail ourselves of the privacy of your cabin, sir? I have much to tell you."

"If that is the case, in private it will be," the captain answered leading the way down to his cabin. "Sit yerself down, and let me hear all about it."

"Can you ask Blackwell to wait outside, sir?"

"Off you go, Blackwell, I'll call you when I need you."

Blackwell scowled his disapproval as he begrudgingly left the cabin, closing the door behind him.

"Now tell me all, Mr Warwick."

"Captain Mendoza is a liar, and not who he says he is. He is not a loyal Portuguese but working for the French."

"And you know all this how?"

"I had these papers and charts he had locked away interpreted by a crew member under the penalty of death if he misled me," he said as he laid them out in front of his captain.

"That does tend to concentrate the mind somewhat." Brownlow smiled. "Go on, Mr Warwick."

"His name is not Mendoza at all. His name is Junot, younger brother of General Junot, who has defected to Napoleon. He was to drop his cargo in the southern states of America, clean up his ship and then transport a French regiment to Hispaniola to bolster the garrison, which is under siege by the slave army. What's more, to deceive us, he was to do this under the Portuguese colours."

Brownlow stopped being a passive listener as the expression on his face grew angrier. George had the feeling of a lightning bolt about to strike as he suddenly stood up and crashed both of his fists down on the table.

"I will have his neck for his treachery. I was going to take him back in chains to England to stand trial, all that has now changed."

"I'm afraid there is more bad news, sir. Three of his henchmen, under their own parole, as well as that of their captain, slit the throat of one of our Marines. I brought his body back with me."

Brownlow went very quiet, thinking of his next course of action. "I think you, and Captain Gates, can be commended for keeping control of the situation, it couldn't have been easy with feelings running so high. Where are these men now?"

"In irons, sir, waiting for the noose and the yardarm," he answered, matter of fact, without any emotion.

"Their blasted captain can join them, and anyone else that steps out of line. Let's go up and see what Mendoza has to say."

Mendoza was unceremoniously hauled onto the deck by two Marines, who had heard of Dicks's death. He had been roughed up and was sporting a large swelling over his right eye. He started to complain of his treatment until he was stopped by an indignant and very angry Brownlow.

"Captain Junot, I think you have some explaining to do."

He was thunderstruck at the revelation and started to bluster. "I am Captain Mendoza…" he started to say and was promptly silenced by a Marine who hit him in the stomach with the butt of his musket. His face fell even further when he recognised the papers Brownlow was holding. As he got his breath back, he straightened up and decided to change tact. "I was simply following my orders, Captain. I am but a simple seaman, like you."

"You follow the orders of a traitor, and the head of a puppet government set up by Napoleon. Following orders is going to get you hanged," Brownlow said, as he turned to

George. "Put him in the longboat, Mr Warwick, take him back to where he belongs."

"My pleasure, sir," he answered.

John Bray grabbed the scruff of Mendoza's shirt and hauled him backwards to the starboard side of the ship. "Climb down, you filthy pig, or I will throw you over."

"Captain, I appeal to you, you have no jurisdiction over my ship or its business, you cannot do this thing."

"Wherever there is one of His Majesty's ships, the rule of English law will be upheld and enforced. Throw him over, Mr Bray," Brownlow ordered.

"All right, I am going, I am going," he whimpered as he climbed over and down into the waiting longboat below.

Before George could go over the side, Brownlow called to him. "Mr Warwick, a moment before you embark, if you please." As Brownlow approached him, he continued. "If the executions do not sit well with you, I will come over and oversee them myself."

George thought for a moment as he considered the captain's offer, and then gave his answer. "It does not sit well we me, sir, but it is my duty, and you have given me command of the *Santa Anna*. I will fulfil the obligations of that command."

"Well said, Mr Warwick, carry on."

George went over the side followed by John Bray, who was detailed to assist him. They rowed over to the Portuguese ship on a gentle calm sea, arriving all too quickly for George's liking. Briggs, sitting just in front of George and Robert, looked at his senior officer who he had grown very fond of, and sensed his foreboding. He couldn't doubt his courage, or his sense of duty, but to hang a man, let alone four of them, was different altogether. They tied up alongside the ship, with Briggs pulling Mendoza to his feet and forcing him to climb up the ladder. George followed, with John Bray coming up behind. As they got to the top and climbed over, John grabbed his arm.

"George, listen to me. I have no compunction whatsoever in hanging any of this filth. I'll do it, Brownlow will never know."

"Belay that, John. I don't expect any man to do something I wouldn't do myself. I command, it is my duty and mine alone. I don't want to hear another word on the subject."

Robert was a little surprised to see Mendoza being brought back as he joined them on the deck.

"He is to hang with the others," John explained, noticing the surprise on Robert's face.

"Captain Gates, please muster all your men. Get the black captives that are on deck back below, and bring up the three prisoners. I want all the Portuguese crew on deck to witness what I am about to do." Robert just stood there and was about to say something when George said harshly, "Just do it, Robert, and whilst you are about it, bring up the captive called Biko, and make sure he is fully clothed."

Robert turned on his heel, recognising the new no nonsense attitude of his friend, and issued his orders. John Bray joined in, lining up the foreign crew along the sides of the ship. A few minutes later, the Portuguese prisoners were brought on deck to join their captain, with a fully clothed Biko following behind. George could see the worry and concern on his face, and went to meet him.

"Don't worry, Biko, this party is not for you," George explained.

Biko looked up at the four nooses, now hanging from the yard above them, and then at the four men who were having their hands tied behind their backs. His glare of hatred was slowly changing to that of satisfaction, as he realised the fate of these four, who had been his people's main abusers. Four lines of men, including crew members of the *Santa Anna*, and the Marines, were lined up behind each rope. George indicated to Biko to stand to one side of him as he addressed those assembled. He looked directly at Mendoza and his men, who were starting to weep in self-pity.

"These men have broken their parole. They have killed one of our own Marines, and they have been assisting Britain's enemies. They have also enslaved, raped and abused the people aboard this ship. In the power vested in me by King George, I now pass sentence." George hesitated, turning quite pale.

Robert and John moved closer to his side, to bolster and let him know he was not alone in this.

"I'll hang the bastards, George, it was one of my men they killed," Robert whispered to him, but George ignored him.

"For the crimes of murder, assisting the enemy, mutiny, and crimes against humanity, I sentence them to hang. Sentences to be carried out with immediate effect, God have mercy on their souls."

The four men were dragged struggling to the nooses, which were placed over their heads and around their necks. They started weeping and begging for their lives, but it was all falling on deaf ears as George gave the order to take the strain. The nooses tightened round their necks, distorting their cries of panic. George closed his eyes tight and shouted, "Haul away!"

When he forced himself to open his eyes and look aloft, he watched the bodies swinging in the breeze. As their legs jerked and convulsed in their death throes, the ropes were tied off against the side of the ship and they were left to hang for all to see.

On board *HMS Broad*, Brownlow watched through his telescope at the scene being played out. He looked up at the figures swinging amongst the rigging with grim satisfaction.

"So you have finally become a commander, Mr Warwick, welcome to our very select club."

FOURTEEN

George retired to the captain's cabin, locking himself in against any intrusion on his self-imposed isolation. No matter how he tried, the sight of the slavers dangling from ropes was constantly in his mind's eye. He hated himself for what he had done. He knew there was no other course, but he still hated himself for it. He heard Robert and John Bray knocking and calling at the door, but he refused to acknowledge them. Eventually they decided to let him stew and get over it in his own time.

He felt the air getting cooler and became aware of a now familiar presence in the small room.

"You isolate yourself from your brother warriors, why?" Wei was sitting opposite him with a puzzled look in his almond-shaped coal black eyes. As George looked up at him, Wei's smile was instant, showing an even set of white teeth and accentuating the scar going down the right side of his face. George glanced down at the sign of the dragon on his chest armour and would have sworn the thing was actually breathing fire. In the absence of any reply, Wei continued. "The means of your enemy's death does not sit easily with you, young warrior, you should have let me take their heads when you had the chance, you would not be feeling this way now."

"I did not know what I know now, Lord Wei. The world would be a better place for the wisdom of hindsight."

"Wisdom indeed, young warrior, but I think you have wisdom well beyond your years, and you have certainly proved your leadership to the one you call Brownlow. I think you will go on to be a leader such as he and your father before you."

There was a knock at the door, with raised voices coming from outside.

"George, open this door, what is going on in there?" John Bray was shouting, as he was joined by Robert.

He looked towards the door and then back at where Wei had been sitting. He had gone, his seat was empty. George took out the key to the chest containing the charts, maps and the jewels, put it in his pocket, and went to the door.

"I am going over to the *Broad* to apprise Captain Brownlow of the situation and to get his orders. Look after things whilst I'm away, please, John."

***

He clambered over the side of the *Broad* and was led in silence to the captain's cabin, all the time watched by the crew, who now viewed him in an altogether different light. He had fought alongside them, sometimes eating and laughing with them, but things could never be the same as before. As he made his way up the deck, all the crew he encountered deferred to him as they saluted, without the normal smile. It was a very sober and morose lieutenant who now stood in front of his commander.

"Sit yerself down, George," Brownlow invited, using his Christian name for the first time. "Blackwell, get Mr Warwick a strong drink of brandy."

Even his captain's attitude seemed to have changed, he thought as he settled into the chair opposite, accepting the welcome drink put in front of him by the steward who then diplomatically withdrew from the cabin.

"To justice, George," Brownlow toasted with a grim smile.

George didn't respond. He drank the brandy down in one before seeking the words to open the conversation. "Thank you, sir, but there is something else I have to discuss with you."

Brownlow considered the serious face in front of him and wondered if he was going to resign his commission.

"One moment, George, please. Don't make any hasty decisions because of what's happened," he started. "Command brings a lot of things to your table, but you mustn't overreact in the heat of the moment."

George wondered what he was going on about and then realised that Brownlow thought he was about to pack it all in. "No, sir, it's nothing like that," he countered as he placed the iron key on the table.

Brownlow looked at the key and then up at George with raised eyebrows. "What is this?"

"A key to a chest on the *Santa Anna*, the same chest that contained the charts and papers, but that is not all it contained," George answered, not knowing how this was going to go down with this strong, but fair disciplinarian.

Brownlow was now all ears, and looked back at him intently, his eyes not leaving George's for an instant "And pray tell me, what else is in the chest, my dear fellow?"

"Six small sacks of pure white diamonds, a small fortune if Robert Gates is to be believed, and I think he does know of these things."

"Does he now? And who else knows about this little haul?" Brownlow asked with a raised eyebrow, remembering with some loathing the cheating lords at the Admiralty.

"No one else, sir, the only other people who could have known, I hanged today," George replied ironically.

George became alarmed as Brownlow suddenly got to his feet and went to the cabin door. He opened it, looked out, and then closed it again before returning to stand opposite George. He sat down and remained silent for some considerable time. This was unlike him, George thought to himself. He suddenly cleared his throat and leant forward to whisper like a conspirator. "You are aware, are you not, how the lords at the Admiralty cheated us of our rightful share from the *Chantelle*?"

"Yes, sir, I am. Lord Fitzwilliam raised the matter with them to no avail. He believes Lord Crowe had a hand in its misappropriation."

"Well I've a mind not to let the buggers cheat me again, George, what do you say to that?"

"If I said what I thought, sir, you could hang me from the yardarm."

Brownlow raised his eyebrows. "And Captain Gates, what would be his position, do you think?"

"He is of the same mind as I, and if I read things correctly, as you, sir."

Brownlow went silent again. His mind was racing, considering the options open to him, remembering how he was cheated of his retirement by the Admiralty. Standing up, he half smiled at George. "Signal the *Santa Anna* and ask Captain Gates to joins us here, if you please. Oh… and ask him to bring the chest over with him, Mr Bray can take care of things over there," Brownlow said determinedly.

An hour later, Robert was standing before his captain and wondering just what George had told him. Had he confessed to Robert's little purloining of the doubloons from the Chantelle, or had he restricted the information to the chest?

"Mr Gates, I understand you have something to show and tell me."

"I have brought the chest over as you ordered, Captain. I understand that you are now in possession of the key."

"Don't be coy, my dear fellow, fetch it in at once."

Robert went to the cabin's door and ordered the two Marines to bring in the chest. Once it was before the captain's table, he ordered the Marines to leave and close the door. Brownlow already had the key in his hand and stooped over the chest to open it. Robert took the opportunity to stare at George over his captain's head and mouth "What?" to him. George ignored him as Brownlow raised the lid and stood looking down into the chest. He looked down at the bags lying in the bottom before reaching down and lifting them one by one, laying them side by side on his table.

"Let's see just what we have, gentlemen. Mr Gates, stand by the door, if you please."

He untied the string around the first bag, tipping the contents carefully onto the table. The pure white diamonds spilled out, glinting in the light from the cabin's window. Brownlow gave an audible sigh as he took them in his fingers before placing them in his other palm and looking at them in wonder.

"What beauties," he said quietly, as Robert and George looked on, mesmerized by the diamonds and the scene before them. "And the other bags?" he queried.

"The same, Captain," Robert answered. "A small fortune for a king, a large one for the likes of us."

Brownlow started to scoop up the diamonds, careful not to miss any, and replaced them in the small sack, tying the string tight, lest they should jump out.

"Can you hazard a guess as to their combined value, Mr Gates?"

Robert looked at George who nodded for him to answer. "I have a cousin who is a merchant banker. He is discreet and more than capable of realising the true value of the stones, sir, but what I can say is that we could all retire early on it."

Brownlow gathered up the sacks one by one before placing them back in the chest. He then sat down behind his desk, staring at both of them for some considerable time, weighing up the situation before speaking. "Do these baubles appear on any manifest anywhere on the ship?"

"No, sir," George answered, "and there are no others alive who are privy to their existence, other than us."

Brownlow went silent again, thinking hard on what was to be done. He eventually made up his mind. "We are taking the slaves to Hispaniola where they will be disembarked. The crew of the *Santa Anna* will be clapped in irons in the *Broad*.

We will burn the ship on the island, just to make sure nothing survives as a record of this."

Robert and George smiled their appreciation at the plan, but their hopes were set back at his next statement.

"I am sure the Admiralty won't miss just one small bag, now would they?"

"One small bag?" Robert asked incredulously. "Are you jesting, sir?"

"Captain," George interceded. "If we divulge the stones, it could set minds thinking, whereas no mention of them at all would be better and more prudent. Besides, the whole crew missed out last time."

"We can't involve the crew, you know how loose some of their tongues can be," Brownlow protested.

"They don't need to know, sir. My cousin can set up a trust or benevolent fund for them under the guise of a wealthy philanthropic benefactor donating the funds anonymously. Nobody but us need know anything different."

Not for the first time, Brownlow went quiet in contemplation, with his eyes switching from one man to the other.

"I'm not sure about this, gentlemen, I will have to give it some thought," he eventually said to sighs from them both.

That evening, all the officers were invited to dine with their captain in his cabin. There was no mention of any diamonds, but the fate of the *Santa Anna* and its cargo was decided. The next day they set sail for Hispaniola and the Free State of Haiti.

***

Standing off the north shore of the island on a glorious sunny day, George eyed the beach and watched as members of the now free black army moved about in what was once a French settlement. There were no signs of the enemy.

"Ready the longboat, Mr Warwick, we must find out how friendly these people are to us. Take a detachment of Marines and speak to their leaders. We will stand off ready for action if need be."

Oh great, thought George, *the shore party would be in direct line of that action.* "Aye, aye, sir. Briggs, you and your men crew the boat."

Lowering the longboat over the side, it was with some trepidation that Briggs remembered his last visit to the island.

They were surprised by the warmth of the greeting they received as they hauled the longboat up the beach. George, with his signature scarf on his head, met the leader and explained the situation to him. They were more than pleased to accept more people on the island and that *Le Scarf* had liberated more slaves. There was no mention of the previous encounter with Baptiste, who seemed to be forgotten.

All that day, George stood on the beach watching the longboats haul their human cargo between the *Santa Anna* and the shore. He kept a special look out for Biko, and was not surprised to see that he and his wife were the last to leave the ship and arrive on the shore. He went to meet them as they disembarked the longboat and nodded to him as he waded ashore.

"Hello, Biko, welcome to your first day of freedom."

"Thank you, my friend, we will not forget you, the legend of *Le Scarf* will go on forever in this part of the world," he said as he grasped George's arm.

"I will say my goodbyes now. I must get back to my ship and deal with the slavers." George got in the longboat and was rowed back to the *Broad* to waves of farewell from Biko and his wife.

Arriving back on board the *Broad*, George was in time to see the Portuguese prisoners being taking down below and clapped in irons. Brownlow had sent Robert and John over to the *Santa Anna* to haul her further out to sea, where they laid gunpowder charges and broke open the hull below the waterline. He watched as the longboats pulled away from the doomed ship and made towards him. As they got within one hundred yards of the *Broad*, the *Santa Anna* erupted with several explosions ripping the ship apart. All hands looked to the stricken ship as it burst into flames and began sinking.

"There goes any evidence, Mr Warwick."

George had been so engrossed in the wrecking of the *Santa Anna* he had failed to hear Captain Brownlow who had appeared at his side.

"Sad to see any ship meet such an end, sir," he responded, "but it was for the best, not because of the evidence, I don't think any existed, but because of the use she had been put to."

"Quite so, quite so, when Mr Gates comes aboard, bring him to my cabin. We must put a line under this."

George and Robert entered the captain's cabin as Blackwell was being dismissed. A decanter of brandy was on the table with three glasses by its side. The captain started to pour.

"Brandy, gentlemen," Brownlow said as he offered the glasses. "A drink to our successful conclusion to this affair." Brownlow smiled. "Just one more thing to do. Jettison the trunk overboard, minus the stones of course, and the charts with the letter from General Junot. All other paperwork will go down with it."

"Are we to take it that all the stones are now included in the deal, sir?" Robert asked, to which Brownlow nodded slowly his consent.

"I'll deal with it tonight, sir," George responded.

"Thank you, Mr Warwick. Good health, gentlemen."

That night, on George's watch, no one saw the trunk go silently overboard and gradually sink below the waves of the warm Caribbean Sea.

FIFTEEN

Two days later, George was with Robert in their quarters, talking quietly about their plans for the future, when they heard shouting coming from above. George grabbed his telescope, rushed up to the quarterdeck, arriving at the same time as Brownlow.

"Sail to starboard, heading northwest!" the lookout yelled.

They went up onto the quarterdeck, joining Bertie Bowden and John Bray, who were scanning the sea ahead. Brownlow was the first to speak.

"A possible merchantman heading for America, Mr Bray, I can't make her out yet." He went to the rail, shouting to the helmsman, "Alter course, nor by nor west."

"Aye, aye, sir," the helmsman answered, as the ship started to respond and began heading on the new course.

"Get some more sail up, Mr Bray, if you please. I'll be in my cabin when you can make her out."

"Aye, aye, sir," John responded, shouting out his orders to the crew.

It was becoming obvious that the ship had seen them and was determined to avoid contact. The *Broad* gradually closed the gap between them.

She's American," said Robert, eyeing the ship through his glass. "A merchantman, probably out of Massachusetts."

"But where has she been, and what is her cargo?" George asked in response.

"America is now a sovereign country, fully independent and not privy to British rule," Robert said, eyeing his friend defiantly.

"All the time America continues to give refuge to deserters, Captain Gates." The voice came from behind them. "Her Majesty's ships are obliged to search and impress those who we find are British." Captain Brownlow had come up to the quarterdeck without either of them noticing. "And I will remind you, sir, of whose uniform you wear."

George sensed the anger rising in his friend at what he felt was an unwarranted slight. He put his hand on his arm to warn and restrain him. "I'm sure Captain Gates didn't mean any disrespect, sir, and he has never given reason for anyone to question where his duty lies."

"That may be so, Mr Warwick, but orders are orders, and we will carry them out to the letter. I hope that is understood." Captain Brownlow ordered the forward gun to be made ready and they pressed on after the American ship.

As they came into range, George went forward, waiting behind the gun for his captain's command. He took out his scarf and examined it, but no warning was forthcoming, and it remained benign with no change of colour. He replaced the scarf inside his jacket.

"Put one across her bows, Mr Warwick, if you please," Brownlow shouted.

"Not too close, Briggs, we don't want to frighten them too much," George cautioned.

Briggs smiled back. "Never fear, Mr Warwick, sir, I'll just get their attention."

When Briggs gave him the thumbs up, George shouted, "Fire!"

The gun roared. He watched as the ball splashed down just twenty feet from the American ship.

"We don't wish to sink them, Mr Warwick," Captain Brownlow reprimanded.

"I could have got a lot closer, sir," Briggs responded quietly, with a winning smile.

"No doubt you could, Briggs, no doubt you could." George smiled back.

Robert watched proceedings from the quarterdeck with some concern. Through his telescope he could see men starting to run along the decks and climb the rigging, drawing in sail, reducing the ship's speed. They were heaving to. Robert had mixed feelings about their actions. He still felt a certain belonging to his old home and wasn't quite sure where his real loyalties lay.

As they came alongside, Captain Brownlow shouted to them, "We are going to board you, remain as you are." He turned to George, who had rejoined him on the poop deck. "Go with Mr Bray, the sergeant, and a detachment of Marines. Board her, and search her thoroughly. Captain Gates will remain with me."

George watched his friend's face contort as he bit his lip. "Aye, sir, with me, John," George responded.

They went down to organise the boarding party before embarking into the longboats. As they neared the American ship, they saw the name *Massachusetts* written boldly on its stern.

George addressed his men in the longboat. "We are looking for anything that suggests anti-British activity, slavery, or any deserters from our Navy. Be courteous, but be firm," he ordered.

Only one rope ladder came over the side. George scaled it athletically, and stood in front of the ship's captain. All others were barred from coming up. He was starting to get the feeling he had been through this before with the Portuguese slaver.

"What is your business aboard my ship, Lieutenant?" a man dressed in civilian clothing asked curtly.

"We intend to search you, sir. Would you be so good as to give me your name and a description of your cargo?"

"I am Captain Poynton out of Massachusetts, and my business is the business of the American government, sir. You have no legal right to search my ship, and I ask that you leave immediately before I have you thrown overboard."

"Well, Captain, I would love to stand around bandying legalities with you, but if you look yonder you will see a ship with thirty-eight cannons, all pointing in your direction. If, as you have threatened, I go overboard, you will be sunk without trace. Now allow the rest of my men on board, and we can get done with this business."

Captain Poynton stared at George, and then out to the *Broad*. He saw that all gun ports were now open on the starboard side and ready for action. He knew he could not bluff any further.

"Very well, this is under protest, and my government will be informed of your act of piracy as soon as we make land." His indignation, and that of his crew, was obvious.

"Your protest is noted, Captain. I will also require the sight of your log and charts." George watched as his men came aboard, and the Marines lined the side of the ship. "Get to it, Sergeant, you know what you are looking for. Please show me to your cabin, sir, and I would also like to see the journals of your midshipmen."

"What on earth for?" Poynton asked, his pale face starting to colour with anger.

"Just do it, Captain. The sooner we finish the sooner you can be on your way."

Poynton turned to a man who was obviously one of his officers. "Collect the journals as requested, Mr Berwick."

The captain turned, leading George to his cabin. The room was neat and tidy, no different to the captain's cabin in the *Broad*. Poynton presented his log book.

"I will also require your manifest, Captain, if you would be so obliging." George was making every effort to be polite, but to remain formal.

A knock at the door revealed Mr Berwick entering with three journals of the junior officers. He handed them to George when indicated to do so by Poynton and then left, leaving the door wide open. George scanned the journals, looking for indicators of events aboard. When he first entered the service as a midshipman he was required to keep a daily journal of events aboard his ship. He suspected, and was proved right, that it was no different for the Americans.

Something caught his eye as he looked out of the cabin door. He saw the sergeant of Marines pushing three men ahead of him at the point of his bayonet. George indicated to the captain to leave the cabin, and follow him as they went to meet them.

"What have we got here, Sergeant?"

"Frenchies, sir, French officers by the look of them, they were skulking below," he answered triumphantly.

The three men were dressed in uniforms of Napoleon's Guard, short blue jackets with brass buttons over white trousers, and black boots.

"Who are you, and what is your business aboard this vessel?" George looked at them in turn, but no answer was forthcoming from the sneering faces in front of him.

"Very well, I will find out from the log and the journals," he said as he went back towards the cabin. "Mr Bray, if you would be so good."

John fell in behind, and when they were out of earshot of the all others he stopped and whispered to him. "Go back and stand behind them, John, let them talk. The contempt they show says they don't think we're up to much."

George entered the cabin, opened up the log, and examined it for any mention of the three Frenchmen. She had sailed out of Marseille some three weeks before, and the men were listed as Colonel Le Cot, and Captains Bruer, and Ferdinand. He scanned the junior officers' journals and picked out several references to the French officers. George went back out onto the deck.

"Which of you gentlemen is Colonel Le Cot?" George eyed the men in front of him, but no one moved or appeared to recognise the name.

John Bray pushed through the three of them and stood with George. He looked at the tallest of the three and saluted. "Colonel Le Cot, I presume. I heard them talking, and this one was ordering the others not to say a word, or they may be shot as spies."

The Frenchman, realising the game was up, saluted and said in heavily accented English, "I am Monsieur Colonel, who am I addressing?"

George came to attention and saluted. "Lieutenant Warwick of his Royal Majesty's Navy and *HMS Broad*, sir. Why are you aboard this vessel and bound for America? And don't tell me you intend to settle there as a civilian," he added sarcastically.

"I am afraid I am not at liberty to answer that, Lieutenant." He smiled ruefully. "Would you, in the same circumstances?"

"No matter," George answered whilst beckoning the sergeant to come forward. "Take the colonel and his officers over to the *Broad*. They are now prisoners of war."

Captain Poynton stepped forward with his men starting to back him. The sergeant pointed his bayonet at the captain's chest, and his Marines lined up in front of the crew, forming a barrier of cold steel.

"You cannot do this," Poynton shouted. "They are guests of the American government, this is an outrage."

"Carry on, Sergeant. Get these three over to the *Broad*." George turned to the captain. "If I have any further trouble from you, sir, I will also start looking at the status of some of your men. Some look decidedly British to me and could be deserters."

Captain Poynton stepped back, waving his men down. "You go too far, sir," he said in resignation of their fate.

When the three protesting Frenchmen were safely in the longboats, George bade the captain farewell and wished him a trouble-free voyage.

"I'm afraid, in the light of your assisting our enemies, we will also be confiscating your log, Captain, as well as the journals." With that, George went over the side to jeering and cursing from the crew, and returned to the *Broad*.

***

"They refuse to talk?" Brownlow queried in exasperation. "Blast their eyes. Well, they can join the other prisoners in chains below. Take them away, Sergeant." He turned to George, saying, "Let the Admiralty decide what to do with them, you have done well, Mr Warwick, we seem to have upset some little game of mischief."

George joined a sullen Robert on deck, who was gazing out at the departing *Massachusetts*. "Sorry, but they did have three French officers on board," George said in their defence.

"That may be George, but America is now a sovereign nation. The trouble with Britain is it thinks it can do what it likes, when it likes, to any nation on earth."

"Steady on, Robert, we're not your enemy," George retorted. "We are just carrying out the orders of our government."

"The trouble is America is being driven into the arms of Britain's enemies by the way your Navy arbitrarily boards them and impresses their men. I hope it does not come to war between our nations, George, for my resolve would be sorely tested."

Robert left him and went below, leaving George very worried for his friend, and for their future friendship.

SIXTEEN

With just another fifty miles to go before they reached the safety of British waters and their home port of Portsmouth, George reflected on the very eventful voyage. Robert's bankers in London should be very pleased with the small fortune that would be put before them, and the Admiralty pleased with the French prisoners.

It being his turn on watch, George was standing on the poop deck. He pulled the grogram lovingly close to his body against the biting northerly wind which was blowing icy spray into his face. His grogram, inherited from his father and made up of wool, mohair, silk, and stiffened with gum, kept out the most severe weather. The scarf wrapped tightly around his neck started to feel warm before he realised it was also starting to throb gently.

Slightly alarmed, he raised the telescope and started to scan the swollen seas around him. He swept the whole horizon in the darkening grey skies before he eventually spotted two sails ahead of them, and travelling in the same direction.

"Request Captain Brownlow to come on deck," he ordered the Marine on guard.

The Marine made his way quickly to the captain's cabin and rapped on the door. Two minutes later, Brownlow appeared, buttoning up his tunic against the icy wind as he made his way back. He was surprised not to see George on the quarterdeck; he looked up the main mast and spotted him in the rigging.

"Not at all like the Caribbean, Mr Warwick," he shouted through cupped hands, trying to compete against the whistling of the icy wind. "What seems to be the problem?"

George looked down at the diminutive looking figure far below as he heard him calling faintly, just making out the request.

"Two sails ahead, sir," he shouted down. "On our course and dead ahead, I can't make them out yet," he added as he saw Robert join the captain on the deck below.

"Down you come, Mr Warwick, let a rating take your place."

Brownlow turned to return to his cabin, almost bumping into Robert as he did so.

"I beg your pardon, Captain," said Robert as he moved aside. "What if they are French, sir, what are you going to do?"

"Do, sir? What am I going to do?" the captain blustered. "Unless you have heard something to the contrary, Mr Gates, we are still at war with France. Well, have you?"

"Well… no, sir…"

"I thought as much, mister. Well, I'll tell you what I am going to do. If they are French I intend to blow the buggers out of the water," he exploded, his face taking on a deepening purple colour.

"That could jeopardise our little fortune, Captain," Robert said unwisely.

"Mr Gates," the captain almost spat in his face. "Duty comes first, your pilfered gemstones a very poor second. We engage the enemy no matter what the cost, and if I get a whiff of you not doing your duty, I will clap you in irons to await trial. Do I make myself clear?" With that he turned on his heel and went back to his cabin.

George arrived on the deck to the sight of an irate Brownlow disappearing into his cabin and a red-faced and very angry Robert standing there watching him.

"Did you hear that? Did you hear what that pompous, bandy legged jackass said to me?"

"I think I caught the gist of it, Robert, and I must say I agree with him. What is more, for what you suggested he could have you hanged from the yardarm without any trial, that is the penalty for dissent or mutiny."

"Now hang on one bloody minute, George. Who the hell mentioned anything about dissent or mutiny? I just pointed out that we could lose everything."

"To a man like Brownlow that was mutiny. What on earth do you think you are doing and saying, Robert? The man is a fierce patriot, and has a strong sense of duty. At the very least he considered that you had insulted him."

"That was not my intention and you bloody well know it."

"No, Robert, I don't. I agree with the old man, duty must come above all things."

"Since when have I not done my duty, above and beyond what is expected of me? You gall me, George, you really do." Robert turned and walked swiftly away without a further look or word.

George watched him go with sorrow, but he had other things on his mind. He spotted Briggs coming towards him. "Up you go, Briggs, make sure you get relieved. I don't want you suffering from the cold. Let me know if there is any change in direction, or speed."

"Aye, aye, sir," the ever-willing Briggs answered, as he started to climb up the foremast.

They stayed on their heading for a further two hours, gradually closing with the two ships up ahead. George went to the captain's cabin. He knocked and entered on command. Brownlow seemed to be expecting him as he smiled at his arrival.

"Well, Mr Warwick, where are they heading?"

"They are staying on their present course, sir. It seems they are heading north toward Scandinavia, possibly Denmark."

"All right, but let's stay with them until we are absolutely sure. Order full sail, and let's close the distance."

George was about to answer, when there was a knock on the cabin's door. Brownlow invited the caller in.

"Yes, Mr Bowden, what is it?"

"Begging you pardon, sir, it's about the French prisoners below."

"Well, what about them?"

"I've learnt to speak a little of their language, for my examination, to lieutenant, sir."

"Yes, yes, get on with it man."

"The Portuguese prisoners told them that you had hanged four of their number for treason and spying. One of the Frenchmen was extremely agitated by this and thinks that they are next for the noose."

"Which one?" Brownlow asked.

"I think his name is Captain Ferdinand, sir. He is frightened to death of Mr Warwick, and keeps referring to him as *Le Scarf.*"

"Go and fetch him, Mr Bowden, if you please. Take a couple of Marines with you, and be so good as to inform Captain Gates his presence is required."

When Bertie had left the cabin, George turned to his captain. "Can I have permission to speak candidly, sir?"

"Yes, Mr Warwick, you may, but I warn you now, I know the subject you are going to mention, and I am not best pleased."

"I am aware of that, sir, but I must intercede on Captain Gates's behalf. He is a brave, gallant and loyal officer of Marines. He has stood shoulder to shoulder with me in battle, not just aboard this ship, but in the *Victory* at Trafalgar, and on the beaches of Hispaniola when we thought we would be slaughtered."

Brownlow turned away from him, faced the stern window and watched the ship's wake as he remained silent, deep in thought. He eventually turned to face George and smiled.

"I hear you, Mr Warwick, and I respect your judgement. I think I may have been too hasty in my assessment of our colonial friend. Of course I am aware of his bravery and his service, but he must learn to guard his tongue and remember whose uniform he wears. Now, let's get back to the business at hand." He gave George a wicked smile and continued, "Now put your scarf on, Mr Warwick, and let's give our French officer a warm reception."

A knock on the door was followed by a very worried French officer being pushed in the cabin by two Marines, with Bertie Bowden and Robert following behind. The prisoner was forced to stand in front of the desk and was physically trembling with fear as he looked down at Brownlow's stern face.

"Wait outside," he ordered the two Marines.

The French captain took the opportunity to look around the cabin at those present. He looked first at Bertie, then at Robert, before catching his breath as he spotted George outlined against the stern window, complete with scarf round his head.

"You, and your colleagues, are spies," Brownlow accused.

The prisoner didn't take his eyes off George, as Bertie translated the captain's words. He tore his eyes away at the accusation and looked straight down at Brownlow.

"Non, non, non!" he pleaded desperately. "I am no spy. I am an infantry officer in the army… no spy," he blurted out in broken English before ranting on in French.

Brownlow eventually held up his hand, not understanding a word he was saying. "Mr Bowden, please let me know what this man is babbling about. I heard the name of *Le Cot* mentioned, as well as *Le Scarf*."

"Colonel Le Cot has told him that almost all of Europe is joining together against the British, including the Russians and Danes. It is their intention to break the British stranglehold held since Trafalgar. He thinks Mr Warwick will hang them because of it."

"Thank you, Mr Bowden," Brownlow said quietly, before adding, "It appears we are at war with most of mainland Europe, gentlemen, including the two ships we are pursuing.

Get this man back below and order full sail. We are going to chase the enemy down before they reach their coastal waters."

"Do we beat to quarters, sir?" George asked as he looked at Robert.

"We do indeed, sir," Brownlow answered bluntly. *"Le Scarf*, eh! You are getting quite a reputation, Mr Warwick. You had better hope you are never captured."

George, Robert, and John Bray were standing on the weather deck after the beat to quarters was given, watching the preparations for war that they had come to know so well. The Portuguese and French prisoners, realising what was going on, started to murmur their concerns and discontent about going into battle chained below decks.

When John left them to go forward, George held out his hand and spoke to his close friend. "We don't go into battle without making our peace, Robert. I spoke to the old man. He agrees that you are a fine and loyal officer and that he may have overreacted, but I still say he was right. You are going to have to watch what you say in future."

Robert took his hand and smiled. "No matter what happens in our lives, George, we will stand together, no nation on earth will stop that."

Later that afternoon, they noticed the two ships were putting up full canvas and making a run for it. They could make out that the ships were Danish frigates, both normally armed with thirty guns. It seemed that they had no stomach for a fight, even though they had superior firepower, as they continued on their heading towards the Danish coast.

"Mr Warwick," Brownlow called out as he headed towards him. "I want every bit of canvas aloft. These cowardly buggers will not escape us."

George watched through his telescope as they closed the distance between the fleeing ships, which did not seem to be handling very well. He noticed the names on their sterns. The one on the left was the ship *Raae* and the other was the *Sorride,* and according to his captain, thirty and twenty-eight guns respectively.

"They outgun us, why are they running, sir, why don't they make a fight of it?"

"Why indeed?" Brownlow remarked.

On board the Danish ships, panic was setting in as they frantically signalled to one another. If Brownlow had been able to see, and read the messages, all would have been clear. Both ships companies had been sorely depleted by a cholera outbreak, contracted from the French out in the Caribbean. They were in no condition to fight, especially after losing their captains and most of their officers. They were only just about managing to sail their ships.

Brownlow and George walked forward to join John Bray and the two-gun crews.

"Mr Warwick, you and Mr Bray man these forward guns. The enemy seems to be staying together and will expect us to veer off and attack them one at a time, only then will they part and fight. They are going to be in for a very big surprise. I want your guns to take out their rudders as we approach, and before we go straight through the middle."

"Through the middle, Captain?" John queried, thinking he must have misheard the plan of action.

"Through their centre, Mr Bray, so you had better be accurate with your gunnery, had you not?"

As their captain went aft to give instructions to the rest of the crew, Robert came forward.

"Did I hear correctly? He is going to sail between the two?"

"It appears so, should be interesting." George grinned.

"Bloody downright arrogance, George, that's what it is."

"We'll see, we'll see. I'm going below to get my gear."

George went below to collect his sword and a pistol. Before returning to the deck above, he tied his scarf around his head. He noticed that it was benign and not changing colour. He wondered why. Normally, going into battle, it started to

209

throb and change colour. He jumped as the figure appeared at his elbow.

"Lord Wei," he acknowledged

"Young warrior," Wei answered. "There is a killer sickness aboard the two ships, you must not board or many of your own men will die."

"So that is why they run."

"Yes, warrior, they have very few skilled men left to run their ships, let alone fight."

"They are still our enemy, Lord Wei, we will still attack, and unless they surrender, we will sink them."

"I understand, and agree with you, just do not go on board either vessel."

George was about to respond when he realised Wei was no longer with him. He made his way up and went forward to his position behind the big guns. His gun crew saw him approach and smiled as they saw the scarf around his head.

"Bar and chain," he ordered as the guns were made ready. "Our primary aim is to take out their rudders. There will be no second chances, if we get the chance for another shot, we will load with grape."

Briggs looked across at George and smiled grimly. "We'll get a second shot off, sir, you can count on it."

On the bridge, Brownlow was shouting his orders. "We are going to take out their tails and leave them rudderless. I want all guns set to fire below the waterline as we fire on both of our flanks. The Danes, like the French and Spanish, will fire up at our rigging, hoping to dismast us. I want total devastation, so guns will be reloaded in double quick time."

He turned and spotted Robert on the weather deck. "Captain Gates, have your Marines forward to support the guns. I want them to take out any sharpshooters in the rigging."

George spotted the Marines coming forward with their muskets, headed by Robert, and starting to line the sides of the ship. Robert grinned at his friend as he saw the familiar scarf round his head.

"Well what do you think, Mr Warwick, or should I call you *Le Scarf*?" he said. "Like old times, isn't it?"

"Well, you seem to have cheered up somewhat, let's hope it is like old times."

"Whatever I think of the old man, he's a wily old fox and a very good tactician. We might just pull this off."

"Whatever happens, Robert, we must not board either vessel."

"Did I hear you right, not board them? What about prize, George, surely we are going for prize?"

"Keep your voice down. I believe there is cholera, or suchlike, on board the ships, that's why they run."

Robert looked puzzled as he looked ahead at the two ships still trying to flee. He eyed his friend quizzically and lowered his voice to a whisper.

"I don't know how you could possibly know that, but it does make sense. They outgun us, so why would they run?" He suddenly thought and added, "Have you had another visit?"

"Yes. Wei warned me, but how do we stop the old man boarding her if the opportunity is there?"

"I think you had better face that when, and if it arises. We have a battle to fight first."

George nodded in resignation as he watched the enemy ships being slowly overhauled. He ducked instinctively as he saw smoke emitting from the stern of the two vessels ahead. The two balls fell harmlessly in front of them as the *Broad* pressed on regardless. As they neared the ships, further shots were fired which were now reaching their target. A ball crashed through the main rigging, but failed to do a great deal of damage.

George looked around at the same time as John Bray, who was manning the other gun. They watched their captain and waited patiently for his orders. The gun crews, in turn, watched their officers and waited for the action to start. Two more cannon balls hit the rigging, causing timber to fall on the deck. The enemy were true to form; they were trying to take out sail to prevent the *Broad* from being able to manoeuvre. The enemy commanders still didn't realise that manoeuvring was the last thing on the English captain's mind. The *Broad* continued on its relentless pursuit as it started to come into range of the enemies' stern.

The commanders of the enemy ships watched in bewilderment as the *Broad* pressed on towards them. Which way was she going to go? Who was going to be the first target? When would she start to manoeuvre? They realised far too late what the English captain was going to do. Panic set in as they shouted out orders to their crews to take evasive action.

"Fire!" Brownlow roared.

The two forward guns fired in unison, sending their deadly chain hurtling towards the enemy ships. The gun crews watched as both sterns started to shatter just above the waterline. The accuracy was devastating as they lost their rudders, unable to continue their evasive action.

The gun crews were busy loading with grapeshot and lifting the elevation of the guns to aim at those manning the wheel. George and Robert were urging their men on, desperately trying to get their guns ready before they passed. Although it was less than two minutes since their last firing, it seemed an eternity before they were ready.

"Fire!" screamed George as his gun came to bear.

"Fire!" screamed John, just a few seconds later.

They both watched, mesmerised, as their deadly loads ripped apart their respective targets, killing all the personnel in the immediate vicinity of the wheels. The *Broad* was now starting to sail between the two ships. The Danes fired in desperation, but the balls were still firing high into the rigging, causing only minor damage. Brownlow waited until the time was right before ordering his guns to fire on the enemy ships.

Cannon after cannon leapt to life as Bertie and Grahame went along the deck behind the gunners on both sides of the ship, ordering them to fire as their turn came.

George and Robert watched as the balls thudded into the now helpless ships, which appeared so close you could almost touch them.

"What's that?" George asked, as he looked up to the mast of the *Sorride* to see a black and yellow flag being hoisted.

"It looks as if you were right, George, that's a flag of quarantine. They must have some sort of plague on board."

Brownlow was shouting for all guns to cease firing as they passed between the two ships and started to heave over to their starboard.

"All officers to me," he ordered, as the ship started a long sweep around.

They all made their way to the quarterdeck where they joined their captain and the surgeon. Brownlow was eying each ship in turn as he noticed that they were now showing the dreaded colours of plague.

"What do you think, Mr Delaforce?" Brownlow asked his surgeon.

"That is a flag of quarantine, Captain, and if it is correct they have plague on board and we shouldn't go anywhere near."

"Mr Warwick, Mr Bray. What are your feelings on this, do you think it genuine, or a ruse to escape us?"

George looked at Robert with relief written all over his face. It couldn't have happened better, how was he going to tell his captain that plague was on board otherwise?

"I think it is genuine, sir," George said eventually. "It would explain why two warships who outgun us decided to run for it. Their complement must be sorely depleted, and they have hardly put up much of a fight, have they?"

Brownlow didn't answer. He put the telescope to his eye and continued to observe each ship in turn, before eventually lowering the glass.

"Mr Bray, see if you can make contact with either of their commanders. No one is to have any physical contact with them under any circumstance. Is that clear? I'll be in my cabin when you've done so."

Aye, sir," John replied. "I'll see if any of them understand signal, sir. If not I will arrange a boat to stand off and talk with them."

All three ships had taken in sail and were now stationary, riding on the gentle grey swell of the Atlantic, as they awaited the outcome.

John, Robert and George joined their captain in his cabin.

"Someone aboard the *Sorride* can read and understand our signals, sir, but just in case of any misunderstanding I had the French prisoner, Captain Ferdinand, standing by. Between us we have learnt what happened."

"Go on, Mr Bray, tell me all."

"Their surgeon was the first to go down with cholera and died a week after contracting the disease, after that they began falling down in droves on both ships, including losing both captains and most of their officers. The ships have mainly been run by skeleton crews of the seamen themselves."

"What is their present status?"

"Poor, Captain. Both ships are now badly damaged. The *Raae* is badly holed and is not able to sail. The *Sorride* can be patched up and could limp to a port."

"Not a British port, mister, that's the last thing we need to take home with us."

Brownlow went quiet, deep in thought, trying to work out what was best to do. It rankled with him to leave an enemy fighting ship afloat, but what was the alternative?

"May I make a suggestion, Captain?" George asked.

"Go ahead, Mr Warwick."

"If the remaining crew is transferred from the *Raae* to the *Sorride*, we can sink the *Raae* and let the Danes continue their journey home on one ship."

"I don't think we have any alternative, Mr Warwick. We could set them adrift in longboats and scuttle both ships, but in the circumstances, I think that may be a little inhumane."

He turned to John. "Get Captain Ferdinand to explain to the *Sorride* what we have decided. There will be no argument. We will destroy the other ship when they have all left safely. If they refuse to do so, I will send both ships to the bottom."

For the remainder of the day they watched in silence as longboat after longboat transferred the Danish sailors from one ship to the other. When the operation was complete, the *Broad* signalled the *Sorride* to get under way and watched as the pathetic looking ship put up sail and started to limp away to the Danish coast.

"Briggs," George shouted out.

"Mr Warwick, sir," he answered as he sprinted to up to him.

"Target practice, Briggs, we sail in close and I want all guns to bear on the enemy ship. Set the guns to fire at, or below the waterline. The intention is to sink her without trace."

Brownlow ordered short sail to be hoisted as they gently sailed towards the empty ghost ship. "Is everything ready, Mr Warwick?"

"Aye, Captain, guns are set to blow out the waterline."

"Then fire when ready."

Robert was standing by his side as they approached broadside on to the target.

"Fortunate, George, thank goodness they had the sense to haul up the 'Q' flag, or you would have had a devil of a job explaining why you didn't want to board them."

George half smiled as he gave the order. "Fire," he shouted.

The starboard guns roared as one as the cannonballs flew to their target.

"Congratulations, Briggs, you seem to have got it right, all guns on target," George praised, as he saw the balls striking the ship along its waterline.

"Come about," shouted Brownlow as he watched the balls strike home. "Good shooting, Mr Warwick, now let's do the same to their lee side."

As the *Broad* came around and traversed the lee of the stricken ship, a further salvo rang out as holes appeared along the side of the already listing ship. Fires broke out below decks, but before they could get a firm hold, the *Raae* started to sink stern first. The whole crew watched with mixed emotions as she started to slide, pushing her prow high in the air, before disappearing below the grey, cold waters of the Atlantic.

"Let's make for home, gentlemen," Brownlow said as he eyed the calm sea.

SEVENTEEN

After two weeks in London, George and Robert arrived at Lord Fitzwilliam's estate in the Hampshire countryside, a few miles north of Fareham on the south coast. It had been a long, arduous campaign, with both of them being glad to be back. They met Harold, the estate manager, as they turned up the driveway leading to the manor in their hired coach. He was busy organising the yearly clearance of the ditches surrounding the estate.

"Hello, Harold, how are you?" George greeted him.

"George!" he exclaimed, "and Mr Gates. We heard you were in Plymouth. His lordship has been expecting you at any time, welcome home."

"Are there any guests here?" George almost pleaded for an affirmative answer.

Harold smiled, knowing what he wanted to hear. "Guests, sir?" he asked.

George frowned, narrowed his eyes, and pointed a finger straight at Harold, as if to warn him.

"All right, yes she's here," he relented, smiling as he bent down to get something from his bag lying at the side of the drive. He put the article to his lips, and blew hard. The resounding noise from the bugle could be heard for miles. "My orders, I'm afraid, as soon as you were spotted."

"Up to the manor," George ordered the driver, "and get a bloody move on, man."

"You didn't ask if Jessica was here," Robert complained.

George laughed loudly. "If Barbara's here so is Jessica." He punched his friend hard in the shoulder, a bit harder than he intended.

"Ease up will you, that bloody well hurt," Robert complained.

The people at the manor heard the bugle call and saw the coach coming up the drive. The buzz of excitement spread everywhere. Lord Fitzwilliam waited for the jubilant, and very girlish, Barbara and Jessica, to join him. They went out together to greet the arrivals.

You couldn't tell who was more pleased, George, Robert, Jessica, or Barbara. They hugged one another in turn, before turning to greet Lord Fitzwilliam.

"My lord." George ventured a bow, before moving forward to shake his hand. "It is a pleasure to be home."

Robert was busy hugging Jessica, and just nodded his assent.

"Likewise, George, it's good to see you both safe and sound. Let's move on into the house and you can tell us of your adventures." Lord Fitzwilliam beamed as if these boys were his own flesh and blood. He jovially led the way inside to the great hall.

They related details of their adventures, making sure to leave out any mention of raking any vessels, so as not to upset the sensitive natures of Barbara and Jessica.

"I think the ladies should retire for a while in order to freshen up," Lord Fitzwilliam spoke for the first time since entering the great hall.

Barbara and Jessica sighed, reacting as if they were facing banishment and a lifelong exile.

"Not already," Barbara pleaded, looking at Jessica for support. "They have only just arrived."

Lord Fitzwilliam would have none of it. "Off with you both, so the men can talk. We won't be long, and you can all meet up for dinner… and no listening on the stairs," he added to the disappointed girls.

They withdrew reluctantly, with Jessica blowing a kiss at an elated, but slightly embarrassed, Robert. As soon as they had gone, Lord Fitzwilliam addressed them.

"I had a letter from Captain Brownlow, which reached me before you got here. I don't know where you have been for the past three days or more, perhaps you would like to explain?"

George and Robert looked like two conspiring criminals, and wondered just what they should say.

"I also know about the battles where you were forced to rake the enemy, which I'm glad to say, you left out in front of the girls."

"George and I decided to go to London for a couple of days, my lord." Robert decided he should say something. "I have a cousin there, and promised him I would visit. It seemed an ideal opportunity to do so, my lord."

"You two can stop with the 'my lord' business this instant, you can both call me Fitz, so there's no mix up as to whom you are addressing. I am well aware who your cousin works for, Robert. What you probably don't know is that one of the directors of the Merchant Bank is Barbara's father, my brother."

Robert and George's mouths gaped wide as their jaws dropped in surprise, verging on shock. They didn't know how to respond, they just gawked at one another.

"I also know what you deposited, and the terms of a trust set up for your crew. The only thing that surprises me about all this is that you managed to carry Brownlow with you." Fitz paused as he looked at their troubled faces. "Don't look so worried you two, it hasn't gone any further, nor will it. The only one missing out on all this is the Admiralty, and they still appear to be satisfied with the prizes you have already laid before them. Seeing as I am one of them, and the fact I don't care, there is no harm done."

Relief was an understatement as George and Robert smiled nervously at one another.

"Thank you, sir, thank you so much." Robert had hold of Fitz's hand, and was pumping away like mad.

"Goes for me too, sir." George took over from where Robert left off.

"All right, all right, I take it that you are pleased. Now you had better retire, and clean up after your journey, dinner is at eight sharp." Lord Fitzwilliam retrieved his right hand, shaking it to get some blood flowing. "Go on, what are you waiting for? We'll discuss your future plans after dinner this evening."

"Oh, by the way, Captain Brownlow took some persuading, sir, and if the Admiralty had been fairer to him and the crew the last time they put prizes before them, as well as rescuing English seamen to boot, it might have been a different story," George said in defence of his captain.

"Off you go, I am well aware of the circumstances. I must admit it did stick in my craw at the time and I told their lordships so. I think the prime reason for me now being on that board is so they can control me. They couldn't be more wrong, and I guarantee one thing, it will never happen on my watch again."

"Thank you, sir." George turned and followed Robert out into the hall. They mounted the stairs together, listening for the girls, who they knew would have been trying to overhear their conversation with Fitz. George put his hand to his ear and gave Robert a knowing grin as they heard the bustle of petticoats fast disappearing ahead of them.

***

Early that evening, George found himself wandering idly in the garden, waiting for Barbara to come out and meet him. He sensed a presence behind him as he turned expectantly.

"Love is on your mind, warrior. You will ask the girl to marry you today, yes?" Wei was standing with his hands on his hips, grinning from ear to ear.

"Don't tell me you see danger in that as well, my lord," he quipped in response.

"There is always danger where the fair sex is concerned, but no, I come to offer my good wishes, and that of my

220

warriors, for your life ahead. If your sons are anything like you, I think we will be kept busy for another generation."

"Thank you. I appreciate your good wishes and your continued protection, my lord."

"Who are you talking to, George?" Barbara asked, appearing silently at his side. Her bright blue-green eyes searched the garden, but all she could see were the roses which were in full bloom.

George jumped at the sound of her voice, and like Barbara, he searched the garden for signs of Wei. He was relieved to see that once again he had disappeared.

"Rehearsing what to say," he replied far too quickly.

"Oh, and pray, what is it that needs such rehearsal and devotion?"

Blushing, he carefully swept the bench with his sleeve. Before inviting Barbara to sit, he removed his coat and laid it on the seat.

"My, aren't we the perfect gentleman." Barbara feigned shyness as she looked up at him from under her long eyelashes.

He was still as smitten as he was when he first met her. Theatrically dropping to one knee, George fumbled inside his jacket pocket, eventually taking out a beautifully mounted sapphire ring surrounded by a cluster of small, pure white diamonds.

"Barbara, will you marry me?" he almost pleaded, holding his breath for the answer.

Tears welled in Barbara's eyes as she looked at the man she loved with all her heart. Her eyes dropped to the beautiful sparkling ring that he held in front of her.

"Oh! George, you know my answer is yes. Yes, yes, yes," she cried.

George let out his breath and then inhaled deeply, trying to control his heart that seemed to be bursting under his shirt. He could hardly believe that this was happening to him. He cursed himself for his past temerity and lack of courage. He thought about the wasted time as he took her hand and they both rose. He kissed her lips lightly a few times, stopped and gazed down at her with a new fire in his eyes, before kissing her in a way neither of them had experienced before.

"Oh, George, I don't think I can wait very long. When can we get married?" she pressed eagerly.

"We will have to consult your parents and mine first. I suggest we tell the others at dinner tonight. Is that alright?" Taking her arm, he gently guided her back to the house, just in time to see the backs of Jessica and Robert disappearing inside.

Through a rising spiral of mist across the lawn, twenty-eight proud Chinese warriors in an arc, looked on approvingly.

***

Rodney and Rebecca arrived at Crompton Manor just after seven p.m. They hugged their son warmly before embracing Robert, who they hoped would soon become their son-in-law. After Robert had left them alone, George spoke to both of his parents.

"Father, I have something to tell you and mother, or should I say, ask you. I want to marry Barbara."

His father burst out laughing. "It's Barbara you should be asking, son, not us."

"I have asked her, and she's accepted me. The only other people we have to ask are her mother and father, and Barbara tends to think they will agree wholeheartedly."

"Of course you have our blessing, George, we couldn't be happier to have Barbara as our daughter," his mother said as she looked at his father in disapproval. "Stop messing around, Rodney, and congratulate the boy."

His father held out his hand and embraced his son. "No words necessary, George, go ahead and marry the girl before she changes her mind. I hope you realise how difficult it will be on a lieutenant's pay."

"I'll speak to you about finances later, Father," George responded.

Mrs Baird joined them for dinner, sitting at the top of the table with Rodney seated on her left. Lord Fitzwilliam was seated at the other end of the table with Rebecca by his side. Mrs Baird didn't look out of place in her prominent position as joint head of the household.

George entered the dining room with Barbara, seating her next to Jessica. He skirted the large table before sitting down next to a grinning Robert. He shot a darting look of accusation at Barbara, who had also noticed the magical atmosphere between Mrs Baird and Fitz, as well as Jessica and Robert. She shook her head as she realised his meaning. Had she been talking, had she told Jessica, had Jessica in turn told others?

"No," Jessica suddenly said across the table. "I haven't said anything"

George looked round the table, embarrassed by the faces peering back at him.

Robert broke the silence. "Something you want to tell us, my old shipmate?" he asked in a mock West Country accent.

George slowly rose to his feet, adjusting his coat as he straightened. "I might as well tell you all now. Barbara and I, subject to her parents' approval, are engaged, and I have asked her to marry me at the earliest date we can arrange."

Barbara looked happily around the table, but was puzzled to be met with a stony silence. Jessica was the first to respond.

"You have stolen our thunder," she complained, as Robert sprang to his feet.

"We were going to tell you tonight that we are engaged to be married as well," Robert protested. "You never said anything to me, did you?" he said accusingly to George.

"I didn't want to marry you, *my old shipmate.*" George imitated the accent Robert had just used. "In any case, you had hardly discussed your own plans with me, had you? Have you even asked my parents yet?"

"Yes, we have, just before dinner, and they said they couldn't be happier."

Barbara and Jessica both rose to their feet to join in the argument, when a thunderous banging on the end of the table stopped them. They all looked down to where Fitz was seated, to see him striking the table with the handle of his dinner knife

"Ladies and gentlemen, can we have some quiet please? Take your seats," he commanded, with the broadest of grins on his face. "It seems as if we all have good news tonight." He beamed at Mrs Baird and simply said, "Anne."

The others looked at each other with some puzzlement. Other than Rodney, they had never ever heard Fitz refer to Mrs Baird by her Christian name. They all turned and looked down the table to a smiling Anne Baird.

She cleared her throat, remained seated, and then said, "Lord Fitzwilliam and I, were also going to break the good news of our intended betrothal, but it seems you have all beaten us to it."

They were all dumbfounded. They hadn't seen this coming. This was completely out of the blue for all of them. George had always known that there was more to their relationship than just master and servant, but he had never guessed that this would happen, not in a million years.

Rodney was on his feet in an instant and went to Fitz's side and began slapping him on his shoulders. "It's not before time, Fitz, congratulations."

"Thank you, Rodney," Fitz coughed back as he looked around at the others with blank faces. "What the hell's wrong with you lot?" Fitz called out. "Don't think we're up to it, eh!"

"No, sir, I mean yes, sir." George was blustering, "I think maybe we were too wrapped up in our own happiness to see it, sir."

Fitz beamed down the table. "Well, before we have dinner and get indigestion, I suggest we get the congratulations over between us." He got to his feet, raising his glass, to which they all responded by standing up. "I hope Rebecca and Rodney will join in when I wish you all a long and happy life."

"To us all," they responded as one.

After dinner, Harold, the estate manager, shepherded the staff out, after first clearing away the dinner plates. He placed the large decanter of port on the table in front of Fitz before speaking. "Is there anything else you require tonight, my lord?"

"If there is, we will get it for ourselves, Harold, thank you, and thank the staff. Now be off away home with you all." Fitz was in an extremely good mood. He waited until the great doors were closed, before addressing his guests.

"Well," he started, rubbing his rotund stomach. "Seeing as Mrs Baird and I don't need anybody's permission to get married, we will be the first up." He poured himself a glass of port and passed the decanter along to Rebecca who passed it to Jessica, who in turn passed it to Barbara. Neither of them poured a drink before Barbara passed the decanter on to Mrs Baird.

"Don't mind if I do." She laughed. "Phew, what an evening," she said, passing the decanter to Rodney by her side.

Eventually George filled his own glass before filling Robert's and passing the decanter back to where it had started.

It was Anne Baird's turn to get to her feet. "Good health, everyone." She beamed.

***

The next day at the farm, George and Robert rose early. They entered the warm kitchen, where Martha was busy baking.

"Is father about?" George asked.

"Out in the barn grooming the horses," she answered. "Breakfast will be in half an hour."

They joined Rodney in the barn, where he was cleaning out the hoof of the shire horse. "Morning, lads." Rodney smiled as he remembered the evening before. "Quite a night, eh!"

The two of them looked at one another, wondering how Rodney was going to take the news of their surprise fortune. Rodney stopped what he was doing, allowing the hoof to fall to the ground.

"What is it?" He looked from one to the other. "You look as if you've just stolen the crown jewels, what's up?"

"There's no easy way to put this, Father, so I think we had better start from the beginning." George began telling his father how they had acquired a small fortune when they had thwarted Lord Crowe and went on to tell him about the diamonds from the slaver.

Twenty minutes later, a disbelieving Rodney was still looking at them both with his mouth wide open, not fully comprehending the situation.

"So, let me get this clear. You have taken proceeds from a prize that should have gone to the crown, you have included Captain Brownlow in your little conspiracy, and you've set up a trust fund for the crew. If Lord Fitzwilliam found out about it, don't you think that others could? If they do find out they most certainly will hang you."

George and Robert spent the whole time he spoke looking down at their feet and wondering what the outcome of their revelation would be.

"Well, it's done now, we can't change that fact. Think yourselves lucky that you have Fitz to protect you. I can see the reasons why you did what you did, and I probably would have done the same. I know Fitz would have."

They both looked up at Rodney with relief written all over their faces. "Does that mean you are all right with it, Mr Warwick?" Robert asked hopefully.

"No it damn well does not," Rodney shot back, "but we are where we are, he is my son, and you are soon to be my son-in-law, although if you had mentioned this last night, I don't know what my reaction would have been. How on earth you got Brownlow to agree to all this is beyond me."

"Fitz also mentioned that," George replied, "but the fact he was cheated out of a comfortable retirement made his mind up for him, especially when we also provided a trust fund for the crew."

"I think a visit to the manor is necessary, we must try and make sure this does not come back to bite you two in your arses," Rodney said sternly.

EIGHTEEN

As they arrived at the manor, Rodney strode out ahead of them, leaving George and Robert trailing behind with Rebecca and Jessica following. George noticed the chestnut mare tethered beside the front entrance. It had been ridden hard and was sweating profusely as Harold arrived to take it to the stables.

As he entered the hall, Rodney bade Anne Baird a good morning. "He's in the study, Rodney, and has company," she said, guessing why he had come so early.

He strode down the hall, knocked on the door and entered without being invited. He was surprised to see Captain Brownlow sitting in conversation with Fitz.

"Come on in, Rodney. You know Abraham Brownlow, don't you?"

"Of course I do, we served long enough together. Good day to you, Brownlow."

"Hello, Warwick, a pleasure to see you again," he responded.

"I wish I could damn well say the same…"

Rodney was cut off by Fitz with a wave of his hand. "Sit down, Rodney, and try to control your temper in my home."

Rodney glared at both in turn before pulling up a chair and facing them. "I'm sorry, Fitz, but the news hit me like a cannon ball. I hope to God we can keep this matter under wraps."

"I'm not going to apologise for my actions, Warwick. You and Lord Fitzwilliam would have both done the same, and probably have done during your service."

"That is me, Brownlow, not my son," Rodney spat out.

"Rodney," Fitz butted in. "George and Robert are grown men. I watched them being cheated by the Admiralty under the influence of Crowe, we would both have done the same."

"It is Crowe I am concerned about, Fitz, he will have a bloodlust where George is concerned and will stop at nothing to harm him."

"My brother, soon to be George's father-in-law, is in charge of the bank in question. No information will ever get out, so don't concern yourself with that," he assured him. "But let us talk practicalities here. If these three suddenly retire, there may be some awkward questions asked by their lordships, but if they return to their positions, there is no reason why anyone should be any the wiser."

"I did what I did in order to make up my pension, which had been raided by the Admiralty and Crowe, but as Lord Fitzwilliam has pointed out, I can't retire now in case it does cause suspicion. I have come all this way to tell George and Robert that, and I hope that they will agree to accompany me back to Plymouth, where we will continue our service on the *Broad*."

"You have new sailing orders?" Fitz asked.

"Yes, we sail in ten days' time under sealed orders of their lordships. My ship is being provisioned as we speak."

"You had better call George and Robert in, Rodney. This does need settling immediately," Fitz said as he got up and went to the door. Rodney followed him into the hall and called to them. As they entered they saw the grim face of Captain Brownlow. Rodney explained to the two of them what had been discussed.

"We have already spoken about this," Robert replied, "and we believe that is exactly what we should do, so if Captain Brownlow will have us, we will return with him."

George nodded in agreement as he added, "Our marriages will have to wait. The girls won't like it, and they probably won't understand, but as my father has already said, we are where we are, and will have to make the best of it."

"I don't want blasted reluctant sailors aboard my ship, sir. If your hearts are not in it, you can both resign your commissions."

"Hold on there, Captain, I think the two of them are referring to the disappointment of their respective young ladies," Fitz countered. "I don't think you could have two more loyal officers than these two."

Brownlow coughed as he thought on what he had just said. "You are quite right, my lord. I am feeling a little tetchy these days." He turned to George and Robert, and smiled. "I apologise to your both, and of course I realise just how conscientious you have been under my command."

"And I apologise to you, Abraham, for being so high and mighty," Rodney chipped in. "Now I think you two had better go and make peace with your girls. I suppose I will have nothing but wailing from Jessica for the next few weeks."

***

After tearful farewells from Jessica and Barbara, the three of them set out for Plymouth, arriving four days later to see *HMS Broad* tied up alongside the jetty. She was low down in the water, suggesting that she had been fully armed, provisioned, and was ready to sail. Briggs was standing with John Bray by the gangplank as their coach pulled up alongside the ship. They both saluted their captain as he stepped down onto the dock. Briggs's face lit up as he saw George and Robert alight after him. George couldn't help smiling as he saw him, realising that he was now a great part of his life.

"Welcome back, Captain. We are fully armed and provisioned, but we seem to be having a problem enlisting a full complement. We have the officers aboard, including the new intake, but we are down on ratings."

Brownlow saluted his lieutenant as Briggs went to the rear of the coach to unload their belongings. "Nice to see you back, sir," he quipped, smiling at George as he went past.

"Thank you, Briggs. Get some help with the rest of the gear, would you? I don't want you ending up with a groin strain."

"Aye, sir," he replied as he shouted to some men loading stores aboard.

"Get the officers together, Mr Bray, and meet me in my cabin as soon as you can," Brownlow ordered.

A few minutes later, all the officers were assembled in the captain's cabin, with John Bray introducing the new lieutenant as Edward Cooper. Two additional midshipmen, John Hudson and Charles Grey, saluted as they were introduced.

"We have two detachments of Marines aboard, Captain Gates. You may introduce yourself to your men when we have finished here." Brownlow then turned to John. "Mr Bray, arrange a party of trusted crew members and go ashore. By hook or by crook, I mean to have a full complement of men when we sail. Offer them wages in advance to encourage them, but if all else fails, press them, and do it quickly."

"What are our orders, sir?" George enquired.

"My orders are sealed, Mr Warwick, to be opened when we are at sea. I can only think our orders are sensitive, and their lordships think the port has ears."

Over the next few hours, George and Robert watched as the press gangs returned with their captives. Some had come willingly, after being offered wages in advance. Others were being manhandled aboard, with varying degrees of cuts and bruises to them. George soon tired of the sight and as Robert moved off to talk to his Marines, he went below to his quarters. He was unpacking his kit as he became aware of Wei's presence.

"So, you have escaped marriage and we go on the ocean again, young warrior. It is a pity you cannot stay on the land. My men are not very good on water."

"Where do you go to when you disappear?"

"That is very difficult to explain. Let us call it, a temporary home among our ancestors."

"How do you get here? Where do you come from?"

Wei looked at George with an ironic smile accentuating the jagged scar down the side of his face as he replied, "I suppose we are what you call immortals, and we exist in the great sky above."

"Why do you come to my aid the way you do?"

"Ah, that is a lot easier to explain, young warrior. You have the scarf of the ancients given to you by your father. He was gifted it by a man who had its protection. The scarf originally belonged to the monks of Tong Binh and protected me in battle, until I had to make a decision: flee with its protection or stand and fight to the death with my loyal warriors. I gave the scarf to my son and sent him away to safety. For the first time I rode into battle without its protection. Twenty-eight of us rode against a horde of over five thousand enemy fighters."

"That must have been a magnificent sight, my lord."

"The ancients thought so. That is why we were made immortal, to protect the deserving owners of the scarf throughout time."

"Do you mean that you have to go on forever?"

Wei never had the chance to answer as a voice shouted from above. George was required on deck. When he lowered his eyes, Wei had gone.

Four hours later, on the highest tide of the year, the *Broad* put to sea with almost a full complement of crew. Once they were out of reach of land, the pressed men were released and instructed as to what was required of them. All officers were ordered to report to Brownlow's cabin where they assembled to await their orders.

"Well, gentlemen, it appears we are to return to Narranga," Brownlow said as his orders lay open on the table in front of him. "Now the extra detachment of Marines becomes clearer, Mr Gates, we are to take the garrison."

"Do we know if the garrison has been reinforced, sir?" Robert asked. "Even with an extra detachment of Marines it's a tall order if it has."

"Quite so, Mr Gates, that is why we are being joined by two other ships which we will rendezvous with off the coast of America. There will be extra Marines aboard those vessels, and you will be in overall command of the attack."

"Do we know what the other two ships will be, sir?" John Bray asked.

"According to my orders, we will meet a ship of the line with a frigate escort. I will be in overall command of the operation and more Marines will fall under the command of Captain Gates. Over the next few weeks we will formulate our plan and train the men for combat ashore."

"A ship of the line, sir, do we know who commands?"

"No, Mr Warwick, we do not, but if I am still in overall command it should be a captain of junior service to me. Do you have a reason to ask?"

"No particular reason, sir, I am just curious," George answered, feeling a little relieved it wouldn't be Admiral Lord Crowe.

Over the next two weeks, they were all busy with their various tasks. George had drawn the short straw to instruct the midshipmen in their duties, as well as assisting John Bray and Briggs in supervising gunnery practice. All the crew, without exception, had to join in with Robert's Marines and take part in close order combat training.

Brownlow looked down on the proceedings with great satisfaction as he saw a disciplined fighting force come into being. He had formulated his plan to take the island. They were now only a few hours from the American coast, and their rendezvous with the other two ships.

"Mr Bray," he shouted down to the weather deck. John checked his stride forward and turned to face the captain. "Have all officers join me for dinner this evening, no exceptions."

Below decks, things were not going so harmoniously. Stubbs, a leading rating, had taken a great dislike to one of the new pressed ratings and was starting to bully him. He had already given the young lad one pasting and was set on giving him another.

At twelve o'clock, Briggs was sitting with his gun team eating their meal from the table slung between the guns. He watched the scowling bully glaring at the younger rating sitting just in front of him, and knew something was about to kick off.

"Have you noticed the bully boy glaring at Johnson again, Briggsy?" Caukwell whispered out of the side of his mouth, as he saw what was going on.

"The lad has to learn to take care of himself, let it ride," Briggs replied, as he looked on.

Stubbs suddenly leapt to his feet and went across to the opposite table. The two ratings sitting alongside Johnson got up and moved out. They didn't want to get in Stubbs's way, lest he should turn his nasty temper on them. As they moved aside, Stubbs struck.

He leant over the rating, bringing his fist down squarely to the side of Johnson's face. The young rating was rocked and slid sideways before recovering slightly and staggering to his feet. He was brave as he put up his fist to defend himself, moving out into the aisle between the diners to face the bigger man.

Stubbs laughed when he saw the stance. Sneering, he brushed aside the smaller man's guard with his left hand and smashed his right fist into his face. Johnson staggered backwards and fell on his backside just behind the table occupied by Briggs and his men. They watched as they saw the dazed man try to rise. Stubbs wasn't going to give him a chance and moved in with his right fist bunched, ready to strike again.

"No you don't Stubbs," Briggs said as he grabbed hold of his wrist as it was hurtling towards its target. This caught the bully off balance, and with a semi pirouette he twisted, turned, and went headlong into the other tables, sending men's meals scattering along the deck. He picked himself up, and with a face reddening with anger, turned to face his new foe.

"Briggs," he sneered as he recognised the culprit who had robbed him of his sport. "You are going to be the sorriest man aboard."

Briggs faced him with his hands up ready to fight. "We'll see about that, Stubbs," he sneered at him. "Let's see how you make out with a man who can handle himself."

Baldwin, one of his gun team came up behind him, pushing a belaying pin into his hand.

"I saw that, Baldwin," Stubbs said angrily. "You'll get yours when I've done here." He turned his attention to Briggs with a sneer. "Can't face me like a man, eh?"

"You've ruined everybody's meals, Stubbs, the sooner I dispatch you, the sooner we can get back to our dinners."

"Hit him with the pin, Briggsy. Show him he does not rule below these decks," another of the ratings called out.

Stubbs might be a bully, but he was not going to lose face, and in spite of the threatening belaying pin in Briggs's hand, he moved forward like a cat, just as George arrived on the scene.

"What's going on here?" he demanded.

On hearing his voice, all the crew immediately sat down, leaving Briggs and Stubbs facing one another. George spotted the pin in Briggs's hand and Johnson, still bruised and battered, on his backside. George immediately grasped the situation.

"If you men have too much energy, I can always arrange further duties for you all. Now, what is going on?"

"Stubbs fell over the table upsetting our meals, sir. You know how clumsy he is, I'm just helping him sort himself out."

"You, Johnson, isn't it? What have you got to say?"

Stubbs looked down at Johnson as he slowly got to his feet, daring him to say something. Briggs also looked at the youth and shook his head.

"I fell, sir," he replied as he saluted.

"Get yourself off to the surgeon, lad. The rest of you get on with your meals." George watched sternly as Stubbs and the men returned to their tables. He looked at Briggs with raised eyebrows as he tried to conceal the pin behind him. "A funny implement to eat your meal with, Mr Briggs," he quipped.

Later that day, the captain sent for George. As he entered the cabin he saw Delaforce, the young surgeon, sitting down opposite Brownlow.

"Come in, Mr Warwick, and sit yerself down," Brownlow invited.

"Good day to you, Surgeon."

"Good day to you, Mr Warwick. It would be a better day if I didn't have extra work because of the crew brawling."

"Mr Delaforce is concerned with having to treat injuries not caused by the general running of the ship, Mr Warwick, and in particular, injuries quite evidently caused by systematic bullying."

"You sent young Johnson to me earlier. His facial injuries were nothing compared to the cracked ribs and bruising he had sustained over several beatings."

George looked at the surgeon and then his captain before answering. "There are always fights below decks, but I think this one is caused by the rating Stubbs. He seems to have set his course against Johnson. Has Johnson made a complaint?"

"No, Mr Warwick, he has not, and I do understand that unless he does, we cannot act. But I have a mind to flog Stubbs for fighting anyway."

George thought for a moment. "I don't see flogging him would do any good, Captain, in fact it would probably make things worse, and set others against the young man. Can you leave this with me for a while? I'll keep them apart until I can sort something out."

***

Later that evening, all the officers dined with their Captain in his cabin. Robert tried to make conversation with George, as did John Bray, but to no avail. George's mind was elsewhere as he just pushed his food around his plate.

"Are you ailing for something, Mr Warwick? I notice you do not touch your meal. I would eat if I was you, tomorrow we may not get the chance."

George got to his feet, pushing his chair out behind him. "If you would excuse me, sir, I have no appetite at present and could do with some air."

"Do you need the attentions of the surgeon?"

"No, sir, just some fresh sea air."

"All right, Mr Warwick, off you go," Brownlow said, excusing him.

George wished his colleagues a good night and left the cabin to make his way along the deck. As he made his way forward, he looked up at the bright starry sky twinkling above the sails and masts. A gentle warm westerly breeze blew through his dark auburn hair as he felt the spray coming up as he neared the prow.

"You are troubled, young warrior." The voice of Wei was at his elbow. As he turned he saw that Wei was not alone. He was accompanied by Liu Mian, his second in command, who was grinning at him.

"You have a problem that is hard to deal with," Lieu Mian stated bluntly. "Why do you not simply cut the man's head off, problem is sorted," he rasped.

"I wish it was that simple," George answered. "I am governed by rules of conduct, and besides, the man in question is a good sailor. I am not allowed to 'cut his head off'," he mimicked.

"Why is it so hard to deal with, young warrior? If the man does not show respect for your authority, why do you not punish him?"

"To punish him without a formal complaint would make matters worse and set the men against the other man, my lord."

"Then why don't you deal with it personally?" Lieu Mian asked.

"Because I am not allowed to fight with the ratings…" George trailed off as he realised they were no longer with him.

"Good evening, sir," John Briggs said as he came forward.

"Briggs," George acknowledged him.

"Begging your pardon, Mr Warwick, but what do you want me to do about Stubbs? He's a bloody idiot and a bully, but he's also a very good sailor."

George thought carefully as he looked at this experienced rating he had come to regard highly, before answering. "Nothing, Briggs, you do nothing. Just keep the two of them apart for now."

"I might have to do something, sir. By interfering and stopping him hitting Johnson again, I think he may now include me in his little spat."

George thought on the words of Wei and Lieu Mian. Why didn't he deal with it personally? The captain wouldn't find out and the crew would remain tight lipped as they always did.

"Tell Stubbs he is to report to me in the orlop, straight away." Briggs looked puzzled and was about to question this last order when George spoke again, "Straightaway, Briggs."

"Aye, aye, sir, straightaway it is."

George made his way down to find Stubbs waiting for him in the semi-darkness, just outside the orlop deck. Although he was nervous, Stubbs still had the smirk of insolence playing on his lips.

"Follow me, Stubbs," George ordered, striding past him to the hold. The Marine on guard at the hold's door sprang to attention, surprised by the sudden visit.

"You can stand guard at the top of the stairs," George told him, but the Marine never moved. "Did you hear me, man? I said at the top of the stairs."

"I'm sorry, sir, I can't do that. My orders are not to move from my post," he stated stubbornly.

George went forward placing his face directly in front of the guard. "I am giving you a direct order, you can fulfil your duties at the top of the stairs, now blasted well move," he shouted into his face.

The Marine jumped with the venom being spat at him. He knew that George was a good friend of his commanding officer, so he turned smartly and made for the stairs. As he watched him go, Stubbs became more nervous as to what was going on.

"In you go, Stubbs," George ordered, as he opened the door to the hold and pushed him in front of him.

Stubbs watched the officer as he started to undo his tunic with realisation starting to dawn on his face.

"Are you going to fight me, sir?" he asked, frowning, not believing his eyes. "I'll be flogged at the very least. The captain could hang me for striking an officer."

"Strip your shirt, Stubbs. There'll be no repercussions for you over this. It is about time you learnt a few lessons and respect for your betters."

Stubbs began to pull his shirt over his head and then just stood against the side of the hold. "You say that now, sir, but what about after? After I give you a beating?"

At that moment, having brushed past the guard at the top of the stairs, Briggs appeared at the doorway to the hold.

"Ah, Briggs, you are just in time to witness this. I have agreed to fight Stubbs and I absolve him of any blame for what follows. Is that clear?"

"Are you sure, sir? He's a dirty fighter, why not let me fight him?"

"Belay that, Briggs. Does that suit you, Stubbs, your very own witness?"

Stubbs sneered at Briggs, grinned as he dropped his shirt to the floor, and flexed the muscles on his tattooed biceps. George removed his shirt to reveal his own lean but well-muscled body. His opponent, for the first time, looked on with some concern, surprised by his apparent toughness. He became even more nervous as he saw George tie his trademark gold-coloured scarf around his head. He was now ready to fight.

"I understand you fight dirty, Stubbs. Well that's all right, no holds barred."

George thought back to the days he'd scrapped with Black Tom. Hard fights, fights at first he had lost, fights he gradually turned the tide on, fights in which he came out on top in the end. He also remembered the tricks his own father had taught him to counter the treachery of Lord Crowe's son, when he had killed him in a duel. Stubbs looked at the scarf on George's head and thought he saw it changing colour. He most certainly didn't like the way things were turning out.

"What are you waiting for, Stubbs?" George said, as he noticed his hesitancy in coming forward. He shot a straight left jab viciously into Stubbs's face, catching him on the bridge of his nose. Before Stubbs could blink, two more rapid right hands hit him as his eyes began to stream with water. Stubbs stumbled backwards, only to be suddenly pushed forward again by Briggs standing in the doorway.

"You asked for it," Stubbs growled as he spat out the blood from his mouth. "Now you're going to get it."

He launched himself forward, swinging with both fists. George parried the first blow but was caught by a left fist high up on his forehead, which sent him back against the side woodwork. Stubbs was fast and strong as he sprang forward with further blows to George's head, who managed to slip the further punches as he sidestepped quickly past Stubbs, snaking out jab after jab into his rib cage. As Stubbs turned, slightly off balance, George hit him with two hard right crosses to the head. Stubbs's first reaction was to raise his arms to protect his head from further damaging blows. George switched to the man's unprotected midriff and piled punch after punch into his ribcage. Stubbs couldn't take the pain as his hands gradually fell away to protect his ribs, with his knees automatically coming up to protect his middle.

The cockiness with which he had started the fight was now slowly disappearing, as Stubbs realised he was going to get a beating. A certain wildness now lit up his eyes as desperation set in. Two more heavy punches to his head sent him reeling backwards. Using the side of the hold to get momentum, he hurled himself at George with his arms wide open in a typical brawler's move.

Having seen the desperation in his eyes, George had half expected such a move, but could do nothing against the brute force hurled against him. He could do nothing but hang on to Stubbs's hair as he was thrown back against the wall with most of the wind being knocked out of him. If Stubbs had let go and moved back at that point, George would have been in serious trouble, but Stubbs hung on desperately, clutching him for dear life.

George got his breath back and recovered as he brought both of his fists down on the exposed neck, causing Stubbs to sink to his knees.

"I think we agreed no rules, Stubbs," George said as he brought his knee up under his jaw, snapping his head back. Stubbs involuntarily released him as he shot upwards with the force. George measured him for the final punch, bringing a vicious right cross over, smashing into his jaw. Stubbs's eyes glazed over as he sank to his backside, before rolling over on his side and lying still.

George realised he was no longer alone as cheers went up from Briggs and other crew members who had got wind of the fight and made their way down the stairs. Robert was standing with his Marine guard, grinning from ear to ear before he turned his attention to the crew present.

"Get back about your duties before I have the lot of you flogged," Robert shouted as he winked at George.

All the crew, with the exception of Briggs, scampered up the stairs to the deck above. Briggs came forward with George's shirt and tunic.

"Bravo, Mr Warwick, sir, let me help you on with your tunic. It was a real pleasure to see such a lesson handed out to a bully. I'll deal with Stubbs and make sure he gets to his hammock."

"Thank you, Briggs, but you had better get him to the Surgeon first, we can't be too careful, can we?"

"Aye, aye, sir," he replied.

Robert came over to George and shook his hand. "Well done, George, let's get back up top."

They failed to notice the two grinning faces of Wei and Liu Mian, standing in the gloom at the back of the hold.

The next morning, as they weighed anchor just off of New York harbour, George was summoned to the captain's cabin where he found an irate surgeon remonstrating with Brownlow.

"Do I understand that our bullying problem is no more, Mr Warwick?" Brownlow enquired sarcastically.

Before he could answer his captain, Delaforce jumped in. "And caused me a lot more work. I thought Stubbs had been keel hauled, he is in a right state."

"Come. Come now, Mr Delaforce, you know full well that keel hauling has been outlawed in today's Navy. Can you leave us now? I wish to talk to Mr Warwick alone."

Brownlow watched Delaforce leave the cabin, and waited for him to close the door before turning his attention back to George, who was still standing in front of his desk, looking down sheepishly at his feet.

"What the blasted hell do you think you were doing, man? What if you had lost, what then?"

George looked over the head of the seated Brownlow as he considered his answer. "You couldn't punish the man without proof, we couldn't stop his bullying without punishment, we seemed to be going around and around without a rudder, sir."

"I'll ask you again, Mr Warwick. What would have happened if you had lost? You would have lost all credibility, becoming absolutely useless to me and the command of this ship."

George knew that his captain had a very valid point. He had taken a great risk to solve this problem. He looked down at Brownlow and held his gaze.

"I go into battle without question and without any regard to my own safety, sir. I take calculated risks and weigh them up against the odds. Stubbs had become such a problem below decks that it was worth the risk. Besides, I knew I had the makings of him."

George watched as Brownlow rose slowly to his feet, not taking his eyes off of him for an instant. He feared the worst.

"I will let it go this time, Mr Warwick, but if I ever catch you brawling with the men again, I'll have your commission. Is that understood?"

"Perfectly, sir," George said as he swallowed hard, knowing he was to get away with it.

"We will be rendezvousing with the other two ships, hopefully sometime today. We'll lie off New York and wait for them. When they do turn up, I want their captains and first officers to join us in the *Broad*. See to it, George, if you please."

George smiled as he heard the rarity of his Christian name being used by his captain, and nodded sternly as he left the cabin.

Three hours later, a ship of the line came into view, escorted by a frigate off its port bow. George and Robert eyed them through their telescopes from the weather deck, trying to make out their names.

"It's the *Bathsheba* with the frigate *Hecla*," John Bray called out from his position by the wheel. You had better signal them to come over as soon as they anchor, George."

George felt uneasy as he watched the ships heading towards them. *HMS Bathsheba* was a third-rate ship of the line with immense gun power. She had been captured from the French at the Battle of Trafalgar and was armed with thirty-two pounder cannons positioned on the lower deck and eighteen pounders on the upper deck bolstered by nine pounders on the top deck, making it more formidable than most armies. He should be pleased to see it, but there was something nagging at him. Was it because it was French and Trafalgar was still raw in his mind?

A further hour passed as they watched the two ships draw in all sail and drop anchors off their starboard bow. Longboats started to pull towards them as their respective officers came over to the *Broad*. As they were piped aboard by Briggs, Brownlow and John Bray went forward to meet them.

The senior captain from the Bathsheba stepped forward, saluted, and held out his hand. "Hello, Abraham." He beamed as he introduced the other captain. "May I present Captain Johnson, of His Majesty's ship, *Hecla*."

"Welcome aboard, Howard. I have already had the pleasure of meeting Captain Johnson, off Cadiz, wasn't it?" he smiled as he took Johnson's hand.

"It was in ninety-eight, Captain, when you led us under their shore batteries and gave them a pasting."

George looked at Robert and winked. "Bloody mutual admiration society," he whispered as Brownlow called him forward.

As George saluted Captain Howard Blake, he got a sensation of the scarf inside his jacket getting warmer and starting to throb.

"Is there something wrong, Lieutenant Warwick?" Blake asked, picking up on George's sudden change of stance.

George recovered quickly and smiled. "No, sir, just a small attack of indigestion. I apologise, Captain."

Brownlow quickly ushered all the officers to his cabin in order to plan their attack on Narranga. As they were seated around the captain's table, Howard Blake dropped a keg of gunpowder on the meeting.

"Admiral Lord Crowe sends his best wishes, Captain, and to you, Lieutenant Warwick."

Brownlow remained stony-faced and didn't react in the slightest. George put his hand under his jacket and felt the vibrating scarf as he shot a quick glance at the open-mouthed and disbelieving Robert.

"I trust you left his lordship in good health, Captain?" Brownlow enquired, with a lot more formality than he had greeted him with earlier.

"He is well, Abraham, but alas, he does not have very good sea legs and he is lying in his cot."

"He's here, aboard the *Bathsheba*?" Brownlow asked incredulously, as he looked at George and Robert. "But the *Bathsheba's* a third rater, I would have thought his rank would have taken him to a first-rate ship of the line."

"Yes, he's aboard. I think he has come along for the ride, but he is not to involve himself in the assault on Narranga. The Admiralty has made it quite clear that you are in charge of the whole operation."

"Well I hope he understands that and sticks to it," Brownlow said quietly but firmly. "Now let's get on with our planning. We will provision all ships over the next two days. Any further provisions will be taken in Narranga, gentlemen."

"What about shore leave for the crews, Abraham?" Blake asked. "Can they go ashore whilst we provision?"

"Small parties at a time from each ship; all hands will be accompanied by officers and returned to their ships before the next parties go ashore. I don't want to be short of men when we sail."

Back on deck, George noticed Briggs scowling at the back of Captain Johnson as he entered the longboat. George had never marked him to be a malicious man, so he watched as they pulled away from the *Broad* before his curiosity eventually got the better of him.

"History, Briggs?" he asked.

"Something like that, Mr Warwick," Briggs replied.

"Well tell me, man, or do I drag it out of you?"

"He's known as 'flogger Johnson' for his free use of the cat, sir. The slightest reason and he'd have the skin off your back."

"That's enough of that, Briggs; we don't want that sort of talk here."

"You did insist, sir, I wouldn't normally say anything, but according to a couple of the ratings who rowed him over, the *Hecla* is very near mutiny."

"About your business, Briggs, this instant," Robert ordered, as he heard him. Briggs moved away down the deck as Robert turned to George. "What do you think?"

"What can we do, even if it's true? He's master and commander of his ship, almost akin to God. Let's sort out who is going ashore and get these provisions organised. In any case, I'm more concerned about Crowe being here."

NINETEEN

George and Bertie Bowden went with the first shore party with Robert following in another longboat accompanied by a squad of Marines. The three longboats pulled up alongside the wooden jetty as the men scrambled ashore. Briggs and his gun crew were in the front party as they made their way towards the taverns of New York. George was surprised to see a heavily bandaged Stubbs amongst them.

Robert left his Marines in the charge of a sergeant and joined George, who was standing on the jetty watching the back of Stubbs heading for the town.

"I'm surprised to see he can make it after the beating you gave him," Robert quipped.

"He's a pretty hardy character, that's for sure," George answered with a wry smile.

"Let's have a look around before we have a drink, George, I haven't seen this place properly for a good few years."

"Fine by me, let's walk awhile." Looking at his friend, George knew he was thinking of his parents. He immediately thought of his own parents, automatically touching the scarf around his neck.

They walked for about an hour, taking in the sights of the growing town before turning back the way they had come.

"I wonder what tavern the men are in," George wondered out loud.

"I think most of the men are in there." Robert laughed as they heard the riotous noises coming from a building by the quayside.

"And in good spirits by the sound of it." George grinned. "Let's see what they are up to."

Stubbs was standing on a table holding court, singing out loud some of the sailors' ditties which did the rounds of the taverns in most ports. He seemed unaffected by his injuries and appeared in high spirits. George spotted Briggs and his men sitting in a corner of the room, cracking jokes between themselves. Briggs noticed the arrival of George and Robert and raised his tankard to them. His men turned and did the same.

George heard the men on Stubbs's table mutter to themselves. "It's Scarf," he heard one say to another. Stubbs stopped dancing and looked to see what had gained his men's attention. He spotted George, and drunkenly got off the table, almost falling over in his haste to get down. He stood to attention and saluted.

"Is everything all right, sir?" he queried without any rancour.

"Carry on, Stubbs, everything is fine," George replied.

They sat down next to Briggs. "Enjoying your shore leave?" George asked.

"Aye, sir, very welcome it is." Briggs raised his tankard again. "You might want to keep an eye on the table in the far corner, over there, sir."

"What's the problem?" Robert asked.

"A few of the locals have been buying some of the men from the *Hecla* drinks, and trying to get them to stay, sir." Briggs looked around the table. "None of our men or the men from the *Bathsheba* are involved, but the crew from the *Hecla* seem to be listening far too closely." Briggs hesitated, and seemed to want to say a whole lot more.

"What is it? You can talk freely with me, and Captain Gates," George assured him.

"I know I can, sir, you are one of the better officers." He looked at George and Robert in turn, and continued. "It seems that Captain Johnson is far too liberal with flogging his men. He even flogs the last man down from the main mast, just because he's last, whether he has committed an offence or not."

They looked over to where the locals were holding court before George answered. "I think we had better get word to

Captain Johnson and tell him to get his men back on board. We need every man for the task that lies before us in Naranga. We can do without any mutiny here." George looked at Stubbs, wondering if he was going to get any trouble from him.

"Right, Briggs, get all our party together and make for the boats, shore leave is up."

Although disappointed, the men knew they had to leave, and most quickly downed the last of their ale, before making for the door. George went over to Stubbs and spoke to him.

"Get you men together, Stubbs, and head for the boats. Shore time is up."

He stood up with tankard in hand, downed the contents in one, gulped, and then belched. "Aye, aye, sir, straightaway, sir, come on you lot, you heard what Mr Warwick said." Every man stood up, moved out from behind the table, and headed silently towards the door.

The crew from the *Bathsheba*, realising what was going on, and not wanting to get involved in any mutiny, also joined them in their exodus.

Robert turned to George, smiling in disbelief and relief. "Bloody hell, what happened there? I thought we were going to have to take them by force."

George just smiled as they made for the door, and went to where the longboats were moored. As they got on board the *Broad*, they reported what they had seen, and heard ashore.

"Have you sent word to Captain Johnson, Mr Warwick?" Brownlow asked.

"No, sir, I thought I had better report to you first," George replied.

"Send a boat over to the *Hecla*. You had better go yourself, Mr Warwick," Brownlow ordered.

Thirty minutes later, George climbed the rope ladder up the waist of *Hecla's* port side, and reported to Captain Johnson. He told him what he had seen, and heard ashore, and that some of his men were in danger of absconding. Johnson, appearing the worse for drink, was livid, his face turning a scarlet colour.

"Mutiny, mutiny, I'll have none of it, sir, I will hang each dog meself!" he screamed into George's face.

George picked up on the man's breath, confirming he was drunk as his eyes were almost popping out of his head. Johnson called for his own officers. A Lieutenant Masters came running to the cabin, alerted by the Marine on guard outside the captain's door.

"Yes, sir, what is it?" Masters asked, as he reported.

"What is it, sir, what is it indeed? It's blasted mutiny, that's what it is, Mr Masters. Your bloody men are mutinying. I have told you time and time again that your lack of resolve for disciplining the men would lead to this sort of thing happening." Johnson moved right up to his officer's face, and was about to strike him, when George moved between them.

"With your permission, Captain, I would like to accompany Mr Masters ashore," he said.

"At least something may get done from a competent officer," Johnson fumed.

George ushered Masters out of the cabin into the fresh, early evening air. "I'm sorry about that, Mr Masters. It wasn't my intention to supersede you in your captain's eyes, rather to diffuse the situation."

"Thank you, Mr... I didn't get your name." Masters looked into George's eyes.

"Warwick, George Warwick. He didn't introduce us, did he?"

"I think my captain is a little worse for wear, as per usual. How do you do, George, please call me Harry." Masters smiled, showing good, even white teeth. He was about twenty-five years of age, slightly built, with a mop of dark hair parted on the right side. He seemed a pleasant and competent officer.

"I wish to signal the *Broad*, Harry. I think we could do with a detachment of our Marines to accompany us ashore."

"What message do you want sending, George?" Masters asked.

"Captain Gates and a detachment of Marines are requested to join me ashore." He turned to watch Masters move away and instruct the signal to be sent.

Thirty minutes later, they pulled alongside the longboat from the *Broad*, with a detachment of Marines headed by Robert Gates. George looked across at his best friend, who was eyeing him questioningly.

"I'll explain when we get ashore," George shouted.

The tide had gone out when they arrived at the port, so they had to scale ladders to reach the pier above. Once up on dry land, George went to Robert, who smiled as he saw him.

"The old man is not too happy about this, George. He says it's Johnson's problem, not ours."

"I disagree, Robert, we need all the men we can get for Naranga, and I mean everyone. We just don't know the strength of the French on the island."

"How are you going to handle this, George?" Robert asked.

"This is Lieutenant Masters, they are his men, and I suggest he goes in first with his party to see if he can talk his men in to coming back peacefully. If not, we will go in with your Marines."

"Thanks for your help, Captain." Masters stretched his hand out, and shook Robert's hand warmly.

"Right, let's get on with it," Robert said, almost impatiently.

They reached the noisy tavern, with Robert and his Marines setting up a perimeter around the building. George was standing at the entrance, observing Masters and his men as they entered the tavern. He watched apprehensively as they approached the party in the corner. Masters was standing talking to them, but instead of complying they just shook their heads. Masters grabbed hold of the man seated at the near end of the table, pulling him from his seat. The others got up immediately and started to shout abuse at him, before one of the locals came up behind him, striking him over the head from behind. George rushed forward as Masters slumped to the tavern's floor. A full-blown riot broke out, with the locals and the crew of the *Hecla* battling the crew sent to get them. George pulled a local off one of the men, who promptly swung a punch at him. George hit him with a right uppercut, knocking him senseless, and then moved forward for the next. Robert came charging in with his Marines, and the fighting came to a halt.

"We are not going back," said one of the seamen, standing in front of his shipmates. "We've been flogged enough for no good reason. Johnson is a tyrant and should be removed from command."

George went in front of the man, looking down at him. "You are committing an act of mutiny, man, you could hang, you silly sod, alongside all of your shipmates here present."

"You might be a good officer, sir, we have heard of you, Scarf they call you." The man went on, "But we can't take any more of Johnson's arbitrary punishments." He tore his shirt off his back to reveal fresh wounds of a flogging. George thought it must be at least four dozen lashes to make such a mess. "This is what I got for being last down from the mainmast. The farthest to go, I was always going to be last. I was expected to carry out my duties whilst he sneered and called me a landlubber. I might have been pressed for this voyage, but I am an experienced seaman, with over fifteen years' service in decent ships."

More locals were piling into the tavern, having heard what was going on, and these men were armed.

George looked around the tavern, quickly realising this could be a very explosive situation. He faced the men again. "You are now committing acts of mutiny. Those who wish to return peacefully, stand to one side with the captain of Marines."

All but three sullenly and reluctantly, moved away from the table to join the Marines, now standing behind Robert.

"Captain Gates, take these men away to the boats and await my arrival."

"Are you bloody daft, George? I can't leave you here with this rabble." Robert was mystified as to what he was going to do.

"Be so good as to do my bidding, Captain Gates, now." George turned to face him, daring him not to comply.

"Sergeant, get these men and your squad to the boats," Robert ordered. "I'll join you in a little while. Pick up Lieutenant Masters before you go."

"Yes, sir." the reply was swift. The sergeant was more than happy to get away from this hostile crowd of civilians. He had two of his Marines pick up the still unconscious form of Masters.

As they left, George looked at the three they had left behind. He was being barracked by the locals, who were starting to push and shove him. He felt the scarf below his tunic start to throb, and knew he was in some considerable danger.

"What's it to be, men?" George asked, looking the men square in the eyes.

"I am sorry, sir, but we do not intend to go back. Johnson will flog us until we are dead." He looked pleadingly at George. "We have no wish to see you harmed, sir, but we three are pressed men who didn't want to be on board in the first place."

The locals were still jostling and pushing when a shot was fired into the ceiling of the tavern.

"No violence towards this officer," the leader of the mutineers shouted out to the locals. "Not all men in the Navy are bad. I have heard from members of his crew. He is a fair and decent, officer."

Robert came pushing through the locals. "Make way, make way, or I'll bring the Marines back."

The locals heard his accent, with one man shouting out. "Where are you from then? You sound like a renegade to me."

"I choose my path in life, as you do," Robert quipped in reply.

"If that's the case, let these three choose their own path," the man shouted back at him.

"We're not going back, sir, no matter what." The three of them were standing stoically side by side.

"All right," George said. "You are pressed men, and didn't enlist voluntarily so, in the circumstances, I am going to withdraw. Captain Gates, come with me, if you please." George watched the three men smile with relief. The leader put out his hand to George. Ignoring the hand, George looked directly into the man's eyes.

"Don't... push... your... luck," he rasped, turning on his heel and leaving with Robert.

After discussing the situation, they both decided to travel straight back to the *Broad*, rather than drop the *Hecla's* crew off at their ship. They would explain everything to Brownlow and leave any decisions to him. Once on board, they made their way to Captain Brownlow's cabin with a now conscious Lieutenant Masters.

Brownlow was not happy and expressed his displeasure at their course of action in no uncertain terms.

"I don't know what you expect me to do, Warwick. I cannot simply involve myself in another command's business; it is for Captain Johnson to deal with. You must return them all to their ship."

"Would you at least hear Lieutenant Masters out, sir?" George pleaded. "All his men are scared to death about going back to the *Hecla*. They say their captain is nothing more than a drunken tyrant who flogs them for no reason."

"Mr Warwick, I will tell you just once more. Return the crew to the *Hecla*, or I will have you and Captain Gates clapped in irons immediately. Do I make myself clear?"

"Yes… sir." George saluted, turned, faced Masters, and simply shrugged his shoulders before leading the three of them out and back to the boat.

The disgruntled crew of the *Hecla* had to be forced over the side before being rowed back to their own ship in complete silence. After unloading them, George immediately turned the boat around and headed back to the *Broad*. He did not trust himself to go on board and face Captain Johnson, lest he lose his temper and do something stupid.

***

Back on *HMS Bathsheba,* Lord Crowe and his trusted henchmen were listening intently to the story of one of the crew who had been inside the tavern with Stubbs and his men. One of the *Broad*'s crew had got very drunk and had been telling him in hushed tones about George's fight with Stubbs.

"Are you sure it wasn't just bar room gossip? Did anyone else hear about the beating given to a rating by Lieutenant Warwick?"

"I'm sure it wasn't just gossip, my lord, the man called Stubbs looked as if he had been keel hauled. He was in one hell of a state, begging you pardon, my lord."

Crowe looked at the rating in front of him and gave him one of his most twisted smiles. "You've done well to bring this to my attention. Say nothing to anybody else. Do you understand? Say nothing. You may have extra grog for a week. Now go."

Crowe turned to his aide, Lieutenant Carter, with triumph written all over his cruel malicious face. "We have him, Carter, at last we have him. Striking and brawling with a rating, as well as allowing three crew members from the *Hecla* to abscond. I think we can call that incitement to mutiny, don't you?"

"Indeed we can, my lord. Do you want me to arrest him?"

"No, not yet. Brownlow will fight me tooth and nail, and at the moment he commands. No, we will wait until we are back in England, or better still, until we are on Narranga. We will seize our opportunity there."

TWENTY

They observed the longboats ferrying the officers from the *Hecla* and *Bathsheba* to the *Broad*. George wasn't the only one to be disappointed at seeing Crowe in the lead boat, sitting alongside Captain Blake. He glanced across at Brownlow who was watching the scene intently with his teeth gritted behind pursed lips.

"Pipe them aboard, Mr Warwick, and then show his lordship to my quarters," Brownlow said sternly, before turning on his heel and striding off. For whatever reason, Brownlow was angry.

George and Robert watched the back of their bow-legged captain disappear below with some concern.

"He's none too happy about Crowe being here, is he?"

"Neither am I, Robert. At least his orders are to stay out of our taking Narranga."

They moved amidships, joining John Bray in the party to receive the officers on deck. Briggs stood by, ready to pipe the officers aboard.

George and Robert held their breath and looked straight ahead as the pipe sounded and Crowe's sharp twisted face appeared as he made the deck. They all saluted and George stepped forward.

"I am to escort you to the captain's quarters, my lord, please come this way."

Crowe smiled maliciously at George as he followed him, whilst the other officers were being piped aboard. As Captain Johnson arrived, Briggs immediately ceased his playing.

"Good day to you, my lord," Brownlow said flatly, without any hint of a warm welcome as he entered his cabin.

Crowe returned the salute, smirking rather than smiling, as he held out his bony hand. "Good day to you, Brownlow," he replied, withdrawing his hand as Brownlow turned away and went behind his desk.

Crowe didn't wait to be asked to sit as he sat down opposite the grim-faced commander. After Brownlow's slight, all pretence of cordiality was now dropped as he almost snarled at him, with some venom. "I have no intention of interfering with your operation in taking Narranga, but you would do well to show some courtesy to my rank," he said.

"You have been piped aboard, you have been shown to my quarters, and I have saluted your rank. I have fulfilled all protocols, my lord. You will receive nothing less, and nothing more."

"Well, we all know where your colours are nailed, don't we, Brownlow?"

Before he could answer, there was a knock at the door and the officers from the other ships were shown in. Brownlow greeted them all by saluting and making a point of shaking all their hands. As Captain Johnson stepped forward, Brownlow became aware of a glaze in his eyes and the smell of alcohol on his breath.

"Please be seated, gentlemen," Brownlow offered, looking relieved as Johnson made it to a chair and slumped down in it. "The sooner we prepare our plans, the sooner we can get underway. Lord Crowe is here as an observer only and will not participate in any of these proceedings," he said, noticing with satisfaction that Crowe was biting into his bottom lip.

They pored over the chart laid out on Brownlow's desk as they discussed their plan of attack to take and hold the island of Narranga. Two hundred Marines were to take part, together with four hundred able bodied seamen taken from all three ships. They were going to approach the island from the north as before, and drop off the invading force before the three ships headed for the Port of Lobo which housed the island's garrison. At precisely five o'clock in the morning, the ships would commence their bombardment of the garrison and breach its walls. The attacking land force had to be in place ready to attack the moment the bombardment finished.

"Captain Gates will be in overall charge of all land forces, with Lieutenants Bray and Warwick as his seconds in command should anything go wrong."

Captain Blake coughed. Brownlow looked up, nodding to him in acknowledgement and giving him permission to speak.

"I have two senior lieutenants in my command…"

Brownlow held up his hand, having already anticipated the objection. "I am aware of the seniority, Captain, but both my officers are well rehearsed in taking the island, having done so before."

Blake thought for a moment as they all looked at him for his response. He smiled congenially at Brownlow before holding up his hands to defer back to him. "You are quite right, Abraham, it would be folly to have it any other way. Please accept my apologies."

Crowe cringed in the corner: he had been hoping for some disagreement allowing him to jump in and take over. Grinding his teeth, he resigned himself to what was being decided.

***

Four days after leaving New York, the three British ships anchored in the clear calm turquoise sea off the northern coast of Naranga, exactly as they had done some months before. They scanned the north of the island, noticing it was still unmanned and deserted.

"You would have thought the French would have learned some valuable lesson from our last visit, wouldn't you?"

"I don't think they have the manpower anymore, Robert. Napoleon is more interested in taking the whole of Europe. He sees these island colonies as a distraction and a waste of resources. Look at Hispaniola, he let that go."

"Let's hope so, me old shipmate, let's hope so," Robert replied absentmindedly, mimicking the accent of one of the Cornish ratings.

George turned to see the crew and Marines lowering the longboats into the warm calm waters of the Caribbean under the direction of John Bray. He noticed Bertie Bowden's peeved attitude toward his fellow midshipman Grahame Johns. Johns was going ashore whilst he, and the other midshipmen, had to remain on board to assist the captain in the running of the ship.

"Mr Bowden, get those men moving, we want to be on the island today, not next week," John Bray shouted as Bertie urged the men on.

"Don't worry, Bertie, you'll see your share of action when you fire on the walls of the garrison. It won't be any picnic when they start firing back at you," George said by way of compensation and encouragement.

Bertie forced a smile as he turned to speak to him. "Yes, sir, I know, but it would have been nice to go ashore with you and Captain Gates."

Two hours later, after the longboats had finished disembarking the men on the shore, they mustered and prepared to move inland. The beach was crowded with over six hundred seamen, including the scarlet jackets of Robert's Marines. Scouting parties had been sent forward to ensure that they weren't surprised by any enemy forces; it was now time to move inland and join them. All of the land force was to rendezvous at the same hill overlooking the port of Lobo as they had done all those months before.

George, standing by Robert's side, gave the order to move forward into the jungle. Briggs had somehow wangled his way through the hordes of seamen, closely followed by Stubbs. They moved forward together, settling in just behind the two leaders. They didn't go unnoticed by the two commanders in front, who just grinned at one another at this new sign of comradeship between these two men.

"Looks as if a firm friendship has developed," Robert said quietly to George, who just smiled back in acknowledgement.

The whole force needed to be in place before dawn when the three ships would start their bombardment of the garrison. They had underestimated the time it would take to move such a force through the jungle. As Robert began to notice just how stretched out the column had become, he became increasingly anxious that they might not make the garrison on time. As he looked behind him, George picked up on his anxiety

"I'll drop back and push them to get a move on. You force the pace on from upfront, Robert."

"All right, George, I don't want them too strung out, or we won't be able to muster in time to fight as a unit."

"Briggs, Stubbs, with me," George ordered. "Make sure that all men know the urgency and that they are to keep up."

He couldn't believe just how strung out the column had become as the three of them urged the men on to almost a running pace. Stubbs and Briggs were invaluable as they encouraged the men forward or booted those that didn't react quickly enough. Robert reached the hilltop with his vanguard of Marines and watched anxiously as the rest of his forces gradually joined him. The sky in the east was getting lighter, throwing a greenish blue haze across the horizon, dawn was not far off. Eventually, looking very exhausted, the last of the stragglers arrived. Robert watched anxiously as they sank to the ground to rest.

"No time to rest, men, we move forward to the town before our ships start their bombardment," Robert shouted. "All officers get your men in order."

The moans were evident as the men struggled to their feet, lifting their backpacks once more onto their shoulders. George moved through them and joined Robert, with Briggs and Stubbs close behind.

"That's the lot," George reported.

"Well done, we should be able to make it if we move now. At least it's all downhill from here."

They moved forward at pace, constantly looking at the eastern sky as it became lighter and lighter. Robert was relieved when the town of Lobo came into sight. He immediately started to dispose the men for attack. He cursed quietly to himself as he heard the bombardment commence.

***

As the sun came up over the horizon, the three British ships of war sailed majestically into the bay housing the port of Lobo. Silhouetted against the bright sky at their backs, they sailed straight for the leeward side of the garrison. They began their turn along the face of the walls before the enemy realised their presence in the harbour. Ship of the line, *HMS Bathsheba* under Blake's command, was the first in line, closely tailed by the *Broad* and *Hecla* in close support.

Captain Blake eyed the fort's walls through his telescope. They were so close he felt he could touch the big guns on the ramparts. He couldn't believe that they had arrived unnoticed by the defenders.

"Let's wake the buggers up," he shouted. "Fire!" he screamed. The *Bathsheba* shook violently as she opened up with all her starboard guns. Sixteen thirty-two pounders on the lower deck, with fifteen eighteen pounders on the upper, together with the nine pounders on the top deck, sent a hail of iron against the walls of granite, without a single shot being returned from the fort.

In the *Broad*, Brownlow watched through his telescope as the shots hit home. Iron was taking its toll against granite as he saw the top walls of the fort crumble and fall away. It was now the *Broad's* turn to make her run, but by now the garrison had awoken and was recovering a little from the shock. Cannon balls started to fall around the ship, sending spurts of water high above the deck. Brownlow, now standing by the wheel, was caught by flying splinters as a cannon ball smashed into the woodwork around him. He went down in a bloodied heap with two others who had been standing by his side. By some miracle, the helmsman was unharmed, and gripped the wheel with all his might as he looked on in horror at the bloodied people around him. On the quarterdeck, Bertie Bowden searched for John Bray to take command. He was nowhere to be seen. Bertie panicked: he had to take command.

"Fire!" the diminutive midshipman shouted out at the top of his voice.

All the guns on the starboard side fired on his command as he rushed aft to the side of his fallen commander. He reached Brownlow, who was now managing to sit up, but he was in a bad way.

"Take command, Mr Bowden," Brownlow said calmly through bloodied lips. "Just follow *Bathsheba*, do what she does."

"Get the captain below," Bertie ordered as two Marines appeared. "Hard to larboard!" he screamed at the helmsman, who was relieved to have someone to tell him what to do.

The *Hecla* followed, firing all its guns at the now disintegrating walls of the garrison. The firing had been so effective it had nullified any reply from the enemy's walls. All three ships tacked to larboard and travelled back the way they had come, now firing all their larboard guns into the stricken garrison. Their job done, they ceased firing. It was now down to the land force to secure the fort.

***

As the bombardment from the sea ceased, Robert ordered his forces to move through the town and on to the garrison. They met little resistance until they reached the outer perimeter of the fort.

They ran forward, urged on by George as a hail of musket fire came from the ramparts guarding the gates. George couldn't believe that the French had failed to close and secure them. "Down!" he screamed as he saw two grenades bounce a few yards ahead of them and start to roll their way. They exploded with a deafening roar, sending out shrapnel and throwing up dirt. George felt the heat pass over him but he was untouched by any fallout. He sprang to his feet, shouting to those that lay on the ground, "On your feet, men, up and at them."

The uninjured Marines reacted instantly and charged forward into the wide-open fort. They were covered by the seamen who fired up at the defenders. Casualties were left behind where they fell as they pressed home their attack, storming through the gates and into the garrison. The light resistance of the defenders was brushed aside as the French were cut down as they appeared.

George was joined by Robert as they looked around at the devastation caused by their ships. There wasn't a wall that hadn't been breached by their deadly force. If an army had been firing cannon at the walls all day, they wouldn't have caused as much damage as they had done.

"Iron against granite," George murmured to himself.

"No contest," Robert replied, overhearing him.

White flags were appearing from windows and doors as the occupants came out slowly and nervously with their hands in the air, uncertain as to their fate.

A French officer stepped forward to meet Robert with his hands in the air. He stopped, drew his sword from his scabbard, and handed it to him without saying a word.

"I accept your surrender," Robert said, taking the sword. "Please ensure all your men and the townspeople do exactly what they are told. If they do, they have nothing to fear from us. Do you understand?"

The officer looked at George with his gold-coloured scarf around his head and addressed Robert. "You are in charge, yes?" he asked nervously.

"I am Captain Gates of His Majesty's Royal Marines, and I am in charge of the land forces, yes."

"You will rein in *Le Scarf*?" he said, still looking at George with notable apprehension.

Robert looked at George and grinned. "You have nothing to fear from Lieutenant Warwick, if you behave," he replied. "Now take me to the command office."

Within an hour, the British forces had rounded up all the French and contained them in the square whilst securing the whole town, and the surrounding area. The Union Jack was hoisted above the rubble that had once been the strong granite walls of the fort.

The three British warships were now anchored in the harbour after taking in their sail. Surgeon Delaforce attended to Captain Brownlow, whose wounds were mainly superficial, but confined him to his cot. John Bray had been located unconscious below decks. He had been hit with timber dislodged by the same cannon fire that had injured Brownlow, but was now recovered and in charge of the *Broad*.

Aboard the *Bathsheba*, Lord Crowe was having a private meeting with his own men without the knowledge of Captain Blake.

"We must keep Warwick and Gates ashore. I will speak to Captain Blake and ensure he is aware of the importance of securing the island with the present land force. Brownlow is laid up, the time to strike is now," Crowe said as his cruel twisted mouth moved behind thin pursed lips. "You, Lieutenant Carter, will go ashore with hand-picked men that we can rely on and trust. You will arrest Warwick and Gates and then signal me when you have done so. I intend to hang them for assisting those mutineers to escape, and for beating a rating almost to death."

Whilst Brownlow was indisposed and with John Bray taking command of the *Broad*, it was down to Captain Blake, as the senior captain, to assume command of all forces; he was completely unaware he was being manipulated by Lord Crowe and gave orders for the land forces to stay in position.

Crowe, watching from the top deck with great satisfaction, saw his team enter the longboat and row ashore. Their orders, as far as Captain Blake was concerned, were to inform Robert Gates to retain all forces in holding positions on the island, but nothing could have been further from their minds and intentions.

George and Robert were interrogating the French officer they had captured, in his own office, when they heard the commotion outside. They were all surprised as Briggs burst through the door.

"What on earth is it, Briggs?" George asked, alarmed and thinking they were under some sort of counter attack. He became aware of his scarf around his neck slowly pulsating, warning him of further impending danger.

"Lieutenant Carter is outside demanding we step aside, sir. He has an armed party and says he must see you immediately."

"Well, let him in, man, what's your problem?" George asked.

Before Briggs could answer, Lieutenant Carter, accompanied by twelve fully armed crew members from The *Bathsheba*, forced his way through the door and pushed him aside.

Robert went forward between George and Carter and stood defiantly in front of him. "What are you up to, Lieutenant, what is the meaning of this?" he demanded.

"I have orders from Admiral Crowe to arrest both you and Lieutenant Warwick, Captain Gates," Carter said with a sneer.

"On what charges, you fool?" Robert asked, drawing his sword and pointing it at Carter's stomach.

"On charges of assisting mutineers in New York, allowing them to abscond, and for the severe beating of a helpless rating aboard *HMS Broad*, for starters."

Briggs moved forward to stand at Robert's side. He wasn't going to allow his officers to be taken without a fight.

"Belay that, Mr Briggs. Stay your hand, Robert," George ordered as he stepped forward.

"I outrank this little gutter rat, George, I can have my Marines in here in an instant."

"No, Robert, we will not set men against our own." George turned to Carter and said, "Does Captain Brownlow know of this?"

"Brownlow was injured in the assault on the garrison; he no longer commands. Lord Crowe and Captain Blake have assumed overall command and have ordered your arrests."

George was shocked and worried. "How is Captain Brownlow, how badly is he hurt?" he asked.

"You should worry about yourself, Lieutenant Warwick. Your fate, and that of Captain Gates, is in Lord Crowe's hands. I am to hold you both here until further notice. You will hand over your arms and come quietly," Carter demanded.

"Do as he says, Robert. Briggs you will leave us now," George ordered as he looked at Carter.

"Briggs can go, there are no charges against him," Carter confirmed as he stepped aside to allow him to pass.

Briggs was reluctant to leave his officers to the mercy of this hated officer and his men, and stood his ground in defiance.

"Very well, I am quite happy to detain you as well…"

Carter was interrupted by George as he shouted at Briggs. "Get out, Briggs, this does not concern you."

Briggs looked first at George and then at Robert, who was handing his sword to Carter before he turned to Briggs. "Off you go, Briggs, you serve no purpose here."

The French officer, who they had been interrogating, looked on bemused, not understanding what was happening. Surely they wouldn't arrest such a man as *Le Scarf*. He was worth more than the lot of them put together. He smiled nervously at Carter as the attention was suddenly turned on him.

"Where is your gaol, you French bastard?" Carter demanded as he moved forward, digging his pistol into the man's middle.

"He's an officer, Carter, treat him with a bit of respect," George warned, looking at Carter with narrowing, fiery eyes.

"It is next door," the Frenchman answered, bowing his head to George, acknowledging his gallantry.

"Right men," Carter shouted. "Let's put these men where they belong, and that includes you, you French scum," he sneered as he dug the pistol into the man's stomach, causing him to double up.

Before they could react, Carter's men moved forward with their bayonets pointed directly at them. George and Robert grabbed the Frenchman before he slumped to the ground, and held him up between them. They were then shoved and pushed out of the office and forced into the gaol next door.

***

A seething Briggs found Stubbs sitting at the bar in the garrison's tavern drinking with other members of their crew. He rushed at him from behind, grabbed his collar and pulled him backwards, lifting him clear off his stool. Stubbs hit the floor hard, and although winded, his instincts took over. He rolled to one side then the other before springing to his feet to face his attacker. Briggs was now looking down at the knife that had miraculously appeared in Stubbs's hand.

"What the blasted hell is wrong with you, Briggs, we've got no quarrel," he blurted out, bemused by what had just happened.

"No quarrel, you bastard, I'll give you no quarrel," Briggs spat out as he drew his own knife and began to circle Stubbs, searching for an opportunity to attack.

"Tell me, for Christ sake, tell me, before I slit your gizzard," Stubbs threatened as he started to move to his left in a crouching position, ready to counter any sudden attack.

"Blabbing to Lord Crowe, or his cronies, about the hiding you took, but richly deserved, from Mr Warwick," Briggs said as he lunged at his stomach.

"You're bloody mad," Stubbs responded as he jumped backwards to avoid the vicious thrust. "I wouldn't entertain Crowe, or any of that lot. I don't know what you're talking about."

Briggs looked at the man he had loathed in the past, spat on the floor in contempt, and was about to lunge again when Caukwell started to shout at both of them.

"It wasn't Stubbs, Briggsy, it was me," Caukwell pleaded as they both looked at him with suspicion. "I got very drunk in the tavern in New York. I was talking to a tar from the *Bathsheba* about what a good officer Mr Warwick was, and how he had dealt with bullying on board."

Both protagonists started to straighten up as they took on board what was being said. Briggs turned to Caukwell. He was determined that someone should answer for his officers' demise, and started to move towards him.

"Hold it there, shipmate," Stubbs shouted. "You've made one mistake, don't go making another. The man was drunk, we've all been there, he doesn't deserve a gutting for it."

Briggs was still seething. Someone should pay for this and he was determined that someone would. He turned back towards Stubbs, the malicious intent still evident in his steely grey blue eyes. It was obvious he was still very dangerous in his present mood. His fellow crew members came up behind him. He was grabbed from behind and his arms were pinned to his sides as Stubbs advanced on him with his knife pointed at his throat.

"Are you going to behave, Briggs? Not one of us would put Mr Warwick, or Mr Gates, in any danger. We would give our lives for them. The important thing now is to get word to Captain Brownlow."

Briggs thought hard, struggling against his instincts to strike out. Gradually his temper subsided as the wildness left his eyes. Stubbs was right, only Brownlow could help them now, and he had been injured. How badly, he didn't know, but he knew that Brownlow was their only hope.

"All right, let me go, someone has to go to the *Broad* and let the captain know what's going on."

Later that day, Briggs and Stubbs concealed themselves amongst some crates on the dock, biding their time to get a boat out to the *Broad*. It wasn't long before the sneering figure of Lord Crowe arrived in a longboat. They watched him stride off with his escort towards the gaol. Stubbs and Briggs stepped into the longboat just as the crew pushed off and started to row back towards the *Bathsheba*. A few yards out, they pulled their pistols from their waistbands and ordered the rowers to make for the *Broad*.

TWENTY-ONE

George felt his scarf pulsating, warning him again of impending danger. Like Robert, he was now shackled to the wall of the small cell within the gaol.

"What's Crowe got in mind?"

"I think I know that," George replied. "He intends to hang me in revenge for his son."

Robert looked at him in frustration and yanked at the chains pinning his arms behind his back. "He wouldn't dare, the Admiralty wouldn't allow it."

"The Admiralty's not here, and Brownlow's injured, how badly, I don't know," George responded. He looked out of the small window of the cell to see Crowe enter the gates of the fort and stride across the compound towards them. "We are about to find out, he's just entered the garrison with more of his men."

A few minutes later, they were manhandled roughly as they were dragged out of the cell and taken to the office. The room had been cleared, with the officer's desk placed against the far wall. Crowe was sitting behind it with his head bowed, studying some papers set out in front of him.

Lieutenant Carter stepped forward and pulled them to the desk by the fronts of their shirts. George noticed there were about fifteen fully armed seamen scattered around the room. Crowe was taking no chances; he wouldn't let them escape. Some time went by as they stood helplessly in front of this tyrant, before he eventually raised his head. George and Robert looked into the most malicious pair of dark, beady eyes they had ever seen, other than those of a snake.

"At last, Warwick, at last you will get your comeuppance," Crowe said with his lip curling harshly. "How I have longed and waited for this day."

"Why are we being held here?" George demanded to know.

"Why are we being held here, my lord?" Crowe repeated his question, adding his title with sarcasm.

George didn't reply or respond. He just looked at Crowe and waited.

"Very well, you are both charged with giving assistance to deserters from *HMS Hecla* and failing in your duty to apprehend and return them to their ship. You, Warwick, are also charged with the savage beating of a helpless rating aboard the *Broad*."

"That is a load of nonsense, my lord," Robert protested. "We were far outnumbered by the locals in New York and Lieutenant Warwick, and myself, managed to get all crews back to their ships, save those three."

Carter stepped forward and punched Robert in the stomach causing him to double up and fall against George. George pushed forward to intercede but was held from behind by two seamen.

"You will only speak when you are told to," Carter spat out in Robert's face.

"You are going to regret that, Carter, mark my words," George promised.

Carter was about to club George with his pistol when Crowe suddenly shouted, "Hold off, Lieutenant, we must not step beyond the bounds of this court. We have witnesses, we will prove our case. There is no need for violence… yet."

"Who do you want first, my lord?" Carter asked, looking at George, leaving no doubt he would be resorting to violence as soon as he was allowed. "Bring in the rating who witnessed the mutiny at the tavern in New York," he ordered.

The door opened, admitting a swarthy looking, very nervous seaman, escorted by two more sailors. It was getting quite crowded in the office.

"Over here, man," Carter ordered, indicating to the rating to stand by the side of the desk to face the two accused. When he had settled, Carter ordered him to state his name.

"Robson, sir, my lord," he added quickly, looking at Crowe and bowing his head. "Of the *Bathsheba*, sir."

"Robson, were you present when three members of the *Hecla* refused to rejoin their ship whilst on leave in New York?" Carter asked firmly.

"Aye, sir, I was that, sir," Robson replied with a nervous grin directed at Crowe. Crowe sneered at him in return.

"Tell this court what happened in that tavern," Carter demanded.

"Lieutenant Warwick and Captain Gates told all crews to rejoin their ships, sir. Some men from the *Hecla* refused and said they were staying, backed up by a lot of locals, sir."

"Never mind the locals, Robson, just get on with the evidence."

"Yes, sir, well, three men still refused after Lieutenant Warwick demanded that they should go back and they stayed in their seats."

"Yes, yes, man, but what happened next?"

"They said they were pressed men, that Captain Jackson was a flogger and they had no intention of returning. More locals came in and started threatening Mr Warwick and Captain Gates, they were all armed…"

"Never mind about the locals, man, what happened next?"

"The officers left, sir."

"Without the mutineers?"

"Yes, sir."

Carter stood back as if admiring his work and looked towards Lord Crowe, who just nodded at him and waved his hand as if expecting more.

Carter caught on with what was expected of him and turned back to the waiting witness.

"Tell the court: did you also talk to a rating about his treatment aboard *HMS Broad* when he was severely beaten by Lieutenant Warwick?"

"Not to the rating, sir, but to one of his shipmates. He told me that Lieutenant Warwick had a man called Stubbs taken to the cargo hold where he gave him a very bad beating, needing the attentions of the ship's surgeon, sir."

George and Robert were listening to the testimony and were eager to have their say, but knew the outcome was going to be a foregone conclusion. They both looked at Crowe as he cleared his throat to speak.

"Is this man Stubbs here to give evidence?" Crowe asked.

"Yes, my lord," Carter replied triumphantly. "He had somehow got back to the *Broad*, but we managed to snaffle him in spite of protests from his new commander." He turned to the two seamen who had escorted Robson in. "Take Robson out and bring in the man Stubbs."

Stubbs was literally pulled kicking and shouting through the door as he was dragged in front of Crowe. He spotted George and Robert and stopped.

"I didn't come voluntarily, Mr Warwick, they forced me here."

"Shut him up," Crowe ordered as Carter stepped forward and struck Stubbs full in the face with his fist. Stubbs didn't even blink or flinch as he looked back defiantly at his attacker.

"You will speak only when spoken to and asked a direct question. Is that understood, Stubbs?"

He stood stock still with defiance written all over him. You could beat a man like Stubbs, but you couldn't make him bend.

"Tell them what they want to know, Stubbs, they've already made up their minds on a verdict anyway," George urged.

"I challenged Mr Warwick to a fight, and he beat me fair and square. He could have had me flogged, but he's more of a man than that, a better man than any of you will ever be."

Stubbs was clubbed to the floor by the two seamen standing behind him.

"Put him in a cell," Carter ordered. "We'll flog him for his insolence later."

George and Robert looked on helplessly as the unconscious Stubbs was dragged out of the room by his feet.

"Do your worst, Crowe. I will see you in hell," Robert shouted.

"And that goes for me as well, Crowe, to hell with you," George snarled as the seamen rushed forward with the butts of their muskets raised.

They both went down under a hail of blows to the great satisfaction of Crowe, who smiled with his twisted mouth as the two unconscious men, badly beaten, were dragged away to join Stubbs in the cells.

***

George awoke in pain. He ached all over as he opened his swollen eyes, squinting even in the gloom of the cell. Stubbs was kneeling over him, encouraging him to consciousness.

"Come on, Mr Warwick, I know you are badly hurt, but try and make the effort."

"Stubbs?" George questioned. "Is that you? Where's Robert?"

"Mr Gates has just woken up like you, sir. He's badly beaten but you will both recover. I've had worse on a night out in Portsmouth, sir."

"Thank you for your home spun encouragement, Stubbs, but I, for one, can do without it," Robert responded as he struggled to his feet and slouched against the wall of the cell. "How are you feeling, George?"

"I've had better days, Robert, that's for sure, but Stubbs is probably right, we'll mend in time for the noose. How are you, Stubbs?"

"I have a lump on my head, Mr Warwick, that's all. Bastards like that can't do much to me. What happens now?"

"Well, I hope that Crowe lets you go after just a flogging. I think Mr Gates and me are for the drop unless Brownlow can come to our aid."

"I don't think he is going to be able to, sir, he was still in his cot when they took me from the *Broad*. I don't think Mr Bray will be able to help."

"What about captains Blake and Jackson, are they aware?"

"I don't think so, Mr Warwick. Blake is too busy in command and thinks that Crowe is helping ashore, and Captain Jackson, according to his crew, is drunk and out of it."

George was about to say something when he heard the keys in the lock, and the door was pulled open. Carter strode in with two seamen by his side.

"Come with me, Stubbs, we are going to accommodate your elsewhere." He laughed.

"Carter, you had better listen and listen well," George said in a threatening voice. "Let Stubbs go back to his ship, if you don't, I swear I will kill you."

Carter laughed loudly. "Where you're going, you are not going to kill anyone, Warwick. Get Stubbs out of here," he ordered his men.

As the door closed, they could hear Stubbs swearing and cursing as he was dragged forcibly along the corridor. The cell started to feel colder as a slight mist started to form.

"Oh, warrior, what have you got yourself into this time? You look as if my horse Lightning has kicked and trampled on you," Wei said, grinning from ear to ear.

"No bloody laughing matter. I wondered where you had got to. Nice of you to turn up, my lord."

"Your life has been threatened, but is not yet in danger, young warrior," Liu Mian answered from behind Wei. "But I do think they intend to hang you."

"No need to sound so bloody pleased about it," Robert quipped at the pair of them.

Wei ignored the remark and, still smiling, answered, "They intend to take you out from this fort, and only the one you call Crowe and his men will witness your execution. They have already erected two gallows for this purpose."

"Only two?" George asked, puzzled.

"Ah, you are concerned for your man who was here with you, yes?" asked Wei. "He is not to hang. He is to be flogged aboard the *Broad* as an example to the rest of the crew."

"Well at least he will be spared the noose," Robert responded.

"Maybe better for him that he wasn't; he will be sentenced to one hundred lashes," Liu Mian said bitterly.

"Is there anything you can do for him, my lord?" George almost begged Wei.

"For him, no, for you two, yes. We will be waiting for the hanging party outside the walls, where we will free you," Wei said, adding, "It will be up to you to do something about your brave man on the ship. Now we must go, they will be coming for you soon."

***

John Bray watched the approaching longboat through his eyeglass. He was puzzled to see Stubbs in the rear, with Lieutenant Carter by his side, who appeared to be holding a pistol pointing directly at him. He wondered what trouble Stubbs had managed to get himself into this time.

"He's to be held in irons until Lord Crowe comes aboard," Carter stated as he pushed Stubbs forward along the deck.

"Just one minute, Lieutenant, on what charge?" asked John.

"Assisting mutineers and obstructing the king's justice," Carter replied.

"What have you got to say about this, Stubbs?"

"I'm not guilty, sir, and they are going to hang Mr Warwick and Captain Gates for assisting mutiny in New York," he managed to say, before being cracked across his face with Carter's pistol.

"Belay that, mister, I'll not have a shackled man assaulted under my command," John said as he watched Carter's face twist. *Crowe's ugliness must be catching,* he thought, as he added, "Oh yes, Lieutenant Carter, I am in charge here and not Lord Crowe." He turned to Briggs, who was standing slightly behind him. "Get Stubbs below and have his wounds tended to."

"He is not to talk to anybody, Lord Crowe's orders," Carter insisted.

John went straight up to Carter and shoved his face right in front of him. "When are you going to remove the wax from your damn ears? I'm in command here until Captain Brownlow tells me differently. Now get off my ship." John turned to Briggs and said, "Belay that last order, take Stubbs straight to the captain's cabin, and send for the surgeon."

"You'll regret this when I tell his lordship of your insolence," Carter blurted out as the crew forced him overboard and into the longboat.

Stubbs was led into the captain's cabin where Brownlow was sitting upright in his cot. He had bandages around his head and his right arm in a sling but looked wide awake and fully aware of his surroundings. After releasing and questioning Stubbs, Brownlow was satisfied that Lord Crowe had overstepped the bounds of his authority. He had signals sent to the *Bathsheba* and the *Hecla*, informing them that he was resuming command of all forces and that they were to answer only to him. He had the garrison signalled to the same effect but unlike the ships, he did not receive any reply.

"Signal captains Blake and Jackson, and tell them I want every available man made ready to enter the garrison on the island. Get our own men ready, Mr Bray, and let's hope we are in time to stop Lord Crowe's folly."

They heard ominous footsteps falling heavily on the stone floored corridor, and held their breath as the lock turned and the door opened. Carter had returned from his trip to the *Broad*, and he didn't seem very happy.

"Get them up and let's get on with this," he ordered. "You are going out to be hanged this instant."

George and Robert were hauled unceremoniously to their feet, their chains were checked, and then they were frogmarched out of the cell, down the corridor, through the front office, and out into the warm afternoon air. Seamen and Marines looked on in amazement as the prisoners were marched out of the garrison between two files of fully armed seamen. As soon as they were clear of the entrance, the garrison's doors were firmly shut behind them to prevent any intervention from those inside.

The party moved off and soon the garrison's walls were out of sight. They walked into a clearing on the edge of the jungle and noticed two nooses hanging from hastily made gallows. Standing in front of the gallows was Lord Crowe, still with that twisted smile on his cruel face.

"You think you don't have any witnesses, my lord Crowe?" George questioned. "Every man here is a potential witness, and therefore a potential threat, if you go through with this."

"Each man is from my estate, Warwick, and can be trusted under pain of death, and that goes for their families as well. You are now going to answer for my son, who you butchered back in England."

"So you have eventually come clean, it was all about your son and not anything that's happened here? He challenged me, thinking he would stick me like a pig. But even then you showed your capacity for treachery by having us ambushed by your footpads on the way to the duel."

"It doesn't matter, Warwick, you are going to die whatever the reason," Crowe vowed.

George and Robert watched the mist emanating from the jungle behind Crowe, who was unaware of the figures forming and rising through it. Robert was the first to laugh loudly, followed by George. Crowe, Carter, and all the men, looked on in amazement at the way these men were going to meet their end.

"We'll see how you laugh dangling at the end of a rope. Get them on the scaffold, Carter, and let's see them writhe!" Crowe screamed.

George and Robert watched the Chinese warriors forming an arc as they advanced on the hanging party. George and Robert were still laughing as they both kicked out viciously at the men who had tried to grab them.

"Give us a hand, mates," one of Crowe's band called out. They were puzzled as to why no one was coming to assist in subduing these prisoners, until they looked around.

The rest of their armed party were all standing around gaping at the advancing group of strange looking warriors, all armed to the teeth and looking very fierce in their black armour with golden dragons emblazoned on their chests. Where on this God's earth had they come from?

The warriors suddenly parted to reveal Lord Wei astride his black stallion. Lightening reared up, kicking out wildly with his forelegs and appearing to breathe smoke and fire from his nostrils. Wei brought him back under control and moved forward ahead of his men.

"Who the hell are they?" Crowe demanded to know as he drew his sword and prepared to face this sinister threat.

"Who are you? I demand to know," Carter shouted out as he drew his sword and stood by his lord's side.

Wei laughed even louder than George and Robert had as he drew his bronze sword and held it above his head before lowering it and pointing it directly at Crowe.

Crowe didn't like this turn of events one bit and stepped back behind Carter. "Come on, you men, meet this rabble head on," he screamed.

"Charge!" Wei shouted as his warriors ran forward with their bronze swords flashing in the afternoon sunlight, screaming at the top of their lungs.

"No prisoners, no one to be left alive," Liu Mian ordered coldly.

George and Robert could only stand and watch as the carnage began. Wei, astride Lightening, made a beeline for Crowe, who was standing, horrified, his mouth gaping wide open as he watched the grinning menace with a scar down his face, come straight at him. Crowe made one silly, desperate lunge but his sword was easily brushed aside by Wei, as he wheeled around on his black stallion, bringing his sword of bronze down through the back of Crowe's skull. By the time Crowe realised he had been mortally wounded, Wei had dismounted and cartwheeled to his front.

"Yieeee!" screamed Wei with a malicious grin, and slashed at Crowe's neck, severing his head from his body.

Carter looked on, horrified, as he was spattered with Crowe's blood. He couldn't believe the lethal punishment being dealt out to his men by these warriors dressed in black, who seemed to flow through them like a gigantic scythe. He watched, his mouth gaping wide open, mesmerised by the acrobatic movements of these fighters from hell, who dealt out death with each slash of their swords. Feeling hopeless, he dropped to his knees in merciful supplication, but it was not to save him. Liu Mian appeared at his side, raised his sword, and brought it swiftly down across the back of his neck. Carter's head rolled away and settled next to Crowe's. They appeared to look directly at one another, each seemingly accusing the other for their predicament.

It was over very quickly. George and Robert, still shackled with their arms pinioned behind them, looked on in amazement. The slaughter of the slave army back on

Hispaniola had been nothing compared to the swiftness of this attack.

Wei approached them with his trademark grin spread across his face. "Don't look so shocked, young warrior. These men were traitors, traitors against you and your king."

"That may well be the case, Wei, but how do we explain such butchery to our own people?"

"You are forever worrying, warrior, you sound more like an old woman than a fighter," Liu Mian said, as he appeared by their side, wiping the blood from his sword with a cloth.

"Do not worry, young warrior, we will dispose of the bodies. You can say that they suddenly left you and disappeared into the jungle. That is where they are going after all," Wei assured them with a laugh. "Your people will be here soon, led by the friend you call Briggs and the brave seaman Stubbs."

"Get these off us before you go," Robert almost pleaded. He watched the Chinese warriors start to collect the dead and their weapons and carry them off towards the jungle. "Well that's great, what do we do now?" he asked as he saw the last one disappear into the trees, kicking the heads of Crowe and Carter in front of him.

"You heard him, Robert. Our people are on the way, it is better that we remain shackled to add weight to our most unlikely story," George said with a nervous grin.

Thirty minutes later, their crew arrived, headed by John Bray, accompanied by Stubbs and Briggs who was in the lead.

"There they are," shouted Briggs, as they all rushed forward to the two battered figures standing by the scaffold. "Thank God we are in time, sir," he said to George as he and Stubbs moved behind them, releasing their chains.

John Bray shook hands with both Robert and George before asking the inevitable question: "Where are Crowe and his men? We expected to find you hanging from a tree in the jungle, George."

"It's a long story, John, but quite simply they just left and went into the jungle."

John looked around the clearing before eying the makeshift scaffold. There were no signs of anyone else having been here. It was a mystery as to why Crowe would leave.

"I think we had better get you two back to the *Broad* for some attention. Lord Crowe can wait awhile," John said.

George looked through his undamaged eye and saw Briggs standing to one side. As he caught his attention Briggs winked, guessing rightly as to what had happened.

TWENTY-TWO

"What happened to Lord Crowe? Where the devil has he gone?" Brownlow asked, pacing the deck alongside John Bray.

He had now recovered from his injuries and was walking the deck of the *Broad* in frustration at the lack of success his search parties were having across the island. He had over eight hundred men scouring the jungle and the shores. They had come up with nothing, not even a glimpse of him, or Carter, nor any of his men.

"We can't do any more, sir," John Bray offered in resignation at their failure. "It's as if they have been spirited off the island."

"No great loss, Mr Bray, but I don't think their lordships back at the Admiralty will be very pleased." Brownlow turned to see George and Robert talking to each other and wondered what really had gone on in that clearing a few days ago. "You had better signal the *Bathsheba* and *Hecla* and tell them to call off the search," he ordered somewhat reluctantly.

Robert watched the signals being hoisted. "Thank goodness for that, George, the longer this went on there was always a chance of someone finding something," he said with a sigh of relief.

"Let's hope it means we're going home, I've missed my family and I'm longing to see Barbara again. Do you think she will marry me still?"

Robert laughed as he put his arm around George's shoulder. "Feeling insecure, my old shipmate?" he joked.

"We've been away some time. I should have married her ages ago. I think I've been a bit of a fool."

"She'll be there for you, George. Never fear, she is as dotty about you as you are about her, and as I am about Jessica," Robert assured him, as his own thoughts turned to the girl he'd left behind. They both noticed Brownlow observing them.

"Mr Warwick, spare me a few minutes of your time, if you please," Brownlow called out, turning on his heel and going down to his cabin. Robert looked apprehensively at George as they both wondered what the captain wanted. George raised his eyebrows in response, as if to ask a question, before shrugging his shoulders and moving off to join Brownlow below.

Blackwell, the captain's steward, was standing just inside the cabin's door. He saluted George in acknowledgement and moved to one side to let him in.

"Sit yerself down, George," Brownlow invited cordially. "Would you partake of a small brandy with me."

George hesitated, surprised by his first name being used again, and by the offer of a drink.

"Two brandies, Blackwell, look sharp about it," Brownlow ordered as the steward looked on, equally surprised by the captain's cordiality and intimacy with this officer.

"Coming right away, sir," he replied, gawping at George, who just smiled back at him. He moved over to the cabinet and poured two brandies into glasses and returned to the table with them on a small tray.

"Your health, Mr Warwick," Brownlow said as he offered George a glass.

"And yours, sir," George replied as he took the glass being offered to him and sipped.

"That will be all, Blackwell, I'll call you if I need you," Brownlow said, dismissing his steward.

When the door closed Brownlow turned to George, staring at him for some considerable time before smiling in some sort of resignation. "I don't suppose we are ever going to find out what happened on the island, are we, George?"

George took another sip from his brandy as he weighed up his response. Did Brownlow suspect something? Well, of course he did. Could he prove anything? No, of course he couldn't.

"It's a mystery, sir, I must confess."

"Confess, confess what?" Brownlow asked, the smile quickly disappearing from his face.

"No, no, sir. I mean, I must confess it's a mystery. I'm as much in the dark as you."

Brownlow looked at him, trying to see what was behind the mask. He sighed in resignation as his smile returned slowly.

"I suppose we are well rid of him. He nearly got away with hanging you, George. Why he changed his mind, I don't know, perhaps he realised he couldn't get away with it and he would have faced ruin on his return to England."

"You are probably right, Captain, who knows?" George replied, wondering what his captain really thought about it.

"We have to come up with some explanation for their lordships back at the Admiralty. The crews from all the ships were privy to this, so it can't be swept away as if it didn't happen."

"I think we must tell them the truth, sir: what actually happened leading up to his disappearance, and the fact you found Captain Gates and me, shackled and in a very bad state of affairs."

"Do you think they will believe it, George? I don't think we need mention Stubbs in all of this. We'll keep to the facts of the so called mutiny in New York. We have enough witnesses from all ships to prove your innocence. Together with the history of your duel with his son, I think we can prove it was malice from a deranged mind brought on by grief."

"I think that about sums it up, sir," George said with relief.

"Tomorrow we will make sail for home. The *Hecla* is to stay in these waters to support the land force being left behind to man the garrison. Captain Blake, with the *Bathsheba*, will also head for England."

George finished his brandy expecting to be dismissed. He made ready to get to his feet, but as he pushed his chair back, Brownlow stopped him.

"One other thing before you go, George. When we make it to England, and this matter of Crowe is settled, I intend to retire. I am getting too old to be battered about. With the monies lodged in Captain Gates's brother's bank, together with a small pension, I am going to be fairly comfortable."

George looked on in surprise: although he knew Brownlow had wanted to retire before, it was still the last thing he expected to hear.

"I am very sorry to hear that, Captain," George replied, recovering from the shock of the news. "If that is the case, I will probably resign my own commission. I can't see myself serving under the likes of Captain Johnson of the *Hecla* and besides, I'm hoping to marry."

Brownlow went quiet, the smile again disappearing from his face as before. George wondered if he had upset him, or had his captain thought of some other problem?

"You disappoint me, Mr Warwick," Brownlow said, looking down at his hands on the desk. "I was hoping you would stay on in the service. The *Broad* needs a good commander, a commander who knows her well, and loves her like I do."

George stared into the captain's eyes as they came up from inspecting his hands and settled on him. George was unsure of what his captain was saying.

"Do I understand you to mean me, sir? That I should have command of the *Broad*?" he asked in disbelief.

"You understand me perfectly, George, I can't think of anyone better to take her over, and I will be recommending that to the Admiralty. What do you think?"

"I can't see the Admiralty agreeing to it, even if I did."

"Well, you have some weeks to consider it before we reach England, but if I were you, Mr Warwick, I would give it some serious consideration before calling it a day. You are a born frigate commander, of that there is no doubt."

As George left the captain's cabin and went on deck, he noticed Robert waiting on the weather deck. George completely ignored him and went straight back down the stairway to his quarters. He needed to think before speaking to anyone, even his best friend.

Robert felt slighted as he watched the broad back of his friend disappear the way he had come. He had made it quite clear that he didn't want to talk to him, at this point in time anyway.

On his way down, George passed Bertie and Grahame on their way up; both saluted and grinned. He entered his cabin and was surprised to see Wei sitting on his bed, wearing his trademark grin.

"Young warrior, why so troubled? They will not find the one you call Crowe, or his men."

"That may be the case, Wei, but they will not stop looking for him. He is a peer of the realm. There are influential people in my country who will demand answers."

"You fight like a warrior, but complain like an old hag. You should not concern yourself with this matter any longer. I understand you have bigger, more important matters to think about."

He looked at Wei and wondered. Did he know everything that was happening, everywhere? It certainly felt like it, and George didn't like it one bit.

"You refer to my captain's recommendation about this ship?" he asked, eying Wei with some suspicion.

"Yes, I do, young warrior, and yes to your other unspoken question," Wei answered truthfully. "Where your safety and security is concerned, my warriors and I are all-knowing. How else can I protect you and fulfil my obligations to the scarf?"

"Well you will have to excuse me, my lord Wei. You have not seen fit to make me privy to what those obligations are, or where they come from."

"Sarcasm does not become you, young warrior…"

"And that's another thing… young warrior. What's with this 'young warrior'? My name is George Warwick," he said indignantly.

"I am sorry, young… Warwick. I will call you Warwick from now on, if that is what you prefer."

George looked at him, relaxed a little, and then smiled. "I am sorry, Wei, you can call me what you want, you deserve that much given your timely interventions on my behalf."

"To answer your question would be a long story. The gold coloured scarf came from the ancients in a far off land. It protected me in my many wars against the dog who called himself the First Emperor, until my last battle, when I gave it to my son for his protection. Since that day, it has been handed down throughout time to those who show courage and valour in adversity, or to those who go to their assistance. Your father was such a person. He showed courage in battle, but he also showed mercy and gave protection to the weak."

"How did he come by it?" George asked eagerly.

"The holder of the scarf was going to be hanged, just like Crowe was going hang you. A priest was going to execute him for not accepting the westerner's faith, and your father shot the priest between the eyes when he refused to release him. The holder of the scarf, in gratitude, and in line with the scarf's creed, gave it to your father who honoured the scarf throughout his life, until he gave it to you, just as I gave it to my son."

George couldn't think of anything to say. Wei's explanation still did not explain the power of the scarf, or the summoning of the warriors. Feeling he was not going to get any more answers, he decided not to question Wei further.

"Very wise… Warwick," Wei said, apparently reading George's mind. "Not even I know all the answers. All I know is that it is my eternal duty to answer the calling of the scarf, and to protect its lawful owner. Now, what will you do about the command of this sea chariot?"

"Ship, Wei, it's called a ship, and I don't know yet. I have many things to consider, like my life back in England. Do I marry? Will Barbara want me to go back to sea? Do I become a farmer? Lots and lots of questions, but no easy answers."

"It is the fair Lady Barbara that occupies your mind. Men have married before and still carried out their duties to their lords and their people. I was married, but still campaigned across my country to protect my people and their way of life."

George sank down on his cot, listening, but remaining silent in thought as he looked down at his feet and wondered what he should do. "My decision will have to wait until after this business with Crowe is finished, and I have spoken to my family…"

"What decision is that, George?"

He looked up to see Robert standing inside the doorway, looking down at him. As always, Wei was nowhere in sight and George was left wondering why he bothered disappearing, seeing that Robert had seen him on numerous occasions before.

"I was talking to Wei, who has decided to do a convenient disappearing act." George could see by the questioning look on Robert's face that he was still expecting an answer. "I'll tell you some other time, Robert. Don't push me on it now, please."

Robert shrugged his shoulders in resignation and left George alone in his quarters. *He'll tell me sooner or later*, he thought, as he stepped out into the cooling easterly breeze of the Caribbean before his thoughts turned to the beautiful Jessica back in England.

***

Robert found George on duty standing by the wheel manned by Stubbs. He acknowledged Stubbs's salute before going up to his friend.

"Are you still going to avoid me, or are you going to tell me what's on your mind?"

"I've not been avoiding you, that's absurd," George answered.

"You've avoided being alone with me, that's for sure."

"I haven't avoided you at all. My duties have kept me busy, Robert."

Robert turned around as Stubbs looked away. He didn't want to be accused of listening to the officers' conversation. George caught Robert's need for privacy as he nodded his head, indicating they should go forward. He resigned himself to the fact he would have to talk to him.

"Let's walk," he said to his friend. "Keep her on this heading, Stubbs," he ordered as he started to move away from the wheel. "Let's go forward, I could do with stretching my legs."

They walked the deck to the foremast, at which point Robert stopped and looked around for signs of any member of the crew. Satisfied they were out of earshot, he leaned against the mast and waited for George's explanation.

"Brownlow is retiring when we get home," George said, opening the somewhat awkward conversation.

Robert looked puzzled. Why should this upset his friend in such a way? He frowned at him before clearing his throat. "You knew it had to come, he's not exactly a spring chicken, is he? Anyway, why should this send you into such a quandary?"

"He's offered me command of the *Broad*," George replied simply.

"He can't do that, George, you know that. It is the Admiralty who decide such things. But even if he could, I thought you would have been bursting with joy at the news."

"With his recommendation backed by Fitz at the Admiralty, and no Crowe to oppose it, he thinks it is a mere formality."

"I still don't understand why you're so glum about it. I would have thought this was your aim, your big ambition, to command your own frigate."

"It is, Robert, leastways it was… but now I'm not so sure. We have money to do whatever we like, but what if Barbara doesn't want me to continue at sea? What if she says she won't marry me unless I stay at home?"

"Oh come off it, George, you were a sailor when she met you, and she knows that it's your driving ambition to have your own command. She might object but she will not make it a deal breaker."

"Let's hope you're right. In any case, I have this business of Crowe to get over when we get back."

"We, George, we have this business to get over. We are joined at the hip on this one," Robert assured him as they both shook hands.

TWENTY-THREE

"You don't have to worry where Crowe is concerned," Fitz assured them. "The only one making a noise about it seems to be his younger brother Marcus, and I think he commands a frigate in the Med."

"When do we appear in front of the Board of Inquiry, sir?" Robert asked, pre-empting George's question. George was seated by his side in the library at the manor.

"In ten days' time, Robert, but don't worry, with the testaments of Captains Blake and Brown, and statements from your crew, I can't see there being any problems. I think you two have bigger things on your plates at the moment." Fitz grinned at the pair of them.

George glanced at his friend, both smiling as they realised what Fitz meant.

"We have set a date for a double wedding in June, Fitz," George responded. "If things go well at the inquiry," he added cautiously.

"Never fear, George, things will go well for you both. Now have you given more thought about the *Broad* and Captain Brownlow's recommendations?" Fitz asked, peering at George with raised eyebrows.

"I have thought of nothing else, but what can I do? I can't even discuss it with Barbara until I have the decision of the Board on Crowe, let alone any promotion."

"I've told him to discuss it, Fitz. Wei has advised him to discuss it with Barbara, but you know what he's like."

"Hang on Robert, it's not you who has to decide..." George was cut off mid-sentence by Fitz.

"Hold your horses, the pair of you. I think you ought to speak to Barbara about your promotion, so if it is offered you can either accept it, or decline it straightaway."

George was quite obviously getting irritated by his two companions, who seemed to have made up their minds for him and weren't going to let it lie.

"All right, I agree. It makes sense to know which way the wind is blowing where Barbara's concerned before I make any decision, I'll grant you that," he conceded reluctantly. "I'll speak to her later today."

***

Harold brought the small open coach around to the front of the manor where he remained standing, holding the chestnut mare's bridle until George and Barbara appeared. They descended the steps with George gallantly helping Barbara to step up into the coach.

"Thank you, Harold, we should be back late afternoon," George informed him as he took the reins and urged the horse forward.

He smiled at Barbara as they went down the drive, out through the gates and turned towards the farm. Barbara looked ravishing. Dressed in a dark green jacket, which more than favoured her honey blonde hair which lay spread across her slender shoulders, she returned his smile with her bluish green eyes sparkling in the warm spring sunshine. *"Oh God,"* he thought, *"how do I control myself, she tests me to the very limit."* He sighed.

"Why the sigh, George?" she asked innocently, unaware of the effect she was having on him.

He thought quickly as he forced himself to concentrate on the road ahead. "I was thinking of the Board of Inquiry and that it would take me away from you for some time," he lied.

"Oh, is that all?" she asked disappointedly, looking away into the countryside and watching the trees going by at the side of the lane, which were now showing signs of leafing.

"Is that all?" he said, noticing the disappointment in her voice. "I am away from you long enough when I am at sea.

When I'm ashore I like to spend every waking moment with you."

"Only every waking moment, George?" she answered as she looked back at him with a mischievous grin.

"Oh, God," he said out loud. "Don't tease me so, Barbara, you just don't know the effect you have on me."

"Have on you!" she exclaimed. "What about you, when you look at me with those deep brown, smouldering, come to bed eyes, how do you think I feel?"

"Whoa," George said as he reined the horse to a stop. He looked directly at her as she held his gaze, still with her eyes sparkling like diamonds; even the stars in the Caribbean at night didn't have the same twinkling intensity. George reached over for her at the same time as she came to him, embracing as their lips met fiercely. He could feel her passion as he felt himself becoming aroused, starting to ache with his need for her.

"Oh, George, I can't wait until we are married, I need you now."

"Hello there!"

The voice stopped them both in their tracks. They hadn't heard any approach and they looked up to see Black Tom astride a dapple-grey Shire horse, standing right in front of them. They broke apart, with Barbara blushing with embarrassment at being caught in such a compromising position.

"Sorry to startle you, George, but you're blocking my way, I need to get past and back to the village."

George looked at the deepening colour of Barbara's cheeks and couldn't help breaking out into a loud belly laugh. Tom's arrival had certainly put paid to their passion.

"I'm sorry, Tom, I'll pull forward and let you through."

Two minutes later, Tom went on his way, grinning from ear to ear. They both looked at one another as Barbara saw the funny side of it and started to laugh with George.

"I think we had better be on our way, George. Just imagine if he had arrived a few minutes later." She smiled at him seductively.

"No you don't, Barbara, don't get me going again," George pleaded as he took the reins and urged the horse forward.

On arrival at the farm they were greeted by George's mother. She explained that Rodney was away at the village getting supplies. George asked her for the use of the parlour in order that he could talk quietly and privately to Barbara.

"I'll get you a ginger beer, George, or would you prefer I wait until you have finished your little talk?" Rebecca asked.

"Later, Mother, we shouldn't be too long," he answered as he closed the door firmly.

"You sit down there, Barbara. I'll sit over here. We don't want a repeat of earlier, do we?"

"Don't we?" she asked wickedly, smiling under her eyelashes at him.

"Barbara, please?" he begged feeling his chest tighten once more.

"I jest, George, never fear," she answered lightly.

George cleared his throat. *This wasn't going to be easy*, he thought. "You know about the inquiry?" he started, watching her nod in recognition. "Well if everything goes well…"

"It will, George, my uncle says it will," she interrupted, "and then we can get married."

"Your uncle is not the Admiralty, we will have to wait and see what the outcome will be," he said in exasperation before continuing. "If it goes well I may be offered command of the *Broad*." He shut his eyes and waited.

Silence. He opened his eyes to make sure she hadn't left the room. Barbara was sitting upright staring at him in amazement.

"Well, what do you think?" he asked.

"I don't know what to think. I did think you might leave the sea, but then again I did wonder what you would do with yourself ashore. I'm sorry, George, I just don't know what to say."

"Then don't say anything yet, especially anything that we may regret. I don't know if I will get offered a command, let alone still retain my rank, at least until this matter of Crowe is settled."

"I agree, let's sleep on it for a few days," Barbara responded, looking down at her small feet and wondering what his decision would be.

***

The Admiralty was alive with senior captains and admirals busily going to and fro, shaking hands with those they knew and those they hoped to get to know better.

George, like Robert, was in full uniform. They were sitting together in the hall leading to the inquiry room. George's apprehension and worry was very evident, as he twisted his hands and fidgeted. He was concerned about his evidence to the Board, and cursing the fact he had caught his white breeches on a nail as he had come out from his lodgings. It wasn't a bad tear and he hoped no one would notice.

"No one will notice, George, you can hardly see it, settle down for goodness sake," Robert said, reading his mind.

"What's that?" Fitz asked, sitting on an opposite bench.

"He's worried about someone seeing a small tear in his breeches," Robert explained.

"For goodness sake, George, concentrate on the matter in hand," Fitz chastised, hardly noticing any damage at all. "Now remember, keep your evidence simple and to the point. Do not embellish anything; they are not fools in there, so the least said the better."

"Why aren't you sitting on the Board, my lord?"

"Because they think I am too close to you and George, Robert. They have accepted my written testament as to Crowe's past behaviour and the outcome of a duel George was forced into. They have also received testaments from Captain Brownlow and Captain Blake, as well as all those present when you were found beaten, shackled, and helpless in that clearing on Narranga. Stubbs's testament is the most compelling though, and should make up their minds for them. Most of them didn't like Crowe anyway."

George was about to respond when the great door opened and a secretary called their names.

"Good luck, you two. Don't forget, keep it simple."

An hour later, Fitz looked up as the great door opened, to see a relieved Robert stride out and head straight for him.

"Well, how did it go?" he asked, as Robert slumped down beside him with a big sigh.

"Fine, as you said, the witness statements seem to have settled the matter, at least as far as I am concerned. They have asked George to stay behind, and I can't understand why. I must admit I'm a little concerned for him."

They waited a further twenty minutes before the great door opened once again, and were relieved to see George emerge with a smile on his face. They both rose to greet him. He just stood in front of them and nodded.

"I take it we have a good result?" Fitz said as he smiled at George and took his hand. "Why the delay?"

"Because of Captain Brownlow's recommendation that I should take command of *HMS Broad*, George answered. "After a brief discussion, Collingwood told me that it was as good as mine, but it would have to be confirmed by a promotions board."

"So did you accept?" Robert asked bluntly.

"No. I didn't have to. I will be notified of the promotions board's sitting. I suppose if I accept their invitation, then I accept the position, if it is offered to me."

"All right, you two, I think we had better get home and let the family know. I think everyone is going to be quite relieved," Fitz said, putting his arms around both men.

They started to walk down the long corridor towards the entrance when they were suddenly brought to an abrupt halt by a figure standing in their way. All three of them looked at the silhouette in amazement as recognition hit them. *It can't be,* thought George, *I saw him die.* The evil twisted face of George's enemy materialised and was standing before them. Pointing at them accusingly was Crowe!

TWENTY-FOUR

Barbara was gazing intently into George's dark brown eyes, holding his stare with her own. Her eyes were sparkling like greenish blue diamonds behind long dark eyelashes, captivating him so he couldn't look away. They could hear the noise of the party inside the manor and wished they were miles away on their own and not just opposite one another at the picnic table.

"Can we go somewhere we won't be disturbed, my love?" Barbara whispered huskily, retaining her unrelenting gaze.

George felt the ache go through him again and he had to fight hard to keep control. "We will be missed, we dare not," he sighed.

"I suppose you're right. I can't wait until we are married, then we won't need any excuse to be alone," she purred in reluctant acceptance.

"Come on in, you two." Rodney's voice cut through the evening's air. "It's much too cold to be hanging about outside."

They looked disappointedly at one another and started to rise from the picnic bench. Barbara stepped back and smoothed her long blue skirt below her slender waist. She bent forward to retrieve her stole from the table, exposing the top of her full, creamy white breast. George caught his breath as he viewed this goddess who had committed herself to him. Never had his self-control and resolve been so sorely tested as this very evening.

"We had better get in," he said quickly, to a knowing smile from Barbara.

Robert and Jessica were waiting for them just inside the hall and watched as they slowly mounted the steps.

"We'll go in together," Robert suggested, leading the way with Jessica on his arm.

The great hall was buzzing with over one hundred guests eating and making merry. George spotted Black Tom with Maggie the barmaid, hurtling around the room with some of the other younger guests to the strains of some jig or other. They nodded to one another as they danced on, before George saw Fitz approaching.

"Ah! There you are, George. I would like to see you and Robert in the library."

This annoyed Barbara, who wanted George to herself for the evening. She showed her displeasure in no uncertain terms. "Uncle, not now, can't you discuss business tomorrow?"

Fitz looked at his beautiful but petulant niece and shook his head slowly. "I am sorry, my dear, I won't keep them long," he answered, apologising to her and Jessica as he turned and led the way.

"Close the door please, Rodney," Fitz requested as he sat down near the great hearth. "Help yourself to drinks, gentlemen," he offered.

Rodney moved over to the chair on the opposite side of the hearth and accepted the drink being offered to him from his son.

"Pull up a chair and sit yerselves down," Fitz invited. "We need to fill your father in on recent events, George."

"Is it true? Did Crowe's younger brother turn up at the inquiry?" Rodney asked incredibly.

"That's not the half of it, Father. When I saw him outlined in the doorway of the long corridor, I thought it was Crowe himself. When he got nearer, I couldn't believe the likeness, in so much I really did think it was Crowe until I realised he was a good deal younger."

"What happened? He couldn't have known about Crowe's demise, so what did he say?"

Their eyes turned to Robert as he took up the story. "He stood there pointing at us, appearing to accuse us, that's why we thought it must be Crowe himself. When we got nearer he spoke to George. His voice was even the same as he rasped out his accusation that George had something to do with his brother's disappearance."

"If it takes me to my dying day, I will prove your guilt, Warwick. You slew my nephew over in Crompton and you have had something to do with my brother's disappearance. Quite what your vicious vendetta with my family is, I don't know, but mark my words, and mark them well, 'I will have you eventually,' he spat out at me," said George.

"Sounds as if he is full of wind like his elder brother," Rodney remarked as he turned to Fitz. "What do you think?"

"Marcus Crowe is no fool, and he's no coward. He is a fairly well experienced captain, still learning his trade, but I have it on good authority he is learning fast. Not like his brother at all, except in looks. I think he will do exactly what he says he will do; he will keep looking for something to hit you with, George. You will need to be on your guard around him."

"I will be cautious, Fitz, but I am not too concerned. There is nothing to be found, so let him keep looking. I am more concerned with Robert and my impending weddings in a month's time."

"And that goes for me too," added Robert, slapping George on his shoulders.

"Well, there seems little point in worrying about something that may never happen," Rodney said as he raised his glass. "To four young people starting out on life." He toasted them.

***

On the eve of the weddings, George, Robert, Rodney and Fitz travelled into Crompton village by coach, driven by Harold, and made for the Boar's Head tavern. As they approached, they heard it was a lot noisier than usual, with boisterous laughter and singing coming from within.

"Pull up here, Harold," Rodney shouted out as they arrived opposite the tavern. "I wonder what gives, there's no festival today, is there?"

"If I didn't know any different, I would have said we were back in Portsmouth, judging by the singing," Fitz commented jovially, whilst Robert and George looked at one another as they stepped down from the coach.

George was the first to the door, pushing it open before ducking and entering ahead of Robert, who bumped into him as he suddenly halted in his tracks. He looked over George's shoulder to see what had caused his friend to stop so abruptly.

"Well I'll be damned!" he exclaimed as he took in the sight before them.

Rodney shouted from just outside the door, "What gives, what's the blasted hold up? Move in for goodness sake."

George stepped to one side to allow them all in. "Take a look for yourself." He grinned as a great cheer went up.

Familiar beaming faces looked back at them, some with reddened cheeks due to the ale and the heat inside the tavern. There appeared to be well over eighty people in the small tavern, and in front of the whole lot stood Briggs and Stubbs, grinning from ear to ear.

"Three cheers for Mr Warwick," Briggs shouted out. Hurrah, hurrah, hurrah." He led the deafening cheers from the rest of them.

Fitz pushed past them and headed for the bar, laughing his head off. "Frederick," he shouted to the landlord. "I'll be picking up the bill, drinks all round, and keep them coming."

"What on earth are you doing here, Briggs?" George asked, beaming with delighted surprise.

"I had a word with the men, sir, and we decided that you and Captain Gates should have a proper send off before you both get shackled tomorrow."

"It is nice to see you all, Briggs," Robert said, adding, "Whatever you men want, put it on the bill, is that understood?"

George went among the men, speaking to them in turn. He noticed that Stubbs had made his peace with Caukwell, who seemed to be slightly the worse for drink. He had his hand on Stubbs's shoulder for support and Stubbs seemed more than happy to give it.

"You all right, Stubbs?" George asked.

"I couldn't be better, Mr Warwick sir, especially now the bar's free." He laughed.

George caught Briggs's eye and motioned with his head for him to move to one side. They pushed through the crowd, moving in the direction of the door.

"It was good of you to organise this…" George started, but was cut off.

"No, no, Mr Warwick, the men wanted to, I only mentioned it to Stubbs and before we knew it a few dozen wanted to come."

"Where on earth are you all staying?"

"James Corey, the shop owner, is allowing us to stay in a barn behind his shop. When he knew why we were here he couldn't do enough for us."

"Well I'll be damned!" George exclaimed as he handed Briggs a small cloth bag.

"What's this, sir?" Briggs asked as he felt the weight of the bag and undid the string. "It's not necessary, Mr Warwick, we are all happy to be here."

"No argument, do you hear? Split it amongst the men. Make sure they get whatever they need whilst they are here. Oh, and I will sort out Mr Corey, all right?"

"Aye, aye, sir," Briggs beamed in acceptance. "I think we'd better get back to the bar."

***

The manor was lit up, and could be seen for miles around as the ladies and workers prepared for the big day. The double wedding was to take place at the small eight hundred year old

Norman church in Compton village, with the reception being held on the lawns of the manor. The workers had already set out the long trestle tables and chairs with the floral arrangements being supervised by Barbara's mother and Mrs Baird.

"Let's hope the weather holds for the big day," Lady Miriam wished out loud.

"Fitz says it is set fair for the next week, and he's usually right in his forecasts," Anne Baird replied. "All those years at sea have given him a nose for it, or so he says," she added as they both laughed.

"Well at least we are on top of things. Everything seems to be as ready as we can get it. Where are the girls?"

"Upstairs with Rebecca, she's putting the final touches to their dresses," Anne replied.

The dresses and veils were of the whitest silk you would ever see. Both Jessica and Barbara were as fully dressed as they would be at their wedding, with Rebecca making final nips and tucks to their bridal gowns.

"There, that should do it," Rebecca declared, standing back and admiring both girls.

They took it in turns to whirl in front of the full length mirror in Barbara's bedroom, smiling in appreciation of the sight they portrayed.

"Oh, Mother," Jessica sighed. "You have done a wonderful job," she said as she moved to her mother's side and hugged her.

Rebecca held out her hand to Barbara, who moved in and joined them. All three embraced. "Thank you, Mrs Warwick, thank you so much," Barbara said sincerely.

"You may as well call me Mother or Rebecca from now on, dear; tomorrow you will become my daughter."

"Oh, that does sound nice," replied Barbara, as she kissed Rebecca on the cheek to smiles of approval from Jessica.

The magical moment was interrupted by a shout from below. Rebecca went to the door to find out what is was about and then came back into the room.

"Mrs Baird, tells me Tom is here to take me back to the farm before the menfolk return from Crompton."

"Rather you than me, Mrs War... Mother," Barbara said, checking herself. "I wonder what state they will be in."

***

Rebecca watched from the kitchen door as George and Robert were hauled off the coach by Rodney as he bade goodnight to Harold.

"Straight back with his lordship, Harold, no stops on the way," he ordered to loud snores coming from Fitz who was slumped in the back. "Mrs Baird will deal with him when you get back."

Rodney half carried, half dragged the two younger men, who were obviously drunk as lords, across the yard and through the kitchen door.

"Sorry about this, dear, I'll get them straight up to bed."

"For goodness sake, Rodney, what kind of state are they going to be in tomorrow morning?" she moaned angrily as she heard him heaving the pair up the narrow stairs, across the landing and into the room above the kitchen.

***

Rodney was awake and up at first light. Rebecca woke to the sounds of him shouting and pulling the two drunken friends from their beds.

"Up and out, you slovenly pair," Rodney shouted as he dragged them from their beds. They hit the floor with a shuddering thud. He didn't give them time to wake up properly before he pushed them to the door and down the stairs. They stumbled and half fell down the stairs, eventually falling into the kitchen where they tried to sit down at the table. Rodney was having none of it.

"No you damn well don't, keep moving and out of the door," he insisted as he carried on pushing.

"Have a heart, Mr Warwick, my head's splitting," Robert complained, holding his forehead and trying to shield his eyes from the glare of the rising sun.

George was about to join in the protest when he received another shove, sending him reeling ominously towards the well and its pump.

"Strip your blouses, you young pups, it's time to sober up. I have just a few short hours to get you presentable and to act with some sort of resemblance as gentlemen and officers of the king."

Rodney took hold of the handle of the pump and started working it until a constant stream of cold water from the spring, some sixty feet below, spurted out. He took hold of George by the scruff of his neck and thrust his head under the freezing water, causing him to gasp.

"Jesus!" he exclaimed, as the icy shock rippled down his athletic torso, causing him to shiver instantly. He tore himself away from his father's grasp as Rodney reached out for the next reluctant victim.

Robert thought to move away, but he was too slow as strong hands held him by the neck and gave him the same freezing baptism. "Oh my God," he shouted as he trembled with the cold and shock. "It's even colder than the North Sea in winter."

Like George before him, he tore himself away from the muscular grip that held him under the torrent. He cursed under his breath as he ran after George, who was already making for the open kitchen door. They both lumbered through the door together as Rebecca laughed loudly at the pathetic sight of them.

Half an hour later they were shaved, dressed and ready for their breakfast. The cold treatment had worked. They now resembled, and felt almost like human beings, but they viewed Rodney across the table with some hostility and suspicion.

At half past ten, Black Tom drove into the yard on a coach pulled by two chestnut mares. He greeted Rodney, who was standing outside the kitchen door.

"Morning, Rodney, everything ready to go?" Black Tom asked, grinning from ear to ear.

"Surprisingly everything's fine, Tom." Rodney grinned back. "They'll be out in a minute," he added as Rebecca appeared followed by the two grooms in full uniform.

Rebecca looked much younger than her years, dressed in a purple gown with a white scarf covering her head. Rodney helped her into the coach and then got in and sat alongside her.

Robert, with his dark hair parted neatly on the left, dressed in a scarlet jacket, white breeches and knee length black boots you could see your face in, climbed up behind Black Tom. He held his hand out to his friend and hauled George up beside him.

George was dressed in his navy-blue lieutenant's jacket fastened with gold-coloured buttons, white breeches and short ankle shoes. He was bareheaded, with his auburn hair swept back out of his eyes for a change. Carrying his tricorn hat tucked under his left arm, he was ready to proceed to the church. George and Robert glanced at one another they both knew what the other was thinking. *Is this what I really want?* They both sighed at the same time.

***

Captain Brownlow was sitting alongside Fitz as the congregation in the small Norman church waited patiently for the service to begin. Most had arrived early, knowing that it would be full and overflowing, such was the popularity of all those involved. Lady Miriam, sitting with Mrs Baird, was joined by Rebecca. They didn't observe the tradition of one family sitting on one side and one on the other; they all sat together.

"Have you got the rings, Fitz?" Brownlow asked.

"Of course I have, Abraham, what kind of fool do you think I am?" he answered, fumbling in his pockets to locate them. He grunted with relief as he felt the small rounded objects in his waistcoat pocket.

A noisy murmur from the packed congregation heralded the arrival of George and Robert. They entered the church and strode purposely down the aisle together to stand in front of the altar. The vicar, standing below the old Jacobean pulpit, looked the epitome of the 'hell and damnation' preacher, but in fact was one of the gentlest and kindest people George had ever known. He smiled his appreciation at the colour and sense of occasion that these two young men brought to his church. He moved forward to shake their hands before slowly walking to the entrance to await the brides' arrivals.

The church became so quiet that you could hear the birds singing in the trees outside. The noise of the carriages arriving made all heads turn in expectation, including Robert's and George's. The two of them caught the disapproving eye of Fitz, who indicated that they should look to their fronts. They did so without any hesitation. As they waited nervously, they heard the low murmuring of appreciation of the congregation as the two brides started down the aisle.

George fought the urge to look around and stared straight ahead, aware that he was starting to tremble. He couldn't decide whether it was with excitement or naked fear. He glanced nervously across at Robert by his side, saw his jawline clench and his Adam's apple bulge as he swallowed. George realised that Robert felt the same.

Eventually, George allowed himself to turn and look at the vision of beauty that had floated gracefully to his side. He caught his breath. He couldn't believe his eyes. How could he have waited so long for this moment? He was so mesmerised by her presence he didn't notice or acknowledge her father, as he stood on the other side of her.

Coughing loudly, the vicar cleared his throat. George reluctantly tore his eyes away and looked to his front. He glanced to his left and caught sight of Jessica on the arm of Rodney. She was standing by the side of a now grinning and triumphant Royal Marine's captain.

***

In beautiful sunshine and a clear blue sky, Briggs and Stubbs were sorting their men out into two lines along the path from the gate to the church's entrance. The villagers looked on in amusement as they formed up behind the sailors who were carrying longboat oars. They had grown fond of these seamen over the past week.

"Get them in some sort of order, will you, Stubbsy?" Briggs complained, as he pulled two men into line on his side of the path, having had his head nearly knocked off by oars.

"I'm doing my best with this drunken rabble," Stubbs answered, as he pulled and pushed men into line, swearing that they were being awkward deliberately.

After much to-ing and fro-ing, they eventually had two lines of sailors, one on either side of the path, all standing to attention holding their oars in a vertical position at their sides. It looked as if it was only the oars managing to hold some of them upright, and they didn't dare look skywards lest they topple over.

Briggs became aware of a slight mist emanating from the graveyard, which was strange on such a bright warm day. He smiled in recognition as he gradually made out the figures of the Chinese warriors starting to materialise amongst the graves. Lord Wei was standing in front of his warriors alongside Liu Mian, his second in command. They had formed an arc behind the line of sailors and were all holding their swords by their sides. The Chinese, villagers and seamen all waited patiently for George and Robert to appear with their brides.

As Briggs heard the commotion coming from inside the church, he realised that the ceremony was now over and that they would soon be emerging from the church, so he took up his station outside the entrance on the opposite side to Stubbs.

***

The service was over in forty-five minutes, with George and a radiant Barbara leading Robert and Jessica back down the aisle. Brilliant sunshine cascaded through the entrance, blinding them as they emerged. The roar of approval was deafening. It took a couple of moments for their eyes to adjust and then they noticed Briggs on one side of the path and Stubbs on the other. Stretching down on either side of the path to the gate was a guard of honour made up of the crew of *HMS Broad*, all standing to attention and holding ships oars upright by their sides.

Briggs put a bosun's whistle to his lips and the high-pitched sound of an officer being piped aboard echoed across the graveyard.

"Three cheers for the happy couples," Stubbs shouted out as the whistle ceased. Three cheers of "hurrah" went along the line, by the villagers at the rear.

Briggs winked at George and Robert, indicating with a nod of his head for them to look to the rear of the crowd. Puzzled at first, they both looked over the shoulders of their men.

"My goodness!" Robert exclaimed as he saw the warriors.

Hearing him, George looked around and mouthed to him, "Only Briggs can see them."

A grinning Wei at the front bowed his head before joining his twenty-seven warriors and raising his bronze sword in a salute. Robert and George smiled at one another as they led their brides to the waiting coaches.

As they were getting into the carriage helped by Harold, Barbara turned to George and asked him, "Are you happy, my love?"

"You couldn't believe how happy," George answered as he kissed her passionately on the lips.

Gasping and breathing in deeply, she pulled away from his embrace and looked into his deep brown, smouldering eyes. "It was nice of your crew to come all this way, George. They must think the world of you and Robert," she murmured in his ear, "but who were those strange, fierce looking men in black costumes, the ones with golden dragons on their fronts, who saluted us so magnificently at the back?"